# THE MAGICIAN

EVER N HAYES

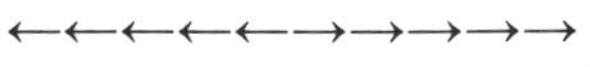

## TITLE / COPYRIGHT PAGE

This is a work of *FICTION*. All of the characters portrayed in this novel are either products of the author's imagination or are used fictitiously. Some elements of this story are however based on factual events, existing truths and real-life people and places. Those references are communicated with the greatest amount of reverence and respect for each respective person, place and/or event and should not be interpreted to any degree otherwise.

***THE MAGICIAN***


Published as an eBook in May 2015 by ENH.
Published in paperback in May 2015 by ENH & CreateSpace
Cover Art by Ana Grigoriu
Genre: Teen / Young Adult Fiction
Word Count: 121,843

←←←←←→→→→→

## CONTRIBUTION CREDITS

Cover Design by Ana Grigoriu of BooksDesign.com
Professional Copy/Content Editing by Katharine D'Souza
Content Editing by Pamela Buttke
Content Editing by Vivian Hart
Content Editing by Anne Hansen
Copy Editing by Beverly Daniels

Few people other than professional editors know the effort it takes just to make a written piece of work acceptable—let alone great. I've been blessed over three books to work with phenomenal editors. And as cover artists go, Ana… wow… you are amazing. That you could pull that masterpiece out my original primitive sketch is incomprehensible. Sheer genius! The people listed above certainly each deserve far more attention and credit for their contributions than I can possibly give. I know how picky and detail oriented I am, so for your every minute of extraordinary effort—thank you! Finally, I'd like to extend significant appreciation to Maxim Magazine's talented and endlessly gracious Joel Randell for the interview opportunity, his constant belief in my writing and voluntary promotion of my work.

*****

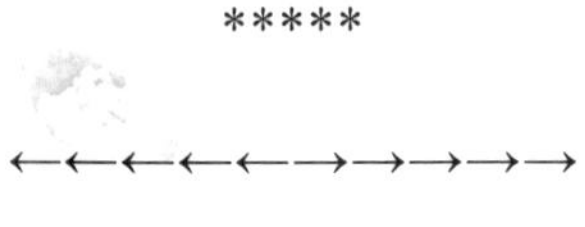

←←←←←→→→→→

## EVER N. HAYES
## PERSONAL & PROFESSIONAL TRIBUTE

*The Magician* is dedicated to my only son and preferred playing/practice partner—Dylan Miles—who has been fascinated with the game since he was two (see photos at back of book). Here's to our hundreds of rounds of golf and mini-golf together, our thousands of golf ball hunts across 41 states (so far), and our infinite sports store H-O-R-S-E (putting) and basement (chipping) contests.

Dermot Desmond once said: "There are three joys of golf: How you play, where you play and who you play with—and the first two are overrated."

I couldn't agree more. To my true "dream foursome" (my kids) and my beautiful wife—and all the other friends and family I am blessed to be able to golf with—thank you all for sharing in this experience with me!

My magazine editor doesn't "let" me praise even the most phenomenal and dedicated golf professionals I meet on my many writing assignments so (since I get to call the shots just this once) I'd like to take that opportunity now. I can't possibly name everyone, but (in random order) Tom Beaudry, Megan Godfrey, Brett Brooks, Kris Strauss, Lauren Harrison, BR Koehnemann, Brian Oar, Steve Wetzler, Mitch Laurance, Sandy Tatum, John Sims, Michael Bixby, Josh Silliman, Mackenzie Monteiro, Dave Gravdahl, Dave Tentis, Kris Schoonover, Mark Neva, Mark Johnson, Jeff Locke, Kent Blaschko, Glenn Hagberg, John Kendall, Darin Fisher, Dave Nordeen, Matt Norgaard, Tim Spanjer, Allison Powers, Lindsey Shindler, Shane Sharp, David Wood, Kathy Reichenbach, Eric Peterson, Frank Soukup, John Cannon, Bill Lang, Jason Deegan, the aforementioned "mean (*but otherwise relatively awesome*) editor" Darin Bunch, and the entire Bachman, Thuringer and Lesnik families—a sincere thank you for all the kindness, support and generosity you've always shown my family and me!

To my parents, Pastor Jack, "Three-Putt" Joe, Kristie "The Great" and "Whipped Down" David… thank you each as well for the support and inspiration you've provided me over the years. I wouldn't be here—with all these people to thank—without the six of you. Lastly to Tom Brady, no matter the results of the witch hunt, and no matter what anyone might say, you are the Greatest Of All Time (QB) and a greater man. Cheers!

←←←←←→→→→→

## MAXIM Magazine EDITOR Joel Randell Goes "20/20" With Author EVER N. HAYES

### (20 Questions with 20-Word Responses)

**Question:** Which of your books was the most challenging to write?
**Answer:** The next one. (*Laughs*) No, the first—"Emergency Exit"—definitely. Series are so hard to set up. Probably won't write another.

**Question:** As a multiple award-winning golf writer, did that make this story easier to tell?
**Answer:** The golf content (20-25%) was easy, yes. But writing it so the non-golfer could understand and appreciate it was definitely challenging.

**Question:** Has golf always been a part of your life?
**Answer:** No. Raised in a family that didn't golf, in a country with no courses. Didn't play until I was 20.

**Question:** Who are your personal heroes and inspirations in golf?
**Answer:** Mr. Palmer, Mr. Nicklaus, Rory McIlroy, David McLay Kidd, Jordan Spieth, Phil Mickelson and many other selfless PGA players.

**Question:** I know you're a HUGE Tom Brady fan. What's your take on "Deflategate"? What would you say to the haters? Share what you want.
**Answer:** I stand by Tom. I think the NFL set this up to get Belichick and got stuck with Tom in the crosshairs. Then it was too late. This should've been handled like the Vikings and Panthers similar transgressions. Instead the league's incompetence has everyone attacking the Greatest (QB) Of All Time, questioning his integrity and legacy over air pressure in a football. Witch-hunt aside, Brady led the Pats to a Super Bowl win on a level playing field against the best defense in the NFL.

**Question:** What is your motivation/purpose for this book?
**Answer:** There are no fictional golf books for teens. Golf deserves better and I'd love to partner with The First Tee. ( www.thefirsttee.org )

**Question:** What's it like being both a golf writer and a novelist?
**Answer:** They're both tons of work. Writers seldom get the credit they should for a task most people hate to do.

**Question:** I've read your "2020 Series" and have no doubt those books would make millions as Summer Blockbusters—similar to Hunger Games & Divergent. Anyone calling on that yet?
**Answer:** It would be incredible to have that happen someday. I need an agent first, and sadly I'm a terrible query writer. (*Laughs*)

**Question:** What is the most frustrating part of being an author?
**Answer:** Collecting Amazon reviews. And trying to get reviewers to remember that ***FICTION***—by definition—shouldn't have to be realistic.
**Question:** Speaking of reader feedback, how do you handle the few critical reviews of your books?
**Answer:** Admittedly, not well. Just a few keystrokes easily cut through the heart, and dampen eight to nine months of effort.

**Question:** But you get TONS of praise. Doesn't that balance the negative?
**Answer:** Honestly and unfortunately, no. It's just like in anything. It takes 100 positives (or more) to counter a single negative.

**Question:** I've noticed you like to respond to your fans, and even some critics, on review posts. As a writer and editor I appreciate your passion and commitment to your readers, but I've also noticed some people find that "fake." What's your take?
**Answer:** I appreciate the people who read my books and want them to know that, even if it's perceived as "fake."

**Question:** How long did it take you to write this book?
**Answer:** 92 days... and just about six months to edit. The cover took forever too, but Ana did an amazing job.

**Question:** Nine months? That's like having a baby. Lots of labor and half the world has no idea what you go through to "deliver" the final product. That a good comparison?
**Answer:** (*Laughs*) Sounds about right, except everyone seems to love babies. And I know someone will find a way to not like this book.

**Question:** Let's talk about that... why wouldn't someone like this book?
**Answer:** If they forget it's written from a 16-year-old's POV... or hate love stories. Or love hating stories. (*Laughs*)

**Question:** Based on your back cover blurb, how much of the book would you say is magic, how much is golf, and how much is just love and life?
**Answer:** Excellent question. Based on word count it's 2% magic, approximately 24% golf, and 74% or more love and life, etc.

**Question:** How about some golf questions? What are your 5 favorite golf courses you've played?
**Answer:** That's tough. So many great ones. Pacific Dunes, Bandon Dunes, the Wilderness at Fortune Bay, Cypress Point and Pebble Beach.

**Question:** What are the top 5 golf courses on your personal "Bucket List"?
Answer: Augusta National (of course), National Golf Links of America, Shinnecock Hills, Old Head (Ireland) and Barnbougle (either) in Australia.

**Question:** What would you say are the five most underrated courses you've played?
**Answer:** Wilderness at Fortune Bay in Minnesota (easily), Ross Bridge in Birmingham, Tetherow in Oregon, Tobacco Road in North Carolina and Troy Burne in Wisconsin.

**Question:** One last golf question. If your next round of golf were your very last one, who would you want to play it with and where would you play it?
**Answer:** My wife, son, and Tom Brady. Augusta National, of course, though Barnbougle (in Australia) would be equally surreal and probably more realistic.

*****

**BONUS:** A publisher or movie studio gives you a $1 million up front for the rights to one of your stories. What do you do with the money?
**Answer:** I've got a lot of bills to pay: medical, dental and academic. That might use it all up there. (*Laughs*) If there was anything left I'd love to send my parents on their dream Alaskan cruise, and support some of my missionary friends (and their families) in Africa. Personally, I'd love to get to Australia and New Zealand with my wife and kids, and maybe open my own miniature golf complex. Get the book on bookshelves at Barnes & Noble and find a way to get a dollar of every sale to go to St. Jude or Mt. Sinai Children's Hospital. Those things… But yeah… mostly pay bills.

←←←←←→→→→→

***"I've spent most of my life golfing - the rest I've just wasted."***

- Author Unknown

←←←←←→→→→→

## ★★★ PRAISE for the "2020" SERIES ★★★

Book 1: **EMERGENCY EXIT** (Rated 4.5 Stars) – 105 Reviews.
(Published April 5, 2014)
First 12 Months Sales/Downloads: 72,800

Book 2: **REDEMPTION** (Rated 4.7 Stars) – 33 Reviews.
(Published November 5, 2014)
First 5 Months Sales/Downloads: 31,300

Book 3: **SCARS & STRIPES**
(Anticipated Release Date: November 15, 2015)

### ★ (Quotes Taken Directly from Amazon.com Reviews) ★

**Summer Blockbuster Written All Over It** – "That should be the final outcome of this series. I hope Ever has been shopping agents!" ★★★★ (*K. Kleinschmidt on April 11, 2015*)

**Sequel Improves on a Solid First Novel** – "A paen to the American Spirit." ★★★★★ (*Anonymous on March 31, 2015*)

**Character Driven Action** – "Plot is plausible and realistic, and the characters never seem bulletproof." ★★★★★ (*C. Nelson on Feb 25, 2015*)

**Huge Twists Make for One-of-a-Kind Action and Drama** – "The author doesn't shy away from taking risks." ★★★★★ (*CafeConLeche. Feb 7, 2015*)

**Fantastic Read!** – "(The 2nd book) kept me more on the edge of my seat than the first did. I love these characters so much! A wild ride. Loved loved loved it!" ★★★★★ (*Kitty on January 11, 2015*)

**Hugely Entertaining Story Despite INSANE PREMISE!** – Some of the fastest paced plotting I've ever known. An absolutely incredible "battle of wits"... and characters who, despite all their emotional baggage, grew on me... Five Stars - ★★★★★ (*Amazon Customer on March 28, 2015*)

←←←←←→→→→→

***"To Find a Man's True Character, Play Golf With Him."***

- P.G. Wodehouse

# ABOUT THE AUTHOR
## "Who is Ever N. Hayes?"

My 4th grade teacher, Mrs. Willett, is directly responsible for my addiction to writing and—in a roundabout way—my decision to author under a pen name.

Two of my favorite stories I received as gifts from her (both of which I still have)—"Where the Red Fern Grows" by Woodrow Rawls and a piece by Samuel Clemens called "The Adventures of Tom Sawyer." Those two men had another commonality (besides awesomeness) in their writing—neither published under their given name.

Woodrow (better known as Wilson Rawls) was a great yet reluctant storyteller, attributing his insecurity to "terrible grammar and spelling"—something I could certainly identify with in my own early years.

Samuel Clemens was quite the opposite. He was an exceptional writer, a man once labeled the "father of American Literature." Of course, most know him better by his pen name—Mark Twain—which he actually didn't start using until he was 27.

As both a professional journalist and author (for the past decade) I've similarly elected to maintain a "dual identity"—to keep my professional and fictional work separate. (*Two names. Same initials.*) Logic: If I were a terrible novelist, my media employers wouldn't be negatively affected. (Just as logical: If I were a terrible journalist I wouldn't have media employers.)

I've been thrilled, and fortunate, to receive recognition (and awards) from the International Network of Golf in the journalism world, (under my given name) and equally fortunate to (thus far) have not embarrassed anyone with my fictional work. (*See the "2020 Series."*)

I write for the love of writing, and am grateful to the many wonderful teachers who instilled that in me, and the many editors I've had since who have molded it into something that hopefully can be appreciated across many platforms—perhaps even on the big screen one day.

←←←←←→→→→→

←←←←←→→→→→

***"Of all the hazards, fear is the worst."***

- Sam Snead

## ←THE ASSIGNMENT→

June 10th, 2017
Southampton, NY

*I should be fishing.*
*Or golfing.*
*I should be doing ANYTHING other than this.*
*But no, I get to work on my writing this summer.*
*Correction. I HAVE to work on my writing this summer.*

*My parents and English teacher gave me the "option" of attending summer school or writing a journal about my life. After careful consideration I've elected to go the "journal" route.*

*Mrs. Willett, you've asked me to cover all the major events in my life. "20,000 words minimum for this project," you said. (Might as well be twenty million!) "Start at the beginning. Give it a catchy title, make it personal—a highlight reel." (More like a lowlight reel.) "Make it good enough and you won't have to do it again next summer." (Good Lord. I'll move to Kansas before that happens.)*

*Remember you asked for this Mrs. Willett. You have NO idea what you're in for!*

*This is the life story of me—"Stellar" Miles Johnson.*

←→

## ←★★★★★ NARRATOR ★★★★★→

### SIX YEARS LATER
### ←Sunday, June 26, 2022→

That's how it all began—the assignment that led to this stack of journals on the table beside me. Sixteen-year-old Stellar penned the story of his life that summer, and gave it to his English teacher. He was right about Mrs. Willett—she had *no idea* what she was in for. *None of us did.*

Mrs. Willett returned all these journals to Stellar's adoptive mother, Kate Parker, later that same year. I asked Kate back then what she was going to do with them and she didn't know. I asked if she thought Stellar would mind if I read them? For that matter, would Kate mind if I read them? There were no outright objections.

I've had them for a few years now. Kate… well… let's just say she didn't want them back.

I get it. And like Kate, after reading the journals, I had no idea what to do with them. I thought they'd make a sensational book in the right hands but was under no illusion "those hands" were my own. And then I got pregnant. And now I'm following doctor's orders, on bed rest—sort of—with enough time and foolish ambition to give this authorship idea a shot. Bookstores full of bookshelves, full of books, suggest plenty of people have had similar notions. I mean, come on, James Patterson has put his name on almost a thousand books—*give or take a few.*

So, how hard could writing *one* book possibly be?

I started by contacting Stellar's family and friends, and asked them to help me fill in the blanks—provide alternative perspectives and/or cover subjects Stellar didn't. That extended family of his came through, *big time*, and now I've got a collection of letters and journals here that will certainly flush the full story out.

I now have enough time, determination and material to write Stellar's book.

It'd be a whole lot easier if I could merely type the story as Stellar wrote it, chronologically and verbatim, exactly as the journals are composed. But I know I can't. Stellar doesn't remember much of his beginning, or at least he gives no indication he does. Nor does he answer any of the education and custodial questions Mrs. Willett asked him in the margins of his first few journals.

*Yes, he was legally adopted by Bernie.* Kate gave me copies of those papers.

*Yes, he was homeschooled for five years.* I have all his state academic reports and tests here as well.

*And no, even Stellar had no idea how he survived living with Ray, or was ever allowed to stay with him for that matter.* Guess kids even slip through the cracks in the Hamptons.

Thank God Ken and Kate were there!

I wish Stellar had covered all those topics more in depth—in his own words, in his own way. But, since he didn't, I'll just have to fill in the blanks as I go along. *Best as I can anyway.*

So here goes... for the most selfless friend I've ever known, and probably the greatest golfer the world has never heard of…

… This is the story of "The Magician."

←★★★★★→

# THE MAGICIAN

**Stellar "Miles" Johnson**

## STELLAR 1: "In the Beginning"

I was raised by a Saint Bernard. It's true. Okay, it's *partially* true. That's at least more believable than saying I was raised by a Squirrel, which incidentally is also true. Okay, it's *also* partially true.

I was born on October 28th, 2000. At least that's what the birth certificate I was found with claims. That piece of paper called me "Miles D. Johnson" though I've never gone by that and don't know what the "D" stands for. *Dumped? Discarded? Disambiguated?* Everyone, as far back as I can remember, has simply called me Stellar. Or Stella.

*I promise I'll explain that.*

I've led an interesting life. I was abandoned, strapped in a car seat, in the back row of St. Paul's Chapel in New York City, on a cool Christmas Eve, in 2001. There were people all around—firemen, cops, emergency workers—but no one saw who left me. The man who "found" me and took me with him was kind, old, wealthy, sad and... well... kind of homeless. *How can you be "kind of homeless?"* He had a home, but didn't live in it. Care to explain? *Not now.*

The man's name was Bernard, but he went by Bernie. He was the first parent figure I ever knew. I say "was" because he died seven years ago—when I was almost ten.

Of what I remember from his early life story he was born and raised in New Orleans, a die-hard Saints fan—*I liked him anyway*. He was a street performer there, an illusionist, a magician. He lost his wife and daughter when a dream vacation to the Big Apple turned into a giant nightmare—on September 11th, 2001. He was supposed to meet them for brunch but was running late. Literally. *He was in Central Park—running.* When the towers came down his wife and daughter were somehow trapped inside. He was just a mile or so away. He lost those he loved most in those buildings. His family was never found. Their remains were scattered here in New York, so he too remained here. He had nowhere else he needed to be, and nothing in New Orleans to go back to.

Bernie was at St. Paul's Chapel on Christmas Eve, alongside dozens of other volunteers, assisting the recovery efforts of those working the World Trade—"Ground Zero"—site across the street. He told me he couldn't stand being there—particularly on Christmas Eve—but he also couldn't bear the thought of leaving. At that point it had been two and a half months since the tragedy, and that was the night Bernie finally gave up all hope. That night, after most everyone else had either gone home or gone to sleep, Bernie knelt at the back of the church to ask God for forgiveness for what he'd decided to do. Instead, he found me—a reason to live.

I don't know for certain what happened to my birth parents. But if the names engraved at the 9/11 Memorial and the parental signatures on my birth certificate are in fact the same people, then my parents were also in the towers when they fell. I've always assumed that to be the case. It was much easier to accept that finality than to believe my own mom and dad didn't want me. You'd think a relative would have taken me in—or "kept me," I should say—since someone had me those two and a half months before abandoning me at St. Paul's. But...

All that matters now is that Bernie wanted me. He always said we were "related by fate." That didn't mean much to me at 14 months, or two years... or even at five or eight.... but it didn't really have to. Bernie was all I had. He was all the family I knew. So I grew up on the streets of New York City with Bernie—Saint Bernard—and let me tell you, I grew up fast. I had to.

By the time I turned eight Bernie had taught me every card trick in the book. I was his eager apprentice, a miniature magician, an amateur of illusion, sleight of hand, and manipulation... but an expert at "guessing" people's cards. Most afternoons and weekends Bernie and I would work opposite corners in Times Square, and money was always good. *Who wouldn't love to help out a cute little blond-haired, blue-eyed kid?*

Over the next couple years we developed quite the reputation downtown. Where cops would usher other performers away after a while, they always seemed to have a soft spot for Bernie and me. They had our backs; cut us a lot of slack. When you make the kind of money Bernie and I did others were regularly gunning for us—crooks and copycats, bullies. We often found ourselves on the run from hostile teenagers, gang members, and other desperate homeless people. We lost a lot of money to those thieves but always seemed to have enough leftover for a nice diner meal for dinner.

You'd think we'd have had far more possessions—and maybe even a permanent address—if we were as successful as I remember us being. And you'd be right. But Saint Bernard was also a Good Samaritan. He helped anyone he thought needed it, any way he possibly could, sharing almost everything—literally—even his home.

Bernie entertained the rich and gave the profits to the poor. He was a Cajun Robin Hood with a buttery-smooth southern drawl. He was Superman without the cape, Batman without the fancy car, Spiderman without Emma Stone. Not quite sure what that made me in any of those metaphors, but I was really just along for the ride. I loved to watch him give almost as much as I loved to watch everyone else receive. Bernie's selflessness and generosity made him beloved by many.

But it also cost him his life.

## STELLAR 2 – "2009"

I'm getting ahead of myself. I need to talk about golf. Bernie loved the game of golf. Every night we'd walk to Times Square to watch sports highlights on the big screens, and we'd stand there a full hour for three minutes of golf clips. Against the big three sports, and hockey, golf seldom received an equivalent share of primetime footage, but it owned all of Bernie's heart.

Bernie was opinionated. He would talk your ear off about golf, about how the bigger courses, new technology, and high round costs were killing the game. How today's professional didn't respect the common fan like the old school player did, and how he thought Rory McIlroy would be the guy to break Jack Nicklaus's major record. Keep in mind Bernie loved Jack—Mr. Nicklaus as he called him. He didn't want anyone to break the Golden Bear's Major record. Bernie loved Tiger for what he'd done for the game, but he never once thought Tiger would get there, and never believed anyone else could either. And then Rory came along. And Bernie believed Rory not only could… but would.

He believed it as early as April of 2009 after watching highlights of Rory in only his *first* Masters—a full two years before the Irish phenom even won his first major. I mentioned people would routinely mock Bernie for that claim, especially back in 09, but not me. Bernie was right far more than he was wrong, and when the US Open came to Long Island that summer, Bernie got us passes. It was one of the rare times he spent the money we made on us. He always said we didn't need it—those we gave it to needed it more. But this, he said, was "for my education."

"You need to see this curly-haired Irish kid," he said. "You need to see how he plays with class, witness his power and mechanics, absorb how much he loves and respects the game." Bernie was selective with such high praise. He was typically far more critical of the "entitled professional athlete." Rory was different though. "Easy to praise," Bernie said. He compared him to "class acts" like Mr. Nicklaus, of course, but also to other golfers like Bobby Jones, Arnold Palmer and Phil Mickelson—and to Tom Brady and Derek Jeter in other sports. "You have to be careful putting athletes on a pedestal," Bernie once told me. "They're all human. Their every move is in the public eye. So much money, so much temptation… they'll make mistakes. Trust me, Rory's biggest adversary is boredom. When you're the greatest, it's hard to maintain the desire to be even greater."

I trusted Bernie. I figured he would know, that he was right. And I looked for what he saw, and loved, in Rory—at Bethpage that summer. We watched the young Irishman closely, followed him through every hole, all four days, and he finished tenth. *At age 20!*

Phil Mickelson finished second. We cheered for him, too. Phil was always the easiest guy to cheer for. He was endlessly gracious and so… human. People liked to criticize Phil for being too nice. Bernie told me those people likely kicked puppies… and hated sunshine, too.

Rory was also very kind… equally human. He even high-fived me as he cut between holes—twice. It was awesome! I didn't need further convincing on Rory—I saw what Bernie saw—and that's probably when I fell in love with golf.

But golf is an expensive sport. A single club can cost over $100, and a round of golf in New York can cost even more. I guess you could say I loved the idea of playing the game, and learned plenty through Bernie's etiquette and history lessons, but I never believed I'd actually be able to participate.

For my ninth birthday Bernie surprised me with a golf club, a Titleist sand wedge he claimed a friend of his received from their corporate headquarters in Massachusetts. I was a little disappointed to find out it was used until, with a smile on his face, Bernie told me who had used it. *Rory McIlroy.*

I carried that wedge with me everywhere. It became the "magic wand" in my act, and the only "toy" I ever really played with. I took advantage of any opportunity to chip whatever I could find—indoors or outdoors—from acorns, to duct tape-wrapped newspaper balls. Chipping morphed from a casual distraction into a compulsive obsession. I loved the whoosh of the club as it cut through grass, the click of a nut glancing off the club's face, and the hop, skip, and spin I could get out of any of them. While Bernie would "nap" or "read the paper" I'd chip away the hours. I knew, of course, he was watching from the little tips he offered here and there. "Keep your head down," "Turn, don't shift," "Follow through," etc. Otherwise he mostly kept his insights to himself.

He always said I was a natural, that you couldn't teach what I had. He'd describe my swing to other street performers with words like "silky smooth, effortless, buttery and stellar." The last one was the word attached to me the most—stellar. It caught on. Bernie called me Stellar, so everyone else called me Stellar. It was years before I answered to Miles again.

## STELLAR 3 – "2010"

Bernie and I didn't have much, but that was certainly more Bernie's choice than it was misfortune. We had what we needed for meals and activities. The rest we gave away. Bernie said he didn't keep money so he didn't have to file taxes, but even at age nine I knew it was never about that. I also knew he filed property taxes on the house he owned, that we never lived in.

Bernie *loved* to see people smile. I may have already mentioned that, but it certainly bears repeating. Every Sunday we'd feed the ducks at the Belvedere Castle and then walk across Central Park to Mount Sinai Children's Hospital, usually right around lunch. That's where Bernie—always in a New Orleans football jersey—became known as Saint Bernard, or Sunday Santa. It was a sight to behold: the gentle, ever smiling, black man filling those hallways with the laughter and cheers of sick and dying children, Bernie fighting back tears as he hugged every last one of them. He'd bring a giant red duffel bag full of little gifts in for the kids, from CDs to DVDs to candy, toys—anything, everything—you name it. That's where most of our money went, and I was okay with it. He had a way of making selflessness seem as simple as breathing—instinctive.

Word spread quickly when Saint Bernard was in the building, and my job was to follow him and record names and personal requests. *Molly wants shoelaces with stars and glitter. Lori would like a Dale Earnhardt Jr. matchbox car. Dylan wants a Calvin & Hobbes book.* I'd write down up to two hundred things each Sunday and within two weeks we'd have every item scratched off the list. He told me it's what drove him, it's why he never took a day off, but he didn't have to explain himself to me. I loved being a part of it. I also loved shopping for the items. The role of Santa's chief assistant never got old.

We had our other routines. Spring, summer and fall we'd walk miles through Central Park, pretty much every weekday. We'd spend Saturdays at the American Museum of Natural History or The Met, at Yankee Stadium, or on a Water Taxi cruising the Hudson or East River. Once a week we'd hit our favorite pizza place under the Brooklyn Bridge, take in the view from 30 Rock or the Empire State Building and, of course, we always stopped at Ground Zero to pay respects to our departed families.

During the winter we pretty much lived indoors. We'd spend our days people-watching at Grand Central Terminal, or touring the museums. We'd see a Broadway show once a week, and regularly go to movies. I had *no idea* back then how expensive Broadway plays were. Guess Bernie considered that part of my education. *The only part of homeschooling I didn't resist.* Snow and ice restricted our street performances, but we never skipped the hospital visits and always made time for Ground Zero.

It was harder to be homeless in the winter. Not just because we made less, but because our "home" at the shelter always got more crowded. For some reason, winter lured the drunks, the fighters, and the bandits into our home, which also brought the police in more and forced us to spend more nights in various hotel rooms. I didn't ask a lot of questions—not about why Bernie took us where he did, or even why we couldn't just stay at his house. Oddly, I just accepted it as "the way it was" and followed along. As I recall, I never once felt like my life was in jeopardy. Bernie always made me feel safe.

Bernie and I had a small walk-in storage locker in downtown Manhattan between Grand Central Terminal and the New York Public Library where we kept our valuables and money. *Bernie didn't trust banks.* Far as we knew, no one else knew about our locker, which was exactly as Bernie intended to keep it.

One February night Bernie got into an argument with a couple drifters over my skateboard—which the men had tried to steal. Bernie used his influence with the shelter manager to have those two men kicked out. He figured they'd come back to stir up more trouble but they didn't. So we kind of forgot about them. *At least I did.*

But they didn't forget about us. A week later we were between Grand Central Terminal and our locker when Bernie noticed two men shadowing us. They walked when we walked, stopped when we stopped. It was obvious. Bernie suddenly grabbed my arm and whispered sharply, "Let's go." That was the *first time* I can honestly remember feeling frightened. We took off down an alley and ran until we were certain we'd lost them. Only then did we continue on to our locker.

By then it was dark. Bernie hated visiting the locker after dark. We were only there a few minutes that night, before hurrying back towards Grand Central Station. We were only two blocks from the station when we heard a woman's scream for help from a dark alley. I could tell Bernie was conflicted. If I hadn't been there he'd have rushed into the alley, but with me there he hesitated. He looked down at me as we heard the desperate plea again. It wasn't in Bernie's makeup to ignore the cries. He felt obligated to go help her. I didn't want him to, but I didn't even try to talk him out of it.

When he told me not to move, to sit on the bench under the street lamp and wait for him to come back, I did as I was told. I didn't object. Bernie disappeared into the alley. He didn't come back out, but the two men who had been following us before did. They didn't see me frozen on the bench. They were too busy rifling through a backpack, Bernie's backpack.

They turned to the right and ran away from my position, tossing Bernie's pack in a dumpster. It was several minutes before I found the courage to stand and venture into the alley.

I found Bernie on his side, in his own blood, beneath a fire escape. He was alive but barely and I could see his mouth moving. I'm certain I was in tears, though I don't actually remember that. I do however remember the terror, the pain in my chest and the degree of difficulty to simply breathe. I remember a woman's body being next to Bernie's, but I mostly ignored her. I knelt beside Bernie's head and leaned down to hear his words, but there were none. Instead, I could hear his teeth chattering on metal. He was trying to spit something out. I reached for the bloody object with shaky fingers. It was a key—a familiar key—the key to our locker. Bernie didn't say a word before he died. I held his hand for those last few breaths and then I lost my mentor, my best friend and the first parent I remember. Bernie's selfless concern for that woman cost him his life. It cost me far *far* more.

I don't know why I didn't stay with Bernie longer that night. I don't know why I didn't try to find help as he slipped away. Maybe I could have done more... or maybe I knew that I couldn't. I really don't know. Looking back now I realize I was in shock, but I've always felt bad for just walking away. And I've felt even worse for not reporting those men. I knew exactly what they looked like. I knew exactly where the police station was. I knew where our shelter was, but I was too afraid those men would be waiting for me there. I didn't go back there. *Not ever*. I didn't do anything I maybe—or probably—should have done. Instead, I returned to our walk-in locker. I opened it and locked myself inside. I cried myself to sleep and didn't even come out the next day. The owner of the storage place found me there *two days later* while reviewing his security tapes.

"You can't stay here, son," he told me.

"I know."

My safety net was gone. I packed all I could into Bernie's backpack, grabbed my sand wedge, and headed for the only other place I felt completely safe.

Mt. Sinai Children's Hospital.

## STELLAR 4 – "Starting Over"

When I walked in the front door of Mt. Sinai I was greeted almost immediately by one of Bernie's favorite nurses, Kristie. She was coming off an overnight shift, and was on her way out, but stayed and kept me company for another ten hours. Somehow she had already heard the news. She wrapped me in a warm hug and escorted me to a lounge where several other nurses gathered around to hear my side of the story. Within the ensuing ten hours at Mt. Sinai, a few phone calls led to funeral arrangements for the next day, with several of the nurses and doctors at Mt. Sinai picking up all of Bernie's burial costs. It was nice to see how much of an impression Bernie had made here. Saint Bernard deserved to be taken care of like that.

Kristie took me to the funeral the next morning and introduced me to a man named Ray Parker. I recognized him but wasn't quite sure from where. He held an envelope full of papers in his trembling hand, filled out and signed by Bernie. *Adoption papers.*

"I know this isn't ideal," Ray said. "It isn't what you ever wanted. But Bernie told Kristie and me a year ago if something should ever happen to him we were to get you out of the city. Kristie isn't really... well... I live out on Long Island, in Southampton, and..."

"Where do I know you from? And why didn't Bernie tell me about this?" I had a thousand other questions but those were the two I asked.

My question seemed to catch him off guard. He looked to Kristie for help but didn't get any so he continued. "My son, Jordan, passed away a year ago—here at Mt. Sinai. Through all your visits I got to know St. B... I got to know Bernie quite well and we... I offered to help him with you if he ever needed me to. He called me one day and asked if we could meet down at the pier."

He continued to explain, but now I remembered. I remembered asking Bernie about the man at the pier that day, and I remember Bernie saying, "I'm securing your future." Bernie had a folder full of papers—these papers. It didn't mean much to an eight-year-old then, but now, at nine, I understood a little more. This was *that* future.

I asked if we could swing by Ground Zero on our way out of town and Ray didn't object. It wouldn't surprise me if Bernie had told Ray the story of his own family, and maybe even mine, in their conversations last year.

This visit to the memorial was different. This wasn't the "see you later" goodbye I had bid my parents every week for the past several years. This was more permanent. *What's more permanent than death though, right?* I felt a pang in my chest as I stood before their engraved names and told them I was moving away.

I didn't know when I'd be back.

## STELLAR 5 – "River Bait & Boats"

I'd never understood the phrase "Jekyll and Hyde" until I moved in with Ray. Turns out Ray didn't want to be my dad. He didn't want another son, or a constant reminder of the one he'd recently lost. His wife kicked him out of the house when their son Jordan died, and Ray had been living alone in a makeshift apartment over his River Bait & Boats shop ever since. There was barely enough room for the two of us in there, and my presence was clearly an unwelcome addition to his hermitage. For the life of me, I don't know why he showed up at the funeral, or ever agreed to take me in. His "sense of obligation" though noble in intent, was moronic in reality.

The person who picked me up at the hospital that day was a mirage, a fraud. Ray wasn't that guy again, at least not for a long, *long* time. This guy's daily routine consisted of working on boat motors, selling bait, yelling and cursing at me, watching TV, and drinking himself unconscious. *I was essentially an orphan, under the "supervision" of a fat, bald and rather ugly Mr. Hannigan.* How Ray managed to get through the Child Services visits without losing custody of me I'll never know… but he did. I had to fend for myself a great deal, but I was used to that thanks to years of life with Bernie. In all honesty, despite my description of the circumstances, I didn't mind things the way they were. Ray didn't care what I did—or even where I slept—and I didn't care to spend much time around him. I did, however, spend a lot of time with his younger brother, Ken.

"Uncle" Ken Parker knew exactly what Ray had become since Jordan's death, and he was just as intent on shielding me from it all. He took me under his wing from the start. He was 30, newly married, a lifelong fisherman, and the co-owner of RB's—River Bait & Boats—manager of boat sales and fishing charters. Ken taught me how to keep the boats shipshape for sale and how to clean the fish he caught each day—mostly pickerel, bass, trout and perch. He would go out every morning, with or without clients, and I'd work on the other boats until he came back. Every evening we'd clean the fish, pack them in ice, and deliver them to a few local restaurants. He'd either take me somewhere for dinner then, or grab a bite to take back to the docks, where we'd sit on a boat and talk until sunset. Then he would go home. Yes, Ray may have been my legal guardian but Uncle Ken was always more of a father figure to me.

I had a bedroom above the bait shop, but I seldom slept in it. I spent as many nights as I could on Ken's boat instead. He owned a brand new 25-foot Sundancer with a bed, bathroom and kitchenette. It was all I needed, I just didn't want to tell anyone, afraid I'd lose my only sanctuary—that I'd have to move back in with Ray.

Lying on that boat, listening to the water gently lap against it, and hearing the gurgling purr of the other boats passing by throughout the night… that was awesome.

I suspect Ken knew I slept out there but he never said a word about it. Every morning I made sure I was up and the boat was spotless before he arrived. If there were a day he wasn't coming in at 5:30 he'd tell me exactly when he would arrive and throw in a wink or a comment like "get a little more sleep."

Like I said, I'm positive he knew.

On my tenth birthday Ken took me fishing with him for the first time. To say I was hooked would be both cliché and the absolute truth. It was a gorgeous day, and he would have easily been booked solid with charters, but it was only he and I—a remarkably generous birthday present. I didn't get—nor did I expect—anything from Ray…not even the words "Happy Birthday." But those meaning-filled hours with Uncle Ken, were easily better than a thousand meaningless words from Ray.

Ken seemed to know everyone out on the water. He gave me the scoop on every boat and its occupants: where they lived, what their house was like, what they did and whatever else he thought I might be interested in. He seemed to like everyone—except for one person, that is.

One day a huge yacht sailed past us. "Whoa," I said. "That thing's—"

"That's my neighbor, Dave." Ken shook his head. "Biggest prick I know. Uh… jerk, I mean. Sorry."

I shrugged it off. The word prick didn't even register as a bad word where I'd come from.

"The guy's got a huge house," Ken continued. "He's got a fake wife—inside and out if you know what I mean—a dozen or so cars, and more money than the US Mint. No matter what anyone else tells you, there is definitely such a thing as *too rich.*"

*From what I'd seen almost everyone in the Hamptons was too rich.* "But if he's your neighbor—" I stopped myself.

Ken seemed to know where I was going. "We have a nice house too, don't get me wrong," he said. "But either floor of Dave's garage has more space than our house and… well… he likes to remind me of that. He's just an egotistical jerk. You'll get to know him better this winter." Uncle Ken smiled at me.

*Wait. What?* "What do you mean?"

"My wife and I—Kate and I—we wanted to know if you'd like to stay in the studio apartment over our garage for the winter. Kate, of course, wants you in our house, but I'm guessing you'd turn that down?"

When I didn't reply immediately he continued. "Anyway, we rent the studio out March through October to an elderly couple from Florida, but November through February… well, it's open. It's empty."

"But—"

"You don't have to decide now. It won't snow for a few more weeks, I'd guess. But if you'd like to, it has heat, a bed, a bathroom, couch and a small kitchen. It's a heckuva lot nicer than the bait shop and… it comes with room service—free dinner every night." He winked at me. "There's a washer and dryer downstairs, and it would make Kate and I feel a whole lot better to have—" His reel suddenly spun like mad and he jumped to attend to it.

He hauled in a huge bass and turned back to me as it flopped around the deck. "Anyway—"

He seemed to think he had to sell the idea more. I was blown away. "Are you serious?" I cut him off.

"Of course." He nodded. "But like I said, you don't have to—"

I wrapped my arms around him. "I'd love to," I said, as he laughed and ruffled my hair with his fishy hands. "But what about Ray?" I pulled away and looked up at Ken. "Will he go for—?"

"I took care of that too. It's totally *your* decision. So what do you think?"

"Uh… is Tom Brady the greatest football player ever?"

"You're asking the wrong guy. As a Jets fan—"

"Never mind. My answer is yes. Absolutely, yes!"

And so it was settled.

Three days later we had the hugest snowstorm—the famous Halloween Blizzard of 2010. I moved into the studio apartment that day.

*My own place. This was going to be awesome!*

## STELLAR 6 – "Winter 2010"

Ken's wife, Kate, was stunningly beautiful. In golf terms I would refer to her as a "hybrid"—a blend of beauties. She was Gisele Bundchen beautiful… Brooklyn Decker, Emma Stone, Katharine McPhee and Carrie Underwood… *that* kind of beautiful. I hadn't yet asked, but I was certain she was a model. She was also an incredible cook. I couldn't understand why Ken ate out so much. I reasoned it had to do with caring for me, since he figured Ray wasn't. Perhaps it had even been Kate's idea. In any case, when she'd get home early from work she'd bring whatever she'd cooked up out to me. It was always something different, always great. If she weren't going to be home by seven, Ken would pick me up something. I told them many times they didn't have to worry about me. I could easily go down to the sub shop on my own. But Kate said the "mother in her" couldn't allow that. She was never overbearing, but I knew it had to be strange for her having a 10-year-old living *alone* in their garage. She would check on me every morning and every night, and routinely invite me over to their house for meals and movies. I turned all of those invitations down. I didn't want to impose on them any more than I already was. Besides, the studio was my home and I loved being out there on my own.

I did try to earn my keep whenever and wherever I could. I shoveled snow from the driveway for Kate before she left for work and before she got home. I'd carry groceries for her, clean out the garage—anything I could think of. She was always on the go. In fact it seemed like she was always gone. Ken would joke she had another life somewhere else, with a better husband and nicer house. In truth, he'd told me she was a lawyer. My original guess was wrong. *Though I had never seen a prettier model.* He called her the "bread winner" of the family; she was a district attorney or something. They had a lot of money and drove nice cars, but they didn't *act* rich. Not like the neighbors anyway. But I'll get to that more later.

I enjoyed watching Ken and Kate together. They were young and playful. They had a lot of snow fights, hugged a lot, kissed a lot, and always seemed to hold hands. Listening to Ken talk about her I tried to imagine my real dad describing my real mom like that before they died. I was convinced they were the same way—always happy, always positive, *always* full of love. I guess you could say Kate was my first crush—like a lot of kids my age have on their teachers. And she was technically my teacher—the only one who helped me with my schoolwork. Yes, Kate was beautiful, fun, funny, athletic and… beautiful. She was perfect. *Or at least as close to perfect as humans get.*

I loved living in the Parker's studio. But it wasn't always easy. I did get lonely from time to time.

I missed Bernie a lot. I had a scrapbook full of ticket stubs, newspaper clippings, drawings and his famous quotes—even a few photos of the two of us together. I probably flipped through that book every day. I often wondered what happened to those two guys who killed him, and all of me hoped there really was such a thing as karma. *If anyone deserved to be kicked in the head by a mule then hit by a bus it was them.* I mentioned I never forgave myself for not going straight to the cops the night Bernie died, and that was true. That was my greatest regret for many years.

One night Kate brought home a bucket of KFC and we sat at my table and ate it together. Ken was out hanging Christmas lights—one of his many winter "jobs." He did it for people who couldn't do it for themselves—mostly the elderly and disabled military veterans. He paid others to help him but he only accepted baked goods as payment from those he helped. *Typical Ken.*

Anyway, Kate could tell something was bothering me that night, and I ended up spilling the entire story of Bernie's death—my guilt and all. It was a difficult conversation, but she really put my mind at ease. I essentially, finally, was able to forgive myself and move on. Kate had a certain… I don't know how to put it. She was just awesome. *She and Ken both were.* And it sure felt great to feel loved again.

Ken and Kate gave me a bike, a skateboard, and my own fishing pole for Christmas that year. We attended the Christmas Eve service at St. Paul's Chapel in Manhattan together—where Bernie had found me nine years earlier. It was the first time I could remember going to an actual church service, and the first time I *ever* felt like I was part of a "real" family.

I look at it this way; I lost a decade of my life in 2010, but at the same time I gained an entire future. As it stands, I think I came out ahead.

## ←★★★★★ NARRATOR ★★★★★→

### ←Sunday, June 26, 2022→

I closed the second notebook and checked my watch. I was starving. *And sooo tired of sitting.* I had moved all over our townhome today—recliner, couch, table, bed, even tried the stairs. It was so hard to stay comfortable with a state fair-worthy watermelon in your belly. 34 weeks tomorrow.

The clock on the wall was two minutes faster than my watch. Either way the 6:15ish felt like 8:30. *Wonder what he's bringing home for dinner*? He should be pulling in any minute.

I could tell from the way Stellar wrote his story that he genuinely cared what his teacher, Mrs. Willett, thought of him. He didn't want her to get any wrong impressions or to see him in any negative light. I did find it interesting what he left out of his rendition—things I knew about him that he for one reason or another didn't feel like sharing*—or remember to.*

Stellar never mentions his parents by name—Derek and Hayley—even though they're listed on his birth certificate. I couldn't tell you why.

He doesn't bring up the two years he spent in the orphanage while Bernie waged an intense battle for legal custody against the aunt that abandoned Stellar in the first place. There's barely a mention of the lavish townhome Bernie owned, that he leased out for free to families in need, while he and Stellar went from shelter to shelter and hotel room to hotel room. Or how that townhome was left to Ray in Bernie's will to pay for raising Stellar*—or what Ray actually did with all that money.*

Additionally, Stellar was diligently homeschooled and tutored for years with only scattered acknowledgements of Bernie and Kate's efforts—and nothing at all about Angela, his private tutor in Southampton. That surprised me. Stellar wasn't one to ever shortchange a person where credit was due. I mean, I get that he hated school, and he was always self-conscious about being perceived as "stupid," but Stellar was brilliant and hard working… and also had an amazing attention to detail that gets almost lost in his version.

I heard the garage door start to open so I put the Mac to sleep. I was tired but eager to pick back up tomorrow morning. *Please, please, please bring Chinese.* The door opened and I saw the pizza box.

"This good?" He walked over and kissed me.

"Exactly what I wanted." I smiled and stole another kiss.

"Excellent!"

*Just tell me it's plain cheese.*

"I got us a Supreme. Hope that's okay."

"You know me too well." I laughed as a victorious grin spread across his face. *Oh well.*

## STELLAR 7 – "2011"

The Parker's neighbor, Dave Dahl, had two daughters—one my age, and one a year or so older. The younger one, Kari, was generally nice but kind of ugly. The older, Taryn, was super pretty but also super snobby. *Trust me, I'm being nice.*

"Takes after her mother," Ken said.

Anyway, Kari was always outside playing with their Labrador, Baxter. Taryn was typically sitting in the bay window of her room or out on her balcony talking on her phone. She couldn't have known I could see into her bedroom, or I'm certain she'd have been more discreet, but I didn't watch when she changed. Okay, sometimes I couldn't help it. But I tried not to. Don't know why I'm even writing this.

Actually, I do know why. The last week of February Taryn had a friend over for a sleepover. It was awe at first sight. I couldn't take my eyes off of her. Long, curly, blonde hair, Yankees cap tugged low, white hoodie and bedazzled jeans. I wanted a closer look and longed for a pair of binoculars—*or a NASA telescope*—so I could see her better (kind of creepy I know). I *had* to see more. But when they started changing that night I didn't watch, not even a peek. I even closed my own shades. It just didn't feel right. I can't explain it. *What 10-year old could?*

Kari was out in the yard the next morning, and I stupidly ran out to the fence to ask her who that girl was in Taryn's room. "Why?" she asked. "Do you love her?"

*Ten-year-old girls are so dumb.* "No," I scoffed, blushing. "Of course not!" *Okay, maybe a little.* The humiliation might have been worth it if Kari had told me the girl's name, but she didn't. She just smiled, coyly abusing the power girls always wield over boys, holding that knowledge out of my reach.

I retreated, defeated, embarrassed I'd even asked. I later realized I had given my secret vantage point away as well. The rest of the week Taryn's bedroom curtains were closed every night. Kari must have told her about my question and Taryn must have figured out what I could see. *Darn again.*

With that Florida couple moving back in on March 1st, I returned to the boat the last day of February… still without a clue as to what the girl in the Yankee hat's name was.

Kate didn't like the idea of me moving back to RB's. That much was quite clear. She and Ken had offered me one of their guest rooms in the house again but I declined. Looking back, I'm actually quite surprised I was even given a choice.

She didn't give me a choice about school though. She said my "adjustment period" was over, and started me on a homeschool curriculum that first day of March. She would drop off my assignments every morning on her way to work, and pick up what I'd finished on her way home. *And I'd better be finished!* I still hated school, but Kate was a better teacher than Bernie. And much *much* prettier.

It was still cool out in early March—upper 40's to low 50's that year—but it was great being back on the boat. It wasn't entirely terrible to see Ray again either. That first day he actually smiled at me and said "hi." *And he appeared to have shaved and showered since October!*

That first Sunday in March Ken was at the boat at 5:30 a.m. sharp, and for the first time ever I wasn't awake when he arrived. He knocked on the door and called into the cabin. "You getting up today?"

I panicked and bolted up, stuffing all my gear in Bernie's old pack. "I'm so sorry," I stammered. "I must not have set the alarm."

Ken laughed. "Don't worry about it. I don't have any charters today. I just thought maybe I'd take you out if you wanted."

"Yes. Absolutely. Of course." I was hoping he'd take me out more that year. I pulled a hooded sweatshirt on.

"Patriots?" Ken teased with a smile. "Where'd you get that crap?"

"From Kate." I said slowly, not wanting to throw her under the bus.

"Figures." He laughed again, ruffling the shaggy hair on my head.

"She's got a huge weakness for handsome blond guys."

"Were you blond once?"

"No," he replied, still smiling. "I'm the exception." He clapped his hands. "Come on, mate. Let's go!"

We cut out of the Shinnecock Canal and into the Peconic River towards the Atlantic. It was a beautiful crisp morning... barely over 40 degrees, but my excitement conquered the cold. We didn't throw out a single line that day, but it was one of my favorite fishing days ever. It felt just like the very first time.

Ken and I talked for several hours, kind of like Kate and I had throughout the winter. We discussed shipwrecks, his favorite fishing spots, the history of all the islands around us, and I finally got up the courage to ask him about that girl.

"Ken, do you know who that girl was at the Dahl's a week or so ago?"

He gave me a puzzled look. "I didn't see any girl over there recently. With Kari or Taryn?"

"Taryn."

"Ah."

"What?" I could hear the sensitivity in my own voice.

"Nothing." Ken shook his head with a smirk. "Sorry, bud, didn't see anyone with Taryn lately. Do you want me to ask them?"

"No." I panicked. "Please don't."

He shoved my shoulder playfully and laughed. "Don't worry, pal. I wouldn't do that to you. Tell me one thing though."

"What?"

"Was she pretty?"

"I don't know." My frustration was evident.

"Didn't get a good look then?"

I couldn't look at him. I shook my head. "Not good enough." That hadn't come out like I'd intended. "I mean—"

"I know what you mean, bud." He revved the motor and turned us back towards shore. "Trust me, man, I know what you mean."

Kate had made us lunch which we ate out on the dock. I hadn't really thought about why we'd come in so early until I noticed Ken was unusually quiet. Something was up.

"Are we going back out?" I asked.

"No." He shook his head. "I can't. I actually have some bad news for you."

Immediately I feared the worst. *He and Kate were moving or he was selling the boat.* It had to be something terrible. "Okay."

"Kate and I are leaving for Hawaii tomorrow for two weeks."

*Okay, that was pretty bad but not absolutely terrible.* "Really? Hawaii? Tomorrow?"

"Yeah. I know it's sudden, bud, very last minute. It's a recent development—as in last week recent—but I still should have mentioned it before. It took all my powers of persuasion to convince Kate you'd be okay but I've always wanted to—"

"I'll be okay."

"Miles, you're ten."

"And a half." He and Kate were the only ones who called me Miles. Ken even introduced me to everyone else as Stellar.

"You're still ten, dude."

"It's not your problem."

"Actually, it kind of is. You've been living on *my* boat, and we both know that, but you can't while we're gone. You have to stay inside with Ray. And you have to promise me you will."

"You're serious?"

"Yes. I'm sorry. If the police were to come by when I'm gone, or if anything happened—"

"Nothing will happen to me."

"But what if it did? Can you even swim?"

I dodged his question. "Did you already buy the tickets?"

"Of course."

"Then you know you need to go. It doesn't matter what I think."

"Miles—"

"I'm fine. Just go."

Ken seemed conflicted, and definitely reluctant to leave me, but he finally stood and nodded. "Okay." He handed me a backpack loaded with books. "Kate prepared two weeks of work for you while we're gone."

My heart sunk. She wasn't even going to come say goodbye. "Fantastic."

Ken smiled. "Hey… we'll be back soon, bud. Tomorrow is Wednesday and I'll see you at 5:30 a.m. two Wednesdays from now. Time will fly, I swear."

I nodded. *Right.*

He held his fist out and I sullenly met it with my own. "You take care, my man. I'll see you soon."

Two weeks is not soon. I forced a smile. "Okay. Say bye to Kate for me."

"Will do, bud."

## STELLAR 8 – "Squirrel"

I *didn't* know how to swim. No one had ever taken me to even a kiddie pool in my life so I didn't understand the threatening nature of water. That ignorance gave me a false sense of security on the docks. I never wore a lifejacket. I should have; I just didn't know I should. The Shinnecock Canal was pretty deep. It had to be to get the bigger boats through, and I spent all day cleaning boats, hanging over the edge—living on the edge. The odds were always in favor of me falling in.

In the first pages of my story I hinted at being raised by a Squirrel. *Kind of.* Well, that Squirrel also saved my life. *Kind of.* It was the night before Ken and Kate came back from Hawaii, an overcast and windy one, and I was finishing up my last boat. I was trying to reach a spot a little further out than I normally tried to reach and the boat suddenly lurched. I lost my footing and fell into the canal. Knowing now how easy it is to swim I feel like a total fool for how difficult I made it on myself that day. I started thrashing like I was the Tasmanian Devil doing the Macarena or like I was being eaten by a school of piranhas. I don't think I had my head above water long enough to scream, but I could hear this sound in my head like barking and it would not stop.

People say your life passes before your eyes in the seconds before you die. I didn't see anything but water. In fact, I wasn't aware of anything other than that the water was freezing cold, I was likely drowning, and that the barking noise never let up. I would sink and the noise would go away, I'd kick a little and it would come back. That noise was the only way I knew up from down. As long as I could hear it I knew I was alive.

And then there was a big splash beside me and I was being hauled to the surface by the back of my shirt. I couldn't see who had me, but he lifted me and carried me up the ladder hanging over the edge of the dock. He gently set me down on the planks, on my side, and then he started licking my face. Or something did.

I don't know what happened to the person who saved my life. I only heard his voice. "You'll be okay, Stella," he said with a strong southern drawl. He sounded like Bernie, but he'd called me "Stella" a couple times already. *Why was he calling me Stella?*

"You'll be okay," the voice said one more time. And that was it.

When I could finally see straight there was no one else around. But there was a dog, a little yapping puppy. *What the…?*

I sat up and looked around me, but there wasn't a single soul in the entire marina. So who had saved me, and where did he go? *There's no way I just imagined that.* I glanced down at the little yapping fur ball fighting my shoelaces.

"Where did you come from?" I asked. The puppy paused his ferocious fight and looked up at me, panting. With his shaggy ears and huge eyes he looked like a... "You look like a squirrel."

The word squirrel set him off again. He started spinning and barking, looking everywhere. *What is it with dogs and squirrels?* "I didn't say I saw a squirrel, you idiot." I laughed and slowly stood, shivering as a strong gust of wind chilled me to the bone. The little yapper went right back to attacking my laces. I bent over and picked him up. "You know what? That's what I'm going to call you—Squirrel."

He barked and licked my face. I laughed again. "It's perfect. Come on now. I need some dry clothes."

I locked him in the cabin of Ken's boat while I changed and rode my bike to the store for some dog food. When I got back I was horrified to see Squirrel had waged war on the seat cushion I usually slept on. He'd torn one corner to shreds already. I didn't know how I'd explain that to Ken. It *definitely* wouldn't help my chances of being able to keep the little nut job.

Ray would *never* have let me keep him, and I didn't want to risk sneaking him up to my room so I kept Squirrel in an old lobster trap on Ken's boat that night.

←←←←←→→→→→

***"Reverse every natural instinct<br>and do the opposite of what you are inclined to do,<br>and you will probably come very close<br>to having a perfect golf swing."***

- Ben Hogan

## STELLAR 9 – "Summer 2011"

One of Squirrel's favorite things to do was retrieve golf balls. *Yes, I still had Squirrel.* Ken didn't mind the dog, actually said it was good for a boy to have a dog. But he did mind the damage. Squirrel was only allowed below deck at night when I was sleeping. *Yes, I was allowed to sleep on the boat again.* Ken bought me a dog-gate and that kept Squirrel out of the cabins of the boats when I cleaned them.

But back to golf. I still had Rory's sand wedge—my magic wand—and carried it with me most everywhere I went. One afternoon I "borrowed" a box of golf balls I'd found behind the counter in the bait shop and began chipping them around the grass. They were considerably easier to hit and control than the acorns and whiffle balls I'd been practicing with to date. Maybe that was because I was actually growing into the wedge now—a little. *Who knows?* I also found when I landed the balls on the turf mats on the dock, I could get them to hop and spin backwards. It added a whole new dimension to my chipping obsession.

Squirrel seemed fascinated by the chipping game. It was one of the few things he'd sit still for. He'd watch the swings, the hops and the spins, and then I'd tell him to go fetch the balls. His Sheltie herding instincts would take over and he'd miraculously bring them all back to me, and sit still while I hit them again. We played this game every day for weeks. One day a guy sitting on the dock across the canal yelled at me. "You ever miss the mat?"

"What?" I yelled back, even though I'd heard him fine.

"Do you ever miss the mat?"

I shrugged. "It's pretty big. But yeah, I've missed it before."

"Son, at best that's a ten-by-ten foot mat. That's not very big."

That was news to me. The slingshot targets I shot at were barely bigger than a quarter—infinitely harder to hit than this. All I was doing was hitting a golf ball fifteen to twenty yards or so. I figured that was a pretty big target for that distance.

"Boy, I've watched you for days hit hundreds of balls, and I don't think I've seen you miss the mat yet."

I still didn't understand the significance. "So?"

"I'm just saying. Odds are pretty good you'd miss quite a bit... especially at your age." The guy shook his head and walked away. *I felt like I should know him from somewhere.*

"Who was that guy?" Ken walked up behind me.

"You don't know him?"

"No." Ken shook his head. "Don't think I've seen him before."

"Me either," I said. *Must not have been a customer then.* "He was just talking to me about golf."

The next day the gray-bearded man was again sitting on the bench across the canal while I was chipping, and this time there was another guy with him—a much younger looking white guy. I went through the box of balls five times, and the sixth time through I noticed the two men had left the bench and crossed over to my side of the canal. They were approaching the shop when Squirrel noticed them and began his frenzied barking. "Squirrel, stop!" I reprimanded him and amazingly he did. "Sit," I said firmly. He did that too. *Incredible!* The tongue-wagging fur ball glanced back and forth between the approaching men and me.

"Son," the tall older man from yesterday held out his hand, "name's Jake. This here is my friend Mr. Martin Birch. He's a golf pro at a local club."

I shook their hands. "Ken's inside if you need him."

"How old are you?" Mr. Birch asked.

"Ten. Almost eleven."

"Seriously?" He and Jake exchanged raised eyebrows.

"Yes sir." I nodded.

"I've seen you hit sixty straight shots to nearly the same spot on that mat—give or take a foot or so." Mr. Birch shook his head and continued, "I've seen you drop and stop it and seen you spin it back. Do you control that?"

"Are you asking if I choose whether to spin it back or not?"

"Yes."

I nodded again.

"Every time?" He knelt down to pet Squirrel and the puppy growled.

"Chill, Squirrel." *Why is this so surprising?* "Yes."

"Can I help you gentlemen?" Ken approached us from the bait shop.

Mr. Birch turned and introduced himself, handing Ken a card. "Name's Martin. I work at The Hills. My cell number is on the back. I'd love to give the kid a free lesson sometime."

"Okay," Ken replied guardedly. "Appreciate you stopping by."

"Mister," I tapped Jake on the arm. "Where do I know you from?"

The man shrugged. "Not sure." He bent over to pat Squirrel's head. The dog didn't growl this time, just wagged his tail.

*That was weird.* Ken and I watched them walk off the docks. Squirrel hates being touched by anyone but me. He'll even growl at Ken.

"Were they asking you about boats?" Ken asked me.

"No. Just golf." I twirled the wedge in my hands. "Do you think they offer free lessons to everyone?"

Ken shook his head. "No way. Not at The Hills."

"What's The Hills?"

"It's that private golf club down the street from our place. One of the five Dave's a member of."

"Oh, *that* kind of place."

"Yes." Ken laughed. "Playground of the wealthy. Garden of the gods."

Bernie was never a fan of private golf clubs or "athletic segregation" as he called it. "Most of the best courses in the world are private," he'd say. "And 98% of us will never get to set foot inside those gates. It ain't right."

I understood his point. So many more people would love the game of golf if they had access to the world's best courses. Ken said even he would golf if they'd let him play Augusta National—annual home of the Masters. *If that doesn't prove Bernie's point, I didn't know what would.*

I saw Jake almost every day Monday through Thursday, every week, for the rest of the summer. He was always there, on the same bench across the canal, eating peanuts or a sandwich, and watching me chip balls from four to five o'clock. I eventually stopped wondering where I knew him from, and just figured it didn't really matter.

By the end of summer I could spin the ball backwards, forwards, left or right on command, and more and more people would gather to watch and occasionally applaud. Having performed magic tricks in front of crowds in New York City, the attention never fazed me, though I still always found it odd. I wasn't doing anything Rory, Phil—or any of the other golfers I watched—couldn't have done just as well. *Or even better.*

This was easy. *It was just golf.*

## STELLAR 10 – "Bullies"

One rainy Friday in mid-September I was inside the bait shop with Squirrel. Ken had gone into town with Kate for the weekend, and Ray had asked me to tend the counter while he ran to the store. I was cashing out my only customer when I noticed a business card sticking out from under the register. It was Martin's—the golf pro from The Hills—with the free lesson offer.

Ken had likely either forgotten about it or not seen any value in it, but I was curious. I waited until Ray came back from the store with his necessities, all beer as far as I could tell, and then asked if I could take off early. He said he was closing up shop anyway, so I could go. I hopped on my bike and rode down Tuckahoe Road to the address on the business card. I showed it to the man in the clubhouse, and he called someone who told him Martin was gone for the weekend. "Sorry, kid," the guard said. "You'll have to come back another day."

I was walking back out to my bike when I saw a man driving an odd-looking golf cart, with a cage-like barrel on the front of it, out on the practice range. He drove it right over the scattered golf balls and the barrel somehow picked them all up. I stood in the light rain and watched, mesmerized by the scene. I didn't even hear the bikes roll up on the gravel behind me.

Suddenly I was falling forward and landing face down in a puddle, having been shoved forcefully from behind. As I tried to push up out of the water I was knocked back down. I rolled just enough to see three boys standing above me, just before one of them kicked me in the stomach.

"What are you doing here, stupid?" the fattest one asked. He spat on me and kicked me again while the other two laughed.

I had muddy water in my mouth and was still trying to stand, but the tallest one kept shoving me back down. "Yeah, stupid, we don't want perverts here."

*Pervert? How was I a pervert?* I wanted to tell them they had the wrong person, but they weren't letting me talk. I finally found a way to stand, but that just gave the third kid the opportunity he'd been waiting for. I tried to duck but didn't make it in time as bony knuckles connected solidly with my left eye. I staggered backwards as someone tripped me—and there I was in that puddle again. I heard them all laughing and one of them said, "Taryn will love this."

I was aware of a motor approaching but I was also still being kicked and shoved down. I felt like I was drowning, but above water this time. It was a strange sensation. Another strange sensation was a voice I heard yelling at the boys, a familiar voice.

I was trying to ball myself up now, to shield my body from as many blows as I could, and then suddenly there weren't any more blows. I struggled to open my eyes, my left eye was already swelling shut, and I saw a man running towards me from the driving range. I lay still on the ground as he picked me up and carried me into the clubhouse. I heard someone say, "Jake, what's going on?"

*Jake? As in the man from the bench across the canal?*

"Some kids were beating this boy in the lot. He needs help."

*And there it was. There was that voice again.*

"Do you know the kid, Jake?"

"I do."

"Do you know where he lives?"

"Yes, sir."

"Can you take him home? We don't want any trouble here."

"Yes, sir. It's okay if I leave now? I was supposed to be here another hour."

"I'll take care of that. I'll get someone else out on the range. Go ahead."

Jake covered me with his jacket and carried me out to his truck.

"My bike," I mumbled.

"I'll get it," he replied.

A minute later I heard Jake load my bike in the back of his old pickup, and then he hopped into the cab beside me. He started up the truck and pulled out of the lot. I was shivering and moaning. It hurt to move and burned too much to open my eyes. "Thank you," I muttered weakly.

"You'll be okay, Stella," he said.

I was right. *I knew exactly who Jake was.*

## STELLAR 11 – "Jake"

"Is your father home?" Jake asked as he pulled up to the bait shop. "I don't see his truck."

"He's not my… No, he's in the city."

"Who takes care of you while he's gone?"

I didn't feel like working up a satisfactory explanation to my complicated living arrangements at that point so I just said, "Really, I'm okay." I reached out to try to open the door but groaned. My ribs ached.

"You must go to the doctor."

"I'll be okay." I made one more lunge to open the door and this time succeeded. I stepped out of the truck and staggered down the dock towards the boat.

"Stella, the house is over here."

"It's locked." I replied, even though I had the key. *And my name is not Stella!*

"You stay on the boat? Your father is okay with that?"

"He's… " *Never mind.* I shook my head and stepped onto the boat. "Can you help me with this door?"

Jake followed me onto the boat and pulled the door open. I ducked inside but he stayed out on the deck. "You can come in," I invited.

"I'll be back," he replied.

I lay down on the bed. I could hear Squirrel barking but it hurt to move. I couldn't handle fending off a loony pup right now.

A half-hour later there was a knock on the door. I didn't answer but I heard it open anyway. And then I was being wrapped in blankets and ice simultaneously. There was a bag of ice on my ribs and a smaller pack on my eye. It felt wonderful. Cold, but wonderful. I heard Jake say at least a dozen times, "You should go to a doctor." But he never forced me to.

All I could think about were the words I'd heard the bullies say. *Pervert and Taryn.* If the "pervert" wasn't just a typically immature insult, and the combination of the two were intentional, then somehow these boys knew Taryn… and had heard the story of me watching her through her bedroom window. *Awesome.* In a little over a month I'd be moving back into the studio over the garage—something I'd really been looking forward to until now. Suddenly I was dreading it.

I drifted off at some point and when I woke it was Saturday morning and Jake was gone. There was a note on the bed beside me.

*Call this number if you need anything. (762) 218-0818*

I sat up slowly. My movement startled Squirrel and he began barking. I crawled across the floor and opened his cage door. He jumped out and leapt into my arms. "Ouch," I groaned as his little legs pummeled me and his tongue lashed my face. "Easy, you crazy dog."

I opened the door and stepped out onto the back deck of the boat. It was a beautiful morning, but the bright sunlight really hurt my head. I turned back inside and glanced in the mirror. My left eye was swollen but not completely shut. The ice had done wonders. How long had Jake stayed?

I grabbed the note off the bed and went to walk Squirrel. Then I stepped into RB's to use the phone.

"What the heck happened to you?"

"It's nothing, Ray. I just fell."

"Into what? A washing machine? A lawn mower?"

"Can I use the phone?"

"First you have to tell me how you got that shiner, and all… that." He gestured at all my cuts and scrapes.

"Forget it." I turned to leave but he gave in.

"Fine, fine. Whatever. Do what you want. You always do anyways."

There were a number of things I could have said then. Instead I just picked up the phone and dialed the number Jake had left me. A female voice answered on the second ring. "Yes."

"Sorry… I thought…" I paused. "Is Jake there?"

"Jake?"

"I'm sorry," I stammered again. "I must have the wrong—"

Another voice on the line interrupted me. "No, no. You have the right number. This is Jake."

"Are you sure?" I asked.

There was a soft chuckle. "Pretty sure I'm me, yes."

*How did the woman not know the name of the man she apparently lived with?* "I wanted to… I was wondering if you could come by RB's today?"

"Are you okay, Stella?"

*I couldn't take it anymore.* "You do know it's Stellar, right?"

Another chuckle. "No, sir, I didn't. I'm terribly sorry 'bout that."

"Well—"

"I'll be there as soon as I can be."

"Thank you," I replied, but the line was already dead.

An hour and a half later there was a knock on my boat door. I opened it to see Jake's wrinkled, gap-toothed grin. "It's good to see you up, Mr. Stellar."

*He finally got the Stellar right.* "That's much better. I'm already being bullied without the girly nickname."

"Why have a nickname at all, sir?"

"My previous owner gave it to me." *Okay, that made me sound like a dog.* "I mean, the guy who used to take care of me—"

"This man, Ken, he's not your father?"

"No." I was worried I shouldn't have revealed that. "But speaking of names, why didn't that woman on the phone know your name was Jake."

Jake chuckled. "My actual name is James. But long ago—when I first move here—the caddie master wrote it down as Jake. Everyone here's called me that since."

"And your wife doesn't know that?"

"Rose?" Another chuckle. "She's not my wife."

"You're living with someone who's not your wife?"

Jake laughed even harder this time. "It's difficult to explain. This twenty questions?"

"I'm sorry." I watched Squirrel lick Jake's hand. "Should I call you Jake? Or James? And you work at The Hills?"

"James is preferred, between you and me, and yes, I'm a caddie and range attendant at The Hills."

"One more question." I did feel like I was asking him a lot of questions. "How did you happen to see me fall in the canal that day? And why did you just take off?"

He held up two fingers to indicate I'd asked two questions but began to answer anyway. "I was on the bench." He pointed across the canal. "And heard the dog go crazy."

"Seriously? So Squirrel isn't yours?"

"Is that another question?"

I playfully reached out to shove him, but the sudden movement hurt too much. I rewound my arm. I liked this guy. He reminded me a lot of Bernie. "I guess it is. You don't have to answer it."

"I don't mind. But no, I'd never seen that dog—Squirrel—before. You were lucky he was there, though."

*Not sure luck was the right word.* "You didn't answer my question about why you left so suddenly after saving me—without staying around to make sure I was okay."

James nodded. "Would you accept that I'd rather not say… but that I knew you would be okay?"

I didn't want to say, "yes" to his question, but I also wanted to respect his privacy. Maybe he was embarrassed, in which case I definitely didn't want to push him. I was just as embarrassed I'd needed to be saved. *Twice now.* "I guess that's okay."

"Appreciate that." James nodded.

"Sure. So, where do you live?"

"Brooklyn."

"Wait, you come out here from Brooklyn every day?"

"No, sir. Just Monday through Thursday."

"So that's why I only see you over there those days." I pointed towards the bench on the other side of the canal. He nodded. "But wait, why were you at The Hills yesterday—on a Friday?"

"The range attendant could not make it in, so they called me."

"Don't they know you live in Brooklyn?"

"No."

*Wow!* "How long have you worked at The Hills?"

"Seven years, sir."

"So, you were in Brooklyn when I called this morning?" He nodded. "James, I would have never asked you to come!"

"It's okay. I wished to check on you anyway."

As I marveled at his thoughtfulness he redirected the conversation. "Care if I ask you a question or two?"

"Not at all."

"These boys that were beating you yesterday… you knew them?"

"No. I only recognized the tall one, and I don't even know from where. Do you?"

"I've seen them around plenty. Two are member kids I believe. The tall one I think is the son of the golf professional at The National. He's quite the player. Any idea why they were beating you?"

I smiled as I came up with the perfect answer to his question. "Would you accept that I'd rather not say?"

James laughed heartily. "Boy… I will indeed." He continued to laugh. "Well played, son."

"Appreciate that," I replied.

Convinced I would be fine, James stayed only another ten minutes and then insisted he needed to get back to Brooklyn. I didn't object, I still felt bad I'd summoned him all the way out here. "I'll see you here Monday?" he asked.

"Sure—yes, I'll be here Monday," I answered.

I knew between now and then I'd have to answer another set of questions. Ken would be back tomorrow afternoon, and there'd be no hiding my swollen eye from him. Ken definitely wouldn't take "I'd rather not say" as an answer.

## STELLAR 12 – "Trick or Trick"

I had never gone Trick or Treating before. *What eleven-year-old American kid could say that?* But it was never important for me, or for anyone I'd been with. Kate insisted I go—that I do it once in my life at least. I said I'd go as long as she went with me. It's not that I was afraid to go by myself. It's just that—you'll laugh—I didn't know what to do.

I went as Batman. Actually, that's overstating it. I wore a Batman mask. We walked through the Parker's neighborhood, rang the doorbells and collected the candy. I have to admit, it was a lot more fun than I'd thought it would be. I had just told Kate "five more" when we walked up the lengthy walkway of a beautiful red house on Oceanview Drive. I rang the doorbell and called out, "Trick or Treat." The door opened almost immediately.

There were two girls standing there, Taryn and a stunning blonde girl with a Jeter jersey and Yankees hat on. *THAT girl!* I was blushing seven shades of red under my mask and ducked my head to not make eye contact with either of them. They were laughing as they dropped candy in my plastic pumpkin and I spun to leave. I hurried down the sidewalk towards Kate. "Let's go," I said urgently.

"Mrs. Parker?" Taryn called out behind me.

"Come on, Kate." I said loud enough for Taryn to hear me, pulling on Kate's arm before she could answer.

"Wait, is that—"

"Please, Kate." I was still pulling on her arm. I was so thankful it was dark. "Please don't say anything."

"Miles…" She followed me down the sidewalk. "What's wrong? Was that Taryn?"

I nodded. "Let's go home, now. Please. I don't feel good."

She didn't argue. We hurried back to their house in silence. She walked me to the garage, to the door of the studio. It was my first night back there. "Miles, can I come up for a bit?"

"I don't think it's a good idea, Mrs. Parker."

"Wait. Mrs. Parker? Since when do you call me—"

"I should call you Mrs. Parker."

"Miles, what's going on?"

"I don't want to talk about it tonight, okay? I'm exhausted." I stepped inside and basically closed the door in her face. Squirrel was yapping from his cage in the garage. He wasn't allowed upstairs when I was gone. I stepped into the garage, let him out of his cage, and let him out to do his business. I stood on the back doorstep and my eyes suddenly filled with tears.

The reality of the social gap between that girl and I suddenly overwhelmed me. That was the biggest house we'd stopped at all night, the most expensive house, right on Shinnecock Bay. The mystery girl's family was obviously filthy, stinking rich—they were probably very important people. I was a nobody… a never-would-be-somebody. She was way *way* out of my league. This girl—whose name I still didn't even know—had sucked all the hope and happiness out of me tonight without saying a word, without doing anything at all. For the first time since I moved to Southampton I felt like there was no future for me here—I could never fit in here. For the first time I could ever remember, self-pity and an associated bitterness entered my life… all because of my feelings of inadequacy around a stupid girl.

Nothing had really changed that night, and yet everything seemingly had. I was at once both intelligent enough to realize how ridiculous that was and yet absolutely incapable of convincing myself to dismiss it. I took Squirrel upstairs with me and went straight to bed. *At 9:30.*

I suddenly felt very lonely. I missed my mom and dad. I missed Bernie. I even missed Kate and wished I could have explained what I was feeling to her earlier. But it was too complicated, and my feelings towards her were becoming more complicated as well. The older I got the hotter she got, and that wasn't good either. I was having thoughts and feelings towards her I needed to control. She was Ken's wife. She needed to be Mrs. Parker to me.

I desperately needed a friend, someone my own age to talk to, who could understand what I was going through. I rolled over and closed my eyes, squeezing Squirrel to me. He licked my face. *Dogs. Why can't girls be more like dogs?* The love of a dog is nearly a given—so simple and unconditional.

I drifted off with the image of that beautiful face under the Yankee cap locked in my head. I still didn't even know her name.

## STELLAR 13 – "The Naked Truth"

A knock on my door woke me the next morning. It was Uncle Ken. "You doing okay?"

"Yeah." My reply was drawn out and loaded with suspicion. "Why?"

"No reason. Kate just said you weren't feeling good last night."

"That's all she said?" *I wouldn't have believed him if he'd said "yes."*

"Kind of."

"What else did she say?"

"Let's go get something to eat."

We drove to a local diner and engaged in a staring contest across two steaming stacks of pancakes.

"Okay." Ken finally broke the ice. "Tell me about this girl."

"Girl?"

Ken laughed. "Right. You have no idea what I'm talking about. Kate completely misread you last night."

I ignored his sarcasm. "I don't want to talk about it."

"Come on, bud. You've got to talk to someone."

I shrugged and stabbed the pancakes to death. "You wouldn't understand."

"Why not?"

"Because you have everything you want, or at least you can have everything you want. You have a beautiful wife, a great job… " The bitterness was about to bring the tears.

"Easy, Miles. Easy." He reached across and grabbed my fork mid-stab. "What don't you have that you want? Besides—"

I looked up at him. "Besides?" "Well, I'd imagine you'd like your parents back."

I shrugged.

"Look, I didn't bring you out here to make you mad. I just thought maybe I could help with what's going on. But if you don't want to talk about it you don't have to talk about it."

I took a couple of bites and looked out the window at the passing cars. Ken didn't know anything about the one-sided fight I'd had with those three boys. I'd never told him. When he asked about my eye I told him I fell riding the skateboard. He hadn't pushed it then—whether he believed me or not. I decided to take a chance. "I don't know her name."

Ken looked at me a few seconds before replying. "I can find out for you."

"I don't want you asking the neighbors."

"I won't."

"So how will you—"

"Kate told me who she is."

I dropped my fork on the plate. "Kate knows her name?"

"No, no, no, I didn't mean that." Ken leaned forward in the booth. "She told me where she lives—which house… *whose* house."

"What do you mean?"

"I assume you saw her at that house Taryn was at last night?"

I nodded.

"That's the mayor's house, Miles."

"Are you serious?" Now I was even more depressed. *I knew she was someone important.* "That's great!" I muttered. Ken had a smile on his face. "It's not funny, Uncle Ken."

"What's wrong with liking the mayor's daughter?"

"It's like me wanting to be president or… " I tried to think of another appropriate comparison. "Or like a Patriots fan *ever* cheering for the Jets."

"You need to work on your similes. There are worse things." He paused and took a big bite of pancake. "Does she know you like her?"

"Heck no. If she even knew who I was she'd hate me."

"Why in the world would you say that?"

"Because she knows I—" I stopped myself. Ken didn't know about the window either.

"She knows you what?"

"Nothing," I shook my head.

"Miles?"

"She thinks I saw her naked." *Man that was hard to say out loud.*

"Whoa!" Ken pushed his plate aside. "What? Why would she—"

"I can see in Taryn's window from the studio."

"Oh boy."

"Wait. It gets worse. I'm even more of an idiot than you think."

"I don't think you're an idiot."

"You will." I looked around to make sure no one else was listening. "I saw her in Taryn's room."

"So you *did* see her naked?"

"No."

"But you could see her in Taryn's room?"

"Yes. I've seen Taryn—" I rolled my hand, allowing the implication to finish the sentence for me. "But not that girl. The night they were in Taryn's room changing I couldn't watch. I wanted to see more of her but not that way. Does that make any sense?"

I couldn't look at him so if he was nodding I didn't know. "Anyway, the next morning I asked Kari who the girl was with her sister. Kari told Taryn I'd asked about her, and Taryn must have figured out where I'd seen them. They must have assumed I saw more. I don't know."

Ken was nodding so I figured he understood what I was saying. "Is it possible you're overreacting? Maybe Taryn doesn't know you've seen her—" He rolled his hand as I had earlier.

I knew then I needed to tell him. I shook my head. "No. Do you remember my black eye and scraped up arm?"

He nodded. "From the skateboard?"

"It wasn't from the skateboard." I continued before he could say anything else. I told him the whole story about going to The Hills, about getting beat up by those three boys, and about the things they'd said.

"Why didn't you tell me about this before?"

I sighed and threw my head back against the cushioned seat behind me. "I couldn't. I didn't want you to get involved."

"Miles… no matter what you want I am involved, and I'm going to remain involved. I'm here for you… for everything. And those things those kids said about you, they're not true. Not at all."

"They kind of are."

"Listen to me… " This time Ken looked around to see if anyone else was listening. "The only way I know how to say this is straightforward. Miles, you're an eleven-year-old boy. You're curious. You see a naked girl you're going to look… it's perfectly normal. Even if she were the ugliest girl on earth, which Taryn is not. It *doesn't* make you a pervert. Trust me, I've been there. When I was your age I… well, let's just say I'd have done the same thing you did… with one difference. I wouldn't have had your conscience or self-control. I'm certain of that. You've got to stop beating yourself up—" He paused, as he realized his poor choice of words there. I smiled. "You know what I mean." He laughed.

"I let someone else do that for me."

He nodded. "Yeah, sorry about that. But hey, you can't keep this stuff from me. I know I'm not your dad, but a guy's gotta have someone to talk to. You need someone to talk to when things happen—when life happens."

"You're not mad at me?"

"Mad? No way, man." He shook his head. "I've done much dumber things than that in my life, trust me. And by the way, you know what you said earlier about me having everything I want, or being able to have everything I want?"

"Yeah."

"That's definitely not true. Perhaps this is TMI for you, but Kate and I can't have kids. Kate is… well… and she can't… you know… give birth. But you want to talk about stupid? I was going to ask her to marry me, and then I find out she can't…" He paused and shook his head. "So I broke up with her instead. How's that for dumb?"

I nodded. "Pretty dumb."

"Yeah." He continued. "This girl who was way *way* out of my league, who gave dumb old me a chance when she could've had pretty much any guy... yeah... sheesh! Selfish and stupid—that was me."

"That's hard to believe." I was understating my shock. I couldn't imagine either of them with anyone else. "But you got her back."

"Yes. Pure luck there. I spent three years trying to find something—someone—better and when I realized the absolute stupidity of my ways it was too late. I found Kate again but she was with another guy. Fortunately for me that guy turned out to be a tool, and I groveled my way back into her good graces. I'm lucky in so many ways to have this second chance, even if I can't have my own kid or kids with her."

"She's amazing." I agreed with him.

"Agreed. But, hey, if I'm being honest, there are still days where it sucks, where we really struggle with our medical misfortunes. Sure, we have enough money to adopt, but I can't lie... it wouldn't be the same as raising our own from birth, you know?"

"I'm sorry," I whispered.

"Shoot, don't be sorry, man. You were right about the other thing. I am married to the most beautiful woman in the world."

Ken paid the tab and we went back to the house. I showered and took Squirrel out for a nice long walk. When we got back to the studio there was a note taped to my door. I pulled it off and opened it to find two words. "Lauren Chambers."

←←←←←→→→→→

***"Golf is deceptively simple and endlessly complicated."***

- Arnold Palmer

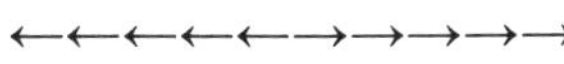

# STELLAR 14 – "2012"

It was different living in the studio this winter. In the four months I was there I never even opened the blinds on the west side of the apartment—not once. I was paranoid that the one time I'd look out I'd see Taryn looking back at me. I had other irrational fears at that time, like getting arrested for spying. It sounds ridiculous, but I didn't exactly understand the law. Guilt always makes the littlest indiscretions seem so much worse. I didn't see Lauren all winter—not once. But I did see those bullies, all three of them, several times. They were always together—the fat one, the bony one, and the tall one. I pointed them out to Ken once and he asked me if I wanted him to run them over. "Can you?" I asked, though I was pretty sure he was kidding.

"No," he said. "It would dent my truck."

I'm also pretty sure that wasn't the only reason. I had learned from Bernie—and even more so from Ken—violence wasn't ever the right answer, but that didn't prevent me from at least entertaining thoughts of physical retribution. If nothing else, I'd pay good money to see a llama spit in their faces.

The second week of March I was chipping golf balls on the docks when I heard a familiar voice call out to me from across the canal. "Good day there, Mr. Stellar."

I smiled and turned around. "James."

"Looks like you've still got the touch, son."

"You seriously are making too big of a deal out of this golf thing."

"Maybe." James nodded his head. "But Mr. Birch wants to know if you can stop by tomorrow. I can pick you up if you need me to."

"Ken's taking me fishing early and then I have a couple homeschool tests." I didn't want to go back to The Hills.

"If I may—you can still do those things. Come after your tests. Just give Mr. Birch an hour. Four o'clock tomorrow."

It was the least I could do considering James had probably set this up especially for me. I sighed heavily. "I'll be there."

James sat on a bench and ate, watching me for another hour or so. Around five, I heard him call out that he was leaving and he'd see me tomorrow. I waved over my shoulder. I'd just missed the mat twice in a row. That almost never happened.

The next afternoon I was on my bike riding over to The Hills when I happened to glance over my shoulder. The sight of three boys on bikes closing in on me caused both my heart and feet to accelerate. *Exactly why I didn't want to come back here.* I pedaled as fast as I could but they were still gaining ground. I pulled into the golf course parking lot and hopped off my bike as they surrounded me.

"I thought I made myself clear, pervert," the fat one said. "You are not welcome here."

"You're going to have to explain the pervert part." *What are you doing? Keep your mouth shut.*

"You like to watch naked girls, do ya?" the short one cut in.

Let. It. Go. "I don't want any trouble guys and I don't know what you're talking about."

"You've never seen Taryn naked?" the tall one asked with a laugh.

"How would I?"

"You live next door to her during the winter."

"And?"

"And she says you've seen her naked. A lot."

*Is there actually such a thing as not a lot naked?* "I think I would remember that."

"You're calling her a liar." The tall one seemed particularly offended.

"That's exactly what he said, Josh." The fat one nodded at the tall one.

"That's not what I heard." A familiar voice challenged the boys from behind me. I glanced back in relief to see James approaching. He was dressed in his full caddie uniform.

"Stay out of this, old man," the fat kid snapped.

"Afraid I can't do that, Caleb," James replied gently. "This boy did no one here any harm. Whatever your beef is with him it's fabricated."

"So you're calling us liars?"

*The bony one was going to be referred to from now on as the dumb one.* "No. No one's calling anyone liars," I said. "It's a misunderstanding, that's all."

"I could have you fired you know." Josh—the tall one—was pointing at James.

"Perhaps you could, sir, but right now you're being videotaped." James pointed at the clubhouse behind him. "I'd be happy to send your dad this video and the one from last year."

He wasn't more specific, but clearly he didn't have to be. If he was bluffing about being taped it worked, because that threat straightened Josh up right away. He looked nervous now.

"So," James continued. "Josh, why don't you, Caleb, and Elliott head on home?"

"We ain't done with you," the dumb one, Elliott, sneered. "We know where you live."

As they rode away I turned to James. "Thank you. Perfect timing."

"What was that all about? What do those boys have against you?"

"It's a long story." I was expecting to go inside but James led me towards the driving range instead. "What are we doing?"

"He's on the range." James pointed at a man standing with a boy at the end of the range. "Giving lessons."

We walked up to Mr. Birch and I noticed James step back. "Stellar, thanks for coming." Mr. Birch said, stepping away from the other boy and holding out his hand. I shook it and watched the other boy launch a ball an awful long way with a driver. "Stellar, this is my son, Nicholas. Nick, come say hi."

Nick looked thrilled to put the club down. He approached and shook my hand. "Is your name really Stellar?"

I nodded. "Yeah."

"Cool," the boy replied.

*Totally not the response I was expecting.* I watched Mr. Birch pull a $5 bill out of his wallet and hand it to Nick. "Grab a couple Cokes, will you?"

"I wanted to watch, Dad."

"Nick, please do as you're told."

I was going to object, to tell Mr. Birch I didn't mind, but I saw James shaking his head at me. I kept my mouth shut.

I spent the next half hour hitting chip shots with Mr. Birch towards a pin about fifty yards away. I had no problem doing everything he asked me to do with the ball at that distance, except spin it forward. I couldn't figure that out on grass. Mr. Birch demonstrated how to pull it off and I worked on that exclusively until I could get the ball to release forward a little. *There... that wasn't so bad.* And then he put a driver in my hand and I lost all control. I hit a dozen shots a dozen different places, none of them over 150 yards. I saw Mr. Birch shaking his head and I knew he was disappointed, but I'd never swung a driver before. I had no idea what to do with it. I heard James say. "He just needs a little practice."

Mr. Birch nodded. "Maybe."

A teenage girl came out of the clubhouse then and yelled for Mr. Birch. "Telephone, Martin."

He walked over to me. "That's enough for today. I gotta go take that call. Good seeing you again." Mr. Birch nodded at James. "Thanks, Jake." He then turned to his son. "Nick, go pick up those balls." Nick nodded as his dad left us.

I stood there for a minute feeling pretty miserable. I felt like I'd just blown some big opportunity. I was convinced Mr. Birch hadn't found in me what he'd been hoping to. *Crap.*

"Shall we?" James asked.

Nick headed out to pick up the eighty-nine balls I'd hit. "Give me a minute," I whispered to James and followed Nick out onto the range.

"You're really good at golf," I said to him.

He laughed. "Me?"

"Yeah. You were crushing that ball."

"Anyone can hit a ball far—" He caught his error too late. "Sorry, I mean, I… I can't do what you do."

"Why is that such a big deal? Aren't shorter shots easier?"

Nick shook his head. "Hardly. Golf is won with the short game. Your accuracy from forty to fifty yards is amazing. Professionals would kill for that on-demand precision."

I didn't respond to his praise. It was nice just to have someone my age to talk to. "Your dad seems nice."

"You should've been there five minutes earlier."

"Why?"

"Never mind."

He didn't seem to want to talk about it and I didn't want to push it. We gathered all the golf balls and took them back to the staging area, setting them up in a pyramid.

"What did Josh want with you?" Nick asked suddenly.

"You saw that?"

"Saw it. Heard about it. I take it you're the kid they beat up a few months ago."

I nodded. "That's me."

"Josh is all talk. He'd be nothing without the two thugs. They're all jerks though. What did he want with you?"

"He thinks I saw this girl Taryn naked." *Maybe I shouldn't have admitted that.*

I saw a smile sweep across Nick's face. "Really? So did you?"

"Maybe," I smiled back.

"So they beat you up?"

I nodded again. "Yep. I take it Taryn is his girlfriend?"

"No," Nick shook his head. "It's his girlfriend's best friend."

The smile vanished from my face, and I suddenly felt like I'd been punched in the stomach. "His girlfriend's best friend?"

"Yeah, they're all in a tight circle—all those rich kids. Caleb, Elliott, Taryn, Josh, Caitlin and his girlfriend Lauren."

*Could it get any worse?* "Lauren, the mayor's daughter?"

"Ex-mayor's daughter, but yes, that's the one. You know her?"

"No," I turned away.

"You ask me she's too good for the other five. The other five drink and smoke already. Not Lauren."

"They're twelve!"

"They're rich. They think they're untouchable."

"But aren't you—"

"Rich?" He knew where I was going. "I guess. But there's a good rich and a bad rich. There's the work for everything kind, and then there's the silver spoon kind—the spoiled rotten rich. Those guys are rotten."

I heard someone yelling Nick's name and looked up. His dad was waving at him from the clubhouse. Nick stood up. "Hey, Stellar, it was nice meeting you. I know it's a ways off still, but if you're not doing anything in June, meet me here at 7 p.m. on the 10th."

"Sure thing," I said as Nick ran off towards his dad. *That was a really specific request.* I walked towards James who was straightening the other pyramids of balls. "Thanks," I said.

"For?"

"Letting me talk to Nick."

"He's a good kid. His dad just wishes he was a better golfer."

"Why does that matter?"

James laughed. "Great question. Fact of the matter is, there's four private clubs all jammed into this one area and each of them has a golf pro with a twelve or thirteen-year-old son. Three of them are almost scratch golfers already. But Nick… he's a fifteen handicap."

"What does that mean?"

"Basically, if those four played a round of golf from the same set of tees Nick would probably lose by fifteen strokes every time. It means he might never be as good as the other three and Mr. Martin has to hear about it from everyone—from the pros at the other clubs. Mr. Martin is trying to coach his boy but it's a terrible idea, him teaching his own son."

"Nick was kind of implying that out there."

James nodded. "Nick doesn't love golf—might not even like it—but Mr. Martin makes him play rounds with the other three every week all summer long. They play 12 matches and the winner gets a cup. Nick's never won a single match in three years—0 for 36. That boy Josh has won 27 of them and all three cups so far."

I could do the math. Josh was great at golf, good-looking, rich and athletic. No wonder Lauren liked him. We walked across the parking lot towards my bike.

"You need a ride, sir?" James nodded over at his truck.

"No thanks, James. I'm good."

"You sure? Them boys may be out there."

"I'll go the other way." I held out my hand to James. "Thank you."

"Of course, sir."

On the ride home I thought about everything Nick and James had said that day—about Josh, Lauren and golf in general. I was curious why Nick wanted to meet me specifically at 7 p.m. on June 10th but I was definitely going to be there. I'd never had a friend my age, and I wasn't about to pass up the chance to make one if this were such an opportunity. That potential reward made the news about Lauren and Josh's relationship a little easier to bear.

I already knew she was out of my league anyway.

## STELLAR 15 – "May 2012"

I remember it wasn't June yet when I first met Avery. I was cleaning boats one Sunday morning when she came strutting out onto the dock. "Whatcha doin?" she asked.

"Who are you, little girl?"

"Avy"

"Avy?"

She shook her head and repeated the exact same thing.

I took a wild guess. "Avery?"

She nodded. "Whatcha doin?"

"Cleaning boats. How old are you?"

She held up five fingers but said, "Four."

"Four?"

She nodded. "Can I watch?"

"You want to help?"

Her eyes got huge. "Can I?"

I handed her a toothbrush and a cup of soapy water. "You see all these cracks here? We just need to scrub them out. Think you can do that?"

She nodded her head vigorously and set to work on them.

"Where's your mom and dad, Avery?"

"I don't have a momma. Daddy is getting suckers."

"Suckers?"

"Yeah. For fissing." She pointed at the bait shop.

"Oh, leeches?"

Avery nodded. "Suckers."

*Cute kid.* I watched her bleached-blonde pigtails bob up and down as she concentrated on scrubbed the cracks thoroughly, tongue pushing out of the corner of her mouth.

"We don't bruss our boat," she said.

"You have a boat?"

"Yep. We live on a boat over there." She pointed down the canal.

"On the other bay?"

"Yep. Sinticotch Bay."

I smiled. *Shinnecock* Bay. "Just you and your dad?"

"Yep. We just moved here from Boston."

"Is that where your mommy lives?"

"I don't have a momma."

I wasn't getting anywhere with that one. A man came staggering out of the bait shop then with a six-pack of beer and a Styrofoam cup, presumably with the "suckers." He squinted into the bright sun, looking all around the docks.

"She's right here, sir," I called out.

"Dang it, Avery," he yelled. "I told you to stay by the door."

"I gotta go," she said, standing. "Tank you for letting me bruss your boat."

"Anytime." I watched her skip away. "Hey, Avery."

She turned and looked back at me.

"My name's Stellar," I said.

She giggled, waved and took off running towards her dad who was staggering away from us towards the bridge. I watched her join him and reach up for his hand. He didn't take it so she just grabbed onto his jeans.

I did something next I hadn't done in a long *long* time. I went into the shop specifically to talk to Ray. "Ray, who was that guy?"

"I don't know." He grunted, not even glancing away from the TV.

"What did his ID say?"

"I didn't look at it."

He *never* checked ID's. "Ray, if that would've been a—"

"There aren't drunk cops out here."

"Wait. He was *drunk*?"

Ray just nodded.

"You know he had a little girl with him?"

"I guess."

"You just said he was drunk. At ten o'clock in the morning on a Sunday."

"And you want me to do what exactly?"

I turned and ran out the door, grabbing my bike and racing off in the direction Avery and her dad had disappeared. I heard Ray yell something after me but I ignored him. I finally caught sight of them when I got to Holzman Lane. They were cutting through the park. I was careful not to let myself be seen by Avery who was looking around at every bird, squirrel and butterfly they passed. At the marina I watched them walk out to an older boat and board it. That had to be theirs. I rode over to one of the marina workers I knew, Thomas, and asked him about that boat.

"They came in about a week ago," Thomas replied. "Why?"

"Do they ever leave?"

"Sure. Of course. The guy's a fisherman. He took his boat your way every morning this past week."

"He catch anything?"

"Everyone catches something. Stellar, what's this about? You sound like you're worried."

"He's got a little girl with him."

"And?"

"He's drunk."

Thomas laughed. "At ten o'clock on Sunday morning?" He was still laughing. "You kids. You don't know what drunk is."

"I *do* know what drunk is. When you're homeless for a decade you have a pretty good idea of what drunk is. He's drunk."

Thomas wasn't laughing anymore. "Sorry, Stellar, I didn't know."

"Don't worry about it." I waved his apology off. "Just do me a favor and keep an eye on the girl will you?"

"Will do. How do you want me to reach you if I have to?"

"You have my uncle's number on you right?"

"It's in the office."

"Call that. Tell him you need to talk to me. I'll fill him in." I waited for Thomas to agree.

"You got it." He nodded. "It's cool of you to watch out for that little girl."

"Someone has to."

I rode back to RB's. When I got there Ken was waiting in the parking lot. "Where'd you go? Ray called me and said you took off after some guy. Did he steal something? Forget something?"

I filled Ken in on the whole story.

"You're taking this whole Batman/Good Samaritan thing a little too far now you know."

"It's not that." I tried to figure out how to best explain my impulsive actions and emotional response to him. "With all I've seen on the streets there's a lot of bad things that happen to little kids who are with alcoholics—parents or not. This little girl was super skinny, she had bruises on her left wrist... my mind just started spinning and imagining all the worst things. I don't know why I followed them, but I do feel better now knowing where she is and knowing Thomas is watching her for me.

Ken smiled. "Whatever you say, Batman."

"If I'm Batman, you know what that makes you, right?"

"*Not* Robin." Ken laughed. "Kate can be Robin. I'll be Alfred."

"Now you're the one taking this too far. You're old, but you're not that old."

"Watch it or I'll throw you in. And James won't be there to save you this time."

I spun my head to look at him. *James had told him?* "You know I can't swim?"

"Yes, and we're going to have to change that. You might fall in again someday."

He didn't seem mad that I hadn't told him, but he didn't have to be. My guilt was bad enough. "I'm sorry," I said.

"Forgiven," he replied. "Just don't do it again." He ruffled my hair as he liked to do. "I'd like to keep you around for a while."

## STELLAR 16 – "Summer 2012 - James"

This was a crazy summer, so I'm going to apologize in advance if I jump all over the place in retelling it. I need to make sure I talk about James, about Nick, about Lauren, Kate and Avery. So, once again, I'm sorry for the mess. But here goes.

I'll start with James. I hadn't seen him in a few months, since that day at The Hills in fact, which was quite strange. I figured once it warmed up, middle of April or so, he'd be on his bench every evening sharing peanuts with the pigeons and watching me hit golf balls before taking the train home. That didn't happen. I didn't see him once in April or May. And it was all kind of Ray's fault.

The first day of each month, Ray, Ken and I met in the RB's shop and discussed schedule and assignments. Ray's never changed. His obligations were to tend the counter and be a worthless drunk. But lately he'd started dating some woman in Manhattan, so he'd actually somewhat cleaned up his act. He'd cut back to just a couple beers a night, if even that, and that was saying something. I didn't want to give him credit for anything yet, but once a week he was shaving and showering, so I was cautiously optimistic about the impact this mystery woman was having.

Anyway, every Friday night he'd head to Manhattan and stay there until Sunday, which left the shop hours to Ken and me on Saturday. If Ken had to take a charter out Kate would usually come hang out in the shop with me, or Ken would call his cousin Joe to help run things. In exchange for us covering the shop for Ray I asked him if he'd invite Avery's dad, Mike, over on Sundays to hang out and watch baseball. Ray hemmed and hawed about it, but Ken backed me up so he eventually went for it. That would give me a few hours every week to catch up with Avery.

June 1st was a Friday and Ray asked if it would be all right if he headed over to Manhattan a little early. Since he'd just given in on Mike and Avery, I told him I'd cover the shop for a couple hours by myself, even though I wasn't supposed to. He went upstairs to get ready while I started cleaning the place up. I'm a little OCD, I won't deny it, and Ray was anything but. I was taking some empty boxes out to the recycle bin when I came across a tall heavy box with "Stellar" written on the top. "What the…?" I said aloud.

Ray had just come downstairs. "What?"

"What's in this box?"

"I don't know."

"It has my name on it."

"So open it."

"But where did it come from?"

"Some black guy dropped it off a couple weeks ago. I just forgot about it. Sorry."

*Some black guy? A couple weeks ago?* I was more curious than angry at the moment, so I let it go and grabbed a pair of scissors off the counter. I sliced the tape on the top of the box and pulled open the tabs. There was an envelope on the top, also with 'Stellar' written on it. *What the heck?* I opened the envelope and read the note.

*Stellar – Was a pleasure getting to know you sir. It is time for me to move on from The Hills, but I wanted to wish you the best. And since I won't be around to further critique your golf game, I thought these might help. Blessings!*

*Your friend – James "Jake" Hill*

"This is dated April 5th, Ray. That's two flipping *months* ago!" I was furious.

"Sorry. Jeez. I told you I forgot, kid."

He was the worst at apologies. *Idiot.* "There's a *huge* difference between two weeks and two months!"

"What's the big deal anyway? Who's it from? What is it?"

I ignored his questions and pulled the paper out of the top of the box revealing a brand new set of Nike golf clubs. *Oh. My. Gosh.* These had to have cost a ton. They had a big "Custom" sticker on them which I removed as I pulled the Nike bag out of the box. The golf bag even had my name—Stellar—stitched on it. *Awesome!* "Holy crap," I mumbled.

Ray had come around the corner to see what was in the box. "Golf clubs? Who the hell got you golf clubs?"

"I did."

"With what? I don't even pay you."

"You think I don't know that?"

"Watch your tone, boy."

*He was right.* "Sorry."

"So where'd you get them?"

"I did some work for a guy, with Ken." I didn't feel good about lying, but I also didn't trust Ray with the truth. "And he tried to give me money but I wouldn't take it so he bought me these clubs I guess."

"Huh." I could tell Ray didn't care. "Well, I need to go."

"Go ahead," I told him, just as eager for him to leave. "I've got it."

Ken had just left with the boat and it had my backpack on it with James's phone number. I needed to call him right away. He was probably wondering why he hadn't heard from me in the two months since he dropped this box off. *Two months!* I felt terrible about that. This was a big deal. No, this was a *huge* deal! I had my own golf clubs, which was awesome, but James wasn't coming back and I had to know why. *That was awful!*

I immediately felt even guiltier I hadn't checked in on him in so long. What kind of a friend was I? As soon as Ken got back I'd call him. I looked at the clock. Four more hours. *It just as well be four days!*

When Ken got back I called the number on the card. A female voice answered again, but this time it was an automated one telling me the number had been disconnected. *What in the world was going on?* I hadn't thought it possible to feel worse than I did before. But clearly it was. Because now I did.

## STELLAR 17 – "Summer 2012 - Avery"

Since the first day I met her I'd seen her almost every day. Every weekday morning they'd go by in their boat, and I'd make sure I was up to wave at her as she passed. She was always looking for me too. They came back in at varying times each day but I was always watching for them.

On Saturday evenings I'd usually ride my bike over to their marina and talk to Thomas, who was still watching them for me. Thomas shared many of my own concerns by now. Avery's dad, Mike, was definitely a heavy drinker and curser, and Thomas said Avery was regularly in tears. Whoever came up with that "sticks and stones" garbage was a total moron. Words often hurt much worse. As far as Thomas had seen, Mike had never hit Avery, but he grabbed her forcefully by the wrist a lot, which explained those bruises I'd seen.

On June 1st I rode over to check on Avery after I locked up the shop. I also wanted to personally invite Mike over on Sunday to hang out with Ray. When I got to the boat Avery was playing with an old doll on the deck. "Where's your dad?" I asked.

"He's sleeping. Doesn't feel good."

*I bet.* "What's your doll's name?"

"It's not my doll. It's mommy's."

I was confused. "Your mommy?"

Avery nodded. "Yes. My momma gave it to me when I was bored. Did you know yestaday was my birthday?"

*By "bored" I knew she meant "born."* "Really? No. I didn't know that. You should've told me. Happy birthday! So, you're five now?"

She held up five fingers. "Yep."

"So what'd you do for your birthday?"

"Nothing. Just played with my doll."

"Did you go out to eat or anything?"

She shook her head.

"Avery, who are you talking to?" Mike yelled from inside the boat.

"Stella."

For some reason it didn't bother me when she said my name that way.

"What does he want?"

"I don't know, Daddy."

Mike staggered up into the sunlight. "Whaddaya want, kid?" He looked like he was in pain.

"Ray sent me to invite you over for the game and dinner on Sunday."

"Who's Ray?"

"The guy you buy bait from every day."

"Oh, you're the bait guy's kid. Yeah, I might come. What time?"

"We close the shop at three on Sunday, so anytime after 3:30 should be good."

"Okay. That should work. Tell him thanks."

Mike turned and scratched his butt as he headed back below deck. *Nice.* "Come on, Avery," he called. "You gotta clean this boat up."

"Hopefully I'll see you Sunday," I said to her as she stood and hopped on the boat.

"Yep. See you Sunday, Stella."

They did come over Sunday around five, and Mike and Ray watched some baseball game. I took Avery out to "my" boat before dinner.

"Can we bruss the boat, Stella?"

"I don't do that on Sundays. But… I got you something, Avery." I held a box out to her.

"What is it?"

"It's a birthday present. You have to open it."

She ripped the wrapping paper off the box. "A doll!" she squealed, scaring Squirrel half to death. "A new doll! I love it, I love it, I love it! Thank you, Stella."

I laughed and Squirrel started tearing around the cabin. *It was almost like she'd never gotten a present before.* "Happy Birthday," I said as she hugged me tightly.

"This is the best birthday pwesent ever!"

That was a heck of a lot of enthusiasm over a doll. "I'm glad you like it."

"Can I play with Squirrel now? I've always wanted a puppy."

I smiled and nodded. "Sure."

They raced around the grass by the bait shop as I sat on the dock and watched. I was suddenly aware of someone standing behind me. I turned slightly and glanced up. It was Mike and he was watching Avery too. "She's had a rough life, that kid."

I didn't know what to say so I didn't say anything.

"She gets attached to things quickly and then loses them. I don't think it's the best idea for you two to be friends. We might not be here long."

"I'm just someone to talk to."

"She's got me for that."

"It has to be hard on her since her mom died though. I lost my mom and—"

"Her mom ain't dead."

*What?* "But she—"

"Look kid, I'm sure you have good intentions, but Avery doesn't need you."

*I couldn't have disagreed more.* "What do you mean her mom isn't dead?"

"She almost is, but she isn't. It's best Avery gets used to the idea—that she thinks Lucy already is. You ever want to wreck her life, just tell the girl her mom's alive. I appreciate the dinner invite, Ray said it was all your idea, but we can't stay. And honestly, I'd appreciate it even more if you'd just leave her alone from now on. You're just going to hurt her."

I said the first thing that came to my head, against my better judgment. "At least I don't physically abuse her like you do."

Mike was obviously caught off-guard by my comment and reacted impulsively, angrily, shoving me off the dock with his foot. I hit the water hard, flat on my back but the rage boiling in me actually kept me composed. *I know it sounds strange.* I kicked to the surface and grabbed onto the dock. I looked up and Mike was holding his hand down to me. Suddenly he went flying over my head and Ray was holding his hand down to me. "Come on, Stellar, grab on." I took Ray's hand and he pulled me up. Mike was floundering in the water now. "He can't swim you idiot." Ray yelled at him. "Get out of here before I call the cops. You're not welcome here anymore."

It was weird to see Ray actually care. "Ray, no, it's okay," I pleaded with him. "It was my fault."

"No, Stellar—no kid deserves to be kicked by an adult. He's lucky. That jack…err… he should be arrested."

Mike was climbing up the ladder and yelling at Avery to follow him. Avery was just standing there looking terrified. I was praying he wouldn't take this out on her. He grabbed her by the arm and dragged her along behind him. I heard Avery say something about her doll, which was still on my boat, but Mike didn't so much as glance back.

I looked up at Ray. "What's he going to do to her?"

For the second or third day since I'd known him Ray was actually being a decent guy. "Hopefully nothing. I'll go check on them later to be sure. The guy drinks too much. Hopefully the water woke him up a little."

*Interesting coming from Ray.* "*He* drinks a lot?"

"Easy there. I get your point, but I've cut back. You know that."

I nodded. I knew he had.

"Why don't you get some dry clothes on, kid? We gotta get you swimming lessons or something. As much as you're out here it's amazing you haven't fallen in before."

The comment sounded sarcastic, like he knew otherwise, but I ignored it and picked up Avery's doll. "I bought her a doll. Her birthday was a few days ago."

"The girl that was just here?"

"Yeah, Avery, she just turned five. She's never had a new doll before."

"That was nice of you. I promise we'll check on her after dinner, okay?" He could tell I was worried about her. "Now get changed and come inside."

We drove over after dinner and there was Avery sitting on the deck of their boat—playing with that old doll.

"She shouldn't be living with him," I said.

Ray was watching her through a pair of binoculars. There was no sign of Mike. "That may be true, but you probably shouldn't be living on that boat by yourself either. Just ask my sister-in-law."

I wasn't touching *that* topic. "At least you've never hurt me—not physically anyway."

Ray lowered the binoculars and looked at me. He could read between the lines.

"Look, Stellar… I know I haven't been an easy guy to get along with. I've had a rough few years and I've really been no good to you—or for you. As negligent as I've been I easily could have lost you too." I knew he was referring to his son's death. "I'm figuring it out little by little, kid. I'm trying… honestly I am. Even if I suck at it."

I nodded, giving him the benefit of the doubt for now. "Okay."

"But you just said I never hurt you. Has Mike hurt Avery?"

I needed to be careful what I said. A lie might get Ray to respond, but could also get me in trouble. *Stick to the truth.* "I don't know for sure," I began, and saw Ray go back to the binoculars. "But last time I was with her she had bruises on her wrists—deep bruises."

"That could be anything."

"I know."

He lowered the binoculars again. "I know you want to help the little girl, Lucy, whatever her name is—"

"It's Avery. I think her mom's name is Lucy."

"Right… but if we call the police on this guy they may take her away from him and who knows what happens to her then. I mean, what if he *hasn't* hurt her?"

*Yet.* But Ray was right, as much as I hated to admit it. "Okay," I said.

Ray put the binoculars away and we drove back to RB's in silence.

I hold myself responsible for what happened next.

## STELLAR 18 – "Too Late"

The sirens woke me just before midnight. There were a lot of them and they were close. I rolled out of bed and threw a sweatshirt on as I ran out onto the dock. I could see the flashing lights from cop cars, fire trucks and ambulances and they were all scrambling towards Shinnecock Bay. My first thought was of Avery. I sprinted for my bike and was met at the door by Ray. "What's going on?" he asked.

"I don't know." I hopped on the bike and raced off with him yelling after me. I flew across the railroad tracks and through the park. I could see a thin pillar of smoke rising above the distant marina. *A fire? Obviously. But what's burning?* Montauk Highway was a maze of emergency vehicles—lights and sirens everywhere. I weaved my way through them and jumped off my bike, sprinting down to the police line that had formed a couple hundred yards from the docks.

"What happened?" I asked one officer who told me to get lost.

I kept asking until I found someone who would actually answer me, an old man from another houseboat. "Boat fire," he said. "One dead—a man."

"Which boat?"

"39."

*Oh, no! That was Avery's slip number.* "What about the girl?"

"Don't know anything about a girl. No mention of a girl. They only found a man. That your dog?"

I glanced down. Somehow Squirrel was at my feet. He must have followed me here. "They should've found a girl too."

"They didn't."

"But there's a girl too." I was almost yelling now. "I can't get anyone to listen to me. Please, can you ask about the girl?"

The old man flagged down a fireman. "This boy says there should have been a girl on the boat too."

"There wasn't a girl," the fireman replied.

"But there should have been." I insisted. "Call the marina manager. He'll tell you."

"Son," he took his hat off and wiped his forehead, "I was one of the first guys here. Trust me. There's been no sign of a girl. I'm sorry."

I looked across the water at where their boat had been pulled up onto the docks. I could hear barking coming from over there. I looked down at my feet and Squirrel was gone. "Sir, my dog is over there."

"I'll get him for you," the fireman replied.

He started off towards Squirrel. The dog's barking was frenetic. I'd only heard him bark like that once before.

That's when it occurred to me. *What if Avery had fallen in? Or jumped in? Or been thrown in? What if Squirrel was barking because... it wasn't possible was it?* "Sir," I yelled after the fireman. He stopped and turned back towards me. "Did you look under the pier?"

"It was a propane-fueled explosion. If she was in the boat she couldn't have survived."

"But what if she was *on* the boat and not *in* it. She might be under the pier by my dog." I could see he was at least entertaining the idea. "Will you please at least let me go check?"

"I can't do that, son. But I'll check for you."

I watched as the fireman jogged over to the pier and walked towards Squirrel. I saw the little dog illuminated by the fireman's flashlight. Squirrel was fixated on one spot, his nose down to the pier, and he was still barking like an insane dog. *She had to be under there.*

The fireman's ensuing yell confirmed my suspicions. "Over here," he called out to two divers who were getting out of their suits. "There's a kid under here."

*Squirrel had done it again.*

A whole crew of men hurried over to that spot on the pier and the divers dove back in the water. A few minutes later they handed a little girl, Avery, up to the firemen. A paramedic took her from the fireman and hurried her off to an ambulance. The fireman came running back over to me with Squirrel in his arms.

"You just saved that kid's life, young man. We would have never looked over there. That was nowhere near the boat."

"Squirrel saved her." I took him from the fireman. "He only barks like that when people are in trouble." *Maybe the pup had a little St. Bernard in him.*

"In any case," the fireman put his hand on my shoulder, "she's alive."

"Can you find out where they're taking her for me, please?"

"Stay here," he said.

I watched him talk to a policeman then another fireman. He came back to me a few minutes later. "They took her to Southampton Hospital. She had some pretty bad facial burns. So you knew these people?"

I shook my head and thanked him, hopping back on my bike, Squirrel under one arm.

"Kid, hey, what's your name?" the fireman called after me as I peddled away, but I pretended I didn't hear him and kept going.

I went back to RB's and told Ray the short version of what had happened. He chewed me out for taking off like I did, but I could tell it was more out of concern than anger. *Maybe he was actually changing.* "At least they found Lucy," he said.

"You mean Avery."

"Right. Avery."

"Ray, I'm going to the hospital."

"Just wait," he said. "I'll be back in a minute."

I sat on the doorstep with my head in my hands while Ray went inside. *If I'd only pushed Ray to call the cops on Mike.* He came back out a few minutes later. "Ken is on his way to pick you up. I'd take you but—"

I waved his excuse off. I could smell the alcohol on him.

"I'm sorry," he said.

I ignored him. *So much for pretending. Ray was still the same guy.*

Ken took me to the hospital but they wouldn't tell us anything there. I tried to explain that I knew her but because we weren't family we had to wait, we couldn't see her. *I could only imagine how lonely and scared Avery had to be right now.* I told them everything I knew about Mike and about Avery's mom. I told them I thought her name was Lucy, that she lived in Boston somewhere, and was supposedly "terminally ill", but none of it seemed to matter to anyone. They didn't have a last name yet for Avery, and I felt dumb I didn't know it either. *How were they ever going to figure it out if the boat had exploded?* They thanked me for trying to help and Ken took me back to RB's. I had given Ken the same version of the story I'd told Ray—without Squirrel or me in it—and he didn't really push me for more.

I felt guilty for not doing more when I could have—for not having Ray call the authorities on Mike. *A deadbeat dad would have been better than a dead one.* I didn't want praise for what happened afterwards, even if it saved Avery's life. Besides, Squirrel was the one who had actually saved her… not me.

I couldn't sleep the rest of the night—my thoughts wouldn't leave me alone. *Now Avery had no one. I could have prevented all of this. Tonight, I could have saved another life.*

## STELLAR 19 – "Headlines"

There was a knock on my door at 6:15 the next morning. "Come in," I answered glumly.

Ken opened the door and stepped into the boat's cabin. "You want to tell me about this?" He threw the local paper on my bed. It flopped open upside down but I could still read the headline fine. *Mystery Boy and Hero Pup Save Little Girl.*

*Oh my gosh. Seriously? How did that get in the paper already?* I turned the paper around to take a closer look.

There was an aerial photo of Shinnecock Bay and the marina where the fire had been but the story was pretty scarce on details. Or, I should say, it just restated everything I already knew. *One person had died in a propane explosion. A little girl had been found under the pier by a boy and his dog. They weren't releasing her name.* The fireman I'd spoken to had been interviewed and called both Squirrel and me heroes. Squirrel was mentioned by name. My name was not in the article. I breathed a sigh of relief. *No one down there must have recognized me in the dark.*

Ken had been waiting for me to finish reading. "Good story, eh?" he asked. "You know anything about that? Because the version I got out of you last night didn't include you and Squirrel saving that girl."

"How is it in the paper already?"

"That's what you have to say?" Ken was pissed. "That's what you think you should say to me right now?"

I couldn't look at him. "It's okay if you're mad at me. I'm mad at me too. I'm no hero."

Ken's irritated tone softened quickly. "What do you mean?"

"Squirrel saved Avery. Not me. I pretty much did the opposite."

"Now hold on." He sat down on the bed beside me. "Ray told me what happened with Mike yesterday. Why do you take these things on alone? Why aren't you bringing this stuff to me?"

"It's not like that."

"Then explain. Because as I see it I should have been down there having a conversation with Mike yesterday after you two went swimming. Then it would have been my call whether or not the cops got called regarding Avery. This shouldn't be on you."

Tears were running down my face now. "I'm sorry," I whispered.

Ken put his arm around my shoulders. "That's what I'm trying to say to you. This is *not* your fault. As I see it, you did way more for that little girl than anyone. You might not see it as enough, but it was far more than anyone else. You should be thankful you were around last night, that you *and your dog* got to know her and that you were there in time to save her life. Because that, Miles, is what you did. You *did* save her life."

I wiped my face and nodded. "I guess."

"Guess all you want, Batman." Ken put his arm around my shoulders. "But I *know*. Now, grab your laundry. We're taking the day off. Kate wants me to bring you home."

"When does she get home?"

"She's home. She took the day off, too. She wants to make you a hero sandwich or something for lunch." Ken playfully punched my shoulder. "Your choice."

I couldn't help but smile a little now. "Toasted peanut butter and honey?"

"Whatever you want, chief."

"Can we stop by the hospital on the way?"

"Actually, I think Kate would like to take you if that's okay. She said she hasn't talked to you in awhile."

"Sounds good to me."

## STELLAR 20 – "Boston Strength"

Kate took me to the hospital hoping she could use her law enforcement connections and legal sway to convince them to let me see Avery. She made a few calls and they finally let us in. Kate stayed out at the desk and let me go in to talk to Avery alone.

Avery was awake but very groggy. Her right arm and neck were wrapped in gauze and she had some bandages on her face. The rest of her was covered by a blanket.

"She's a tough little girl," a pretty, young nurse said as she walked me in.

"She's from Boston," I replied, as if that was sufficient explanation. "Hey, little girl."

"Hi ya, Stella."

"I brought you a friend." I held up the doll I'd given her earlier. "And… I have a secret for you."

She ripped the doll from my hands with a smile. "Okay."

"My real name is Miles. But only special people call me that. Would you like to call me Miles?"

She nodded her head. "Is that your mommy?"

I glanced behind me at Kate, who was watching us talk. "Kind of. My mommy died when I was a baby. Kate takes care of me now."

Strangely talking about dead mothers perked her up. "Really? Your mommy died like mine?"

I thought about what Mike had said to me about his wife, Avery's mother. I nodded. "Yeah, like yours." It felt terrible to lie to her but this was not the time to tell her otherwise.

"Miles, have you seen my daddy?"

*She didn't know?* I shook my head. "No, sorry, I haven't. Have you asked anyone else?"

"No. I just waked up."

Kate knocked on the window and waved at me as a nurse walked in. "I need this little lady here to get some more rest," she said with a smile. "You're welcome to come back tomorrow."

"I will." I squeezed Avery's hand. "I'll be back to see you tomorrow, okay?"

"Thanks, Stella."

"Miles," I corrected her with a whisper.

She smiled. "Thanks, Miles."

I gave her a thumbs up and stepped out into the hall with Kate. "What's going on?"

"The police have a few things they'd like you to look at. You up for that?"

"Sure." I shrugged. "Why not?"

Kate took me into another room full of tables with items scattered all over them from the boat. “This is all the stuff they salvaged last night and this morning,” she said. “And this is Officer Kennedy. He’ll walk you through it.”

Officer Kennedy shook my hand. “Miles, is this—”

“Jack,” Kate cut in. “He goes by Stellar.”

I looked up at Kate with a smile. She nodded at me and winked.

“Sorry, Stellar, this the guy? The little girl’s father?” Officer Kennedy held up a half-burnt driver’s license. “Michael Layne?”

“Yes. That’s him.”

“The address says Framingham, I’m guessing in Massachusetts but—”

“It is.” I nodded. “They came here from Massachusetts.”

“Good.” Jack—Officer Kennedy—nodded. “Alright, there was a safe on the boat, but it didn’t have much in it—a couple hundred bucks, a few photos, and some bills. Do you know anything about the girl’s father? Was he in the hospital recently or something?

“Tell him what you know,” Kate urged me. “It’s okay. The more you tell them the better for Avery.”

I took a deep breath. *Okay. You can do this.* “Avery just turned five last week. She thinks her mom is dead because her dad always told her that. But her dad told me yesterday she wasn’t dead yet. Her dad was a big-time drunk. If those bills are from a rehab clinic or something then they’re his.”

“They’re not.” Officer Jack looked at Kate. “They’re from the Dana Farber Cancer Institute in Boston. But there’s no legible patient name.”

“That could be where her mother was,” I exclaimed.

Kate and Officer Jack were both nodding. “Or,” Kate said, “That could be where her mother is.”

“We have to find out.” I was stating the obvious I knew, but it needed to be said. “Her name’s Lucy. Can we call and ask?”

Officer Kennedy left the room to do that. He came back a few minutes later. “You were right, son, and she’s still there.”

“Did you talk to her?”

He shook his head. “No. Not yet.”

I turned and looked at Kate. She smiled. “Want to go to Boston?”

“Can we?”

Kate looked at Officer Kennedy, who shrugged. “That’s not my department,” he said.

“It’s a little unorthodox,” Kate admitted. “And we might have to wait until someone else talks to her first, but I’ll make a few more calls. Who knows?”

“Seriously?”

She put an arm around me. "Of course. Let me see what I can do." She looked at her watch. "It's been a couple years since I've done it, but if I remember correctly, the Cross Sound Ferry should take us four to five hours. We'd be there by three or so, we could have dinner and catch the late ferry back tonight."

Somehow it all worked out. Kate made a few calls and our visit was green-lighted. She called Ken to see if he wanted to go with us, but he thought he should hang around in case Ray needed help at RB's. Kate and I got in her black Range Rover and headed for the ferry docks out by Plum Island. We were going to meet Avery's mother. *Wait... I'm going to meet Avery's mom?*

Maybe I should've thought that through more. *What was I going to say?*

## STELLAR 21 – "Lucy Layne"

It was the first time I'd ever been on that ferry. Ken and I had fished around Plum Island many times, but seeing Gardiners Bay from the top deck of a ferry was a different experience. Boston always seems so far away from New York, but it's really just right there… like New Jersey, kind of.

*Okay, so Boston is nothing like New Jersey.*

When we got to the hospital we were directed to Lucy's room. Kate knocked and we were invited in. Kate introduced herself and then me.

"What can I help you two with?"

I was trying not to stare. I'd been to Mt. Sinai so many times with Bernie I'd gotten used to seeing people with a thousand tubes running to and from them like spider webs. Bald, pale, and paper-thin, I was used to all of that. But it had been a few years and looking at Lucy now, well, it brought a lot of memories back. And Lucy looked worse than most of the people I was ever allowed to see.

Kate looked at me and I looked at her. I had it all worked out in my head before we got there what I was going to tell Lucy and now my mind was blank. Kate seemed to read that blankness through my expression.

"Lucy," Kate took her hand, "I don't know how to say this."

"I already know why you're here so however you say it you're not exactly going to kill me—though I wish you would."

"You know about the accident?"

Lucy nodded. "Yes."

"You know your husband, or ex-husband, is dead?"

"Yes."

"So they told you your daughter is alive… in New York."

"Yes and yes. Like I said…" There were tears in Lucy's eyes, but I'm not certain they were emotional by the grimace on her face. She was definitely in some physical pain. "If you came all the way here to surprise me, well, surprise… I already knew." She started pressing the clicker in her hand to summon a nurse.

This was *not* going *at all* like I thought it would. I was beginning to think coming here was a terrible idea.

The nurse came in as Kate's phone rang. The nurse asked her to take the phone outside if she needed to answer it and to leave it off when she came back in. She gave Lucy some medication for her pain. The nurse then followed Kate out of the room and I was alone with Lucy. And suddenly I was very nervous.

"You don't have to be afraid of me," Lucy said.

"I'm not."

Lucy smiled a "yeah, right" smile. "How old are you? And how do you know Avery?" There was still an edge to her voice.

"Eleven," I answered glumly. "She helped me clean boats and waved to me every day as they passed through the canal. She loved my dog and always played with this doll she pretended was you. I just wanted to be a friend. I knew you were sick but—"

"Mike told you I was sick?"

I nodded again. "Yeah, he told me. He said Avery had no one but him and I should leave her alone because she didn't need someone else who would just… " My voice trailed off as I realized Lucy might not care.

"Why do *you* care?" she asked me.

I shrugged. "Someone had to."

She was staring at me now. "And you really do care, don't you?"

I nodded. "It's hard not to. She's a great kid." I moved over by the window. "I lost my parents when I was little. Never even knew them."

Lucy nodded towards the hallway. "That's not your mom?"

I shook my head. "Not really. *But kind of.* I help her husband out with his boats and stay with them during the winter. They've kind of adopted me because I had no one else. I know how much of a difference it made to me to have them… I thought maybe I could help your daughter out too, even if she did have a dad. Looks like I failed there."

Lucy's glare was completely gone now. She reached out for my hand. "Son, you came all the way to Boston from New York to tell a little girl's mom that her daughter was alone. That's not failing."

"What difference did it make though?" We both had tears in our eyes at that point, though this time I'm pretty sure hers were emotional. "I'm sorry," I added. "I didn't mean to upset you."

"Can I ask you something?" Lucy squeezed my hand.

I nodded. "Sure."

"How is she… really?"

I looked at Avery's mom. This was more what I was expecting. "She's lonely. She has no one."

"Except you."

I shook my head. "Not sure how much good I'm doing her now."

"Don't underestimate yourself so much." She waited for me to look at her again and smiled. "Can I ask you something else?"

"Of course."

"What were you hoping to find? What were you hoping I'd say?"

I paused before answering. "I don't know. I guess I hoped you'd be healthy enough to come with us and take care of her. That maybe Mike was exaggerating when he told me how sick you were."

"Does Avery know you came to find me?"

"No. Avery doesn't know you're alive. Even when we found you we didn't say anything. We didn't know what the right thing was."

Lucy looked momentarily relieved. She sighed deeply. "The doctors told me two months ago I had less than a month to live. I honestly had no idea why they were keeping me alive—how I was staying alive. Maybe now it makes a little sense. Maybe—and I don't even know if I believe this stuff—but maybe the man upstairs knew I needed to be here a little longer."

I shrugged. "Maybe. Or maybe the doctors were wrong altogether. Maybe you'll beat it."

She smiled a sad smile and shook her head. "They're not wrong. I wish they were. I wish this were a new beginning—that I could just go pick Avery up with you right now… "

"But you won't?"

Another lengthy head shake. "I can't."

I nodded. I understood.

Lucy wiped her eyes again. "Did I do the right thing?"

*You realize you're asking an eleven-year-old that question?* "Uhh… I don't know. I really don't."

"If I were your mom, would you want to know I was alive, even if it was just for another day or week or month?"

"I don't know. I think so. But maybe not."

Lucy nodded. "So you understand my dilemma? Why I didn't want her to see me… *especially* not like this?"

"I don't know. I mean, you've had this cancer for five years?"

"No, no, no… just three," she corrected. "We decided two years ago it would be best if Mike moved on without me so Avery wouldn't have to watch me die. She was still young enough to not really know me, if that makes sense. We didn't want this to be her last memories." She gestured at all the tubes and machines. "Or, I should say, I didn't want this to be her last memories."

"So your husband didn't agree with this?"

"Mike? No. He… he definitely didn't agree."

"Did he drink when you were still together?"

"Drink? No. Why do you ask that?"

Kate came back in then glancing back and forth between Lucy and me. "Everything okay in here? I'm sorry, that was work. I'm never supposed to shut this phone off."

"She's a lawyer," I said—pretty much to Lucy's back.

"So what will happen to my baby?" Lucy whispered, but we both heard her.

Lucy and Kate spoke for a few minutes while I tried to wrap my head around everything I'd just learned, and what this all meant for Avery.

Finally I heard Kate say, "Are you absolutely sure you don't want her to know about you? I'd be happy to bring her to you."

"No. Please no. This can *not* be the best thing for her. She can not see me like this—can't watch me live, or die, like this. Not… not ever."

I understood and even agreed now. Avery had just lost her dad. If anything she'd been at some kind of peace about losing her mom already. Bringing her back to Lucy like this now and then having her lose her mother all over—that would crush anyone. As much as it felt wrong for Avery to not even know Lucy was alive, I had to admit it would be almost as bad for her to know Lucy was living like this.

Kate put one of her business cards on the bedside table insisting Lucy not hesitate to call if she needed anything at all. I wasn't sure how Kate could possibly help her. I also didn't know what else I could even say at that point. Kate took my hand and led me towards the door. "We should go," she whispered.

"Son." I heard Lucy speak behind me.

"Yes?" I turned back towards her.

"Can I ask you one last question?"

Kate let go of my hand and I walked back over to Lucy's bed. "Sure."

She finally turned her face enough to look at mine. The sadness was unmistakable. "Are you happy? In life I mean. Are you happy?"

I nodded but felt like I needed to say more. My voice cracked as I said, "yes" so I repeated it. "Mostly, yes."

"Thank you for coming to see me. More importantly, thank you for all you've done for Avery."

"I'm sorry I couldn't do more—that I can't do more."

"You did enough, young man. You did enough."

Kate and I left the hospital and I had an uneasy sort of peace wash over me. *I did enough.* That seemed to be the common theme, and it felt good to hear it from the people I cared about—even Avery's mother. *If only I could feel as convinced.*

We had dinner at Jerry Remy's Seaport—never seen such a big TV outside Times Square—and then caught the late ferry back to Long Island.

I had mixed emotions about seeing Avery the next day. It wasn't my place or duty to tell her what was going to happen to her, which was a great relief. But it also didn't feel right pretending like I didn't know. The foster care system was hit or miss—Russian roulette—and telling her otherwise would be a lie.

Kate told me it would all happen fast—she'd be gone probably in the next two to three days. I made a silent vow to be at her side until that time came. This little girl deserved a lot better than she was getting.

## STELLAR 22 – "The Next Three Days"

I was at the hospital the next morning when visiting hours began. Avery was extremely happy to see me. Clearly she hadn't gotten the bad news yet—or she was on a lot of medication.

The burns on her face and neck weren't terrible. They'd leave scars but they could be covered up almost completely if she wanted to. Her arm burns were the worst, and looked terribly painful, but I knew better than to stare at them or really talk about them at all. She did also have some cuts, scrapes and a broken collarbone but that was, amazingly, the extent of her injuries. It didn't seem right to suggest it, given all the other drama and trauma in her life, but she was lucky to be alive.

I sat and talked to Avery for an hour or so before a parade of people in sunglasses and suits walked in—*the bad news bearers*. I asked to stay with her but my request was denied and I was ushered out into the hall. The nurse muttered something about "child services." I had figured as much, though they looked more like the FBI. *They couldn't have recruited Carrie Underwood or someone else compassionate and pretty for that, instead of the all-business legion of gloom?* I tried to call Kate but she was in a meeting at work. Ken was out on the boat and didn't answer his phone either.

When the parade left, I hurried back into Avery's room. All the sunshine and enthusiasm were gone. The happy girl I'd left in here a half hour ago was now glum and bummed. "You okay?" I asked.

"I don't have no daddy neither anymore."

"They told you that?"

She nodded. "They said he's in heaven with momma."

I found it odd that was the explanation they gave her, considering her mom was still alive, but I also knew I couldn't tell Avery that. "If that's the case, then I'd say your daddy's pretty lucky."

She looked up at me in surprise. "You think so?"

"Of course. I mean, obviously you'll miss him, and that's perfectly okay… but I'm sure your momma was probably happy to see him. Don't you think? I mean, now they can both watch over you together."

"Does it work that way?"

I didn't know if I believed what I was saying but it definitely seemed to be helping her, so I kept going. "I like to think my mom and dad are watching over me. I look up at the clouds and the stars and I imagine them up there somewhere smiling down at me."

"Aren't you sad though, Stella? Don't you get lonely?"

"Sometimes. But I have a new family, and pretty soon you will too. Soon you'll be as happy as I am."

"Okay," she said.

*Okay?* That wasn't what I was expecting but she seemed to be accepting and processing what I'd said. She also looked like she needed a hug. I wasn't big on hugs, unless it was Kate giving them, but Avery didn't have anyone else. I put my arm around her and she squeezed me, burying her face into my shirt and sniffling. "I'm sorry," I said. That felt like a totally stupid and inadequate thing to say at this point, but I had no idea what else to say. "It will all be better soon." *Don't make any promises!* "You'll get through this, Avery… I promise." *Great job!*

The next day some of those same suits came and took Avery from the hospital. They had to pry her away from me. I felt horrible. Her cries wrenched at my heart like nothing else ever had. I went back to the Parker's house and sat on the back steps of the garage until Kate got home that night. She must have seen the light on out back because she came around the garage and found me.

"There you are. Have you been here all day?"

I nodded.

"I've been looking…" She sounded ready to really chew me out but she cut herself short. "Are you… Have you eaten anything?"

I shook my head.

"Will you come inside so I can make you something?"

"I'm not hungry."

"Would you come inside and talk to me?"

"I don't want to talk."

"Miles, I saw you called. I tried to call you back. I also tried to come home earlier, but there was a very important… " She let her voice trail off. "Anyway, I'm sorry. I tried."

"It's okay. I'm not mad at you."

"Miles."

There was urgency in her voice. I glanced up to try to read her face and reassure her. "Kate, I'm fine."

"Would you come inside please?" She extended her hand down to me, clearly not convinced. "Come watch TV with me."

"Okay." I nodded, took her hand and stood up.

Kate led me into their house and over to the living room couch. She turned the TV on. "Will you be okay here for a few minutes while I take a shower? I'll be right back."

I nodded.

I heard the water start a minute later and settled back onto the couch, closing my eyes. I was asleep in seconds. When I woke up I was covered by a blanket and the room was flooded with sunlight. *It was the next day.* It took me a second to get my bearings and then suddenly I could hear the voices and smell the bacon and coffee. I flipped off the covers and tiptoed into the kitchen to find Ken and Kate standing at the stove.

"Hey, bud." Ken held his fist out to me. "Sleep good?"

I connected with him and nodded as Kate looked up from flipping pancakes to smile at me. She was in gray yoga pants and a thin light blue t-shirt.

"Sorry for falling asleep," I mumbled, blushing, certain I hadn't averted my eyes from her shirt in time.

"Hey, you obviously needed it." She smiled. "Ken, can you take over here? I'll be right back."

She hurried upstairs while Ken moved to the stove. When she came back down a minute later she had a less transparent t-shirt on. *Yeah, she'd caught me.*

She scooped some pancakes onto my plate. "You feeling better?"

I couldn't look her in the eyes but nodded. "I guess." I was starving, and back to eleven-year-old boy thoughts, so I must have been.

I caught the long sideways glance between Kate and Ken and watched him whisper something in her ear. *Something was up.*

"We have something to talk to you about," Ken said softly.

Kate sat down next to me and put her hand on my hand. "Miles…" She stopped suddenly and tears filled her eyes. She shook her head. "Ken… can you—"

He nodded. "Miles… There isn't an easy way to say this." I watched them exchange another uneasy glance and Kate wiped her eyes.

"You guys are scaring me," I whispered to Kate.

"Avery's mom died yesterday," Ken said.

This was one of those times where you hear someone say something and you swear you didn't hear them right—when it's not at all what you're expecting to hear. *Not sure what I was actually anticipating.* I looked up at Ken. "*What?*"

"Avery's mom," Kate replied. "I got a call from the hospital in Boston yesterday. She passed away."

My appetite was gone again. Suddenly all the anger and bitterness I'd managed to contain yesterday took over. "This sucks." I dropped my fork on the plate and shoved back from the counter. "This sucks! What did Avery do to deserve any of this? How does God live with Himself? Huh? Why does He take parents away from kids when they really need them? How can He possibly need them more than we do?"

I ran out the kitchen door. I heard Kate yell my name and Ken tell her to let me go. I hopped on my bike and rode through town. I biked until I was tired—until I found myself at the end of Far Pond Road, on the shore of Shinnecock Bay. I'd never come down here before, so no one would know to look for me here. That was just as well—I wanted to be alone for a while.

## STELLAR 23 – "No Safe Place"

I saw a cartoon once where this storm cloud followed this character around zapping him over and over with lightning bolts. No matter what the character did to try to get away it didn't work. The character would hide in "safe" places and still get hit. It was funny and surreal at the same time—the epitome of what I was going through… the epitome of what I was about to experience.

I hadn't been on the beach five minutes when I heard tires on the gravel behind me. I turned around expecting to see Ken or Kate, but there were three boys there instead—Larry, Curly, and Moe as Ken called them. *Crap.* But this time there were three other people biking not too far behind them, also coming towards me. Three girls to be exact… Taryn, Lauren and another girl I assumed must be Caitlin from what Nick had said at the golf course.

"Look who we have here, boys." The dumb one, Elliott, tossed his bike on the ground. The girls had parked beside them now.

"What are you doing, Elliott?" Taryn asked him.

"Just having a little fun."

Caleb turned to Taryn. "Isn't this the kid?"

Taryn nodded but didn't say anything.

"I thought you said you didn't see Taryn naked." Caleb had a big smile on his face as he poked his finger firmly into my chest.

I winced but didn't say anything. My eyes were on Josh.

"You know what we do to liars?" Caleb wasn't going to let this go.

"Hey, where's your bodyguard today?" Josh chimed in.

"Leave him alone, Josh." Lauren surprised me when she spoke up.

"Oh, so you're going to defend him now?" Josh smirked and looked around again. He was acting nervous. I saw him put his hand in his pocket and pull out something red. A Swiss Army knife. *Crap again.*

"If he says he didn't—"

"Don't tell me you believe that crap," Josh scoffed, rolling his eyes at Lauren. "He'd never admit it, especially not with you here."

"Guys, please, I don't want any trouble." I took two steps back.

"Oh, did you hear that?" Caleb sneered. "He doesn't want any trouble."

"Caleb—"

"Shut up, Taryn," Elliott snapped.

"Don't tell her to shut up, Elliott." Lauren snapped.

"Or what?" Caleb challenged her.

Lauren hopped off her bike. "Do you really want to find out?"

*I did.* Caleb backed down and Lauren turned back to Josh.

"Come on, Josh," she said. "Let's leave him alone. Your dad said you better not touch him."

"Yeah," Caleb laughed. "But my dad didn't say anything—"

"Caleb, seriously… shut up." Josh glared at him. "Or I'll let Lauren whup you." Josh stepped towards me then, and I took a step back. *Was he going to stab me right here?*

"Josh—" Lauren moved towards me as well.

"Lauren, I'm not going to do anything to him. Chill out. I just have a message for him."

He stepped up close to me and my eyes didn't leave his. "I didn't get to make my point to you last time because of the black knight, but let me make this clear." He was speaking in a hushed tone so no one else could hear him. "Hero or not you are not welcome here. Don't talk to these girls, don't talk to our friends, don't come near our courses and don't ever—never—watch Taryn again. Do we understand each other?"

I nodded.

"I need to hear you say it."

"Come on, Josh, this is stupid. He hasn't done anything wrong."

"Lauren," Josh glanced back at her, "enough. Stay out of this or I'll dump you."

"Please do," I muttered.

"What?" Josh spun back to face me.

"I said 'I do.' I hear you." I snuck a peak at Lauren's face and was suddenly aware she'd understood me. I blushed and looked down.

"There," he smirked. "Was that so hard? Now… you tell anyone we had this conversation and this… " He held up the pocketknife, "will be for you."

He flipped the blade open and I took another step back, but he wasn't coming for me. Instead he turned and walked over to my bike and slashed my tires as Lauren yelled at him and the others laughed. I watched Lauren get on her bike and ride away before everyone else. She was clearly upset and wanted nothing to do with this. I could tell by the look on Taryn's face she wasn't sold on this bullying act either. Caitlin on the other hand was laughing hysterically with the boys.

"Have a fun ride home." Josh smiled at me.

They got on their bikes and rode away. I waited until they had disappeared around the corner before moving over to my bike.

That conversation had told me a few things. Somehow Josh's dad knew he'd been in a fight with me and had told him to leave me alone. Taryn didn't seem to hate me. Lauren definitely didn't. Josh was the leader of the group. He had said the words "hero or *not*" so somehow he'd put the whole thing from the other night together, probably thanks to the newspaper. *Great!* I looked down at my bike and lifted it upright. This was going to be a long walk home.

I had only gone about a mile when a familiar truck rounded the corner and pulled up to me. Ken rolled down the window. "Want a ride?"

"How'd you know I was here?"

"Well, I could tell you Kate and I have been driving all over looking for you, which incidentally is true, or I could tell you some girl called me and told me you needed a ride." He looked down at my tires. "Which is also true. And I can see why. Care to tell me what happened?"

I shook my head.

"I figured as much." He didn't sound mad or disappointed. "Boys and their pocketknives."

"What?" *How much had Lauren told him?*

"Nothing." He hopped out of the truck and lifted my bike into the back. "You know, bud, at some point you've got to stop protecting these people who keep picking on you."

I climbed up into the cab beside him. "What good would that do?"

"Well, if I knew who was doing this—"

"You don't know who's doing this?" I cut him off. He looked over at me. *I shouldn't have snapped at him.* "I'm sorry."

"You're right," he said. "I do know who is doing this. Or at least I assume it's those same three boys, and that this still has to do with you seeing Taryn and Lauren naked?"

"I didn't see Lauren naked."

"You know what I mean."

I nodded. *I did.* Suddenly I had a question for Ken. "Can I ask you something?"

"Of course."

We had pulled out onto the street and were heading back towards the marina. "Did you by chance say anything to Josh's dad about the fight?"

He said "no" but he paused. He was hiding something.

"You told me you want me to trust you, but how can I trust—"

"Your friend did."

*What? What friend?* "My friend?"

"George."

"James?"

"Yes, James. I was close."

*Not even.* "How do you know that?"

"Small town." Uncle Ken pulled over to the side of the road.

It wasn't a small town, but I knew what he meant. People talk. Ken's neighbor… he talks.

"Is that why James doesn't come by anymore? Did you tell him not to? It wasn't his fault—"

"No. Absolutely not! I didn't say anything to him. Haven't seen him or had a single conversation with him. You haven't either, I take it?"

I believed him. I shook my head. "Josh did this to me because he thinks I told on him about the fight."

"That's what I was afraid of." Ken nodded.

"So what do we tell Kate about the fight? About the tires?"

"She knows about the fight. She's already given The Hills her two cents on how it was handled."

"Crap."

"It's okay, Miles. You know Kate. She can handle herself. She's a fighter for those she loves. Sometimes even for me." He winked and nudged me.

I allowed myself the smallest of smiles.

"How would you feel if we don't tell her about the tires at all? Would you feel guilty about that?"

I thought about it for a minute. I didn't think I would. "Maybe… no… I guess not."

"So, how about we get them fixed and tell her I just found you by the bay."

"But what about the phone call?"

"The girl called me, not Kate. I told Kate I'd found you but didn't say anything about the girl's call."

"Do you know who it was who called you?"

Ken smiled. "I have a pretty good idea."

*I did too.* At least I knew who I wanted it to be. "Will you feel guilty about not telling her?"

Ken laughed. "No, I guess not." He nudged me again playfully. "I can keep the secret for you. But only for you. Okay?"

"Okay."

We stopped by a bike shop and got new tires then headed back to their house. Kate came out of the house as we got out of the truck. I walked up to her and gave her a huge hug. "I'm sorry," I said quietly.

"You, dear boy, have *nothing* to be sorry for. Life hasn't been very good to you, but we're going to do all we can to change that."

Ken walked up and put his arm around her. "Anyone else hungry?"

Kate and I each raised a hand.

"How bout something special then?" Ken asked.

"What do you have in mind?" Kate asked.

"Miles?" He looked at me. "Wait… don't tell me. Toasted peanut butter and honey?"

"You know me." I gave them both a full grin.

"We do." Kate put her arm around me. "And we love you."

## ←★★★★★ NARRATOR ★★★★★→

### ←Monday, June 27, 2014→

I grabbed a Kleenex and blew my nose. My husband looked away from the game he had on the TV. "You okay, babe?"

"Yeah." I nodded. "These announcers just make me cry."

"They are pretty terrible." He knew that wasn't what had prompted the tears. "You sure you're—"

"I'm fine." I blew my nose again, sounding and feeling like an elephant. "Don't ever get pregnant."

"I'll keep that in mind." He smiled and turned back to the television.

I looked down at the laptop. That was enough writing for today. Rereading the whole story on Avery had pierced my heart… and tear ducts. I couldn't imagine growing up without a mom and dad… couldn't imagine the hardships she'd experienced—the impossible truths she'd faced at such a young age. That Miles had become so personally involved in trying to "rescue" her was no surprise at all. The first time I met him I knew he wasn't like anyone else I'd known. I snapped the laptop shut and began the two-minute process of standing up.

"Need help, babe?"

"No. I'm good." He watched me struggle to find a comfortable way to lift myself from the recliner. "This chair is too small."

"I know it is."

*We both knew it wasn't.* "Dang it all."

He laughed and slid off the couch, extending a hand down to me.

I took his hand and he pulled me up. "I almost had it."

"I know you did."

*We both knew I didn't.*

It was a restless night for me, and it had nothing to do with my physical discomfort. I wanted to keep on writing. I needed to keep on writing.

At 3:53 a.m. I gave up on sleep and slowly made my way down the steps, through the living room and into the kitchen. I flipped on a light and opened the freezer door, prompting a loosely placed, half-empty, bucket of vanilla ice cream to assault me. "Good try," I muttered, shoving it back in. "Too much sugar." I popped a couple frozen gummy bears in my mouth instead.

And got back to work.

←←←←←→→→→→

***"The object of golf is not just to win.<br>It is to play like a gentleman, and win."***

- Phil Mickelson

## STELLAR 24 – "Summer 2012 – Nick"

Nick told me to meet him at The Hills Golf Club at 7 p.m. on June 10th. I was there at 6:30. So was Nick. He looked surprised to see me. "You remembered. And you're early."

"You were pretty specific about the date and time," I replied. "And you're early too."

"I don't have a choice."

"Let's just say I was curious about why you wanted me here."

"How'd you like a summer job?"

"I already have one."

"Well, how'd you like another one?"

Not sure what I'd been expecting but it wasn't this. I didn't need another job and didn't know how Uncle Ken would feel about it. "Okay… I don't know… what is it?"

"My dad gives me $20 a day to pick up all the range balls and restack the pyramids. I'll split that $20 with you every day you're here by 7 p.m."

"It has to be seven?"

Nick slowly nodded but then paused. "Not necessarily, I guess. Why?"

"I typically can't leave the marina until 7:00 depending on when I get my uncle's boat cleaned. If it could be 7:30 I could be here every day but Saturday."

"Okay. I could do 7:30. My dad shouldn't care. The range closes at seven. Sunset isn't until 8:30 or so, so it wouldn't be dark until nine, pretty much all the way through August… that should work. I'll check with my parents to be sure, but I think it should be fine."

"So you just wanted me to come out here and help you stack balls."

Nick began to slowly nod again. "Yes. Well, kind of."

*I knew there had to be something else. He didn't really need my help to stack the balls.* "Okay… " I waited for him to continue. He looked embarrassed now.

"I… I was hoping maybe you'd help me with my short game."

"Seriously?" I laughed then covered my mouth. *He was serious.*

"What?"

"You brought me here to help you with golf?" *That was ridiculous.* I didn't even know how I did what I did. I just did it.

"What? Why is that funny?"

"You're a great golfer, Nick. Your dad is *the* golf pro—"

"But I can't do what you can do."

"And I can't do what you can do either. I could never hit the long ball like you."

"So I could teach you. We could help each other."

The idea quickly went from preposterous to semi-logical. I began to nod then too. *I'd love to hit a driver like Nick could.* "You know what? Maybe it isn't such a terrible idea after all. Your dad wouldn't care?"

"I haven't said anything to my dad, but I told my mom about the idea. She doesn't like Dad forcing me to play Josh, Brett and Toby for this stupid Summer Cup either. She asked me to give it one more year, and I told her I would if she'd let me practice with you. She's the one who has to pick me up when I'm done, and she's good friends with the chief security officer. You won't get in trouble for being here… "

I didn't need any more convincing, but I did have some concerns. "Won't you get teased for working with me? What if Josh, Caleb and Elliott find out?"

"Look, I get teased by everyone already. I've never even won a single match. I've never even been close. Not once. *0 for 36.* It's humiliating to see the scores posted and see my 90's with their low 80's and upper 70's. Dad gets teased about it and then gets mad at me for it. It can't get any worse."

"But won't your dad—"

"Let me worry about my dad." He walked away from me and started picking up the range balls. "It's totally up to you, Stellar."

I stood there for a moment and watched him. I'd wanted someone my age to hang out with for so long that nothing seemed like a strong enough reason to walk away from this opportunity. A friend. Free golf at The Hills—even if it was just hitting balls on the practice range. *Why the heck not?*

I grabbed the other bag off the ground and scurried after Nick. "I'm in," I called out.

He turned and flashed a huge smile. "Excellent."

## STELLAR 25 – "Second Best Day Ever"

Nick and I collected range balls and practiced together six nights a week for the next two weeks. Ken and Kate didn't have a problem with me taking on the extra responsibilities since it didn't affect anything at RB's, and they were thrilled I had someone my age to hang out with. Kate had one condition—I wasn't allowed to ride my bike home in the dark.

So she started picking me up. She would come early to watch us hit balls out into the far reaches of the headlight beams and Nick's mom—Carrie—would as well. They would sit, talk, laugh, and drink ice tea or flavored water on the lift gate of Carrie's truck. They quickly became as close of friends as Nick and me, which led to us all spending more time together away from The Hills as well.

The four of us started watching a great show on the Golf Channel called The Big Break. I swear Carrie and Kate were more hooked on that show than Nick and I—except for the all-girls Atlantis season of course. The Big Break led to us watching actual tournaments together—either Kate and I, or me and Nick. Kate and I had watched one of my favorite golfers, Bubba Watson, win the Masters back in April—the one tournament I'd always watched with Bernie. It was definitely a different experience watching golf with her. She knew almost nothing about golf. I remember her clapping once when a golfer got an "8." The announcer called it a "snowman" and Kate clapped. "That's pretty rare isn't it?" she asked.

"Yes, Kate, a snowman is somewhat rare on the PGA Tour."

"He didn't seem all that thrilled," she said.

"I would imagine he had higher expectations."

I was careful not to make too much fun of her. I appreciated her interest in golf, in whatever capacity, and that she'd take the time to sit down with me and watch it. I now followed Bubba, Phil and Rory, of course, in every event they played. I loved Bubba's tenacity, and his unapologetic passion for the game. I understood some people disliked him for those very things, but I didn't let that influence me, just as I hoped Bubba didn't let it get to him. *It stood to reason that if people could find a reason to hate God, they could find a reason to hate anyone.*

I liked Bubba for another unique reason. His swing was 100% self-taught, just as mine was. Well, I guess that's not entirely true. I was learning a lot from following Rory. It was his buttery smooth mechanics that I would practice in front of the TV, on the Wii. It was his effortless swing I tried to replicate while practicing with Nick—to varied degrees of success. Okay, so Nick was kind of teaching me too. So disregard my earlier point.

But, golf was my life again, like it hadn't been since I was hanging out with Bernie. There were some days I still really missed Bernie, particularly when I'd stumble across a pile of acorns. Some days I'd talk to him as if he could hear me, as if he could see me. I had a feeling he'd be pretty happy for me that I'd found someone like Nick.

I know I was thrilled.

Nick's first Summer Cup round was coming up at The National, on June 30th. There'd be four more rounds in July and three in August before the last week of the month where they'd play a round four days in a row—one at each course—to end the event. Josh was expected to win most of them *and* the Cup. As I mentioned earlier he'd won 27 of the 36 rounds so far and all three Cups. Toby had won eight rounds and Brett had taken the other. Nick didn't need any more reminders—especially from his dad—that he hadn't yet won one.

Nick hadn't played a round of golf since we'd started working together, and he was nervous about how our sessions would translate onto the course. I was convinced he'd be fine. His short game had come a long way, and I believed he was actually hitting his driver even further than before.

For these events each boy had his own caddie. I knew from watching golf on TV caddies were paid to carry your clubs, keep them clean, rake the bunkers, etc. But most of all caddies were valued, and rewarded, for their detailed course knowledge. The best ones had to know every break and curve of the greens, every yardage distance for every shot, and how to best keep their "client's" golf ball out of trouble on the course, often in spite of the golfer's ability. *Or total lack thereof.* Caddying sounded fun to me, but James always said it was a lot of work. For the most part they didn't use carts at these clubs, so the caddies would carry very heavy golf bags for eighteen holes all over the course. And often the clients that made you work the hardest tipped the worst.

In any case, the boys in this Summer Cup had the best caddies from each respective club. *Of course.* The stakes of pride were ridiculous! *No wonder Nick hated it.*

Josh's caddie was actually his father, Jason. His dad left little of Josh's game—and future—to chance. Everyone was convinced Josh was going pro eventually. He'd been playing in tournaments almost his entire life. His dad had played on a couple of the "mini tours," and Josh had been professionally instructed by one PGA coach after another since he was Avery's age—five. He'd always had everything he wanted—clothes, shoes, video games… a certain girl named Lauren. He attended the same private Catholic school as Nick, and Lauren, but I knew even that was a sham. Nick said he was barely ever there. He was always on the golf course at The National. *Or beating up new kids.*

Toby's dad was head golf pro at the club Nick called "Long Neck", adjacent to The National. He was pretty much the opposite of Jason, Josh's dad—completely uninvolved in his son's life. Nick said Toby had abandonment issues and a crazy temper. He snapped clubs, threw others in the water, cursed all the time, and constantly berated his caddie. I had a feeling I wasn't going to like Toby much.

Brett hailed from The Club, the fourth exclusive golf club in Southampton. Nick didn't have anything bad to say about Brett—quite the opposite in fact. Brett was courteous, a walking encyclopedia of golf knowledge and rules, and he was quiet as a mouse. "He doesn't talk unless he's reciting a rule, complimenting others or accepting praise," Nick said.

I asked Nick why he didn't hang out with Brett more and he just shrugged. "He only talks about golf." I made a mental note to myself at that point to *never* talk too much about golf.

Nick's caddie was a fat man appropriately named Rolls. How he walked a full 18-hole round carrying golf clubs without having a heart attack was anyone's guess. Nick said he was nice enough, but also extremely stubborn and critical. He wouldn't let Nick hit the shot he wanted to hit if he thought it was the wrong one. And every time Nick did something wrong Rolls would tell him. Nick's dad said it was exactly what Nick needed to improve—to toughen up—but Nick didn't trust Rolls at all, and liked him even less.

The day of the first Summer Cup match was a long one for me at the marina. My mind was at The Hills with Nick while I tended the shop at RB's. I kept checking the clock on the wall and guessing which hole they might be on. I was hoping Nick would call me at some point with an update but he didn't. At seven o'clock I locked up the shop and helped Ken with the boats. He drove me home at nine, still with no word from Nick.

When we pulled into the Parker's driveway that night there were three other cars parked there. I gave Ken a curious look and he smiled over at me. *He knew something I didn't.* "What's going on?"

"Kate and I have a surprise for you, bud."

"Okay… "

Ken put his arm around my shoulders and led me to the house. When I opened the door to the kitchen it was full of people, but I only saw one. She was sitting in a chair at the table, her hair tied up in pigtails, her mouth—and face—full of something chocolate. I heard laughter all around me as my expression turned to pure shock. *What was going on?*

"Stella!" the little girl squealed.

"Avery?"

She hopped out of the chair and charged towards me. I knelt and she threw her arms around my neck. "Of course, silly." She squeezed me tightly.

Avery? "What the—"

"She's going to be living with us permanently now, Miles," Kate said quietly. She was kneeling beside us with her hand on my shoulder. "I hope that's okay."

I had tears in my eyes, I was so happy to see her. "What? What do you—"

"We adopted her," Kate said, tears running down her cheeks as well. "She's our daughter now."

"Are you kidding me?" I looked around the room. I recognized everyone now. Kate's parents, Ken's mom, Ray and his wife... wait. *Ray's wife? What was she doing here?*

"Totally serious," Ken said.

I looked at him. "How long have you known?"

He laughed. "Hang on, son. There's more."

*More? How could there possibly be more?* I didn't know what to say, so I just stared at him as he kept talking. "A lady in Boston got the ball rolling the day you and Kate visited her. The next day Michelle..." Ken pointed at Ray's wife, "... picked her up for us while the process got finalized. Avery's been staying with Michelle the past few weeks."

I knew "the lady" was Lucy, but I had so many questions. "But... "

Ken held up his hand. "The lady had *one* condition for us being Avery's parents."

"And?" I was looking around the room for clues but all I saw were smiles. No one else was giving anything away. "*And?*"

"She couldn't be an only child," Ken continued.

*Wait. What?* "So you and Kate are... " *That's not possible.* "But I thought you couldn't..." I looked back and forth between the two of them as they each shook their head.

"No, honey, we're not pregnant," Kate whispered, blushing, with a quiet laugh, then turned to Ken.

Ken held an envelope in his hand. "But we are *your* parents now, too," he said. "Thanks to Ray."

The shocked expression returned to my face, as both the papers he held and the words he spoke registered. Ray had signed over permanent custody of me to them. Ken and Kate were now legally my parents. Avery was now legally my—"

"You my big bwutha, Stella." The little girl beamed and squeezed me tightly again.

*Avery was now my sister.* "This is the best day of my life," I whispered and everyone in the room laughed.

Kate kissed my cheek. "Ours too, honey... ours too."

## STELLAR 26 – "Love Bites"

The next morning I hopped on my bike and raced over to Nick's house. Carrie answered the door. "Nick's not home, Stellar. He and his dad are at the course."

"Do you know when they'll be home?"

"Sorry, Stellar—I don't. Midafternoon maybe?"

I was disappointed I still didn't know how his round had gone. "Guess I'll just see him tonight then."

"Everything okay?" Carrie asked.

"Yeah. All good. Thanks, Mrs. B." I hopped back on my bike and rode off.

Nick was already out on the range picking up balls when Kate dropped me off. I raced out towards him. "Hey, how'd it go yesterday?"

"Terrible." He didn't even look up. "I suck."

"You've got to give me more than that."

"Okay." He kicked a golf ball about twenty yards. "How about I *never* want to play this stupid sport again."

"So the practice didn't help?"

Nick shook his head but didn't say no. Instead he sighed deeply. "I was only one down to Josh through eleven holes."

"Nick, that's fantastic!" I was trying to step in front of him to get him to look at me but to no avail.

"Then I fell apart. I ended up finishing ten shots behind Josh and five behind the other two." He shook his head.

"Okay." I was trying to put a positive spin on his sour mood. "So what do we need to work on?"

"Everything!" Nick kicked another golf ball. "I can't hit sand shots, can't chip and can't read the greens. My putting is terrible and Rolls is an awful caddie." Nick paused. "I *hate* that guy."

"How'd your dad take it?"

Nick laughed. "Yeah… not well. After Fat Man called me a few names and basically told my dad he thought I was beyond help, my dad chewed me out for not letting Fat Man "help" me. Dad even tore up my scorecard and threw it in the trash. My best round ever wasn't good enough for him."

"That totally doesn't sound like your dad."

"Yeah. That's what everyone who doesn't know him would say."

*I shouldn't have said that last part.* "Sorry, that's not what—"

Nick waved off my apology. "It's not your fault. I know what you meant. My dad is not my problem. He's under a lot of pressure, too. He's the only one whose kid sucks."

We continued picking up balls in silence. It wasn't until we were stacking the last pyramid that Nick said something else. "Your girlfriend was there yesterday."

"She was?" I answered before thinking, watching a small smirk cross Nick's face. "I… what do you mean?"

"Everyone knows you like her."

"Who knows? Josh knows? Did you say something?"

"Yeah. He definitely knows. But no, I didn't say anything."

"So how would he know?"

"Those two argue all the time. Josh is a punk at school—a bully—and Lauren hates that. When Josh slashed your tires they almost broke up."

*Almost?* Nick had my undivided attention now. "That doesn't explain how he would know I like her. And how do *you* know all this anyway?"

"You're quite the hot topic around here. You and your dog."

A car pulled up behind us then and Carrie got out. She walked up to us. "You two doing all right?"

"We're fine, Mom." Nick nodded as she mussed his hair.

"Hey Stellar," Carrie said. "I just talked to Kate. Did you tell Nick your news?"

Nick spun to look at me as I shook my head. "No."

"What news?" Nick asked. "Sorry, man, I kinda dominated the—"

"It's nothing." My mind was completely on Lauren now.

Another set of headlights swung into the parking lot then and I recognized the silhouette of Ken's truck. I didn't give Kate a chance to get out. "I can't practice tonight," I said, walking away from Nick and Carrie.

"Stellar, are you sure you're okay?" Carrie asked.

"Yeah." I waved. "I'll see you tomorrow night, Nick."

I heard Nick ask his mom what she was talking about, but didn't hear her reply. I hopped into the back seat of the truck next to Avery.

"Hi, Stella!"

"Hey Avery."

"No practice tonight?" Kate asked.

"Nope. Nick's not feeling well," I lied. I just wanted to go home.

Kate waved at Nick and Carrie, then took us home.

An hour later Kate came into my room to tuck me in. "How are you doing?"

"I'm okay. Just tired."

I could tell there was something on her mind as she sat on my bed and watched me brush my teeth in the mirror. "Miles, do me a favor, will you?"

"Of course. What do you need?"

"I need you to be honest with me."

"Okay." I stopped brushing and turned to face her.

"I mean always." She continued. "I know I'm not physically your mother, but legally you are my son and I love you. I don't want to see you hurt and I don't want you to hurt me."

"What are you talking about? How did I hurt you?"

"I just talked to Carrie."

*Crap.* "And?"

"Nick is fine. You lied—"

"I'm sorry." I knew what she was saying now. "Kate… "

She didn't reply or interrupt me. She was waiting for me to continue.

I sighed. "You wouldn't understand."

"Try me."

"There's this girl."

"Lauren?"

I sighed again. *Seems everyone knew.* "I'm not even going to ask how you… never mind. Let's just say I like her. I really really like her… which doesn't seem possible I know, given I've never said anything other than "trick or treat" to her." I saw Kate smile but I kept going. "But she likes this other boy—"

"Josh?"

*Seriously?* "Do you just want to tell this?"

Kate laughed. "Sorry—no. Continue please."

"Lauren is Josh's girlfriend." I didn't know for sure that they were, but didn't know how else to say it.

Kate laughed again then quickly apologized… *again*. "Miles, you need to understand something. At twelve or thirteen being someone's girlfriend basically means you don't ever talk to them. It's almost like an arranged marriage—you might not even like the other person."

"You mean you can have a boyfriend you don't even like?" *That was about the stupidest thing I'd ever heard.*

"I did."

"That doesn't make any sense." *I clearly had a lot to learn about love.*

"Tell me about it." Kate nodded.

"So you think Josh and Lauren might be like that?"

Kate paused and finally shrugged. "I can't say for certain—and definitely can't speak for Josh—but I'd say there's a good chance Lauren feels that way."

"Seriously?"

Kate laughed. "I mean come on… it *is* Josh."

That was simultaneously the best and meanest thing I think I'd ever heard Kate say. I gave her a huge hug. "Thank you."

She kissed the top of my head. "Anytime."

## STELLAR 27 – "Summer 2012 Wrap Up"

I don't remember much from the rest of the summer Avery and I were adopted—other than golf that is. I do know it felt as if we'd been brother and sister forever. I loved having her around. She and I were glued to the TV in early August, watching Rory turn in one of the most dominant performances in Tour history—at the PGA Championship in South Carolina. *Avery refers to him as "Whoa-wee." It's adorable!* And then Kate and Carrie took Nick, Avery and I to the final round of the FedEx Cup event at TPC Boston, where we got to see Rory hold off Tiger in an epic finish. It was surreal. But real.

Life was good back in Southampton, too. Nick and I picked up balls and practiced together the rest of the summer. Kate would bring Avery to watch us and then Avery would help us pick up the pyramids we'd scatter. The burns on her arms had left some pretty nasty scars but I'd gotten used to them. Kate did a good job of masking the deepest scar on her face with a little make-up, but people would still point and whisper. People were still mean. Fortunately Avery was largely immune to their cruelty. I thought she was adorable just the way she was, and Ken and Kate always told her the same. I don't think she had *any* doubt she was loved.

Nick's short game had vastly improved over the summer, but he continued to struggle with putting. His parents had his eyes checked out and they were definitely part of the problem. His left eye had serious cataract issues, resulting in significant visual distortion.

He struggled on the course the rest of the summer. Josh won every single one of the twelve Cup rounds and his fourth consecutive Summer Cup. With every round he played, Nick seemed to hate golf more, but he'd made a deal with his mother that he'd finish out the season. I knew if his dad allowed it, he'd probably never golf again after that.

I didn't try to convince him otherwise, though I believed if I were allowed to play with him at The Hills he'd change his mind. I thought I could make him love the game and have fun with it again, but I wasn't a member—no way we could afford it—and non-members weren't allowed on the course at The Hills—not to watch, play or caddie. *Certainly not non-member kids.*

I only saw Lauren a few times that summer, mostly at the Shopping Centre or grocery store. If it was possible, she got prettier every single day, and the few opportunities I had to actually say the word "hello" to her I chickened out, taking evasive measures instead.

There were no other run-ins with Josh, Caleb, Elliott, Taryn or Caitlin that summer. I stayed pretty busy down at RB's and the marina with Ken, and that was not the kind of place you'd ever see any of them. *We didn't have million dollar yachts or cruise ships there.*

When the school year began, Ken and Kate enrolled Avery in a local Montessori. They hoped private school would help fill in whatever academic gaps she might have from the chaotic and traumatic life she'd lived to this point. Private school had also been a specific request of her mother's in her will.

On several occasions I heard Ken and Kate talking about putting me in an actual school too—instead of homeschooling—but Ray had sold Ken his half of RB's in mid-August and moved into the city. He'd dried up, straightened up, and moved back in with his wife, Michelle, so Ken needed my help more than ever. In fact, even my help wasn't nearly enough.

We needed someone to tend the shop full-time during the week, and Ken's cousin, Joe, could only work weekends. I was capable, of course, but not yet even twelve, and Kate refused to let me be down there alone. So, it needed to be an adult. Kate got Nick's mom, Carrie, to help her track down the current phone number for James from his employment application at The Hills—Nick's dad must have been able to look it up. Ken got ahold of James and offered him the job over the phone. James accepted and shocked the crap out of me when I walked in one morning and found him behind the counter. *Talk about an awesome surprise!* It was great not just to see him and talk to him again, but also to be able to finally thank him in person for his amazingly generous gift—my golf clubs. *And to make him promise never to leave me like that again!*

So, James was back in my life, and Nick and I remained as close as ever, even after school started up. He'd come down to the marina some evenings after school and help James clean the shop or me scrub the boats. His dad had someone else picking up the balls on the range now, but we'd still go there occasionally to chip a pyramid at dusk in the headlight beams of Carrie's car.

The eleventh year of my life was the most eventful and runaway best I'd ever had. So many changes: James was back, I had a best friend, a new sister, new parents, a game I loved, and a girl… well, a girl that made me feel like no one else ever had before.

A girl who could probably have anyone she wanted—*ever*—and would *never* in a million years pick me.

But I think I loved her.

## *←Author Note→*

*If you've ever read a book where you feel like you missed something, or one where pages are physically missing, it can be pretty frustrating. Especially if you like the book. (Happened to me with The Horse Whisperer. Wish it had happened at the end of Old Yeller.) Unfortunately, you might feel similarly frustrated now. Somehow I'm missing one of Stellar's journals—Journal #4.*

*Let me be clear that at this point it's easier for me to accept, as a pregnant woman, that I've lost my mind, than it is to come to terms with the possibility I've lost even a page of Stellar's writing. But... I've searched every box, every inch of this townhome, through all my school stuff, etc. with no luck. And so, unfortunately, there is no written record of anything that happened in his life from October of 2012 to June of 2013—assuming, of course, that's what he'd covered in that journal.*

*From my conversations with Kate over the years and ensuing journals, I can fill in bits and pieces of the story, but there's no way it will be as complete or authentic as Stellar's version would be. So... my apologies in advance for the "incomplete" nature of this ONE "improvised" chapter.*

## ←★★★★★ AUTHOR ★★★★★→

Stellar turned twelve on October 28, 2012—the same day Hurricane Sandy hit New York. *Largest Atlantic hurricane on record!* Ken had boarded up River Bait and Boats, and the Parkers had all gone into Manhattan to stay with Ray and Michelle for the duration of the storm. They stopped briefly at Ground Zero that afternoon—Stellar wanted to show Avery where his parents were—then went out for dinner to celebrate... at McDonalds. A lot of places were shuttered up that night and remained so through November 2nd or 3rd. The mayor even cancelled the New York City Marathon on November 4th.

Sandy destroyed RB's, the marina, and most of their boats. I know it took them almost a full month to get everything fixed and replaced. Ken debated not even coming back to Southampton, selling the shop and house and moving elsewhere, but Kate wouldn't hear of it. She didn't want to separate Nick and Miles, didn't want to add any more drama to Avery's life, and she had grown really close to Nick's mother, Carrie.

I'm glad the Parkers decided to come back. That first week of November was actually the first time I spoke to both Avery and Stellar.

My dad was on the committee that filed the restitution claim for Southampton with the state, and I was with him the day he stopped to evaluate Ken's River Bait and Boats.

I'd seen Stellar around plenty but never talked to him. He always seemed so quiet and shy back then. His dog on the other hand was anything but. That little hairball came charging right up to me, yapping like crazy. I knelt down to pet him and almost bumped heads with Avery. "This your dog?"

"Squirrel is my brother's," she replied, in the cutest little voice.

"His name is Squirrel?" I almost laughed. "What's yours?"

She didn't reply. But Stellar spoke up from behind me. "Come on, Avery. Let's go."

"That's my brother," Avery whispered, picking Squirrel up.

I stood and turned towards the sound of his voice. "Cute dog," I said, smiling at him.

He didn't smile back—barely even looked at me. "Thanks."

That was all he said. His little sister scurried over to him and took his hand, and they walked away from me. "Nice meeting you," I called out. I saw Stellar's head nod but he didn't reply.

Avery glanced back and said, "You too."

Then they were gone.

The next day, November 7th, we got our first snow of the season thanks to a freak nor'easter named Athena. The day after that the power was down almost everywhere. No one had real wood-burning fireplaces anymore so almost everyone on Long Island froze. *What a crazy two weeks!*

Stellar started taking swimming lessons at the local aquatic center after Thanksgiving. Ken wouldn't take him out on his deep-sea fishing charters until he could "tread water for an hour and swim a half-mile in a pool without stopping." Stellar was determined to accomplish both by the next summer—2013.

His family once again attended the Christmas Eve service at the church where St. Bernard "found him." I remember Kate telling me how emotional those services were for him—reliving all those memories. On the one hand he was thrilled with the life he had at that point, but he still missed Bernie and, even though he never actually knew them, he still missed his birth parents.

The somber mood on Christmas Eve was replaced with ecstasy on Christmas morning when "Santa" got him a Junior Membership to The Hills, which I know for a fact he considered to be *the* greatest tangible gift he ever received. *Top three for sure.* Stellar, of course, would say that getting a little sister and parents earlier that year was the gift of a lifetime, and not just to be PC. That was Stellar's way.

I promised at the outset this was a story about golf… trust me, it still is. There's a whole lot more to come. But it's always been interesting to me how it almost wasn't. If the Parkers hadn't come back to Southampton after Hurricane Sandy a whole lot of things would have been different. This would *not* be a golf story. This wouldn't be a story at all. At least I know I wouldn't be the one writing it.

And then there was Calvin.

One of James's good friends that he'd worked with at The Hills started picking up a few hours at RB's on weeknights, mostly cleaning boats. His name was Calvin, a black man from Puerto Rico, who mostly went by "Cal." He was soft-spoken and self-conscious of a slight speech impediment, but also very kind *and* a very hard worker. Stellar and Ken both spoke very highly of him. He fit in perfectly at RB's.

Cal was also on the maintenance crew at The Hills, and one of his jobs was to change the pin placements—move the flags—on the greens early every morning. Sometime in April or May Stellar started heading to the club before sunrise with Cal, just to help him move the pins. Nick thought he was insane to get up so early, but Stellar loved that job… though he wasn't paid a dime for it.

Never having played a single round of golf on an actual course, Stellar was fascinated with the greens—every bump, hump, dip and curve. He could recite all eighteen pin placements, *and their significance*, daily and hole-by-hole, if you'd let him. I'm sure Kate and James did. I know Nick didn't. Nick still hated golf, but Stellar's attention to detail and near photographic memory was impossible to ignore… impossible to forget.

Nick was still intent on giving up golf, but Stellar and James convinced him to give it another year—one last shot. Nick agreed, but on one condition: Stellar had to caddie for him for the 2013 Summer Cup. His dad took some convincing but Carrie backed Nick up. She made it pretty clear to Nick's dad, Martin, that either Stellar would caddie for Nick or Nick would never golf again. Martin reluctantly gave in.

That's where the story picks back up from Stellar's point of view, where the next journal in the stack begins: Summer of 2013.

## STELLAR 28 – "Digging Holes"

I remember the first time I ever swore. It coincided with the first time I saw Lauren in a bikini. It was hot. She was hot. I was hot. *Three very different contexts for the same word.*

I usually didn't get to go to the beach during the summer, but when Cal started helping us at RB's, Ken started giving me some days off… or at least half-days.

Nick and I biked over to the beach by her house on Saturday, June 1st. I was going to fish. We were going to fish. That didn't happen. Manure happened. As in "divine manure." That's where I let the "Holy S" slip—where a tan blonde girl in a white bikini blew my twelve-year-old mind. I found a way to stare at Lauren and count her two-piece polka dots for three full hours. I distinctly remember Nick saying at one point. "It would be a whole lot less awkward if you'd just go over there and lick her face."

Maybe he was right.

I didn't though. I had feelings coursing through me I still didn't have a very good handle on. There's no way I could have walked up to her without falling down, or talked to her without swallowing my tongue… not with her in a swimsuit.

I kept my distance.

I saw her glance our direction a few times, but every time she did I ducked behind a rock, or Nick. And every time Nick would sigh or shake his head, or both. I knew it was dumb, but I couldn't let her see me. We could have left… but I still wanted to see her.

Finally, she packed up, covered up, and took off. I could breathe again.

"You can come out now," Nick said sarcastically.

"You ready to go?" I asked, making sure she was completely gone.

"For almost three hours now," Nick replied.

"Sorry." I honestly did feel bad.

"Don't worry about it. I get it. She's the prettiest girl in school."

*Try "in the world."* I'd been steadily dating her in my dreams for months now, ever since I'd heard she'd finally ended whatever she had going with Josh. And those dreams… man, I hated waking up from those dreams.

I was curious what had been the final straw, and/or what took her so long to permanently leave that loser in the dust… but, in truth, I didn't really care. All that mattered was that now I might actually have a chance to ask her out. Of course, I had to find the courage to say "hi" to her first.

Nick's first match of the 2013 Summer Cup was coming up in exactly two weeks on June 15th. I was itching to get out on the course and play a round of golf with him.

On my membership plan—which was some kind of custom one Kate had negotiated with Martin—I wasn't allowed to play on weekends. I could practice any weekday from 5 a.m. to 8 a.m. and 5 p.m. until dark, but nowhere in between. Bottom line: I hadn't even *played* the course yet.

Nonetheless, I knew the greens by heart. For almost two months I'd been coming out with Cal at 5 a.m. to move the pins. Cal was a golf nut, though he'd never played for pretty much the same reason as me.

"It's a rich man's game in New York," he'd say. "But I l-l-loves to watch it."

His stuttering would really fluster him at times—when he got nervous or excited. He did everything he could to avoid words with the letter 'L'—somewhat challenging at "The Hills Golf Club." Truth be told, he seldom spoke to anyone at The Hills, or anywhere else for that matter. But James and I… he'd talk our ears off, and if it was just the three of us—or just he and I—Cal seldom stuttered.

Cal's main responsibility at The Hills was rolling the greens and moving the cup—golf hole—on each green. The mowers would come through and cut them and Cal would follow, rolling them to make them carpet-smooth. Once he finished rolling them he'd cut a new hole and move the pin—the flag—to that location.

They do the same on every course in America daily, but I guarantee you few places have a crewmember who puts as much thought into where the cup should go. Cal would check the weather, the wind, the temperature, and firmness of the greens. He'd roll a dozen balls, daily, from the fringe—the edge of the green—to each pin position he marked. He did that to make sure it was fair for any reasonable approach shot.

He cut the holes in different parts of the green based on the majority of people who would be playing it that day. On senior and women's league days it was always somewhere in the middle. For casual, celebrity, and corporate events, they were usually drilled in one of the back corners—giving the most room for error. For championship events the pins were mostly placed directly behind the bunkers or in precarious positions near sharp breaks or steep drops.

Naturally, some spots were more challenging than others, but seldom did anyone complain. Cal had been "the pin man" for two years now and wanted the people playing to enjoy the game, not hate it. He was also well aware of the history of The Hills—the first 18-hole course on the east coast—and of the significance of "the little things" at a legendary club like that one.

I took my apprenticeship with Cal with similar artistic dedication. I learned about each bump and break on every one of the greens at The Hills from him. He would point out the turf subtleties to me as he plotted his pin positions. Sometimes he'd repeat himself, or contradict himself, but I didn't mind. I soaked it all in—put my photographic memory to work.

I've never known anyone like Cal in many ways, but in golf he... well... he could see every minor indentation on a seemingly flat surface and could dictate how every imperfection or intended design feature would affect a rolling ball. *And I thought my attention to detail was special.*

Cal enjoyed testing me. He'd ask me about the conditions and tell me about the golfers scheduled to play the course that day. Then he'd challenge me to predict where he'd put the pin and why. If I guessed correctly within a foot or so he'd let me cut the hole. *My record was five out of eighteen at that point.*

(I personally think "within a foot" was a little unfair, but this was a privilege to me and I never objected out loud.)

Cal would finish the pin setting by bending over with a tiny pair of scissors and neatly trimming the longer blades of grass around the freshly dug hole. He was a perfectionist—an artist working on a masterpiece in obscurity. *Exactly the way he liked it.*

Cal's mentoring greatly benefitted my golf game. All I'd ever done in golf thus far was chip and putt, and I'd mostly only putted around the furniture in our basement. Now, with my membership, I began putting on the practice green at The Hills every day. I would roll balls when no one was around and watch how they broke from every angle. My photographic memory came in handy there as well.

One more note about Cal's professional pin-setting routine. He carried a small notebook in his back pocket with a hand-drawn diagram of the greens at The Hills. He'd dissected every green into anywhere from twelve to twenty-four little boxes based on topographical details most ants wouldn't notice, and each box was labeled with a letter. He tracked not only how many times he put the pin in each box, but the exact dates he put them there. "Don't want to hear from no Department of Redundancy Department," he joked. *But he was also serious.* He told me he started a new notebook every year. Now *that* is dedication!

I didn't miss his smile the day I brought my own little notebook out and began drawing out the greens. "Just a second," he said. He reached into his backpack and pulled out a leather bound flipbook. "Use this."

It was an official yardage guide for The Hills. "Guard it with your l-l-life. They ain't cheap." He didn't often stutter around me—unless he was nervous or excited. It must have really moved him to have a copycat.

I still have that yardage guide—three years later. I'm holding it in my hand right now as I try to remember all these details for this journal entry. It's full of my notes, notes no one but Cal could possibly make heads or tails out of. And I wouldn't sell it for a million dollars.

## ←★★★★★ NARRATOR ★★★★★→

### ←Tuesday, June 28, 2022→

"I don't understand golf."

"What's that?" My husband popped his head out of the bathroom, toothbrush wedged in his mouth. "What'd you say?"

I powered off the computer and set it on the nightstand beside me. "Golf. I don't get the addiction… don't understand the allure. I mean why pay hundreds to thousands of dollars to always be angry and frustrated, and to constantly pursue a mostly hopeless cause. It's like playing the lottery, except for the fact that you *could actually win* something from the lottery. Golf can't be good for your health… or self-esteem."

"Your dad played all the time."

"Exactly. And he always came home bitter at the game… or at his clubs, or the balls, or at "Johnny Cell Phone" who wouldn't shut up during his swing. I mean… if it doesn't make you happy, why keep playing?"

"It's hard to explain." He shut off the bathroom light and walked towards the bed. "I've loved *and* hated the game… It's hard to explain."

"You said that already."

He laughed. "Maybe you should just come with me sometime."

I shut off the lamp on my side. "Once was enough for me."

"I understand that. I guess I just hoped that maybe over time you'd change your—"

"It's not gonna happen." It came out more forcefully than I'd intended, but I absolutely meant it. "You want to skydive? I'll skydive with you. You want to have a baby? I'll have it for you. But I'll never golf again. And you *know* why."

"You're right. I'm sorry." His immediate apology was sincere. I knew that. He understood exactly where I was coming from.

"I'm sorry too," I replied. "I didn't mean to bite your head off." I was quiet for a few seconds, then tried to ease the tension with a joke. "But speaking of bites… I *am* hungry."

"Of course you are," he teased, as I scooted up against him under the covers. "You want me to go get you something?"

"No. Just hold me."

He shut off his lamp. "I can do that." He wrapped his arm around me and was silent for a few minutes. Just when I thought he was asleep he whispered in my ear. "You're right... golf *is* a dumb game." He kissed my cheek. "But a part of me will always love it."

I nodded and closed my eyes, unwilling to confess aloud what I knew was true in my heart.

*A part of me would always love it too.*

←←←←←→→→→→

***"A kid grows up a lot faster on the golf course."***

\- Jack Nicklaus

## STELLAR 29 – "The First Round"

I triple bogeyed the first hole I played—three over par. It was embarrassing. Almost like I had never swung a golf club in my life. I'd never even heard of first-tee jitters before, but I could only compare the feeling in my stomach and the shaking in my hands on that tee box at The Hills to the first day Lauren talked to me. I shanked that conversation with her as badly as I did my first ever tee shot, and Nick's response was the same as mine had been with Lauren. "Calm down."

I did settle down. But I didn't play much better. Interestingly enough, my erratic play prompted Nick to enter a sort of instructor mode, and in that mode he played phenomenally. He was so tuned in to adjusting my flaws that he was subconsciously reinforcing the same basics in his own game. He was basically playing error free. His tee shots were crisp and long, his irons were dialed in—he looked like he should be winning *all* the Summer Cup matches. And then he got to the greens and there—in my comfort zone—he was lost. His putting was terrible. That's where I learned how to help *him*.

Course management is critical in golf. If you play the game right and always set up your next shot to your skill set strengths, you can make the game much easier and score a whole lot better. But golf is a game of millimeters more than it is inches. A millimeter off can result in mishits and missed putts. *An inch off and you might miss the ball altogether.*

We played The Hills from the green tees—the Summer Cup tees—at around 6250 yards. It felt really long to me. At the end of the round I didn't have to see the scorecard to know I'd shot a 94. Nick bested me by ten strokes, easily should have been twenty. I had twenty-four putts over the eighteen holes. Nick had thirty-six. I could provide a much more scientific breakdown, as I did for Cal and James, but I doubt anyone else would care. Suffice it to say there was plenty of room for improvement—in both our games.

As we approached the clubhouse after our round my heart skipped a beat. There were three boys standing there with their bikes watching us approach. Josh, Caleb and Elliott. *Crap.*

"What do you guys want?" Nick snapped.

"Were you out playing with your girlfriend?" Elliott—the dumb one—sneered.

"Shut up, Elliott," Josh turned on him, and the bony idiot shrunk back.

Josh attacking Elliott surprised me. *What is this?*

"What'd you shoot?" Josh asked Nick.

"Eighty-four."

"And this one?" Josh nodded in my direction.

I opened my mouth to reply but Nick cut me off. "Stellar didn't keep score."

"Convenient." Caleb smiled, not learning Elliott's lesson. He got a glare from Josh too.

"Stellar could beat you with one club." Nick turned to Caleb then towards Elliott. "You too."

"Bull," Elliott retorted, glancing nervously at Josh who let it go.

"One club?" Josh asked.

"One club."

"Nick, don't—"

He waved me off.

"How many rounds has he played?" Josh was taking this seriously for some reason.

"Just finished his first."

Caleb and Elliott were shaking their heads, but neither said another word. They were letting Josh pick their battles for them.

"How much you want to bet?" Josh asked.

"What's it worth to you?" Nick asked.

"Nick…" I didn't like where this was going.

"How 'bout something small, like…" Josh looked in his wallet. "$500?"

*Five hundred!?* "Nick, come on—"

"Okay." Nick nodded. "Either of these guys beats him, I'll pay you $500. But…" He waited for Caleb and Elliott to stop celebrating, "I don't want your money."

"Okay." Josh looked confused. "Not that it'll matter anyway, but what do you want?"

"He beats them, and they leave him alone."

*Whoa!* Now I saw what he was doing. I also noticed he wasn't including Josh in that bet. But I still had to beat these guys. I didn't know if I could do it with a full set of clubs. And certainly didn't think I could with *one* club!

"What do you mean?" Josh asked. "That's it? You just want them to leave him alone?"

"That's it." Nick's eyes were locked with Josh's. "They don't touch him, tease him. I don't want either of them to even talk to him again."

I didn't even object now. I was waiting to see if Josh would take the bet. He was eyeing me up and down. You'd think he'd have been confident, but he seemed to think Nick had something up his sleeve. I didn't know which response I was hoping he'd give.

"When would we play?" Josh seemed pretty close to agreeing.

"Tomorrow morning," Nick replied. "7:30 a.m."

Josh nodded and held out his hand. "Deal."

Nick shook his hand and stood still beside me as Josh corralled the other two away. We watched them bike down the road and then Nick spoke, "Let's go."

"Nick, what did you just do? That was stupid."

"Don't worry about it. You'll be fine."

"I can't beat them with one club."

"Maybe you will. Maybe you won't. I don't care either way."

"So why make the bet?"

"I was making a point with Josh. He's a smart kid. Obnoxious, arrogant, and spoiled, but smart." Nick looked at me then. "You don't know him like I do. I just got through to him on his level—his competitive level. He'll respect both of us for this if you even make it close."

"But $500? Why not $20."

Nick laughed and clapped me on the back. "Josh wouldn't have taken me seriously for $20. These guys wipe their butts with $20s."

I had a hard time imagining that, but understood the gist of what he was saying. This wasn't about the money.

When I got to RB's that afternoon, I told Cal and James about the wager but begged them not to mention it to Ken. The $500 Nick had put on the line was as stunning to the two of them as it was to me, but they also understood the purpose.

I struggled through my chores at the marina that night and skipped off to bed earlier than usual. Cal picked me up the next morning to set the pins, but neither of us said more than five words the entire two hours. Cal dropped me off at the clubhouse just after seven and stepped inside to refill his coffee mug.

I could see Josh out on the range with Caleb and Elliott, but there was no sign of Nick yet. At 7:20 I was beginning to get a little worried. It would be terrible if he didn't show. It would probably make everything much *much* worse. At 7:28 I could see a car coming down the road and recognized it as Carrie's. Finally!

When Nick stepped out of the car the expression on his face was hard to read. He looked upset—sad, angry, embarrassed—or something.

"What's going on?" I asked him.

"Bet's off," he replied.

"What? Why?" I wasn't expecting that. I saw Nick glance back at his mother.

"Dad found out."

"How?" I asked. But I knew how. Josh had to have run his mouth.

"I have to go. I'm grounded."

"Nick—"

"I'll see you later."

"Nick, I'm sorry."

He waved my apology off and got back into the car. They drove away and I stood there watching them leave.

"What's going on?" Cal's voice behind me made me jump.

"The bet's off. Somehow Nick's parents found out about it."

Josh, Caleb and Elliott joined us then. Josh had a huge smirk on his face. "Too bad about Nick, eh?"

"You did that on purpose?"

"You think I didn't know you two were trying to punk me—to make me look stupid?"

*Prank?* "You thought that was a joke?"

"Come on. You beating these guys with one club?" Josh shook his head. "That is a joke."

"I'm here aren't I?" I was angry now. "Would I be here if it were a joke?"

Josh paused. He knew I had a point.

Caleb reached out and grabbed my shirt. "You know what isn't a joke? Us beating you with one club."

"L-l-leave the boy al-l-lone." Cal reached out for Caleb's arm. Caleb shrunk back at Cal's touch, releasing my shirt.

"Stay out of this M.C. Stammer," Elliott growled.

"Yeah, black man... " Caleb laughed nervously, clearly not even comfortable with his own racist superhero reference. *But he finished it anyway.* "Robin here can take care of herself."

"Cal," I turned to him and saw a fire in his eyes I'd never seen before. "It's okay."

Cal reached into his pocket and pulled his wallet out, snapping it open and removing five crisp hundred-dollar bills. He held them out towards Josh. "You want proof it's not a joke?" he asked.

"Cal, don't. You can't afford that." I could see his hand shaking but knew it wasn't nerves. He was angry.

Josh was staring back at Cal, an expression of partial shock on his face. "Are you serious?"

Cal didn't blink, his arm still extended.

"Cal, it's not worth it." I tried to reason with him.

"It is to me," he whispered back.

Josh took his money. "We're off at eight," he snapped at me, then grabbed the other two by the arm and pulled them away.

I turned to Cal. "Why did you do that? You could get fired for that—for me."

"Son," he looked at me calmly, "I don't need this job that much. And in any case… I believe in you."

I shook my head. "But why?"

"You're special." Cal smiled. "I knows it. Now go... " He patted me on the shoulder. "Take that Rory wedge of yours and give it your best shot. Go and be the best version of you."

## STELLAR 30 – "91"

I lost. To both of them. Calvin lost his money. Calvin lost his job. Josh made sure of it. As soon as the match was over he went into the clubhouse and put the $500 on Martin's desk. "I know you don't allow your employees to gamble, and that black man Stellar hangs out with just took that same bet your son made yesterday. Too bad about him. He seemed like a nice enough guy."

Understand I heard all of this from Ken, who heard it from Kate, who heard it from Carrie who heard it from Martin. It might not be verbatim, but it's all the same to me. Josh was his usual smug self and Martin didn't like it, but Martin was stuck. He had to fire Calvin immediately or word would have spread to the other three clubs. Martin's job and reputation would have been on the line. Employees gambled all the time on little things, amongst themselves, but with members… it was another thing entirely. Martin couldn't allow it.

He offered Cal his money back as severance but Cal wouldn't take it. Cal did however ask they consider allowing me to stay on as the "pin-setter." Martin said he'd think about it, but I wasn't yet thirteen… I knew he wouldn't go for it. *I'd lost my "job" too.*

As Josh was leaving Martin's office, Martin stopped him. "Was it close?" he asked.

"Caleb beat him by three. Elliott got him by two."

"Over eighteen holes?"

Josh nodded.

"With what club?"

"Some wedge."

"No putter?"

"No putter." Josh confirmed. "You get that he lost though, right?"

"Yeah," Martin said. "I caught that part."

I was grounded a few days later for throwing a punch at Josh. I got a black eye, bloody lip, and lectures from Ken, Kate, James and Cal as a result. And I didn't even land the punch.

Ken hired Cal on full-time and gave him a $500 signing bonus. When I thanked Ken he pretended like he didn't know what I was talking about. "I give that to all new hires," he said.

I asked James if that was true, and he neither confirmed nor denied it. As he and Cal were the only two full-time employees Ken had ever hired, I didn't have much further I could take my investigation.

I wasn't allowed to see or talk to Nick for the next two weeks. He finished fourth in his first two Summer Cup matches with Rolls as his caddie.

I was a little worried about how he'd react to seeing me, considering how much trouble I'd gotten everyone into—and the fact I'd lost in the end.

I knocked on the door to his house. Carrie opened the door, greeting me with a warm smile. "He's in the back yard."

As I approached Nick his face lit up. He hopped out of the swing and ran towards me, holding his hand up for a high-five. *Not at all the reaction I was expecting.*

"Dude," he said with a grin. "I'm so glad to see you."

"I thought you might be mad at me."

"Mad? For what? For shooting a 91 with just a wedge? For doing what every boy our age has always wanted to do but never could—taking a swing at that punk… "

"But I lost. And you lost. And Cal lost."

"I don't see it that way." Nick shook his head. "And I'd bet Cal doesn't either."

"Is your mom still mad at me? Or you?"

"Nah, man. She loves you. And she can't stay mad at me. No one can."

"I thought maybe your parents would forbid you from hanging out with me."

"Stellar, between the two of us I'm the bad influence. I told them it was all my idea and they know it was. This wasn't your fault."

I wished I could believe that. I felt terrible for Cal. He loved that job more than anything. It was far more glamorous and interesting than working at the marina. Paid better too. But Cal didn't seem to care about the money. He'd also told me he knew what he was doing when he picked up the wager with Josh. He wasn't disappointed I lost. He was just disappointed I let my anger turn to violence—even with cause. "You've got to be a better man than the next guy," he said. "You've always got to try to be the best version of you." *He seemed to like that phrase.*

I've had a lot of role models in life—Jordan Spieth, Rory, Brady, and Derek Jeter among them—but few people influence you like the ones you love… like those who have loved *me.*

I've been blessed to know, love and be loved by great people—people like Bernie, Ken, Kate, James and Cal. Sometimes I just needed a little wake-up call.

## STELLAR 31 – "Down Goes Frazier"

There are monumental moments in sports: Ali taking Frazier down, Jordan hitting "The Shot(s)" against Cleveland and Utah, David Tyree making me—and the Patriots—cry, Jeter hitting a home run for his 3000$^{th}$ hit… I remember some clearer than others, specifically those in my "era." But I don't ever remember being impacted by anything in sports as much as I was by what happened on July 22, 2013.

If you're doing a web search right now you won't find this story. If you're skipping ahead in this journal entry you'll also miss the headline, cause I'm going to say it right here: Nick won a Summer Cup event. Yes, that's right: Nick beat Josh.

It was the first time I caddied for him. And the *last* time. The event was at The National—Josh's home course. Nick played a perfect game. He was bombing the ball off the tee, splitting fairways, and playing a masterfully strategic round of golf. It was a beautiful day, little to no wind and mid to upper 60's when we teed off. This wasn't a fluke—no battle against the elements.

They were all square through nine holes, two up on the other two, Brett and Toby. And that's when it all got interesting.

Nick started to believe in himself. Josh started to curse, slam his clubs, glare at both of us, and act like the spoiled little brat Nick always said he was. I'd never seen this side of Josh, and it didn't seem Brett and Toby had either. Proper golf etiquette went out the window altogether on the back nine. Josh would talk or cough loudly during Nick's tee shots. He'd walk ahead of Nick while he was hitting from the fairway, sometimes directly in the line of fire. And he'd pace back and forth across Nick's putting line on the greens. The caddies were reluctant to call Josh on his boorish behavior and Nick, to his credit, mostly ignored it. But I could tell by the growing smile on Nick's face—hole-by-hole—that not only was he aware of Josh's desperate moves, but he was enjoying the fact they didn't faze him at all. If anything they made Nick play better.

The opposite was true for Josh. He was down by one through twelve holes, down by three through fifteen and only finished the round because a DQ would have eliminated him from Cup contention. Josh lost to Nick by eight strokes. He ended up tied with Toby and two behind Brett.

So what was the difference between that round and the fifty other Summer Cup rounds Nick had played the past four years? Why did he win that day? If you'd have asked Josh why he lost he'd have said he just didn't care that day, didn't feel good, or was hurt somehow—or some combination of the three. We heard all his excuses at school that fall. *Yes, I started actual school that fall. More on that later.* But I only cared what Nick thought. And Nick told everyone it was his caddie—his best friend. Nick told everyone he won because of *me*. The 72 was "because of me."

I say that mostly to prove the point that I think a great caddie makes a world of difference in golf. The best ones seldom get the credit they deserve. *Mostly the players keep that credit to themselves.* In a game where temperament is as important as knowledge, and confidence is as critical as skill, the world's greatest players typically have the world's greatest caddies.

Nick had the greatest round of his life that day because he was relaxed. He had fun. He was always skillful, but that day it all came together in one complete package. If I was the glue, I'm thrilled. But Nick still had to hit the shots.

After that round Nick told his parents he was done with competitive golf, he was done with the Summer Cup. I knew how badly he wanted to beat Josh—just once. And now, having done so, on Josh's home turf no less, Nick was content to move on. I supported his decision, even if I loved the experience of caddying for him. For one thing, it would forever drive Josh nuts knowing the last time they'd played, Nick had won. That kind of victory was far better than punching Josh in the face. Josh could recover from a bruised eye so much easier than he could a bruised ego.

Another thing I noticed is that Nick's dad didn't object to his son stepping away from the game. Sure, he'd have loved to see if Nick could have gone on to challenge for—or win—the Summer Cup that year. But Mr. Birch had learned a few things about Josh that allowed him to see why his son hated playing those matches so much. I'm sure Mr. Birch took some flack from Josh's dad and maybe even the other local pros for his son "quitting." But I'm also sure it gave Mr. Birch a similar satisfaction to that of his son, knowing Nick had beaten the local "anointed one" in his last ever match.

Nick's victory had other benefits. Josh was too embarrassed to show his face around The Hills. We didn't see him at the club the rest of the summer. We'd see him at the beach, pool, or local movie theater from time to time, but he made a point of staying far *far* away from us. That kept his stooges away from us, too.

Nick and I continued to golf together until school started. We never kept score, playing more a game of H-O-R-S-E on the course than we did a structured round of golf. We also started playing night-golf with these awesome glow-in-the-dark golf balls. The Hills had very little water on course so we lost very few balls, and Nick's dad gave us these rings to put in the cups to see where we were going. *Talk about an addicting twist to the game!*

Nick and his dad began a new tradition of their own that summer. They started golfing every Sunday evening, just the two of them. They used to play together, of course, but these rounds were the polar opposite of those from earlier years.

I'd like to think I helped Nick with his golf game that summer, but more than anything I'd like to think I helped him and his dad find common ground—a friendship. At a time when most boys our age were running away from their parents, especially their dads, I finally had a dad of my own, and Nick and his dad were closer than they'd ever been.

There was no more pressure on the golf course for Nick—no tension, no arguments, no anger. Nick preferred the "you against yourself" and the "you against the course" mentalities of the game. He had no aspirations of being a professional golfer, and his dad had finally accepted that.

I wasn't blessed with such a curse. My love for the game itself had never been greater—and my skill set never more complete—but I'd also just gotten my first true taste of competition and I desperately wanted more.

First I had to go to school. A real brick and mortar school—*if that's even what buildings are made out of anymore.* No more homeschool. No more tutoring. *It sucked.*

I could blame it all on Avery. She was of age for Kindergarten but was insistent that she be like her "big brother" and stay home, or work at the marina. *See what I mean?* Kate sat me down for a bargaining session in late August, though I pretty much held no chips, and I reluctantly agreed to give school a shot, just for Avery. *Darned cute little sisters!*

And so, that first Friday of September, my seven-years-younger little sister and I shared our very first day of school.

## STELLAR 32 – "Perfect Attendance"

I had perfect attendance the first week of the 2013-14 school year. So it was a one-day week. *Still counts!* Kate had attended Catholic school as a child, so it was very important to her that Avery and I do the same. You don't argue with Kate. *At least you shouldn't.* (And not just because of her 128-13 record in court as a District Attorney.) And so my education began at the Rockville Academy in Southampton, a community K-8 pool/school for three of the local Catholic churches.

There were 22 kids in my eighth grade class, sixteen boys and six girls. I didn't know *any* of them by name and only remembered seeing a few of them ever around town. *Southampton does have 60,000 residents.* These kids were reciting religious things I'd never heard of and everyone but me raised their hand when the teacher asked if we attended church every Sunday. I'd still only been to two church services ever, unless you counted funerals—then I'd been to three. Yeah, I was kind of an outsider. *One day in and I was already "that" kid.*

Nick, Josh, Lauren, Taryn, Caitlin, Caleb and Elliott were all in ninth grade. Ordinarily that would have put them all at the Catholic high school, but the high school was adding a new building, so 9th grade was going to be taught at Rockville for the next two years. Their core classes were all self-contained—a flip from ours, which was kind of backwards. Their specials rotated with ours though, which meant they had to share classes with us junior high kids. So we interacted with them at morning break, lunch, and all of our electives throughout the day.

We had to have *one* music class so—*since I refused to sing*—Kate had signed me up for band. I was "assigned" an instrument called a viola. I just knew I was going to hurt someone with that thing.

I only had two classes with Lauren, art and media, and then lunch and morning break. Everyone had to take art, so it was just random luck we ended up in that class together. But media was technically an extra English class Kate made me take, one grouped by ability, meaning Lauren was apparently as terrible with language as I was. *Which was pretty awful.*

I only had one class with Nick—math. And that was only because I tested out of both seventh and eighth grade math and was put in a ninth grade accelerated class with Nick and five other kids—all girls. Normally it would have been an online class, but with the 9th grade here this year, I "lucked out." *I got to see Nick every day for at least an hour at school.* Josh, Caleb and Elliott were not in any accelerated classes. *Just thought I'd point that out.*

School was okay. I felt stupid in English and brilliant in math, somewhere in between in everything else.

My attention to detail and perfectionist nature was both a detriment and a positive in art. We hopped from one project to the next too fast for my liking. I felt like I was barely beginning while others were finishing. It was maddening. I don't think I completed a single project that year—except when we made paper and popcorn chains for Christmas. *There's only so many ways you can mess up gluing and putting a needle through popcorn.*

I maintained my perfect attendance through October 27th. Then, as part of my "contract" with Kate I was allowed to go fishing with Ken on my birthday, October 28th. I hadn't missed a single birthday yet because of school, and I wasn't about to start now.

Nick and I biked home from school together every day we could. I always had a lot of homework, so I didn't go to the marina during the week anymore. I made up for that on weekends, when I seldom left the marina, except to go to church. We were required to attend at least twice a month—for school. *So much for free will.*

Business was booming for Ken as the economy had come full circle. He was selling boats almost as fast as he could get them in, and his charter schedule was booked out for weeks. Kate had stepped down as District Attorney and opened her own private law office out in Southampton, so she could dictate her own hours and be home with us more during the week.

Avery turned six on November 8th and we got our first snow on November 12th in what was an insane winter on Long Island—nearly 60 inches of snow in all.

We attended the Christmas Eve service at St. Paul's Chapel across from Ground Zero again this year. Something in me always stirred when I was there, so close to where I lost my birth parents (and later Bernie) in what seemed like a lifetime ago. Plus, 2013 was the year Nick and his parents came with us, which was pretty cool as well. We walked through Times Square and the toy store with the Ferris wheel. That was another great Christmas.

I don't remember much else between Christmas 2013 and Thursday, April 10th, 2014, but I do recall Nick and I were really into swimming. Nick had hit quite a growth spurt that year and that greatly benefitted him in the water. No one could keep up with him but that didn't keep me from trying.

Nick and I took CPR classes together and tried out for the Junior Lifeguard program. We *both* made it. The kid who not too long ago had nearly drowned—*twice*—was now a lifeguard. *Ha! How bout them apples?*

You're probably wondering why I specifically mentioned Thursday, April 10th a paragraph ago. Believe me, I wish that date didn't stand out in my mind. That day—that week—changed everything.

## STELLAR 33 – "April 10, 2014"

Nick wasn't at school on April 10th. His house was dark when I rode over later that afternoon, and he wasn't at The Hills either. In fact, there was a sign on the front door of the clubhouse that said the course was closed for the day. *Was it some holiday I didn't know of?*

I rode back home and asked Kate if she knew what was going on. She didn't but she told me she'd call Carrie and find out where they were. I ran up to my room to see if he'd left me a note on one of our video game message boards. He hadn't.

I jumped up from my chair and turned to head back downstairs when I saw Kate standing in the doorway, her hand over her mouth, tears in her eyes. *This wasn't good.* "What? What's wrong, Kate?

She was shaking her head now. "Miles…"

"Did something happen to Nick?" I could feel the panic gaining momentum inside me.

She shook her head again, firmer this time. "No."

She took a couple steps towards me and wrapped me in her arms. I could feel her chest shaking as she fought back sobs. "His dad had a heart attack last night," she whispered. I knew heart attacks weren't always fatal, but before I could even ask she confirmed my fears. "He didn't make it."

I was stunned. She sat down on my bed and I sat beside her. I knew Nick's dad had just celebrated his 40th birthday a few weeks ago. He'd just gone golfing with Nick last—crap—he'd just gone golfing with Nick last night. "Was Nick with him when—"

"No," Kate anticipated the question, "it happened in his sleep. Carrie… Carrie didn't even know."

I didn't know a whole lot about heart attacks, but I'd always envisioned them as these violent episodes. It didn't seem possible someone could have one "peacefully."

"He went to bed early and when she went to bed she…" Kate stopped short and started sobbing again.

"I need to find Nick," I said suddenly.

Kate covered her mouth again and nodded. "He's at his grandparents tonight in the city. Carrie said he'd be home tomorrow if you want to stop by after school."

"I have to wait until *after* school?"

Kate began to nod, but I could see her conviction on that wavering. "Tell you what… when Nick gets home I'll come get you and take you over there—whatever time that is."

"Okay." I nodded. *Fair compromise.*

When I got to school the next morning there was a vibe to it I'd never experienced before. Apparently word had gotten around about Nick's dad. I kept my head down and walked through the halls from class to class without saying a word to anyone. Everyone knew how close I was to Nick, but no one said anything to me, until art class.

I was already at my table with my head down when I felt a cold hand on mine. I jerked my hand back and glanced up into that beautiful face—Lauren Chambers.

"Sorry," she said. "I just wanted to say I'm sorry."

I opened my mouth to speak, but couldn't, so I just nodded. She gave me a weak smile and then walked past me, patting my shoulder softly as she passed. I turned and watched her walk to her table. She sat and looked at me again. I looked away and focused on my right hand—the one she'd just touched. It looked the same but felt completely different. Those cold fingers of hers had burnt right through my skin. I was *never* going to wash that hand. I don't remember a single thing from the rest of that day until Kate picked me up.

We rode in silence to the Birch's house. Kate parked the car and opened her door. I grabbed her arm. "What do I say to him?"

She closed her door again and turned to face me. "I don't know."

"It's stupid to ask if he's okay, right? I mean… he can't be."

"I know what you mean, honey." She took my left hand. "When I spoke with Carrie last night she mostly just cried. I let her do all the talking. I let her say goodbye when she was ready. I didn't know… I understand exactly how you feel."

I wasn't quite ready to go inside yet. "Lauren touched me today," I mumbled. *Didn't quite come out like I'd wanted it to.*

It also caught Kate off guard. "Really?" She chuckled softly. "Touched you, huh?"

"Just my hand," I quickly interjected. "She just touched my hand."

"On purpose, I assume?" Kate asked with a smile.

"Yes." I nodded.

"That counts as a touch then in my book."

"Yeah." I agreed. "Mine too."

Nick and Carrie both met us at the door. Kate and Carrie immediately dissolved into a sobbing, hugging mess. Nick and I just looked at each other, then at them, then back at each other. "You want to go out back?" Nick finally asked.

I nodded, and we headed back to his old swing set.

We sat swinging in silence for a solid five minutes before Nick spoke. "I didn't get to say goodbye. I didn't get to tell him I loved him."

*That seemed to happen to a lot of people.* I wasn't sure what he wanted me to say, if anything, but my instincts took over. "You golfed with him yesterday afternoon, right?"

"Yeah."

"Then he knew you loved him."

There was another lengthy pause. "You think?"

"Yeah. Parents are weird like that. They read into those things."

"True. Mom kinda said the same thing." He stopped swinging. "Stellar, do you think it would have been harder to lose Bernie now than when you did?"

That was an unexpected question but one with an easy answer. "If you mean at this age? Definitely. Much harder."

Nick nodded again. "Yeah, I suppose so."

I was watching his face carefully for clues on what I should say or do next.

He sighed deeply. "I feel like I kind of just got to know him, you know? I mean, I knew him, but we just started getting really close this past year."

"You have golf to thank for that."

"I have you to thank for that." He pointed at me.

I wasn't comfortable accepting all the credit, or even most of it. "Nick, what you and your dad had was what every child wants, and deserves, with a dad. And you two created that on your own."

"I shot my best score ever yesterday. 71."

*Sudden topic switch.* "Nice." *What else could I say?*

"And then he died."

There was no appropriate response to that either.

"I don't think I'll ever golf again," he continued, tears pooling in his eyes, with one escaping and rolling down his cheek.

"You think that's what your dad would want?" I glanced up and could see Kate and Carrie watching us from the window.

Nick shook his head and wiped his eyes. "No," he admitted. "But I'll never be able to think of anything other than my dad on a golf course again."

I nodded. "I get that. But maybe we should hold off on the never and forevers for now."

He wiped his nose with his arm and hopped off the swing. "Yeah, maybe. Let's go inside?"

"Cool." I followed him towards the door.

I considered telling him about Lauren touching me but ultimately decided against it. She'd only done so because of "my loss" through Nick's loss, and I no longer felt comfortable with even the implication of benefitting from his tragedy. As soon as we got inside I took a deep breath and washed my hands.

## STELLAR 34 – "Making Lemonade"

The next time I saw Lauren was at the funeral for Nick's dad. And I didn't just see her… I sat next to her. And I didn't just sit next to her… I talked to her. Part of me felt terrible for missing every word of the entire service, but I couldn't help it. I was inches from the girl of my dreams. I could smell her. *She smelled like lilacs or lavender… something like that.* I could feel her, without actually touching her. *It's like our auras were connected.* I could hear her breathing and was mesmerized by her beauty in that body-fitting black dress that didn't go anywhere near her knees when she sat. There was a frog in my throat, butterflies in my stomach, a pulse in my toes, and my knees shook when I stood with her, but when she said, "Hi, Stellar." I said "Hi" back. And then she told me I looked nice. *She* told *me* I looked nice.

Care to guess what I said back? Think of what a nervous, love-struck teenage boy would say in response to that…

"You look nice, too." That's what I said to the most beautiful girl on the face of the planet. I shook my head. *That was stupid.* I was thinking supercali-angel-ish-sweet-holycrap-amazing, or something a little more… dramatic. I went with "nice." *Idiot.*

Keep in mind this was a little over two years ago, but I still remember inhaling every time she exhaled. I remember running out of film on my mental camera. I remember wishing the service would never end—*a kid wishing a church service would never end.* And then, when it did end, she asked me if I'd sit next to her at the reception afterwards.

*No. Way. Let me think about that for a second.* Inwardly I was doing backflips, cartwheels and other gymnastic moves I can't do outwardly. "Uh… sure." That's what I said. *Idiot squared!*

The reception was rather somber. I could tell Nick hated it. He sat there as dozens of old people came up and ruffled his hair, kissed his cheeks and apologized for his dad's death. I felt terrible for him in so many different capacities.

His mom, though she maintained a smile, clearly didn't feel much different. Kate stood by her throughout, gently urging people on who got a little too personal, touchy or chatty.

I had become overwhelmed with guilt again about having my dreams come true as Nick lived out his worst nightmare. I honestly wanted to talk to Lauren a lot more than I did, but I sensed she didn't mind sitting there in silence. I believe she knew I wanted to be with Nick, but not because I didn't want to be with her. I think that angel sitting three feet to my left was every bit as intuitive as she was beautiful, and it only made me like her more.

About a half hour into the reception I saw Nick slip out the door. I turned and looked at Lauren and she just nodded. "Go ahead," she said.

I started stammering and stuttering, trying to explain that I didn't want to leave her, but she just smiled that incredible smile and said, "It's okay, I understand. You should go make sure he's okay."

As I stood to walk away she gently called my name, "Stellar?" I turned to look at her. "Thanks for sitting with me."

"Anytime," I said. *And I mean that literally... 24/7/365.* I was somewhat impressed I actually said what I meant. Around Lauren that was quite rare, as rare as getting something good in a retail pack of sports cards anymore.

I found Nick sitting on the back steps of the church. "You didn't have to leave her," Nick said. "I know that had to be hard."

"Nowhere near as hard as sitting there watching everyone torture you."

Nick laughed, a genuine laugh. "Yeah... that was pretty awful. Why do old ladies kiss kids they don't know?"

"You got me."

"I did get $20 from one who told me to go get something that would make me happy."

"Better than a quarter, I guess. Got anything in mind?"

"Not for $20."

"How 'bout shakes and fries at Fells?" A lively, familiar female voice almost sang behind us. I hadn't even heard anyone come out the door. Our heads spun and took in the splendor of the two girls standing there—Lauren and Taryn. Lauren had added a Yankees cap to her perfect fitting, short, black dress. *Trust me—she pulled the look off flawlessly.* Taryn was in a similarly cut—and equally short white dress. Prettiest I'd ever seen her look... *by far.*

"Taryn just got here," Lauren explained. "We followed Stellar." She nodded at me. "Hope you don't mind."

I looked to Nick, not quite sure how he'd feel about Taryn being there and caught an odd expression on his face. Not only did he "not mind" but he seemed particularly "happy" to see Taryn. Her dress had certainly impressed him as well. "Sure." He stood up. "Fells would be great."

Fells was a local sports bar, a popular Yankees fan hangout. They had delicious fries and ice cream, which were even better mixed together. I didn't figure Nick would be hungry, and maybe he wasn't, but he certainly was open to the idea of getting away with these two angels. If nothing else it would take his mind off all the misery in that church. "Let me just ask mom," he said.

We all went in and checked with our parents. Carrie and Kate were terrible at hiding their surprise but awesome at not making a scene in front of the girls. Ken offered to drive us, but we wanted to walk. Nick and I wanted to make this "date" last as long as humanly possible. Nick led the girls away and Ken whispered my name, "Miles."

I turned back to him and saw his hand extended in a closed fist, a smile plastered across his face. “Have fun.”

I smiled back and met his fist with my own. “I’ll try.”

I turned back towards Nick and the girls and saw Lauren standing there watching us, waiting for me. *Did she see that fist bump?* I felt my face flush, immediately kicking myself, but her expression didn’t give anything away. She just stood there and smiled—at me.

Looking back now, at that point in time, nothing else really mattered.

Though we were very much “Lady and the Tramp” then, Lauren and I didn’t share a milkshake at Fells. We didn’t kiss. We didn’t hug. We didn’t hold hands. The six times we touched were all incidental—well, there was one high five. There was nothing at all romantic about that *way* too short two hours. But I remember every minute of it. More than anything I remember Nick smiling, laughing and being able to escape for a while. I remember him actually saying, after Taryn had hugged him and the girls had left, “That was a great way to end a terrible day.”

*Amen to that!*

## STELLAR 35 – "Girls"

Girls are hard to understand. *And the award for "Understatement of the Year" goes to Stellar Johnson-Parker!* There have been countless books written on the subject, but seriously… how can their thought processes be so alien to a high IQ, relatively rational male?

Nick and I had the greatest time with Lauren and Taryn the day of Mr. Birch's funeral—*not sure how else to put it*—and then the next day Taryn was apparently Josh's new girlfriend and Lauren wouldn't even look at me, much less talk to me. *What the heck did I do? What did Nick do?*

I realize I was only thirteen, but just when I thought I might really "have" a girl, just when I thought there might be hope, suddenly I was back to square one. They're evil in that way—pure wicked. They get you wrapped around their finger, drowning in the thought of them, and then they yank you around like a yo-yo and make you want to put your face through a mirror.

I felt even worse for Nick then, since Taryn had essentially been helping him get through the loss of his father. And then there she was at Josh's locker, laughing at all his stupid jokes, looking up at him like he was some god. *Puh-lease!*

*Aaargh!* I hated girls.

Don't get me wrong. I loved them, too. They were too beautiful to actually hate, but they're insane! They drove me insane!

The thirteenth year of my life sucked. If I were stacking 2014 up against any other individual year it might very well have been my worst one. Not only did Lauren seem to forget I existed, but Nick wouldn't golf with me, or anyone, since his dad had died. Ken and Kate were having some issues, my face broke out in every imaginable way, my voice cracked all the time when I spoke or sang, and Hollywood split the last book of the Hunger Games trilogy into two movies over two years. It was a terrible year.

I was already considered shy and reserved before, and became even more so thanks to the issues I just mentioned. I continued to golf all the time, but always by myself. Golf was my escape from the elements of life that drove me crazy—*everything*, in other words. Golf was the one thing I was good at, the one thing I could control.

The bullies were back to picking on me again—Josh, Caleb and Idiot, or Elliott… *whatever his name is*. But not when Lauren was around. They were all nice to me then. *Strange. Fake.*

I heard every name in the book thrown my way those days, accompanied by choruses of mean-spirited laughter. I disliked the name "volcano face" the most, because it was the most accurate thanks to all the zits.

I looked terrible and felt even worse about it. It was embarrassing to say the very least. To make matters worse, *yes, worse*, Nick had gone into a deep dark shell of his own—something I blamed Taryn for—and I don't think I ever felt more alone. And I do mean EVER!

I can think of only one highlight between the funeral for Nick's dad and my birthday in late October. On September 17th Kate took me to Radio City Music Hall for the Live! finale of America's Got Talent. We'd watched the entire season together, pulling for Mat Franco—the magician—from the very beginning. *What would you expect from me?*

Amazingly, not only did Mat make it to the finale, but he won the entire thing! He was so original, so awesome, so deserving. Watching Mat really made me miss performing on the streets with Bernie, not far from where we were that night. And all those memories… let's just say there were a few tears shed. But that night was definitely a highlight. Kate is the best!

My birthday came and went with much less fanfare. Kate let me skip school again to fish with Ken, but the only thing I caught was a cold. I stayed home the rest of the week not because I was actually sick, though I claimed to be. I was just miserable. And I'm pretty sure I made everyone around me miserable, too. I was *NOT* a happy child. I didn't want to be fourteen and this ugly. I didn't want to be fourteen and this lonely. Even Avery and Squirrel couldn't cheer me up. Trust me, *that* was saying something. I'd come a long way in a year, a long way the wrong way.

For Christmas, at school, we created a special art project that we spent two months on and drew names for who we'd give ours to. The theme was "Love"—of course—and of *ALL* the dumb luck in the world I got Lauren. I wanted to just draw a giant question mark and give her that.

It's kind of hard to explain the "love" in my actual project. There were no hearts, xoxo's, people kissing or anything so obvious. It was more reflective—more me. I painted a golfer standing on a hill overlooking New York City, staring over the water towards a giant moon. It probably didn't say "love" to very many people, but to me it did. To me it symbolized a love of where I came from—a love and appreciation for Bernie and my parents. It was dark. It was detailed. It was somewhat sad. But I loved it. And I hated to give it away. *I hated to give it to Lauren.*

I even asked the teacher if I could make another one at home and switch them. She didn't let me.

I couldn't even look at Lauren when I gave it to her. I left it on her desk and walked away. I heard quite the commotion behind me—mostly "wows" and other exclamatory remarks—as I sat and stared blankly at the front of the room. I knew how good it was and figured she might even like it, but it physically hurt to give it to her, and I was honestly trying not to cry.

I remember the kid sitting next to me asking if I was going to look at mine. I glanced down at the back of the frame on my desk. *Nice frame at least.* I sighed and flipped it over and wouldn't doubt that my eyes nearly popped out of my head. There was another chorus of appreciative oohs and aahs around me as the other students gathered around my desk. I believe the word "wow" even came out of my mouth—*without my voice cracking.*

As first impressions go, I thought this drawing was just as beautiful as mine—if not more. *Who drew this?* It was a brick wall with a large LEGO-shaped heart perfectly chiseled out of it, and I mean *perfectly.* The wall had graffiti all over it with words like "apology," "forgiveness," and "second chances" boldly leaping off the paper. The more I looked at it the more incredible it got. I remember thinking "if only this were from Lauren", but I knew it wasn't. Lauren had drawn Graham's name. *Everyone* in the class knew that. I glanced over at Graham to see what he thought of his, of what Lauren had given him, and he was giving me the coldest glare in return. *What the heck?* Then I heard the voice behind me that always gives me chills. *Beauty was addressing the Beast.*

"So, what do you think, Stellar?"

I froze, unable to turn around and look at *her.* I knew for an absolute certainty my voice would crack if I spoke so much as a word, so I just nodded my head.

"Do you like it?"

I continued to nod. *How did I have her drawing?* I muttered the word "amazing" but still didn't turn to look at her.

"I figured you deserved this," she whispered in my ear, or at least close to it, and then returned to her desk.

*Why? What did I do to deserve this?*

I couldn't get myself to look at Graham again. Now I understood why he was upset. Every boy in school—or at least in our class—had a crush on Lauren and would have wanted her drawing. Graham should have gotten it, but somehow Lauren had traded for my name—something that wasn't allowed. I glanced up at the teacher *AND SHE WINKED AT ME! She knew about this? But???* She had allowed Lauren to trade for my name. I was so confused.

Lauren was sending me a message. The only thought running through my head at that time was what *exactly* does this mean? She was, after all, *a girl.*

## STELLAR 36 – "Christmas 2014"

On December 7th, Nick and his mom moved into the studio apartment above the garage at our place. Actually, Nick moved into my room with me for the first few weeks. Ken had hired a crew to come in and permanently seal up one of the three garage stalls—converting it into a connected bedroom/office. Carrie didn't want Ken and Kate to do that on their account, but Ken insisted that had been the plan all along. *A plan I'd never heard of.* In any case, the conversion was well underway and Nick stayed in my room until they finished it.

Nick's mom didn't have a lot of money after his dad died. I'm not sure how life insurance works, but it definitely didn't work for them. Carrie had been "unoccupied" at the time, as she put it, but now she was trying to find a job and she didn't want Nick coming home to an empty house. Kate being Kate, she became the "fixer" for the situation—or Katwoman, per our familial "Batman" roles. She insisted Carrie and Nick take over the studio and pushed Ken to give them a little extra space with that garage conversion. *That's how it actually went down.*

It was great having Nick around more. We had swimming together almost every day after school throughout the winter, and then we'd grab a sandwich with chips or fries somewhere and head home. We'd work on homework for an hour or two, play another hour or two of Madden or Call of Duty, and then go to bed, where we'd typically talk for another hour or two before finally drifting off. *Yeah... okay... so it was awesome!*

Carrie started working part-time at Kate's law office the week before Christmas. It was enough to pay for what she needed to cover, and the position essentially came with lodging, so it was a pretty good deal for Carrie and Nick. *And for the rest of us by extension.*

You might be wondering how I remember some of these less significant things from a couple years ago. Or perhaps you don't see the relevance at all. Maybe there is none. But I remembered them so I wrote them down. Suffice it to say the little events I remember in my life were usually tethered to much bigger events: moments or occasions I'll never forget. That is definitely the case with the Birch's transition to our place.

Kate decided to throw a huge Christmas party, essentially a housewarming celebration for Carrie and Nick. Kate and Carrie made a list of their closest friends from the area and sent out invitations. Unbeknownst to me, one of those invitations made it to the home of Mr. and Mrs. Sam and Susan Chambers. You would think the former mayor would have had a hundred better places to be on December 23rd.

Apparently that wasn't the case. I answered the doorbell to find two large blurs bookending a gorgeous blonde in a long white coat, with a white stocking cap, black boots and a brilliant smile. *Holy... Hot... Wow...*

My turtleneck immediately became thirty times less comfortable, and that much more ugly. I quickly glanced behind me at Kate who just smiled back. *A little advanced notice on this one would have been fantastic!*

Nick and I had made it a habit of saying "Merry Christmas" to every guest we greeted at the door. My tongue unfortunately picked that moment to get a bit tangled—okay… tied in knots. Had I just kept my dumb mouth shut and moved out of their way they'd have entered and I wouldn't have made such a giant fool out of myself. Instead, I stood there, blocking their entry, and managed to so eloquently say "Merry Kissmas." *Clear as flipping day!*

I turned twelve shades of red in the next three seconds and was relieved to see someone else coming up the walk behind them. I stepped past the Chambers and basically yelled "Merry CHRISTMAS" to the next startled guests essentially to either prove I was capable of saying the right words or to insinuate I had actually said those words to the Chambers as well… and they'd just heard me wrong. Either way, I doubt I fooled anyone, but I certainly made one of myself.

I relinquished my door greeting duty to Avery a minute later. She was much cuter in general, and certainly much more adorable when she butchered the word Christmas. I tried to inconspicuously shadow Lauren around our house for the next twenty minutes. *Epic fail.*

Nick and I eventually grabbed some food and headed upstairs to watch TV. I caught one last glance of Lauren chatting with a couple of her friends from school—friends I'd never once spoken to. *And vice versa.* To my knowledge, Lauren didn't even see me leave.

"Holy balls, Nick, did you see what Lauren was wearing?"

"You mean the Lauren with the semi-transparent white dress, that leaves so little and yet so very much to the imagination? The most beautiful girl on Long Island. That one?"

"Yeah." I was blushing again. "That one."

"Nope." He smiled. "Didn't see her."

"Didn't see who?"

*And there she was.* I almost threw my plate of food across the room she'd startled me so much. *How much of that did she hear?* "No… no one," I stammered. *Idiot!*

"This your room, Stellar?"

Lauren was in *my* room. "Yes." I nodded. Suddenly I started to panic. *Lauren was in my room!* I frantically glanced at her yearbook picture I had cut out and thumbtacked up by my bed. It was right behind her head. If Lauren turned even a couple of inches to her right she'd be staring right at it.

But she didn't turn her head at all. Instead she sat down directly across from me in my "L-shaped" gaming chair. That chair wasn't meant for someone in a short, tight dress—I'll put it that way. She didn't stay there long, but *thankfully* she did stay in my room.

Nick, Lauren and I hung out and talked for a good hour before her mother called up for her. Or, I should say, Nick and Lauren talked. I mostly listened and counted the stitches on her dress—or stared, if that's the better way to put it. I was soaking up every word, every smile, and every second of having Lauren in my room. *Ridiculous in hindsight, but truth at the moment.*

Nick was so comfortable around her—so smooth, so relaxed, and happy—I'll readily admit to being quite envious of his demeanor. I was *the* polar opposite. Granted, Nick had sufficient reason to be so confident. He was every bit *the* best looking guy in our class as much as Lauren was *the* girl. He was as athletic as Josh, as smart as me; they'd be the perfect couple if Nick didn't already know how much I liked her. But, I should at least say this, it was never lost on me how happy Lauren made Nick. Given all he'd been through, part of me thought I should tell him to go after her. *I said "a part" not "all."* I mean, if anyone were going to have her besides me, I'd have eventually been okay with the lucky guy being Nick.

But Nick seemed to have no such motives. He claimed they'd always been more brother/sister than anything since birth, almost as literally as you can get. Born in the same hospital, not only were their birthdays merely a day apart, July 4th and 5th, but Nick was exactly—only—three hours and fifty-seven minutes older than her. Their mothers were actually in labor simultaneously in adjacent rooms.

They were that close at birth and lived nearly as close to each other in Southampton for the next six years—literally *only* three doors down. They learned how to bike together, swim together, and had been in the same class since pre-K. Nick liked to remind me he'd already seen her naked—even if it was at the age of two. *And he certainly didn't remember it.* Lauren remembered him as being the first boy to ever tell her he loved her—on her seventh birthday. That was a big joke to them now.

Those expressions of affection came so easily when we were little, when we didn't realize what we were saying. Love didn't feel remotely complicated then. At this point, I had a better chance of getting struck by lightning riding a unicorn in a Chicago Cubs championship parade, than I did of getting those three words out, especially aloud—*especially to Lauren*—even if I was 99.3% certain that's how I felt.

Nick excused himself, supposedly to use the bathroom, leaving Lauren and me alone for a moment. As she bent over to put her boots back on, her mom called her name again.

"Coming, Mom," she hollered back. "Man." She glanced up at me. "We spend hours waiting for our parents day after day while they drone on and on, but they can't wait two lousy minutes for us?" She laughed that beautiful laugh and shook her beautiful blonde head.

"Yeah." I was trying to think of something clever to say and trying in vain to not look down the front of her dress. I wanted to be cool like Nick *for just five flipping seconds*. I couldn't do it. I had nothing.

"I like your room," she said with a smile, standing up and shaking her long curly hair out of her face.

"Thank you," I mumbled.

"I have to say it would look even better with my picture on the wall, though. Uh… the picture from art class, I mean," she added quickly, blushing as she seemed to realize how I might twist her words. "Not 'my picture' like my picture, picture, but… you know… sheesh! Anyway, I have your moon on my wall. I mean…" *Even that didn't come out quite right.*

"Oh yeah." I tried to save her.

"I sound like an idiot." She laughed.

*Welcome to my world.* "Not at all."

"I hope you at least liked my drawing."

*Don't say "yeah" again.* I nodded. "I love it."

Lauren laughed. "I get it. I got that one. You *love* it."

I hadn't intended the project-themed play on words. I was really just trying to survive the conversation without further embarrassment.

"So, where is it?" she asked.

"Lauren!" Her mother called up again. "Let's go."

I was saved by her mother—saved from having to lie about where her picture actually was. *Under my pillow at the moment.*

"Okay then." She rolled her eyes. "Guess I'll see you at school?"

I nodded again. "Yeah." And then it happened.

Lauren leaned in towards me before I realized what she was doing—*or I'd quite possibly have punched her*—and she kissed my cheek. "Merry Kissmas to you too," she said with a laugh. And then she was gone.

I didn't even care she'd heard my slip-up earlier and was teasing me now. I watched her run down the stairs, stunned, and then turned to find Nick staring at me from the bathroom door. "Did she just kiss you?" He was smiling. He knew the answer.

I was frozen in place. I remember touching my cheek with my fingers and nodding. "Yeah," I said. There were no other words.

*Lauren Chambers just kissed me.*

## ←★★★★★ NARRATOR ★★★★★→

### ←Thursday, June 30, 2022→

"How's the book coming?" My husband's sudden presence behind the couch startled me.

"Good Lord." I placed my hand on my chest and took a deep breath. "You almost scared the baby out of me."

"Sorry." He laughed and kissed my cheek. "I'm wearing boots. Loud boots. I figured—"

"Guess I was really lost in the writing."

"Hopefully that's a good thing?" He kissed my cheek again. "You done with Stellar's journals yet?"

"No, but it's going good. I'm up to the end of 2014 now, which means I've only got two years left of his journals, and then this other stack." I nodded at the journals and letters from friends and family on the other table.

"Still think you'll get it all done by Monday?" He tapped July 4, 2022 on the wall calendar with his pinkie.

"Kind of up to this one." I rubbed my belly, quickly searching for protruding knees or elbows. "I sure hope to."

Tomorrow was July 1st already. I had to keep pushing… before I had to start pushing.

"Anything I can do to help?" he asked.

"Leave." I said with a smile.

He leaned over for one last kiss. "Okay then."

## STELLAR 37 – "Spring 2015"

Girls are hard to understand. Different verse, same chorus. Don't worry, I won't go off on a tangent like last time. However, I've got to get some of this off my chest. Lauren kisses me on December 23rd and then she pretends I don't exist for the next few months. I was under some illusion that we had made a lasting connection at my house, somehow believing she and I would at least be friends at school.

Nope. I returned to being too visible to everyone else... and invisible to Lauren.

I was still an eighth grader. She was still a ninth grader. She was still the prettiest girl in school. I was still... me. *Or "Frankenface" according to Josh and the Hillbilly Bunch.*

And speaking of Josh. Lauren started sitting with him again at lunch. *By "with" I mean at the same table.* There she was, smiling at him, giving him those eyes, fluttering those lashes. She'd toss her long flowing blonde hair back and laugh and Josh would laugh with her. It made me sick to my stomach. Literally, on one occasion. *Though that might have been the "Tuna Noodle Surprise."*

I'm trying to think of a better way to explain how frustrated I was at whatever it was Josh and Lauren had going on. Honestly, I don't think that I can. It was far more exasperating than trying to untangle six billion Christmas lights every year for Ken. It was more maddening than watching the Patriots lose to the Ravens or Jets, and every bit as agonizing as sitting through forty-five minutes of commercials in a one-hour TV show. Nothing compares. Nothing comes close.

Only Josh could have made me feel worse, and he often did. From time to time he would look at me and grin. He'd pretend to laugh at something she'd said and touch her arm. He knew exactly what he was doing to me. I don't *ever* remember hating anyone like I hated Josh then. *Not even the NFL Commissioner.*

One day I was particularly salty sitting beside Nick at lunch. I was grinding my blueberry muffin into powder with my hand when he laughed at me and nodded at the muffin. "Picturing that as someone's head?"

"Huh?" I looked up at him and then down at my hand. I hadn't even known I was doing it. *I had actually really been looking forward to eating that muffin.* "No. Well... yeah, maybe. He's killing me."

"And he knows he is," Nick countered. "You're letting him."

"And what am I supposed to do?"

"Forget about him. Forget about her."

I laughed and shook my head. "Right. You clearly don't understand."

"Actually, I do—better than you'd think. I know exactly what it's like to really like someone and not be able to have her."

*Whatever.* I didn't believe him one bit. *Who could he not have? Who wouldn't jump at the chance to be Nick's girlfriend?* "Right," I said. "Of course you do."

The bell rang then, and I didn't pursue the conversation any further. I was actually kind of mad at Nick then, too. I wanted him to back me up. I wanted him to walk over to Josh's table and pour chocolate milk all over the jerk's head. Somehow at that point in time I perceived Nick as *less* of a friend for not being as upset as I was. I didn't really listen to what he was saying. In fact, knowing how he felt about golf at that point—knowing he wouldn't go anywhere near a course—I used golf as my escape from him. I started living at the golf course, or at least spending every free minute of daylight there—with James or Cal, but no one else. Basically I dodged Nick like Lauren dodged me. I was no better than she was.

I'm embarrassed about my behavior looking back, but it's the way it was… the way I was. I can't change it now. But I definitely regret it.

This next entry is a particularly hard entry for me to write, because I know I'm supposed to write about myself—to basically praise myself—something I don't like to do. For all I know you won't even read this, no one will. This is likely a colossal waste of time. Either that or you'll read it and nominate it for a Pulitzer, or something, and everyone in the world will find out how I feel about Lauren. Not sure which scenario would be worse.

Hopefully you'll read just enough of the journals to grade them and give them back to me so I can burn them. The less people know about me the better.

←←←←←→→→→→

***"You must work very hard to become a natural golfer."***

- Gary Player

←←←←←→→→→→

## STELLAR 38 – "The Magician"

Nick swam as much as I golfed the summer of 2015. We almost never saw each other. We attended the grand opening of the One World Observatory together in Manhattan, in late May, and that was pretty much it until school started up again in September.

Kate and Carrie were clearly worried about our relationship, but we just had different priorities at the time. I didn't want to swim because Lauren was always there, which meant Josh was as well, with his band of buttheads. Nick didn't want to golf because the game and any course reminded him of his dad. We were content to go our separate ways.

I was playing in Montauk, with Calvin caddying for me, the day I posted my first score in the 70's from the tips. 78—sometime in mid-June I think. I was partnered up with three people—I assumed were college kids—who were riding in carts while Calvin carried my clubs and we walked. Those guys could crush it off the tee, but they had relatively weak short games. I had twelve one-putts in that round.

After the round, one of the guys came over and asked who my instructor was.

"This here kid is l-l-like Bubba Watson," Calvin told him. "All self-taught."

*If only.* I shook my head. "I'm no Bubba."

"Dude," the guy (who could have passed for PGA player Paul Casey's identical twin brother) stuck out his hand. "Name's Chandler."

I shook his hand. He had a crushing grip. "Stellar." I winced.

"Stellar?" He smiled. "Love it. Don't be modest about that game, my friend. How old are you anyway?"

"He's fourteen," Calvin replied.

"Almost fifteen," I corrected.

"Fourteen, fifteen, 240 to 250 off the tee and a short game like that. That wedge of yours is like an extension of your arm, that swing is pure butter. You're going places, kid. You'd win our junior club championship for sure."

"I don't know about that. I've got a lot to work on."

Chandler laughed. "Well, keep working at it then. You made my assistant pros look like chumps today." At that point I realized they weren't college kids. He reached into his wallet and pulled out a card. "If you're ever in the Hartford area give me a call."

I looked at the card he'd handed me. Chandler Green was the Head Golf Professional at a private club in Farmington, Connecticut. "Thanks," I mumbled.

"I'm serious," he said. "It is private, but you're welcome anytime, both of you." He nodded at Calvin. "I'll slip you on somewhere."

I didn't figure I was going to be in Connecticut anytime soon, especially not for golf, so I pretty much dismissed the offer. Then, sometime in mid-July Ken told me he needed to make a boating supply run to Hartford. He was taking Calvin with him and asked if I wanted to go along. Since James had to run RB's and Cal was going with Ken I didn't have much else for alternatives, so I shrugged and went along.

It wasn't until three hours later when we pulled into the Country Club parking lot in Farmington that I even realized Cal wasn't along to help Ken. Calvin hopped out of the truck and pulled my clubs out of the back. *What the…?*

Before I could ask if Chandler even knew we were coming he strode out of the clubhouse towards our truck. Ken introduced himself to Chandler in person. *Apparently they had spoken over the phone several times.* They'd been planning this for a while. I turned and gave Cal a knowing look, and he winked at me.

"I'll be back in five hours," Ken said. "Let me know what I owe you."

"It's all on me." Chandler clapped him on the back. "I'll take care of the kid for you."

We stepped into the red barn-looking pro shop and he reintroduced me to the two assistants we'd played with at Montauk. Chandler then excused himself from work and joined Calvin and me for the front nine.

I started with three straight birdies and then eagled the par 3 fourth hole. Immediately a stunned silence fell over the tee box, as there was no doubt where the ball had come to rest. Chandler turned to me as I muttered the word "finally" and he burst into laughter.

"Finally?" He was still laughing. "You just got a hole-in-one at fourteen years old and you go with the word *finally*?" He gave me a high five then that almost broke my hand. There was a club member playing with us who stood speechless, simply shaking his head.

"Forty-two years," he muttered. "I've been playing forty-two years and have never had one." He shook my hand then—much more gently than Chandler had. "Son, I'd be running around screaming like a child if I'd done what you just did. What's scary is you looked like you were trying to do that."

"I always am," I replied, and Chandler burst into laughter again.

"What I mean," the other gentleman, Tom, explained, "is that it looked like you tried to land the ball just short of that pin, hop it past and then pull it back. It was like it was on a string. Your caddie doesn't even look surprised."

I turned to Calvin, who still hadn't done anything but stand there and watch me, and I whispered to him. "That *was* what I tried to do."

Calvin smiled at me. "It's okay if you don't share that part."

But Chandler had heard us, and he made a rather unusual request. We were all about to leave the tee box and I heard him say, "Hit another one."

"What?" Tom exclaimed, though he'd heard the instructions clearly. "You're kidding, right?"

Chandler shook his head. "Not at all."

I already had my hand out, and Calvin was digging into my bag for another Nike ball.

"You can't be serious?" Tom was beside himself. "You have to at least let the kid go up and get his ball out of the hole first. He may never get another one."

I heard Calvin whisper beside me. "Oh, I'd bet the contrary."

"Hey," Chandler continued in all seriousness. "Camilo Villegas had two aces at the Masters' Par 3 contest just a couple months ago. It can happen."

That was true, I'd seen it on ESPN. Even Jack Nicklaus had one in that contest… at 75 years old. In any case I didn't question Chandler. I teed up another ball, same club and distance—7 iron from 142 yards—and put the ball in motion with a similar arc and path to that of the ace. This time the ball landed about two yards short of the pin, hopped past it about eight to ten feet and then whipped back towards the cup. There was a notable clang as the ball hit the pin, but this one didn't quite drop. It remained just outside the cup. *Wow! Even I wasn't honestly expecting that.*

I glanced back at Chandler and now he was shaking his head. "Amazing," he mumbled. "Even your 7-iron thinks it's a wedge."

"The kid's a magician," Tom added. "Now I see why they call you Stellar."

"Has nothing to do with his game," Calvin replied. *Though it kind of did.*

"It does now," Chandler disagreed. "I've never seen anything like that in my life."

"You don't have to tell anyone about this."

"Seriously?" Chandler looked at me, almost choking on his surprise. "Of course we do."

"I'm serious." I nodded. "I just want to play."

"It'll be in the Hartford paper."

"Doesn't have to be," Cal said.

"You really don't want me to call it in?" Chandler was looking directly at me.

I shook my head.

"Stellar," Chandler said. "If this is about not buying drinks—"

"Buying drinks?" I didn't even know that unwritten rule.

"It's not about buying drinks," Calvin assured Chandler. "Kid just wants to pl-l-lay."

"Sure," Chandler nodded. "I can dig that… no problem. It's your ace, young man."

"Unbelievable!" Tom was still shaking his head. "Were that my shot I'd be walking through the clubhouse with a megaphone and hugging all the waitresses and cart girls." He elbowed Chandler. "Especially Brittlyn."

I laughed at those visuals as Tom's meaty hand thumped me on the back. "That was pure magic, kid. Unbelievable!"

Tom and Chandler left Calvin and me at the turn. I saw Calvin hand Chandler a folded up piece of paper, and only later found out it was a hundred dollar bill to buy everyone in the clubhouse drinks. "Don't worry," Calvin assured me. "He won't tell anyone it was you."

I didn't believe him. *With good reason.* We finished off the rest of the round on our own, and by "we" I mean "me playing and Calvin caddying." It was a beautiful afternoon and I loved the course. Dating back to the 1890's, it was—as Chandler described it—"a classic course, as pure and simple as they ever were built."

I did get to meet "Tom's Brittlyn" on the 14th hole when she brought complimentary beverages out to us. I could certainly see why Tom wanted to hug her. At first glance I honestly thought she was Meghan Hardin from Golf Channel's Big Break. *Look her up.* She was smoking hot, though probably only twenty or so—*at least forty years younger than Tom.* I should clarify that she wasn't quite Lauren hot to me—no one was—but Brittlyn was dang close.

Ken was waiting for Calvin and me as we walked off the 18th green. I looked at him suspiciously to see if Chandler had said anything to him about the hole-in-one. There was no indication he had.

"Chandler had to take off," Ken said, taking my clubs from Calvin. "But he wanted me to give you this." He held out a large manila envelope.

I looked at the envelope but didn't open it. "Thanks."

"Well, aren't you going to open it?" Ken asked.

"Maybe later," I replied.

When Ken stopped for gas I slit the top of the envelope open and glanced inside. I pulled out a scorecard that had been signed by Chandler and Tom with my "1" on the fourth hole circled. I glanced up at Calvin who winked at me. "Nice," he said. The envelope also contained a painted postcard of the fourth hole, which I assumed they sold in the shop. There was writing on the back in silver ink.

*"To the Magician—Hope to see you again soon." – Chandler Green*

*Magician.* I smiled as I instantly thought of Bernie. That nickname meant a lot of different things to me, almost none of them golf related at that point. But, as Chandler had stated at the course, maybe that was about to change.

Ken hopped back in and glanced at the card in my hands. "What's that a picture of?"

"One of the holes," I replied casually.

"You guys have fun?" Ken glanced over at Calvin who nodded and looked back at me, winking again.

"Yes, sir," he said.

"Yes, sir," I agreed.

"Good. Think I'll be doing regular business in the area from now on, probably once a week. Would be great to have you guys tag along."

"Sounds good to me." I nodded. *Fantastic* was a more appropriate adjective.

We took the Cross Sound Ferry back to Southampton that evening, past Plum and Fishers islands. The hole-in-one really sank in we watched the sun set. You could say Ken's little "Batman" had adopted a Joker-like grin. But I knew enough to not let a few good bounces and a little luck go to my head. I could play another ten thousand rounds and never record another ace. That hole just happened to be in the perfect place, with just the right amount of flat landing space, for me to be able to do what I know how to do. So while it was a special moment in a special day, in the grand scheme of things it wasn't a big deal to me.

*It was just a hole-in-one.*

I dozed off to the conversation between Ken and Calvin in the front seat, though I wasn't yet completely out when I heard Calvin say, "That's some special boy you have there, sir. You should be mighty proud of him."

"Yes, Calvin." Ken agreed. "He is. And I am."

There was a lengthy pause and then Ken added. "So what do I owe you for the drinks?"

## STELLAR 39 – "OB"

Pretty much every weekend Calvin and I rode along with Ken to Farmington and I either played with or was given instruction, or "tweaking", by Coach. That's what I mostly called Chandler now—Coach.

Though he was technically the club's primary golf instructor, Chandler had very few students. There were two pretty ladies who he said paid him way too much, didn't wear enough of anything except makeup, and weren't there for the lessons. He had two junior golfers—one boy and one girl—whose parents were essentially trying to *buy* their Tour cards. *Coach didn't believe either of them would ever make it to a tour, unless it was at the Smithsonian.* And then there was an old man who Coach said was the "single most consistent golfer he'd ever seen in his life." Consistent is typically a compliment in golf. Not in this instance.

This man, Coach called him OB, was almost ninety and had a goal of shooting less than his age just once. He'd never come close, hadn't even cracked the century mark for that matter. This guy wasn't a golfer. *Not. At. All.* He didn't have an athletic bone in his body. In the first 88 years of his life he'd only picked up a putter to play mini-golf with his one kid and two grandkids. His wife was the golfer. She only played in the women's league once a week. But she came to the club every single day to get away from OB and his preference for alcohol over conversation. No one remembered *ever* seeing OB here until the day she died, seven years ago. Rumor was, when his wife came here, he went to the bar. He was at the bar every single night.

Until seven years ago. Since her funeral he'd come to the course every day it was open and he hadn't been seen down at the bar once. Rain, shine and even occasionally in snow, OB would putt for an hour before the course opened, play nine holes, eat an early lunch, putt for another hour, play the last nine holes, then eat an early dinner and go home to bed. On Saturdays he'd come to the course and sit in the Ranger's cart. He'd ride around and watch the golfers, never talking to anyone, never once leaving that cart—mostly just shaking his head and cursing "the modern day club-wielding Neanderthals in clown outfits." Then, on Sundays, he'd come to the course at 3 p.m. for his one-hour lesson with Chandler. That pattern of life, that cycle, he wouldn't compromise. Not for a day. Not if he was sick, tired or sick *and* tired. That consistency was one honorable quality about the man. It just didn't make sense. If you were so terrible… why play?

Everything else about OB was, well… less honorable. I'd never met a sailor or heard one curse, but Coach swore OB could render a sailor speechless *and* make a rapper cry. The man wouldn't smile, he was rude if he ever said anything at all, and he was—*how do I say this properly*— well… he was gassy. Man did he smell! Thank God he didn't smoke or he'd explode!

OB golfed with his wife's hickories—100 year old wooden sticks. He'd never even tried a modern club. Best as anyone knew he'd never hit a drive over 120 yards. He'd seldom hit a fairway shot over eighty. He couldn't chip if his life depended on it, not even a tooth. *His were all fake.* But he also never lost a ball. Every shot was dead straight, no more than ten feet off the ground, and every time he hit the ball he cursed it—the ball. Everything was the ball's fault. I mentioned he never lost a ball, so the OB in his name didn't stand for what I thought it did—*Out of Bounds*—but whatever it was Coach wouldn't tell me. I did know however, that Stubborn was his middle name and like me, OB preferred to golf alone. *Or maybe no one else would golf with him.* I'd noticed on the tee sheet in the clubhouse that the word "single" was always written under OB's name, and the two tee times behind him were always blocked.

I'm not sure what Chandler's connection to OB actually was—he wouldn't talk about it. He took the old man's tongue-lashings and curses with a nod and replied with humble apologies. *As if Coach had anything to apologize for.* I didn't get it. I'm also not sure why Coach gave OB lessons—he never listened. He never changed a thing, he never improved. He hit the ball the same way every time and yelled the same "d" word at it every time. He was consistently terrible in everything. Well… almost everything. The guy could putt lights out! *No joke!*

In late August Ken dropped Calvin and me off at the club and Coach told me he had a different kind of lesson for me that day.

"Sure," I said. "What do you have in mind?"

"I want you to spend the day with OB."

*Wait… what?* I glanced at Calvin and he was staring back at me, pretty much expressionless. "You're serious?" Chandler was nodding his head. "That guy hates me." I objected.

"Hang on," Chandler raised his hand, stopping me. "He doesn't hate *you* specifically. He hates everyone. Well… almost everyone."

Calvin failed to conceal his smile quickly enough. I glared at him. *Come on Cal… tell him this is a terrible idea. Calvin didn't.*

"Well?" Chandler was looking at me, likely expecting another objection.

I didn't give one. "Fine. But you know I don't like playing with people."

"You've golfed with me a dozen times. You played with Tom. You played with my assistants and me at Montauk."

"I didn't want to."

"Hey now… "

"Coach, it's nothing personal. Calvin made me play with you guys at Montauk that day, and when I'm here I feel like I have to play with you… "

"Or you wouldn't?"

I shrugged. "I like to play alone."

"Stellar, it's good for you to play with other people, to learn to adjust your game's rhythm to theirs and so on. It's especially good for you to play with people you don't like, people who make you uncomfortable. It puts a different kind of stress on you."

"Well, then I should be pretty stressed out today."

Calvin couldn't prevent his laugh then, and I gave him another glare. *Thanks a lot for your help.*

He nodded and winked at me as if he could read my mind.

"So where is he then?" I asked.

"Just finished putting," Chandler replied. "You ready?"

"No."

"Good."

We walked to the first tee to meet OB. I don't think I've ever seen an adult throw a temper tantrum, but what took place on that tee box would be hard to describe as anything else. *Great.* He was as thrilled as I was.

Calvin nudged me and nodded towards OB. *Seriously?* I gave him a look to say, *"Do I have to?"* Calvin just nodded in his direction again. I sighed deeply and dragged my feet across the tee box extending my hand towards OB's.

"Get lost, kid," he snarled. *(I know, as my English teacher, you'd tell me people can't snarl. I beg to differ.)*

I dropped my hand and retreated to Calvin's side. "That was fun," I muttered.

Understand as close as Calvin and I were then, he still almost never spoke to me in full sentences. He was more of a listener, a nodder, a simple "yes, sir, no, sir, sure, or maybe" kind of guy. So it caught me completely off guard when he chose that moment to say, "You're better than that, sir."

I looked at him and absorbed the admonishment. Calvin was not a chastiser, not bluntly anyway. If anything he was my greatest defender, my greatest supporter. I knew he was right. "Sorry," I whispered.

He nodded and handed me my sand wedge.

"Cal, this hole's 290."

"Stay with him," Cal replied.

"What?" I'd heard him; I just didn't think I'd heard him right.

Cal pointed at the orange ball out in the fairway. *Great. He plays with orange balls too?* "Stay with him," Cal repeated.

I started to shake my head then thought better of it. I kept my words and thoughts to myself. *This is going to suck.*

## STELLAR 40 – "OB Continued"

*That was the best round of my life.*

Sure, I've scored better since then, but I've never experienced the game of golf as I did that day—or been so transformed.

My discomfort on the first tee was increased exponentially when Coach informed me he wouldn't be able to play today; he had too much work to do. I watched him shake hands with Calvin, they exchanged a few words, and then it was just me, Cal and OB—us and Mr. Orange Balls.

I hung on to my bitterness through the first three wedge shots of the first hole, with my approach settling about ten feet from the pin. I wanted to tell Calvin I should have been there in two instead of three, but he was tending the pin for OB who managed to drain a 30-footer for par. *Wow. Where'd that come from?*

"Nice putt, sir," Calvin said to OB, handing him his orange ball. OB grunted and wandered off towards the second tee box without even waiting for me to putt out. I missed my putt and settled for an angry bogey.

I followed Calvin up to the second tee and shook my head when he held the wedge out again. "No way, Cal. I can't lose to this guy."

Calvin placed his other hand on top of my driver in the bag as I tried to wrestle it free. "Then don't," he said matter-of-factly, "just—"

"Follow his ball," I muttered, snatching the wedge from him.

At that point my competitive juices went into overdrive. I became motivated to show Calvin just how dumb this exercise was—to show him exactly how close I could get to OB's ball. I glanced back at Calvin. "How far out is he?"

"One twenty-two, one twenty-three maybe?"

"One twenty-two and a half it is," I muttered under my breath as I dialed in and shaped a beautiful, high, arching shot to within a few feet of OB's ball.

Calvin was beside me before I could look back at him, taking the club from my hands. "Close enough?" I asked.

"That's up to you, sir," Calvin replied without a trace of sarcasm.

I watched him walk off. *What was that supposed to mean?* I hurried after Cal. "Cal, wait up." He slowed but didn't stop. "What's the point of this? Why can't I just play my own game from my own tee boxes? What's wrong with the way I've been playing for the past four years?"

"Nothing wrong, sir."

"So, why then? Why this… whatever this is?"

"Maybe this ain't about your game at all."

We'd caught up to OB by now so the Q&A paused there. I'd expected him to have hit already, but he was looking back at me with a scowl. "Suppose it's your turn," he said. He didn't even swear.

"Okay, thanks," I mumbled. I was about eight inches short of OB's ball. "What do we got, Cal?"

"I expect it's nine short of a Benjamin, sir."

"Benjamin?" I asked. *Why was he suddenly talking in code?*

Though OB turned away from me I still heard his clear translation. "Hundred," he said. "Like the bill. You're ninety-one out."

*Ah.* I looked at Calvin who was holding a sand wedge out to me. I couldn't quite risk attacking the pin with that and he knew it, but I took the club anyway. I started looking for where the best place was about eighty yards out to put my ball. I picked the target and struck another pure shot to within a couple feet of the intended spot.

"Perfect set up," OB said. "About seven yards to the pin."

*He was talking to me now? What the heck was this?* I gave Cal a bewildered look and though he turned away to watch OB's ball sail towards mine, I didn't miss the crack of a smile splitting across his face.

I don't want to get too golf technical here, so I'll skip the other hole-by-hole details, but I came into the ninth hole needing a par for a 45 on the front, which would be my worst nine-hole score of the year, from the shortest tees on the easiest course I'd played pretty much ever. I got my 45. Nine was OB's first triple bogey (three over par) and triple putt of the day, which gave him a 49 on the front—easily his best nine holes in years.

It was then that I figured out what this round was about. It wasn't about me at all. *Though the lesson still was.*

When we entered the clubhouse for lunch I figured Calvin and I would get our own table, but OB was directly ahead of us and I heard the waitress address him. By the voice I knew it was Meghan Hardin's replica, Brittlyn. "I have your table ready, dear." She pointed towards the patio where there was a small table with a single setting.

"Actually, it's three of us today, honey." He paused. "Please."

*Think I just found the one person OB didn't hate.* I saw a smile wash across Brittlyn's face and noticed a couple other diners turn towards us in obvious surprise. *Seems OB's reputation was well established.* OB ignored them all. "Right—right this way," Brittlyn said cheerily, sashaying her way towards the patio.

I grabbed Cal's arm. "I'm gonna wash up."

"Yes, sir." He nodded.

As I emerged from the restroom I heard someone call my name.

I turned and saw Brittlyn gliding towards me in those super short tan shorts and that tight white, see-through polo with all four buttons undone. *Her typical attire.*

"How's the round going with OB?" she asked cheerily, her soft cool fingers brushing against my arm, creating quite the internal stir in me.

"Okay," I replied, doing my best to keep my eyes up on her face, though that plunging neckline begged a few peeks. I swallowed hard as she touched my arm again. *I was sooo thankful she didn't know what she was doing to me.* "You're a waitress too?"

"One hour a day—when he's here anyway. You need anything?"

"N-n-no," I stuttered. "I'm good." *Stay cool. Please stay cool.*

"Let me know if you do," she almost sang as she skipped away.

I turned and watched that backside sway from side to side. *Wow! College girls.* Six years difference wasn't that much was it? *If things didn't work out with Lauren, of course.*

As I returned to our table, Cal glanced up at me. "You okay?"

"Yeah, why?"

"No reason," Cal replied as Brittlyn skipped past us and back to her beverage cart. "You look a little—"

"I'm fine."

"Hey, Cal," Brittlyn called out.

"Miss Brittlyn." Cal nodded.

*I was even more transparent than her shirt, and I knew it.*

OB broke 100 for the first time in his life that day, and he got a par on the 18th hole to do so for a 98. He and Cal had quite the conversation going on throughout the back nine and though I did hear OB swear from time to time it was with no regularity, no consistency.

And that putting… he was an incredible putter. Best pace I've ever seen with the flat stick. I told him exactly that as *he* approached *me* on the 18th green to shake hands. "Thanks, kid," he said in reply. "A few years of mini golf. Any chance you'll be here next week?"

*Who was this man?* "Uh, I don't know."

"That's alright, kid." OB smiled, as he had quite a bit today. "If you is you are."

*If you is you are.* I liked that.

I watched Cal shake hands with OB and heard OB thank him. "That's some kid you've got there," OB said. And then he thanked Cal again.

*What did I do exactly?*

Cal and I sat on a bench in the parking lot, waiting for Ken. I was quiet. Cal was playing his harmonica. "Cal," I finally broke my silence. "What did I do?"

"Pardon?"

"What did I do? I mean… I sucked today. How did that help him?"

"I don't feel like sucked is the right word, sir."

"But how did you know he'd break a hundred—"

"Tear the Benjamin?"

"What?"

"Say it. Tear the Benjamin."

"I'm not—that's not—it's not even a real expression. No golfer has ever used that to say they broke a hundred."

Cal laughed. "Says you."

"Okay, whatever, but how did you know my playing bad would help him play good?"

Cal contemplated his answer for a few seconds before finally replying with, "I didn't."

"Really?"

"No, sir." Calvin shook his head. "It all was Mr. Chandler's idea. And the round in truth had *nothing* to do with scores. A man like OB... well, you give that man some kindness and maybe he can find confidence. With confidence in his tools maybe he can build a boat that floats."

My head was swimming. "Enough with the similes—"

"Metaphors."

"Whatever. Why not just have him play against a five-year-old then—for confidence?"

"Because..." Calvin spoke slowly. "A five-year old might make him look bad. And..." he looked directly at me for the last line. "A five-year-old wouldn't get anything out of the lesson."

Somewhere in my head and heart—coded or not—everything Calvin said and did that day made sense. He gave me an ego check while I gave OB a confidence boost.

I golfed with OB several more times that summer, and every time I did he broke 100. *I'm not sure which of us felt better about that fact.* He wasn't always pleasant, and he still loved to curse his neon orange golf ball, but the OB initials no longer meant what they used to at the club—*Old Bastard*. He was now Oscar Brown to me, and to many others. Oscar, the billionaire, who had given a million dollars to the club every year since his wife had passed—the reason he was never billed for anything... and why he always got what he wanted. *Including Brittlyn as his waitress at lunch.*

I was given *far* too much credit for Oscar's "magical" transformation that summer. *If anything it was the other way around.* I wanted to beat that old man that first day we played to show him how great I was. But what would that have really accomplished? A nearly fifteen-year-old, ten handicap, destroying a ninety-year-old man who had never once "torn a Benjamin." *Copyright it Calvin.*

No. Cal deserves all the credit for that day. He had the hard job, the nearly impossible task of reigning in the ferocious egos and attitudes he was stumping with. Cal worked his magic.

*Cal was the real magician.*

## ←★★★★★ NARRATOR ★★★★★→

### ←Thursday, June 30, 2022→

Contractions suck, and I'm not referring to the "couldn't, wouldn't, shouldn't" kind. I'm talking about the double-you-over, tie-your-stomach-in-a-pretzel, uppercut-to-the-windpipe type that pregnant women get. And contrary to the popular opinion of the voices in my head, punching the floor did not help.

*Praise the good Lord if you're a boy, or a man.*

I was bent in half on the couch, trying to regain my breath when I heard the voice of the one responsible for my condition. "Toe touches?"

I lifted my head and glared at him. "Say that again. I dare you."

His smile was suddenly replaced with concern. "Are you okay? I'm sorry, I didn't—"

"No—I'm fine. It's just Braxton Hicks."

"Oh." Now he looked confused too. "Should I know who that is?"

I shook my head. *Obviously not.* "Not who, what. They're contractions… kind of—I think."

"Do you need to go to the doctor?" He knelt beside me.

I shook my head. "No. They've been relatively frequent the past couple days." I saw relief flood his face. "They just haven't quite been this… contracting. This one was nasty."

"Sounds fun." He was trying to lighten the mood.

It didn't work. "You'll never know."

He knew better than to reply to that. He stood up. "I'm gonna go run. That okay?"

I nodded. "Hey, does Brittlyn still work at the club?"

"Brittlyn?" He walked down the hall towards the garage door.

"Yes, the hot blonde with the great—"

"I know who you're talking about," he cut me off. "Yes, I think she's still there."

"You *think* she's still there?"

He didn't answer right away. "She's still there. Why?"

"No reason."

I knew he didn't believe me and I saw him look back at me, waiting for me to continue. But I'd gotten the answer I needed. I just smiled at him.

"Love you." I said.

He mumbled something back that probably wasn't 'I love you." Then stepped out the door.

## STELLAR 41 – "Ignorance and Reality"

Nick and I had worked out most of our differences by the end of summer—in large part because most of our differences were imaginary. I had taken it upon myself, thanks to Cal's lessons or parables, or whatever you want to call them, and apologized to Nick for my moronic behavior since that day in the lunchroom. He claimed he didn't even remember us fighting about anything. *Could I really have made that much out of nothing?* Maybe Nick was just taking his own angle on the high road. I didn't know.

It still didn't change the amount of time we were spending together, as swimming remained his entire life, and golf, fishing, and cleaning boats was mine. I can't help but look back now though, and know I still took him for granted.

That all changed when school started. I was in ninth grade the fall of 2015. Nick, Lauren, Josh, Caleb, Elliott, Caitlin, Taryn and everyone else, they were all sophomores. They were now over at the Catholic high school. Now we were on very different schedules. Now we didn't even see each other at night or on weekends much. *And we lived on the same property!* It sucked. I started to really kick myself for letting my friendship with Nick slip through the cracks. I never took mulligans in golf, but I'd have taken a do-over in life at that time if it had been offered.

I didn't have even one good friend at my school. Trust me, I know I could have tried harder to make new friends. I could have done a lot of things better. Instead I got worse. Instead I got pretty moody, rude and… well… brooding. I started shutting myself in my room, throwing the headphones on and tuning everything and everyone out. I stopped hanging out with Avery, stopped talking to Kate, and started making excuses to not go down to the marina and help out Ken, Cal and James. I was an idiot. It was only a year ago and I probably haven't grown up all that much since, but I can see it pretty clearly now and I can easily admit it. I was stupid. All the things I was mad at myself for doing to Nick I started doing to everyone else in my life. Kate said it was hormones. I think that's a cop-out. Every one of them deserved better than they got from me last year. Hormones may be responsible for a lot of things I did—and maybe even do—but they didn't replace my brain cells. I should have known better.

Fortunately, Kate is pretty stubborn. She's a million wonderful things, but she's especially perceptive, intelligent, and stubborn. A hundred times I tried to shut her out and she was there a hundred and one. She and Carrie must have been on the same page in regards to the relationship of their sons, because they decided to take us to Hawaii over an extended Thanksgiving break. Avery stayed home with Ken.

Kate called the Hawaii trip an "intervention." I didn't care what she called it. She could call it doing homework, getting a root canal or eating broccoli—I was going to Hawaii. Nick and I were going to Hawaii together.

It was an eye-opening trip to say the absolute very least.

There may be nothing in life more bipolar than the difference between reality and ignorance. Take airplane flights for example. I'd never been on a plane before. I'd seen a billion of them pass over Long Island heading to La Guardia, Boston, Newark, JFK or somewhere else nearby, but I had no idea what it was actually like to fly on one.

I figured they were much faster—for starters. *Ridiculously so.* I honestly believed we'd board at JFK and a few quick hours later we'd hop off to a crowd of hot, young, half-dressed women in coconut bras and hula skirts… in Hawaii. *Ha!* Ha ha.

Our twenty-hour travel day began with a four-hour flight to Dallas, followed by a three-hour flight to Los Angeles, and another six hours plus to the Big Island. *Airplanes apparently aren't time machines.*

When we got off the plane it was almost dark. There was one half-dressed woman at the airport but she wasn't Hawaiian, she was French (or Canadian), and drunk, and most definitely not worth looking at. The two women who greeted us with leis were clearly locals but were also middle-aged and dressed rather conservatively… and the flower necklaces were $10 each. We passed. *All that anticipation for nothing.*

The airport itself was kind of cool. It was actually an open-air-port. *Must not snow. Why can't we just move there?* My ignorant "surprises" continued beyond the realm of aviation. Turns out our hotel rooms weren't made out of bamboo and they weren't constructed over the water—*not sure which state or country I thought we were going to.* The North Shore of Oahu, was on a different island—*Oahu, obviously*—so there weren't thirty-foot waves breaking on our beach. But then we didn't really have a beach either. The Waikoloa shoreline was mostly white coral, lava rocks and a gazillion tiny pebbles. They had running water and electricity at the Hilton and there were no cockroaches crawling around in our bathtub. *Gosh, where did I think we were going?* I remember being surprised by many of these dumb little things. *And I'm sure there were more I don't remember.*

Nick and I got to share a room in Hawaii, though it was connected to Kate and Carrie's. One of the rooms had a king bed, the other had two queens. Nick and I got the room with two queens because Kate didn't want it to be awkward for us, which actually kind of made it more awkward because then we couldn't stop thinking about our moms sharing a bed. *Yeah, I know… teenage boys!*

Hawaii was also the first time I ever saw Kate in a swimsuit—a bikini no less. I'm going to leave my observations at that. She's supposed to be—or in fact, is—my mother. Nick, on the other hand, couldn't stop staring. *He almost needed a bib.*

Fortunately, there was no shortage of beauty around the resort to redirect his attention. I'd always wondered why there never seemed to be attractive girls at the waterparks and resorts we visited back home. Now it made sense. All the hot girls were here… testing the theory on how little material it took to make a swimsuit.

It's strange to reflect on it now—to think of it that way now—knowing I was in a completely different frame of mind while I was there. While Nick was constantly tapping me to point out various girls, each one impressive in their own right, I was considerably less impressed because I was comparing every one of them to Lauren. And, truthfully, *none* of them compared.

Nick finally called me on it. "Will you please stop it? You're never going to find anyone more beautiful than Lauren, trust me. Just enjoy the view."

"I know," I said, only reading halfway into his words at that point. "I am." But I wasn't. I was just missing Lauren.

And then we met Lola.

Lola was sixteen, same as Nick, but with a body several years more "enhanced" than any other 16-year-old girl I knew. She reminded me of the blonde girl from "Never Back Down", a movie Nick and I had watched nearly fifty times together—visualizing Josh as the antagonist, of course. She made me stop thinking about Lauren, for a while. She pretty much made me stop thinking, period.

The only problem was she had the exact same effect on Nick. And anyone but a blind girl, when forced to make a choice between us, would *always* be more interested in Nick.

*Come to think of it blind girls probably would be too. Nick even sounded handsome.*

## STELLAR 42 – "Lola from Nola"

You never forget a name like Lola Laughlin—or "LOL" as she called herself—particularly not in the social media age. Lola loved to laugh. And Lola was loud.

She was from New Orleans, and let's just say that the word "inhibitions" was not in her vocabulary. Whereas, for Nick and me, "inhibited" was pretty much our collective middle name.

We met her the day after we arrived in Hawaii. It was her last day, and night, at the resort, and she was bent on making it her most memorable. Kate and Carrie had given Nick and I our "rules and limitations" but they pretty much consisted of "don't get eaten by a shark, or die." As long as we stayed on the property we could do what we wanted. *We were on our own!*

We were snorkeling in the hotel's huge private cove just after lunch, when this girl in a pure white bikini swam up to us and yelled something at us through her snorkel.

"What?" I yelled back, also through my snorkel.

She removed the snorkel from her mouth and smiled. That was my first impression and dang, it was a good one. She was *stunning.*

"You look ridiculous," she said, laughing.

"That's what you were yelling at me?" I was trying to get a better look at the rest of her without being too obvious, but the rest of her was under the churning water by the waterfall. Nick had no such dilemma. He hadn't yet seen the face that went with the body he was examining below the surface. I grabbed his snorkel and yanked him up.

"No," the girl giggled. "I said, 'come check this out'."

"Check what out?" I asked.

"Baby sea turtle," she replied. "It's adorable."

At that point she could have asked me to go count sand and I'd have jumped at the chance. "Where?"

"Follow me," she said.

I didn't need to be asked twice. I was right, well, *behind* her.

Keeping my eyes on Lola was not a problem but keeping my mind on what I was supposed to be looking for was something entirely different. I don't think I blinked once in the two or three minutes I followed Lola's tan churning legs and white bikini bottom through the water. She pointed out the baby turtles—there were two of them—and I remember seeing them… but I don't remember *seeing* them. *If that makes sense?*

After finding the turtles we headed towards shallow water where I got my first glimpse of her full body—up close and from the front—and I nearly swallowed my snorkel. She tapped my head and I reluctantly lifted my face above water with hers.

The snorkel was already out of her mouth, mask off, beaming smile. She was so perfectly tanned. I was so translucently not. "Wasn't that amazing?" she asked.

I nodded. *Yes. It most definitely was.*

"Did you see it?"

*Not sure we're talking about the same "it" but...* "Yes." I nodded again. I was at a loss for what to do or say so I dropped my face down in the water a little bit and proceeded to swallow a mouthful of saltwater—something you really shouldn't do.

I immediately reacted by spitting the rest of what was in my mouth directly into her face. Talk about first impressions. I'll never forget her expression, or Nick's for that matter, as I turned tomato red and wished I could vanish or beat myself to death with the nearest rock.

But it didn't bother her. In fact, she started giggling. Then laughing hysterically. And then she filled her mouth with water and spit in my face. The next thing I knew the three of us were engaged in an all out llama war, which turned into a dunking contest, a chicken fight and all kinds of "too much fun."

Somewhere in there Lola introduced herself by name and the three of us began a twelve-hour friendship that I could fill an entire journal with. I could, but I won't. *In the best interests of everyone involved.*

Nick and I have somewhat different versions of that day. Nick remembers swimming with dolphins, paddle boarding, building a huge sand castle on the lagoon's beach, skipping rocks, the incredible meal and sunset at Kamuela Provision Company, taking a gondola ride through the resort's canals, and then falling asleep by the pool with a headache. That's what Nick got out of the day.

I remember all of that with Lola, too, but most of all, I remember a kiss. I remember a long, wet, OMG kiss. In baseball terms, I managed to stretch my first career single into a double. And then I immediately wished I'd stayed at first base. In fact, I wished I hadn't "swung" at all. I wish I'd walked... away. Don't get me wrong... I desperately and pathetically pursued Lola all day—like a dog chasing a car. But I didn't expect to catch her, and when I did, well... I didn't know what to do. Lola wasn't who I wanted to be doing that with... she wasn't who I wanted my first *real* kiss to be from.

*Too late.* I suddenly felt crazy guilty. I bumbled and apologized my way through the somewhat fictional onset of a stomachache, and proceeded to lead an extremely confused Nick on a steeplechase race over beach chairs back to our room. Call me insane, stupid, conflicted... whatever you want—you're right—but I felt terrible... like I no longer deserved a shot with Lauren at all. I honestly felt like I'd cheated on a girlfriend who wasn't even mine. The only saving grace was Nick had been asleep for it all. Or I would have felt so much worse.

## STELLAR 43 – "The Truth About Nick"

Yeah... Nick wasn't asleep for any of it. He saw it all. He was surprised it happened, but happy for me. He'd been trying to get me to forget about Lauren on that trip, and celebrated the fact that I apparently had. That's the nutshell version of the truth.

Given my feelings of guilt and unworthiness I went along with it. Especially when Nick continued his confession by taking me back to the "argument" in the lunchroom that had created the rift between us in the first place. I'd told him that day that he'd never understand what it was like to really want someone and not be able to have her. Turns out I was *way* wrong. He *completely* understood. There was a girl he'd always wanted too, a girl he'd always liked, but a girl he couldn't have—not without losing his best friend.

*Nick had always wanted Lauren.*

I was stunned at the time. *You probably could have heard crickets chirping if the ocean hadn't been so loud.* I was blindsided. *Not sure how in the world I didn't see it.* It's not like he hadn't essentially told me as much a hundred different times. He'd just never pushed it—he hadn't ever acted on his feelings... *because of me*. Forget trying to measure my guilt at that moment. *Or my insecurity.*

I had little doubt then that the feelings were likely mutual for Lauren. I saw how she looked at him, smiled at him, and how she used to sit by him at lunch until Nick all but forced her to sit by me. *Which is when she started sitting with Josh again.* Nick's loyalty to me had been so consistent and obvious... but I'd never seen it for what it was—support—and always held it against him for what it wasn't—indifference. He'd been a true friend, the rarest of friends, willing to sacrifice what he wanted most to not jeopardize his friendship with me.

*Dang that guy!* I was blown away.

I didn't feel like a million apologies that night could possibly be sufficient, but Nick wasn't even looking for one. He was essentially seeking permission to pursue Lauren without verbally asking for it. So I basically gave it to him. And I lied.

I told him the whole experience with Lola had convinced me there were other fish in the sea besides Lauren. The entire Hawaii trip had encouraged me to branch out more. I told Nick about a girl in Farmington that I really liked, and would probably make a move on. I spoke of Brittlyn to Nick like she was my age, and legitimately a girlfriend candidate. He'd never meet her anyway. *Or so I thought.*

I sold the story well. And Nick opened up to me about his feelings for Lauren—everything he'd kept contained for years. His happiness waxed as mine waned. His heart swelled as mine broke. It hurt, but it was the right thing to do. It was time for me to get out of the way of destiny.

## ←★★★★★ NARRATOR ★★★★★→

### ←Thursday, June 30, 2022→

I was down to Stellar's last journal.

On the one hand, I was thrilled to be so close to finishing *his* side of the story, eager to let the world get to know him through the rest of us—through this other stack of journals and letters.

On the other hand, I also knew this was merely the halfway point—essentially the intermission. The second act was about to begin, and the greatest challenge was easily still ahead of me. As Stellar's introspective wrapped up I now had to, as seamlessly as possible—chronologically *and* logically—blend in the diverse writing styles and perspectives of everyone else.

No problem. *Right.*

Doubt hadn't just crept into my mind. It was throwing a massive block party in there. I honestly didn't know if I could finish this.

I popped open a Dr. Pepper, pulled a well-loved children's classic off the bookshelf beside me, and sipped my way through Watty Piper's "The Little Engine That Could."

The soda wasn't exactly my physician's prescription, I know, but that caffeine kick sure perked me up. And Mr. Piper's pages picked a perfect time to inspire me.

Suddenly, my confidence was back on track. "You can do this," I whispered to myself.

*Yes... I think I can!*

## ←★★★★★ CALVIN JACKSON ★★★★★→
**Letter (Part 1 of 6)**

I was asked to write a letter of recall regarding Mr. Stellar Parker. I apologize that it has taken me so long to do so. Summarizing five years of life into five or so pages is no talent of mine. But I've done my best and expressed my feelings for this boy as effectively as my own words can humbly express.

Stellar loved his magic. Yessir. He did as a boy and he did as a young man. I never saw him perform on the streets, but he'd regularly do card tricks for James and me at Mr. Parker's bait and boat shop, and more just for me throughout our golf travels together. He frequently said of himself that he was "never the master and ever the apprentice". *A perfectionist's point of view, no doubt.* I remember those times with Stellar clearly and fondly—his joy, his smile, his laugh. They were all part of the magical effect he had on people.

I've never met a better person. *Miss Kate being the possible exception.* I've definitely never met a better golfer, though his *consistency* certainly could have been improved on. But Stellar, when he was on his game, weren't many that could compete with that boy.

Stellar didn't see it proper to accept credit for his greatness nor for any of his accomplishments or contributions to those around him. His incredible talents he always left understated. He misperceived himself as ordinary, though he was in a class far from that. As he saw it he succeeded because of good fortune, hard work, and a few people that carried him wherever he went. He was most always that humble, too. Trust me, I didn't carry him so much as he carried me. What Stellar didn't know is that he made changes in the lives of others just by being who he was. A boy like that, looking up to people like he did, that affects you. It makes you want to be a better person, to set the best possible example. Least it sure did me.

I'd long lost the belief in myself, or rather in my own potential, until that boy made me feel valuable. In turn I've never believed in anyone more than Mr. Stellar. Life sure wasn't much fun for me when I met the boy. I'd just turned fifty; two decades removed from the early midlife crisis where my wife left me and took my only child, my son, with her. He didn't talk to me no more. They hadn't returned so much as a single call or letter in seven years. Can't say as I blamed him, or either of them. They had moved on. But I couldn't.

When they left I was best friends with a bartender and his various longneck pals. I couldn't see what I was doing to my family, didn't know what I had till it was gone. I can see clearly now. I can't take it back. I wish for all the world I could. In Hollywood I may have gotten a second chance. But mulligans—do overs—are harder to come by in the real world, specially when you need them most—when you make the biggest of mistakes.

I do however feel like God gave me a mulligan at fatherhood through Stellar. He was kind of a son to all of us; Mr. Parker, James and me. The man I always dreamed my own boy would become, that's the man I got to know and watch grow in Stellar.

I had no real friends in New York but James, and nothing else I cared for here save my maintenance job, my corner stool at the corner bar, and my fishing pole. I loved that job though, more than anything, cutting those greens and placing those pins... it was artistry for a man who couldn't scratch out stick figures on paper. It was golfing for a lover of the sport who'd never been able to afford to play it. But some of the people were terrible, some of those members unbelievable. Didn't matter none if you were courteous to them, some of those rich folk looked at and treated me like I was beneath them... and the constant mockery of my stutter, it destroyed me.

James and I, we stayed a long time for the money. But there comes a time when the money you need isn't worth the toll it takes on you to gain it. We could have, and maybe should have, left a long time before we did. But then we'd never have met Mr. Stellar. James will say, same as me, that we both was glad we stuck with it for just that one reason.

A handful of liars cost James his job not long before I decided to leave. James is a great man, a gentle man. He'd have never taken the money they said he did, wouldn't have jeopardized his employment for $200, nor would he have spoken to or accosted that woman as she accused him. She was drunk and had fallen—split her lip when her face hit the railing on those steps. James was helping her up, just helping her. She told some lies, and people took her word without considering his. It is what it is.

But the way James was treated, that burned Stellar. I could see it. I could feel it. He went against the grain and stuck by a black man in an all-white court of public opinion. I suspect Stellar didn't write much about it himself. Wasn't his way. But I'll write it so his story includes it—as it certainly should. The boy took heat for his support of James at the club, and I know he did at school, though he'd never admit it to James or me. Miss Kate knew though. She confessed as much one day. That boy didn't see right and wrong by color, he saw it as it was. All the Parkers was that way.

My transition from golf to boats and fishing was facilitated by Stellar. He maintained forever that he had none to do with Mr. Parker offering me that job, that it was all James. That is not how James recalls it. Of course, the boy was somewhat responsible for James's job as well. Stellar, he always looked out for others, largely to his own expense. That boy, he was selfless. That boy, he was special.

I wanted to tell the world with this letter, anyone who will listen that is, that Stellar Parker's life was an inspiration to me from the day I saw him standing by that fence watching me mow the greens. He waved at me like I was someone of significance, like my tractor was a parade float. The boy could turn a frown upside down and make a rain cloud retract its drops. He brought out the sunshine on the darkest of days and led this man to the fountain of youth.

I fear anything I say that can close approach a proper description of the Stellar I knew and loved would be misconstrued as cliché. That is the unfortunate reality.

The truth of it all is, as Stellar's story goes, that I saw in my years with him a collection of magic shows, a series of inexplicable performances, on and off the golf course. Some would deem them miracles, random acts of God—his friendship with OB at the club being one. But Stellar, he never believed that God took sides, not ever in life nor even in sports for his beloved Patriots, and he always believed that the right and the good would overcome the wrong and the bad. I don't know where he got it from, not after all that boy went through in his life. But those magical acts I mentioned, he deserved them. He earned them. And the first of the five golf-related ones I witnessed happened in Tampa, Florida in the spring of 2016.

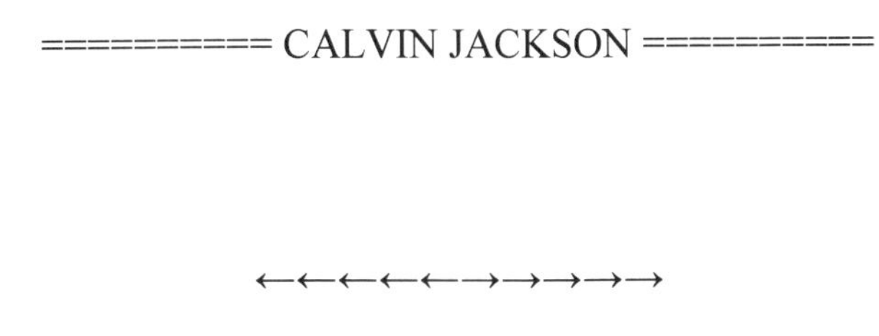

========== CALVIN JACKSON ==========

***"He missed putts because of the uproar of butterflies in the adjoining meadows."***

\- P.G. Wodehouse

## STELLAR 44 – "Nuclear Mistletoe"

And they lived happily ever after.

Good for *them*, whoever "*they*" is. It sure wasn't Nick and Lauren. It should have been, but this isn't a fairy tale. The perfect guy doesn't get thc pcrfcct girl in this story.

Nick asked Lauren out at Christmas 2015 and she said no. *Yeah, that's not what I was expecting either.* Apparently I wasn't in the way of the two of them after all. My permission for them to marry and have Duggars of kids together was irrelevant to Lauren. She said no.

Nick was as stunned as me. Okay, to be fair, he was probably more stunned than I was.

"What happened?" I asked him.

"I have no idea."

"Did she say why?"

"Josh."

"That's what she said?"

Nick nodded but said, "Not exactly."

"Well, which is it? You think it's Josh?" I shook my head. "There's no way she picked Josh over you." I was angry. *Maybe even angrier than Nick.* "Do you want me to go beat the crap out of him?"

"He'd kill you."

I at least got a small smile out of him. "Yeah." I nodded. "You're probably right."

"This wasn't the way I saw this going." Nick looked miserable. "Not at all. I mean… do you know what I mean?"

*Uh. Yeah.* "I'm with you, Nick. I'd take you over Josh any day."

Another small sad smile. "Thanks."

I was sick of Josh. Absolutely sick of the jerk. It was one thing for him to mess with me, to bully me, to strut his life in front of me with that hundred-dollar haircut and stupid smug grin of his. It was another for him to mess with my matchmaking career—to mess with Nick. Josh didn't deserve Lauren. I have no idea what she saw in him. *Other than the muscular, popular, rich and almost famous parts.*

I couldn't do much about it at school since he was at a different one now, and I knew Nick would be respectful of Lauren's wishes. He'd be respectful of Lauren in general. Nick would stay out of the way.

But I wanted to get in the way, specifically in Josh's way. And there was only one way I knew to do it without getting run over.

Josh was on the fast track to stardom. He'd played in a dozen American Junior Golf Association events in 2015 and he'd won four of them at age 16. *He never once finished outside the Top 10.*

He'd had his picture in the local paper infinite times—shots of him holding trophies beside Jordan Spieth, Justin Rose, and even with Rory McIlroy at a Nike event he won. He was listed as "one to watch" by several national sports magazines. He had everything going for him. I wasn't jealous, but I hated it. *It's not the same thing, believe me.*

I mentioned to Coach Chandler that I was interested in entering some events to get a feel for competitive golf.

"It's a different animal," he said.

"I don't care if it's a werewolf," was my reply. *Yeah, it didn't make sense to him either.*

I didn't tell him why exactly I was so motivated to play, and the first two events he entered me in did not go very well. I began to question whether I'd ever be able to compete with the area's junior elite. *And Josh was better than all of them.* Maybe my plan to mess with Josh wasn't going to work. Maybe I'd only amount to a bug on his metaphorical windshield—just a squashed streak of blood and guts on Richie Rich's Porsche.

There was an American Junior Golf Association (AJGA) Open at Innisbrook in Florida in early April of 2016 that Coach had inquired about. Somehow he managed to get me on a waitlist of sorts, the second alternate, and I got the call two days before the event telling me I could play in the qualifier if I could make it there. Ken was a little skeptical about forking over significant money for travel expenses and golf, but I told him it was probably the last event I'd ever enter. *I honestly believed that.* When Cal offered to cover half of it Ken refused his money. "No, Calvin, I've got this one. *Just this one*." He looked at me.

I nodded. *Understood.*

So, Kate, Cal and I headed to Tampa Bay.

Innisbrook Resort was huge, like a city in and of itself. We were staying in a two-bedroom suite just off the North Course, the host course for the qualifier and first two rounds of the tournament. The resort had several other golf courses, including the Copperhead course—a PGA stop with one of the toughest closing stretches on tour. If I made it to Saturday, I'd get to play that. But that was getting ahead of myself. I needed to try to make it to Thursday first.

The place was pretty fancy and expansive—biggest resort property I'd been on this side of the Hilton Waikoloa in Hawaii. But it was still a small world. A small social media world.

"You'll never guess who's here," Kate said at dinner.

I guessed anyway. "Josh?"

She looked up from her phone in surprise. "How'd you know?"

"It's a big event, and he's the defending champion. It made sense he'd be here. I'll never see him though."

I was wrong. Not only was he staying in the same building we were, but we ran into him and his mom in the parking lot the next morning. I said hello. He didn't. *Shocker.*

"Nice to see you two getting along," Kate said with a smile.

"Isn't it?"

"Don't let him get to you."

I nodded. *I'll try.*

Something strange happened to me that day. I was expecting the nerves to be as unnerving as they'd been my first two competitive events, if not a little more because Josh was here. I was wrong about that, too. I warmed up with the strangest sense of calm. Cal stood behind me watching me carefully and didn't say a word until I was finished. I finally turned to him. "I don't know what's going on!"

"Never seen you hit so good," he said.

"I know." I shook my head. "Maybe it's the elevation?"

"Florida doesn't have elevation."

"Okay, then who knows? It's just the driving range though."

But it wasn't. I went out and posted a 72 in my qualifier, 18 consecutive pars—the magic number to move on. I did the same thing in the first round of the event on Thursday—18 more pars—ending with the same score as Josh, in fact. *Weird.*

I think that pissed him off. Especially when I did it the next day, too—my third 72 in a row. 18 more pars. And again, Josh shot the exact same score as me.

We were in a tie for fourth at that point with one round left to play.

I didn't say much to Kate or Cal at dinner. I was busy memorizing the yardage guide for the Copperhead course. A few reporters had tried to come talk to me, but Cal had shooed them away insisting that if they still wanted to talk to me after tomorrow's round, I would be happy to. Lots of people were murmuring and pointing at me everywhere I went. I didn't know what the big deal was. I was in fourth place, and wasn't playing particularly well. *I still didn't have a single birdie!*

Kate hadn't even asked me about my rounds yet, none of them, though I was certain Cal was keeping her updated. I didn't take it the wrong way. I knew she cared. But as long as I was happy, she was willing to give me, and my thoughts, plenty of space.

Cal was also keeping his opinions to himself. Well, most of them.

"You go out and post a 60 tomorrow and you'll probably win," he said as we finished eating.

I almost snorted chocolate milk through my nose. I wiped my face, laughing as Kate shook her head in feigned disgust. "A 60?" I coughed. "Twelve under par on one of the hardest courses the PGA Tour plays… and you think that *might* be good enough?"

"Pretty sure Mr. Spieth shot a 62 at age fourteen—"

"I'm no Jordan Spieth, if that's what you're getting at, and 60 is a ridiculous score at any age. I would love a bird though. At least one."

"What kind?" Kate asked without looking up.

Cal and I looked at her, then at each other, and I burst out laughing again.

Kate glanced up from her magazine. "What? What's so funny?"

"Nothing," I said, still laughing.

"Miss Kate," Cal said. "By 'bird' he was referring to the term for scoring one stroke better than par on a hole."

"I thought that was an eagle," she replied.

I was almost crying now. "That's *two* under par on a hole."

"Young man…" She pointed her finger at me.

"I'm sorry." I did my best to settle back down. I couldn't look at her though, and didn't dare look at Cal. "Can we order dessert?" I asked, failing to catch an escaping hiccup.

"No," Kate said immediately with a mock glare, but she held the dessert menu out towards me anyway. "You're lucky I love you."

"If I may, sir?" Cal was back to business. "Could I make a strategic suggestion?"

"Go ahead, Cal."

"Now that we've established there's no reason to pursue the course record tomorrow, I'd like to talk about the weather."

I knew there was a reason he'd brought up the 60 and Jordan Spieth. Reality check. *Typical Cal.* "What about the weather?"

"It's supposed to be a mite windy tomorrow morning," he continued. "So, I was thinking we might play the course a bit differently."

"Differently?" I asked.

"Different."

"You're the boss." I shrugged. "I'll do whatever you want me to do."

I saw Kate smile as Cal calmly accepted my deference. "What?" I asked her.

"You guys are so cute," she said. "I clearly don't know what you're talking about, but it's still cute."

At fifteen I didn't exactly like being referred to as cute, but I accepted things from Kate I wouldn't take from anyone else. Besides, I think she was playing dumb. I'd seen golf books on Kate's nightstand recently. She'd tried to cover them with a pillow one night when I'd approached her side of the bed, but she wasn't quick enough. I think she knew a lot more about the sport than she was letting on. And I knew that she was learning about it for my benefit. That was Kate, it's just who she always was. She always put everyone else first—the most selfless person I knew.

## STELLAR 45 – "Head of the Snake"

A storm was brewing. The sky was dark and the wind was howling, but there was no rain at 10:20 when Josh and I teed off. The event went on as scheduled.

With cameras watching, Josh came up to me at the first tee and forced himself into a fake smile and handshake. "Too bad you can't get anything other than a par," he whispered.

"I know, right?" I agreed tongue-in-cheek, since we were tied. "Then I wouldn't be so far behind you."

I watched him open his mouth to say something else, but no words came out. He turned away and stormed over to his bag.

"Easy, mister," Cal muttered beside me. "You play your game."

"I am," I replied with a grin. Cal raised an eyebrow and I dropped the smile. "Fine. I will. Promise."

"If you promise…" he whispered.

"Yeah, yeah… I know." I nodded. "Deliver."

"All I'm saying." Cal stepped away.

*Right.* That was *never* "all" he was saying.

Today, in the final round there was a guy carrying a sign around with our names and scores on it. Josh and I both had a big red "E" beside our name—even par. The starter announced our names, and Josh stepped up to hit first. The first hole was playing 535 yards, and Josh did more than cut that in half with his tee shot, splitting the fairway. "Beat that," he mumbled as we passed each other on the tee box. *Sportsmanship.*

I couldn't and I knew it. And I didn't. I ended up in a bunker about 250 out on the left. I salvaged a five on that hole. Josh got a four. I saw the scorekeeper take the "E" away beside Josh's name and note his birdie with a "-1."

Calvin saw me watching that and handed me my driver. "Wasn't no wind on that one, sir. Be patient."

We recorded a pair of 4's on the second hole, and Josh set himself up perfectly on the third hole—about 160 out between the two ponds guarding the fairway. I laid up a little shorter, about 180 to the flag.

"Good amount of wind up there," Cal whispered. I looked at the swirling treetops. "More than it appears," he added. "And it ain't consistent."

I waited for him to hand me my six-iron. He gave me my five instead. "Five?"

"Keep it down. Cutter l-l-left to right."

His stutter suggested nerves, perhaps even a degree of uncertainty in that decision, but I remained calm and did as I was told. My ball ended up just short of the green.

Cal picked up my bag and nodded. “Just fine.”

Josh’s ball found the bunker just right of the green. I heard him curse and saw him glare at his caddy. *Classic Josh.*

I got up and down from my position for another 4. Josh missed his 10-foot par putt, and the scorekeeper put the red “E” next to his name again. *Back to all square.*

Josh dropped to +1 on the fourth hole and +2 after the fifth hole. He was having major trouble with the trees but refused to take anything other than driver off the tee box, even though his caddie was insisting on it. It cost him again on six as he bogeyed to fall to +3. I still had an “E” next to my name. *Even Steven.*

Josh got a lucky bounce off a tree on seven and managed to birdie the next three holes. I recorded a par on all three. We made the turn tied.

And that’s when the wheels came off. *Josh’s wheels.*

We get a lot of strong wind on the eastern tip of Long Island. I’d played in it at its worst, and typically not well I might add. Calvin would later tell me that this had to be the strongest wind I’d ever played in and maybe he was right, but it barely affected my game or demeanor.

Josh bogeyed ten, doubled eleven and tripled twelve to plummet to +6. On the twelfth hole the “E” blew off the sign by my name, but the scorekeeper chased it down and put it back up there. That was the most work he had to do for me all day.

Josh triple bogeyed thirteen, doubled fourteen and finally got a par on fifteen. He was at +11 now. He’d been berating his caddie for the past six holes unlike anything I’d ever heard a golfer say. The caddie looked like he wanted to quit. At one point when he walked off to use the restroom I didn’t think he’d bother to come back.

Josh’s mother, Marcy, hadn’t followed us for even a single hole today. The wind was so terrible not many people had. But Kate had been with us the entire way. Occasionally she and Calvin would exchange looks and a few words, but she never said a thing to me.

I should have birdied both fourteen and fifteen. I’m not one to make excuses, but the wind definitely moved my ball on both of those four-foot putts. As we approached the sixteenth tee box we came upon a giant bronze statue of a Copperhead. The course designer must have had a fascination with snakes. There was a plaque beneath the statue that read:

*“You Are Entering THE SNAKE PIT.*

*The Moccasin, The Rattler and the Copperhead are Among the Most Difficult Finishing Holes on the PGA TOUR! Play Well.”*

So I did—recording a par on all three. I finished with that capital "E" beside my name. Josh ended with a +18 beside his. He shot a 90 in the final round. I won the tournament by six strokes over the kid who had been in first at the beginning of the day, but had also shot a 90.

After the round I was told that I was the first golfer anyone could ever remember shooting fifty-four consecutive pars in a tournament. Calvin was quick to remind every reporter who brought it up that I'd actually had eighteen more in Wednesday's qualifier—72 pars in a row.

I spent almost two hours talking to people who had never cared about me or perhaps even heard about me before today. Most of the other players came up and congratulated me in one form or another, in one language or another. Not Josh. He just left.

One reporter suggested my performance was a modern day miracle—perhaps the greatest feat he'd ever witnessed.

Cal was quick to temper that. "He's just a boy. And golf is just a game."

"He's a magician," the reporter replied. "And sometimes there's more to golf than the game."

They were both right. *And there was that word again.*

## STELLAR 46 – "Everything Changes"

People look at you different when you're somebody. I mean, obviously everybody is somebody, but most of us just walk through life with zero recognition factor, like nobodies. When I got back to New York I was under no illusion that my social status had changed. And then I got my first autograph request.

Autographs are weird. They're just a scribble on a ball, a picture, a piece of paper... or whatever. I don't understand their actual value. They're someone's signature that no one else will ever really care you got—probably not even yourself after a while. I didn't like signing autographs. Not even my first one.

I don't want to sound ungrateful or uppity in any way. That probably all came out wrong. Perhaps I should explain myself better. *Considering I have collected a few autographs myself.* Signing your name for someone when you don't feel like you're any more special than they are is... well... awkward. I mean, I get people wanting Brady's autograph, or Rory's, Jeter's, etc. Those guys are Major and World Champions... big time *somebodies*. But I was a fifteen-year-old kid who had just won a *junior* golf tournament in Florida. My autograph, in my honest and humble opinion, was no more valuable than a Bingo winner's at the local American Legion.

Winning the tournament in Florida changed a few other things for me. For one, Ken independently determined that my competitive golf career wasn't yet over. At dinner one night he informed me I was registered for the Thunderbird Invitational in Arizona in late May.

"But I thought that was it?" I said. "That Florida was my last tournament."

"Well, I know that's what I said, but the Invitational is a big event. All the best junior golfers in the country will be there. Unless, of course, you don't want to play anymore?"

"No. I mean yes—of course I want to keep playing. But Arizona?"

"We can afford it if you really want to do it." Kate cut in.

"I definitely do."

"There is one catch though," Ken continued.

"Okay... "

"Because of deadlines we can't guarantee you'll get to play any other events before then. You could be going into one of the world's biggest junior golf tournaments cold."

*Cold in Arizona... interesting concept.* "Just gives me a little more time to practice," I said.

I did play once more competitively before the invitational in Arizona—a 36-hole tournament with no cut. *Unfortunately.*

It was a junior all-star event in Jersey that Coach Chandler got me into. He was there for it, as were Kate, Ken, James and Nick's mom. They all wanted to see me play. Nick didn't come, but it was golf. I understood why, and definitely didn't hold that against him. *Good call actually.* According to the registration sheet Josh was supposed to be there as well, he'd even paid the fee, but for some reason didn't show up. *Dumb call on his part.* He missed the perfect opportunity to humiliate me, or at least pile on to my humiliation.

Who knows what got under my skin or what happened to all the Florida magic, but I was a complete and utter mess. I followed up an ugly 88 with a barely better 86 and finished at 30 over par. *In last place.*

I was beyond embarrassed, and all but begged to drop out of the invitational in Arizona. I figured Ken and Kate would support the idea—or at least not object to it. Surely they wouldn't want to just throw all that money away. *Au contraire.*

They insisted I follow through on "my" commitment, and that my golf "could only get better."

Calvin agreed, in typical Calvin fashion. "You ain't got no more bad swings in you, sir. And I assure you, Josh still has many."

That's right… Josh was going to be there. *Great.*

## ←★★★★★ CALVIN JACKSON ★★★★★→
**Letter (Part 2 of 6)**

72 pars in a row… I ain't never seen such a thing. Ain't never heard of it neither. Hard for any golfer to imagine such an impressive imperfection. You see, to golfers a "perfect" score is a round below par… *well* below par. Par generally represents the ceiling for the recreational golfer and the basement for the professional. It's the bipolar line between those who aspire to shoot it and those who are deeply disappointed when they do. A perfect round is one with multiple birdies, and pars at the very worst. And that's just for eighteen holes. 72 pars in a row over four rounds, over four days? I would've never expected such a result under any circumstances. Wouldn't ever believe anyone capable.

For a fifteen-year-old boy to have such calm, such control, to be so unflappable in the most flappable of weather and circumstances, "crazy" falls crazy short of describing it.

A reporter approached me after the final round and asked how many years I'd been a caddie. I seen his jaw near hit the floor when I told him I ain't done it but a year. "How'd you keep the boy so focused?" he asked.

"That boy gets his eyes on a particular prize," I replied. "Don't take nothing to keep them there."

"So he wants to go pro?" the reporter asked.

I chuckled. "Not less he has to."

The bewildered expression that crossed that man's face was priceless. He'd never understand what meant what to that boy. Stellar didn't play the game of golf for himself. It was a mode of transportation to a destination in his heart, another dimension he could exist in with his parents, with Bernie, and with a few other people he'd like to be spending time with.

T'was then I got to thinking about my role in this relationship. I was there for the boy's first ace in Farmington. I watched him closely. Was no big deal to him. I saw him nearly repeat the magic with his very next swing. Still no big deal. He gave no thought to his mechanics, always focused on the objective of each individual shot. That ability to compartmentalize, to have such short recall and such controlled nearsighted vision, he could do anything he wanted to in this game.

So what did he want to do? That was always the question.

We had great conversations in our practice rounds. But God's honest truth, they were never about golf. He and James, they spoke of golf all the time. Can't say that Stellar and I ever discussed it in a round, not beyond the last or next shot anyway. When a round was over he didn't like to dwell on it much, not if it was good, not if it was bad. He knew the next round wouldn't be the same.

So we discussed what was really important to him: his parents, Avery, Nick, the Saint Paul Chapel renovations, Tom Brady and the Patriots, etc. We discussed life. *And Miss Lauren, of course.*

Mr. Stellar had his priorities in line, on and off the golf course, and I greatly admired that of him.

But not everyone understood or appreciated Stellar's perceived competitive indifference as I did—Mr. Parker for one. After Stellar's lackluster performance in New Jersey, Mr. Parker asked me if Florida had been a fluke, if Stellar had just been lucky.

"No, sir," I told him. "The boy just has to want to win."

"You're saying he didn't care? He didn't want to win this event?" I looked at Mr. Parker and debated how to answer that so as to not get his head steaming more. "Well, sir… no. But he'll surely want the next one."

"Yeah, well, about that… I've decided to pull him from the Arizona tournament."

I opened my mouth to object, but quickly reconsidered. It was his call. Stellar was his son. Mr. Parker eyed me. "What?"

"Nothing, sir."

"You don't think that's a good move?"

"I don't, sir."

Mr. Parker was silent a minute. "After that disaster in Jersey, you think it's wise to put him up against the best kids in the country? You really think he can handle that—that he can just turn it on and off like that?"

"I think so… yes."

"I don't see how that's possible." Mr. Parker shook his head.

Nonetheless, when I requested that he reconsider his position he agreed to do just that—he'd discuss it with Miss Kate. He also agreed to not be hard on the boy. "I won't say a word about it," he promised. "Golf is your department. I'll leave all that to you… for now."

*Message received.*

The next day he informed me that he and Miss Kate had elected to keep Stellar in the Arizona event. "I hope you're right," he said.

I hoped I was, too.

←←←←←→→→→→

***"Golf tournaments are not usually won by making the heroic shot, but instead by not making the disastrous ones."***

- Jack Nicklaus

## STELLAR 47 – "Phoenix Invitational—May 2016"

Humility is insensitive. It doesn't care who you are or what you've done. It's a wrecking ball in a greenhouse, a baseball bat to the back of the knees. It destroys you—typically before a captive audience—and then tattoos a "kick me" sign on your back. The Karate Kid can recover. He gets back up. The knight in Monty Python and the Holy Grail… he fights on without his arms and legs. Those brave kids at Mt. Sinai Children's Hospital… I don't know how they do it, how they bounce back from the devastation life throws at them. They're brave and resilient. *HEROES.*

I'm an idiot. I flew to Phoenix with a sense of dread… *about playing golf.* It kept me up at night—several nights. I didn't want to go. I'd tried any number of things to get out of it. I even asked a kid with a broken arm how he did it, not just because I was curious, but to see if that was an option for me. *I'm not kidding.* There was nothing in me that thought playing in that event was a good idea—nothing in me that believed the outcome would be any different than the debacle in New Jersey. I was embarrassed, stressed out and scared. *Because of golf.*

Trust me, the true humiliation is in reflecting on all that immaturity now. But at the time, it's where I was at—feeling sorry for myself… wondering what I'd gotten myself into. My 72 consecutive pars were long forgotten. In fact, in the program it even said I'd had a streak of 27 consecutive pars in Florida. No one cared anymore. I was yesterday's news, and inaccurate news at that.

Josh on the other hand was on a roll. He was the shooting star to my crashed meteor. He'd won his last three events since Tampa, and one look at him surrounded by cameras and microphones was reason enough to believe this would be his fourth.

I did my best to avoid him the night before the event and figured by the weekend I'd be on my way home and he'd be on his way to the podium.

I can't explain my 62 on Wednesday. I'd never even shot in the 60's before. Not once. Ten birdies, eight pars and a six shot lead over Josh. *They had to have set the place up too easy.* I was the lowest seeded golfer in the tournament so I was out first. There was virtually no crowd, not even at the range yet, and no spectators followed me. *Exactly the way I liked it.* It was a beautiful morning on the Talon Course at Grayhawk Golf Club in Scottsdale. I was kind of in awe of the place—essentially a shrine to hometown hero Phil Mickelson. I had zero experience with desert golf, but when you hit 14 fairways the desert part never comes into play.

We were back at the hotel before Josh even teed off. Kate told me his score later. He was in second with a 68—likely counting on that being the lead. I'm guessing he was a tad surprised and upset to learn it wasn't, and even more surprised and upset to be down *SIX... to me!*

We switched over to Grayhawk's other course—the Raptor—on Thursday. Initially I was disappointed. I loved that other course. But my disappointment didn't last long. The Raptor rocked too. I was surprised to see Josh waiting for me on the first tee. Neither Kate nor Cal had told me I'd be playing with him today. I hadn't figured our pairings from Wednesday would change. Guess they did it differently in Arizona.

I shook the hand of the starter and the official who'd be carrying our sign, then extended my hand to Josh and his caddie. Josh ignored it and glared at his caddie when he didn't. I smiled at Josh. "Good luck to you."

He replied with something similar in sound but with just two words and an entirely different meaning. Cal didn't take it too kindly, but I pulled him away. "Don't worry about it," I said. "It's gamesmanship."

"There's no room for them words out here," Cal muttered.

"I've heard worse," I mumbled back.

Cal shook his head. "There's no excuse for fishermen neither."

I bogeyed the first hole—we started on the back—and didn't miss Josh's comment about snapping my par streak. Guess he didn't know I'd snapped, tweaked, hyperextended and amputated the snot out of that streak in Jersey. *Or he'd been holding onto that line for months.*

Josh birdied the hole so he was now two strokes closer. As he slid past me towards the next tee he whispered in my ear. "At this rate we'll be tied in a couple holes."

"You good?" Cal asked me as I watched Josh walk away.

"Yessir." I nodded. "I'm good."

"What'd he say?"

"He likes my shoes."

"Truth?"

"More or less."

"Kind of an odd thing to say."

"Well... he's weird."

Three holes later my six stroke lead had been whittled down to one. I was struggling, and Josh was getting cockier with every passing hole, particularly on the tee box. All he was missing was the Shooter McGavin collar flip and smoking guns—*from Happy Gilmore*. Even his mom looked embarrassed, which is probably all I had to say.

The fourteenth hole was playing downwind but a little long today—around 429—and Josh left himself about 90 yards out. I settled about sixty yards behind him, right next to the one-fifty marker.

"Heck of a shot with your five-iron," Josh scoffed, mocking my tendency to leave the big dog in the bag. "Oh… " He looked at my club. "Sorry, that *was* your driver. My bad."

I watched him high-five a few rambunctious dudes in the gallery and saunter off down the fairway. I handed Cal my driver.

"You good?" he asked, for the thirtieth or so time already that day.

I nodded. I was right where I wanted to be—next to that yardage marker. With the helping wind this was a perfect nine-iron. I knew the split second I hit the shot that it was going to hit the hole or pin, it was going to be dang close. Instead it went in. I holed out from 148 for eagle. Out of the corner of my eye I saw Josh throw his hands up. *In disbelief, mind you, not in support.* I heard him swear clear as day.

Cal hurried to catch up to me. "I about gave you the eight," he said with a laugh.

"I'd have given it back."

"No, you wouldn't have."

*He was right.*

My hole-out must have flustered Josh because he bladed a wedge across the green and didn't get up and down from there. He managed a bogey. And my lead was back to four.

In typical Josh fashion he took the next tee box and set up to hit, only to be pulled back by his caddie. "You lost honors," he whispered.

Josh cursed again, in embarrassment this time, glared at his caddie and picked his ball up. "Lucky shot," he muttered brushing against me as we passed each other.

"How you feeling?" Cal asked me.

"Fine. Why?"

"Drivable par four today—only playing 292." Cal was examining the yardage book. "Pin's in the middle of the green. Wind ain't hurting—"

"You're going to let me hit driver?"

"I think you could. Four shot lead… "

I was a little reluctant to change my approach, even with that lead, but Cal seemed to like the idea. "Shoot. Sure, I'll go for it."

Cal gave me the driver and I let the ball fly. I've never had a 300 yard drive before, not to my knowledge anyway, and I didn't get one here.

*It went exactly 292 yards.*

I saw the people around the green jumping up and down like mad, heard the roar and then heard Cal beside me mumble "Mary, mother of—" before he was cut off by Josh's best Samuel L. Jackson imitation.

*Wow.* I looked at Cal with a questioning look. "Did that—"

He nodded with a huge grin. "Yessir."

There were a hundred or so people following Josh and I around and they were all going crazy. Par three aces were rare. Par four aces were like unicorns—*and should really be called that.* No one ever *ever* expects to see one… or really even considers them within the realm of possibility.

"Wow… now *that* was a lucky shot." I said for Josh's benefit, winking at him. His mouth was still open, his head shaking back and forth like Lee Trevino's in Happy Gilmore. *Okay, so I've seen that movie a few dozen times.*

I'd have bet my life I couldn't do that again, not in ten thousand shots. It was the first driver I hit that day and ended up being the last. After Josh struggled to another double I had a nine shot advantage.

Josh had nothing to say to me on the next tee. He nearly walked a full circle around the tee box just to stay away from me. I managed to birdie sixteen, seventeen and eighteen for a back nine 29. Josh got a par on each. I was up twelve.

On the front I bogeyed the first, got pars on two and three and then pulled off five consecutive birdies. That put me at a 28 through eight on the front and a 57 overall. I needed a birdie to shoot a 60. I wound up with a bogey for a 29-33 = 62. Another 62. *Where was this coming from?*

Josh's caddie shook my hand again after the round, even told Cal he was "lucky". His golfer had already left the 18th green without a word or handshake for anyone. I never asked what Josh shot, but Kate said it was a 72. Par. Good enough to keep him in second.

At dinner Cal sat down next to me and pulled out the scorecard. "I know you don't care to go over these after a round, but I wanted to show you something." He pointed at the scores consecutively from hole eleven through eighteen and then back to the first. I'd scored 5, 4, 3, 2, 1, 2, 3, 4, 5 over that nine-hole stretch. I smiled. That *was* interesting.

"Heckuva round, son," Calvin gently patted my shoulder. And that was the last he said of it around me.

Kate was much more effusive, much less restrained. She kissed me darn near a hundred times and was so excited on the phone calls to Ken and later to Carrie that I had to leave the hotel room—both times.

Josh, now 16 strokes out of first, withdrew from the tournament with an "undisclosed injury". He flew back to New York that night.

I held myself together on Saturday for an even par 72, winning the event by a dozen strokes. I left Phoenix just as my Patriots had four months earlier: on top of the world.

## STELLAR 48 – "Summer Break"

I broke my arm on July 6, 2016. And let me be clear… it wasn't to get out of a golf tournament. It royally messed up my life. That's when, using Ken's nautical conversion of a popular saying, "The ship hit the sand." That's when, with my game at its all-time best, playing golf was suddenly out of the question. For the first time in my life I had two official handicaps. *And both involved the use of the word "scratch."*

I'm not comfortable discussing how it happened. Enough stories have already been written on that. But let's just say having your arm in a cast during the summer is about the least convenient thing in the world.

Of course it was my right arm. It couldn't have been my left. I did everything with my right arm *before* that day. From July 7th to September 5th I did almost nothing with it.

The first week I mostly spent feeling sorry for myself. Everyone was worrying about me. The police wanted to talk to me. The doctors wanted to see me. The reporters were constantly calling. Seemed everyone wanted to see me, to talk to me… everyone except Lauren, that is. She apparently didn't care about me at all.

With me out of commission for a while Nick filled in at the marina. Ken was paying him well, and Nick was a fast learner of everything. The position quickly transitioned from a "couple hours a day, a couple days a week" to full-time by the end of July. He was always busy. I was always bored. Nick was never home. Instead of getting by on Madden and Call of Duty with him, I was stuck playing UNO and Yahtzee with Avery. Don't get me wrong, I love her to death, but that kid wins at *everything*, and that gets old *really* fast. So yeah, I was jealous of Nick and his daily activity list… jealous of his life. In fact, I noticed I was starting to get jealous of all kinds of things… really strange things; kids jumping rope, cats climbing trees, people shaking hands, mothers singing "Little Bunny Foo Foo" to their babies—anything that involved the movement of right hands. *Or paws.* I was losing my mind.

Being useless and alone all summer gave me plenty of time for thinking, and most of that time was spent thinking of (hmmm)… Lauren.

With Nick admittedly still stuck on her, and me openly denying I was, it was an interesting time of my life to be sure. You can lie to other people all you want, and if you're convincing you might get away with it. But you don't get away with lying to yourself. Your heart and mind know you all too well. Lauren was the girl I wanted to marry.

I already knew that at fifteen. I also knew that if I couldn't figure out a way to get past her… I was going to be alone forever.

I broke my arm on July 6th, and it messed up my life. But I'd do it again in a heartbeat.

## ←★★★★★ NICK BIRCH ★★★★★→
### Journal (Part 1 of 3)

### ←Wednesday, July 6, 2016→

Sweet sixteen. What's so sweet about it?

Okay, so that's a Stellar line, who got it from Avery, who got it from some grumpy guppy on one of her favorite Nickelodeon cartoons.

Anyway… My birthday was Monday. Lauren's was yesterday. Normally, since I'm only required to write once a week, I save my writing for Sunday. Can't do that this week. Not after last night.

Lauren was having a bonfire on the beach, just off Sunset Avenue near River Bait & Boats, for her birthday party this year. It was a beautiful night. So bright it was hard to believe the moon wasn't out—that the stars could give off that much light. Stellar and I had been invited, but so had Josh, Caleb, Elliott, Taryn, Caitlin and everyone else in my class who Stellar didn't want to see, hear or be anywhere near. He had decided not to go—to hang out at the marina and wait for Ken to get back from a night-fishing charter. I made the fateful decision to swing by and try to change his mind.

I've known Stellar for a few years now. He's the kid that makes split second decisions the right way—determining almost immediately the difference between instinct and intelligence. *Occasionally there's no difference at all.* I can't say I've ever known anyone else like that. He's been "wrong place wrong time" on so many occasions in his life that it only makes sense he'd get a few of the opposite as well. There was the entire Avery story. And then there was last night. *The definition of "right place right time."*

Because I haven't written much in my journal yet—this is only my fourth entry—there are a few things I should probably establish. 1. I HATE writing by hand. (*Why couldn't this assignment have been a blog?*) 2. Stellar would pretty much end our friendship if he were to read this post. 3. I'm typically an excellent swimmer. And 4. Today is the first time I've ever had to put the word "typically" in that sentence.

I found Stellar out on the docks last night; putter in hand, tapping a golf ball back and forth between a couple lampposts. His dog, Squirrel, was down there with him, perched at the end of the dock watching the occasional boat pass.

"Aren't you worried about losing the ball?"

Stellar glanced back at me and smiled. "No. It's a floater and I've got my ball retriever just in case." He pointed to the long metal stick leaning against one of the lampposts. "What are you doing here? I figured you'd be at the party. It is kind of yours, too, you know?"

"Yeah. Mom told me I should at least stop by for some cake... since she bought it."

"What time is it, Nick?"

I looked at my watch. "Half past ten. Why?"

"Couldn't you just say 10:30 like a normal person?"

"You want to talk about normal?"

Stellar laughed. "How 'bout we don't. Ken said he'd be back by now. Wonder what's keeping him."

It wasn't ten seconds later that we heard screeching tires just north of us on the sharp bend of Sunset Avenue right next to the canal. We both spun and watched as a car slid sideways under the streetlamps and flipped once, crashing through the guardrail, and hurdling into the canal.

This is what I'm talking about regarding Stellar's instincts. I stood there stunned for a second, but Stellar was already running down the edge of the canal towards the spot where the car had entered the water. I yelled at him to wait for me and took off after him, but he didn't look back.

I saw Stellar run and jump off the edge of the canal into the water like he was cliff jumping. "Stellar, wait... "

Doesn't do much good to yell that to someone who is already in the air.

I was only twenty yards or so behind him and quickly caught up to where he'd gone in. All I could see below me were bubbles and darkness.

I mentioned earlier that swimming is one of my greatest strengths. What I left out is that I have a paralyzing fear of dark water. I wanted to help Stellar, but...

Stellar is not a fantastic swimmer. But one thing he can do is hold his breath—he can make it up to 90 seconds at the pool. So I started counting. That's how I "helped."

The canal was about twenty feet deep here, but as my eyes adjusted to the darkness I could make out two dim lights, presumably the car's headlights, shining up from the bottom. My best friend was down there somewhere. He'd gone in without the slightest hesitation. I should've been able to join him, to help him, but I stood frozen in place... counting.

========== NICK BIRCH ==========

## ←★★★★★ TARYN DAHL ★★★★★→
### Letter

I never liked Stellar Parker. What kind of a name is Stellar anyway? Sounded like someone pretty full of himself. Turns out he wasn't—*nowhere* close—but I didn't know that at the time.

I remember when he moved into the Parker's garage apartment—long before I'd ever met him. He was shy, he was quiet, I thought he was a pervert. My little sister told me one day that he'd admitted to seeing me and Lauren naked—that he'd been spying on us from the apartment over the Parker's garage with binoculars.

I later found out that wasn't exactly true. He'd never seen either of us naked—kind of me I guess, but not "*naked* naked" if you know what I mean. And even then he hadn't been spying on me. He just happened to see me changing a couple times and what boy wouldn't have watched? I'm not defending him, or what he did, but I also shouldn't have done what I did. I spread a bunch of rumors around about him, many of them involving the word "pervert." I got Caleb, Elliott and Josh to beat him up one day, and told them I'd give them each $20 to do so. I encouraged them to keep roughing him up, even got them to slash his bike tires once—which didn't quite go as planned—but acted like it was all Josh's idea. I wanted to let Stellar know who was boss in our neighborhood, to send the message that you don't mess with us. You don't mess with me.

My agenda would have worked if it weren't for Lauren. She felt sorry for him. She thought he was kind of cute. *I thought she needed to get her eyes checked... or entertain a full-fledged neurological exam.* She actually even liked the pimple-faced kid. She told me I needed to stop bullying him if I wanted to stay her friend. That's a heck of a statement from someone you've considered your best friend your entire life, taking sides with someone she hadn't even spoken to yet.

I tried to manipulate her, making up lies about Stellar to her, too, but she didn't budge. I didn't get it. I didn't see it. But I also didn't care, because I'd always liked Josh and he'd always had his heart and eyes set on Lauren. They'd been "boyfriend-girlfriend" since well before either of them understood what that actually meant, and yet Lauren had never looked at Josh like she looked at Stellar. She'd never spoken of Josh like she spoke of Stellar. I also didn't get that. *She didn't even know him!* But like I said, if it opened the door to Josh for me, even the slightest bit, I wasn't going to miss the opportunity to slip in.

Josh was special. He was taller and more muscular than everyone else our age—even if he was the oldest kid in our class. He had this chiseled look and the cutest dimples. He was drop-dead gorgeous.

He was also the richest kid any of us knew. He was the only one in our class with an *indoor* swimming pool at his house. His parents were never home, so he could do whatever he wanted whenever he wanted to. We held some pretty epic swim parties at his place. He had anything and everything any of us wanted, including alcohol, and most of our parents wouldn't have noticed if we were drunk as fish. *Except Lauren's and Nick's.*

Josh had an older brother, Skip, who used to buy us alcohol for our parties. Skip also had a car. When Josh turned sixteen Skip started letting him drive that car when his parents weren't home. As a result, Josh was twenty degrees cooler than every other boy any of us knew. As a sophomore in high school we all held him up as if he was a sophomore in college. It was pretty ridiculous. My mom once referred to him as "The Fonz"—something I didn't understand then, but find rather appropriate in hindsight now. Every boy wanted to be him, well, most boys anyway, and every girl wanted to be with him. Well, every girl but one I guess.

We were having a beach party for Lauren's 16th birthday on July 5th, 2016 not far from Ray's Bait & Boats. Josh's brother was home and his parents were out, so he let Josh take the car—trunk loaded with beer—down to the beach. There were about fifty kids and no parents at the party, so it got pretty wild pretty fast. I don't know for certain, but if I had to guess I'd say Josh was already drunk when he drove Caitlin, Caleb, Elliott and me down to the beach. We didn't see a problem with it at the time, couldn't imagine the potential consequences.

He'd had a rough few weeks since Stellar had whupped him in Arizona. I don't know much about golf, but I know Josh had played in three events since then and done terrible in each of them including the one the past weekend in Texas. He came back in a sour mood on Sunday and had been looking forward to letting loose that night.

Josh knew that Lauren had a soft spot in her heart for Stellar, it was probably, *no, definitely*, the biggest source of conflict between the two of them. Josh told everyone that he and Lauren were dating, but you'd never have heard Lauren say that. I was her best friend. Trust me, I'd have known.

When Nick asked her out at Christmas she implied that she couldn't because of Josh, but it wasn't because she was dating him. It was because she was afraid of what Josh would do to Stellar if he didn't feel like he had to be nice to Stellar for Lauren's sake.

Lauren liked Nick enough to where she'd have gone out with him. Nick was almost as handsome as Josh but infinitely more kind and genuine. She'd known Nick forever and liked him enough, but not the way she liked Stellar. Again, I totally didn't get it, but that was Lauren.

So the party that night was a little awkward on that front. Nick had been avoiding Lauren for months, pretty much since he'd asked her out at Christmas, but their parents had still tried to set up this party together. *As they had for the past fourteen years.* I knew Stellar wouldn't be there even though it was technically Nick's birthday party, too. But I was curious as to whether or not Nick would show. By ten o'clock he still hadn't.

Around ten o'clock I was made aware that we were out of beer, and Josh was trashed—he couldn't have driven under any circumstance. I was more than a little pissed at him at that point for basically ignoring me the whole party. I'd been intending to have him all to myself that night. Instead, he'd been all over Lauren the past couple hours. She was tolerating him, as she usually did, but I could tell he was getting worse, and for perhaps the first time I started to see some of what she didn't like in him.

I was with Josh when he called his brother and told him he'd pay him triple for more beer and not tell their parents about "some prostitute named Hallie or Howie"... something like that. *His slurred speech was hard to understand.* His brother agreed to the deal but needed someone to come pick it all up, so Josh volunteered me.

I was torn. I didn't want to leave Lauren with him, but I also didn't want to watch him with her anymore. I also knew there were only two people who were sober enough to drive. Lauren—who would have never driven a car without a license—and me. Josh putting his arm around me sealed the deal. "Okay, I'll go," I said.

I still should have refused. I still should have known better. My leaving to go get that beer was a bad move for so many reasons. 1. I'd never driven by myself before. 2. I'd never driven at night. 3. Lauren had begged me not to go—not to leave her with Josh, and 4. I was sixteen and going to pick up beer for a party to impress a guy. *It takes incredibly low self-confidence to be so desperate.*

I drove slowly to his house. As far as I know I did everything right. Skip helped me load up the trunk and then disappeared back into the house with some super short, blond, half-dressed chick. *Perhaps that was the prostitute Josh had referred to?*

I started driving back towards the beach, and my driving confidence was high. I had the radio on now and the windows down. I'd remembered to buckle my seat belt and even drove past two cop cars without drawing even a glance. *Piece of cake.* And then I turned onto Sunset Avenue.

I drove past Ray's Bait & Boats and turned right and then my cell phone screen lit up and I reached over for it. Somehow in the process of picking up the phone I leaned my foot on the gas and the car took off. Things happened so fast and so slow at once. I had enough time to note that the one-word text was from Lauren—"Help"—before I dropped the phone and whipped my head up. Sudden panic took over as I saw the guardrails approaching. I simultaneously turned the steering wheel sharp left and tried to apply the brake… but I missed the brake and punched the gas pedal further to the floor.

The tires started squealing, and I began screaming. The car went sideways and airborne, crashing through the guardrail and launching into the canal.

The car hit the water hard, the impact slamming my head against the doorframe. If the cold water hadn't shocked me as it poured in through the open windows I'd likely have been knocked completely out.

I continued to panic, struggling against my seatbelt, trying desperately to unfasten it but it wouldn't budge. I felt like I'd been down there in the dark for minutes already. I knew I was dead. And then my door was opening, and someone was unfastening my seatbelt. As an arm slipped around my chest and pulled me free from the car I blacked out.

When I came to, Nick was kissing me. For a second I wondered if it was a dream. Then I realized he was giving me CPR. And then I threw up—or at least spit out a ton of water. I coughed as Nick backed away and breathed a huge sigh of relief. Nick had saved my life.

Suddenly I was aware of someone else lying beside me. I shook my head to clear the cobwebs and turned my face towards the body next to mine. It was Stellar. *Wait a second...* Nick was totally dry. Stellar was soaked. *Stellar had saved my life?*

Then there were lights and sirens coming from everywhere. Nick had dialed 9-1-1 when we were in the water.

I should have been able to say something other than "thank you" at that moment. My mind was swimming with things I wanted to say. But that was all I whispered. "Thank you."

The ambulance took Stellar and me away. Stellar had landed on a piece of the guardrail when he dove in and broken his arm, and Nick stayed behind with the cops to give his version of the story.

Lauren's "Help" text was forgotten for the moment, and every grudge I'd ever had against Stellar was permanently put to rest. I reached over and took his hand.

"Ow," he said.

"Thank you," I replied. "Seriously."

*Talk about "right place, right time."*

========== TARYN DAHL ==========

## ←★★★★★ NICK BIRCH ★★★★★→
### Journal (Part 2 of 3)

### ←Sunday, July 10, 2016→

Josh made a lot of mistakes Tuesday night. He's paying for all of them right now. After Taryn came clean about what happened, the police flew out to the beach and broke up the party. They even took Josh away in handcuffs. *Yes, that made the front page of the local paper.*

His driver's permit was revoked. He received a steep fine for public intoxication, or something like that, and for a few other violations. *Unfortunately his family wouldn't even feel the financial toll.* He was grounded indefinitely and suspended from all AJGA sanctioned golf events for a year. His parents were humiliated, and his brother was booked for providing alcohol to minors and soliciting a prostitute. It was a major mess, a big time black eye for one of the "Royal Families" of Southampton. Seems immeasurable wealth and political connections only provide you with so much immunity to real life.

Immunity. Josh messed up there, too. He took things a little too far with Lauren, probably figuring he could get away with it—being who he was. He had tried to force himself on her at the beach, and she'd fought him off. In drunken anger he'd closed-fist punched her in the face, twice, which was what had prompted the "Help" text to Taryn. Lauren's parents hadn't taken that news lightly, but they also hadn't gone public with it yet. The outside world didn't know about that despicable side of Josh, yet.

Lauren told me Josh *and his parents* came to their house Wednesday night and spent almost an hour apologizing and pleading with her parents to not press charges. Mr. and Mrs. Chambers didn't want to send a message of tolerance in any way, but ultimately they left it up to Lauren. For whatever reason, she let it go. She accepted Josh's tearful apology. She said she could forgive him, if he got help.

*Help?* The help he needed involved his roleplaying a piñata in a circle of people with baseball bats. I couldn't believe it. This was the one opportunity to shut that punk up, to take away his power—humiliate him as he'd humiliated so many. I'd have jumped at the chance. But Lauren had her reasons—*or reason*—and my own rage towards what Josh had done to her blinded me to why she didn't want the whole world to know about it.

Mr. and Mrs. Chambers did however issue a restraining order for Josh. He was not to communicate with Lauren at school or anywhere else in any context or capacity for a full year. Our school assisted that order, publicly stating in Friday's paper that Josh had been expelled. *Hallelujah!* That world, at least, would be a better place.

But enough about Josh.

They tested Taryn's blood alcohol level at the hospital, and she was 0.01 below the legal limit. *One of only two kids at the party that passed—including Lauren, of course.* Taryn still got in a lot of trouble for the drinking—especially the combining it with driving part—from her parents. But she wasn't dead. She should have been, probably would have been had it just been me there, but thanks to Stellar she was still alive. Her parents visited Stellar at the hospital Wednesday afternoon while I was there, and though I stepped into the hall, I overheard plenty of weeping, gratitude and even apologies—for what the broken arm now meant for Stellar and his summer.

Stellar, of course, blew it all off. And he wanted nothing to do with the media side of the ordeal. The mayor wanted to have a televised ceremony to present him a medal. *Right.* Stellar got the medal on Thursday, but there was no ceremony. He never did make a public statement of any kind. Stellar kept his thoughts and feelings to himself, except for when he told the Dahl's. "I did what anyone would have done." *Yeah... not quite.* I knew from being there that absolutely wasn't true.

I also knew the details would get out somehow, and they did. It took considerable effort from both Ken and Kate to keep the news vans off their lawn and the cameras away from their home—away from Stellar. Finally, yesterday, the last of the news crews and vehicles left. The local media world had moved on to another story.

Curiously Lauren hadn't stopped by to see Stellar yet. I hadn't even seen her since several days before the party, and had only spoken to her by phone on Friday afternoon. That's when she told me what Josh had done to her. She told me her parents were keeping her in the house and out of the public eye, and made me promise not to mention any of what she'd shared with me to Stellar.

"I will tell him when I'm ready to talk about it," she had said. "Nick, I mean it. It better come from me."

As I already mentioned I was furious at Josh. And *naturally* I wanted to tell Stellar everything immediately. But I agreed to honor Lauren's request, figuring she just needed a couple more days, even though I didn't understand why. *Was it a beauty thing? Insecurity? Did she not want Stellar to see the bruises on her face? Was that all? Was she worried he'd think less of her? (Laughable)*

In any case, I knew Stellar was assuming Lauren's absence meant she didn't care. That's 100% how he was taking it, and I couldn't really blame him. *Though I knew better than anyone that wasn't true.* It's been five days now, and she still hasn't come by. That would bother me too. Frankly, I'm running out of reasons to give him, and starting to feel pretty guilty about what I know.

*What would you have done, Mrs. Willett? What should I have done?* Knowing and being so close to both sides, it's the hardest secret I've ever had to keep—other than liking Lauren of course—but I've kept my mouth shut so far. Ultimately, I've done as Lauren asked, which means that ultimately… I'm failing Stellar *miserably.*

When I got off the phone with Lauren on Friday I went over to the Parker's house. Kate met me at the door. "Mrs. Chambers just called me," she said.

*What did that have to do with me?* "Oh yeah?"

"She says you just talked to Lauren… that Lauren told you what Josh did."

"Uhh… yeah." *So her mom was listening to our conversation?*

"You can't tell Miles what happened to her—do you understand? You can't say a thing to him. Nick, you know he'll sprint over there immediately, and you know how Lauren would feel about that."

Truthfully, I still had intended to tell Stellar at that point, and was just going to make him promise not to throw me under the bus. Kate actually changed my mind. Picturing Stellar tearing out of the house in a panic sealed the deal. "Yeah, I got it. I won't say anything."

Maybe I'm being naïve. A part of me suspects this is about more than just Stellar seeing Lauren. Stellar wouldn't care what she looks like—he'd think she's beautiful no matter what. But he'd want to kill Josh.

*Ah.*

Maybe I was right. Maybe this was about something else entirely.

I hung out with Stellar Friday night, all day yesterday and today. Not once did he bring up his heroics from Tuesday night… or what I had *(or hadn't)* done to help. *Well… I guess he did thank me for dialing 9-1-1.* Taryn came over after dinner last night—Saturday—to check on him, and ended up staying pretty late playing UNO with him, Avery and me. *That pigtailed little rascal won every game.*

When Taryn had to leave, Kate and Stellar walked her to the front door. I watched Taryn hug Stellar, and heard her say, "I'm really sorry about your arm."

"I'll live," he replied.

"I will too." She hugged him again. "Thanks to you."

========== NICK BIRCH ==========

## STELLAR 49 – "August in Suffolk County"

I hadn't seen Lauren in what felt like forever. She was conspicuously absent among those who had come by to check on me. I didn't want attention from anyone else for what I'd done but, if I'm being honest, I was hoping for some attention from Lauren. I was hoping she'd come thank me for saving her best friend. I thought it was a given that she would sooner or later. But she didn't *ever*. I knew Nick had spoken with her several times, that Kate had spoken with her parents, that Taryn had even asked her to come by, but she still hadn't. At first it just hurt. Then it made me mad.

When the doorbell rang on August 5th at 10:30 a.m. I was still in bed. I heard Kate answer the door through the vent in the floor, since the front door was directly below my room, and heard the words that could get me showered and dressed in world record time. "Hi, Lauren."

I flew down the stairs and there she was—the most beautiful girl in the world—in cut-off jean shorts and a plaid shirt over a white cami. "Oh… hi," I said. "I didn't know you were here." *Liar liar.*

She smiled. "I hope that's okay?"

"Sure." My voice cracked and I cleared my throat. *Come on!* "Sure—of course it is."

Kate stood up. "I'll leave you two alone."

"Thank you, Mrs. Parker."

"Of course, Lauren. It's good to see you."

"Can I get you anything?" I asked. "A drink or something to eat? Are you hungry?"

She held up the glass in one hand and the cookie in her other hand—*they'd been there all along.* "I think I'm good." She giggled.

*Calm. The. Heck. Down.* "Are you looking for Nick?"

"No." She shook her head. "I just saw him at the marina. I came here for you. I came here to see you."

I needed to sit down. "Oh," I said, in all my infinite wisdom.

"Do you want to go somewhere with me?"

*Anywhere in the whole wide world. I can pack for life in minutes.* "Sure… I guess. I mean yes." I shook my head. Idiot! "What do you have in mind?"

"My mom and dad are outside waiting for me. We're going to Block Island. I wanted to see if you'd come with me."

"Taryn coming, too?" Lauren always took Taryn out there with her.

"Not today." Lauren shook her head.

*Just me and you?*

She seemed to read my mind. "Just us. Well… and my parents, of course."

Block Island is only about fifteen miles east of Montauk. It's actually part of Rhode Island. I've been out there countless times with Ken—it's where he typically picks up bait and fuel when he's running low on a charter trip. There are several ferries that run back and forth from a few ports around here, but most of Southampton heads there via Montauk.

Block Island is a popular day trip for kids at our school during the summer. *Albeit an expensive one*. The island is only ten square miles with a population just over 1,000, but it has great biking and hiking trails, lighthouses, rich fishing holes and tons of wide-open beaches. I've heard it described as "romantic without the crowds, but still beautiful when packed", and most people have no idea how easy it is to get out there.

As I said, I've been out there a dozen times but I've never explored the island. *Similar to counting a state or country as "visited" when you've only been to their airport.* Ken and Kate had spent the night out there on several occasions—it was their annual Valentine's Day escape—but I never had. I'd never left the port.

I turned to ask Kate if I could go, but before I'd even spoken a word she called out from the kitchen. "You guys have fun. Just don't get your cast wet."

"We won't be swimming, Mrs. Parker," Lauren called back. "Don't worry."

*No swimming?* There went seeing Lauren in a swimsuit. "Bye, Kate," I said.

Squirrel followed us to the front door. "I love your dog."

"We… " I swallowed hard, catching myself before I almost really stuck my foot in my mouth. *Careful!* "Squirrel clearly loves you, too."

Lauren's parents sat inside on the ferry ride over to Block Island. Lauren and I went out on the deck and stood by the rails, watching the birds circle and the waves splash on the rocks, as we pulled away from Montauk.

"I love this ride," Lauren said.

I glanced sideways at her. She had her sunglasses on; head tossed back, long curly blonde hair blowing in the wind, her straw hat clutched in her hand. She had three hair-ties on her left wrist and easily could have pulled her hair up, but I was *sooo* thankful she didn't. She looked like a model standing in front of one of those giant blowing fans. *Stunning!* She turned towards me and smiled, those million watts almost frying my internal circuit board. "Yeah. It's awesome," I managed.

"So how's your arm?"

"Orange." I tapped my neon cast.

“I see that.” She laughed. *I’d have listed the rest of the colors of the rainbow for more laughs like that.* “Why’d you go with that color?”

“They were out of pink.”

There was that beautiful sound again. She thought I was kidding, and I let her think that, but I was serious. I’d let Avery pick the color at the hospital, and thank God they were out of pink. I smiled at Lauren. I wanted to ask her what this was about? Why did she ask me to come along with her? *Why me?* But I also didn’t want to spoil the moment with my voice.

“I’ve missed you,” she said suddenly.

I almost choked. “What?” *Did she say what I think she just said?*

She paused before saying it again. “I said I’ve missed you.”

*Yep.* “You could’ve come see me,” I replied

She nodded. “Yeah. About that… I’m sorry. I could have.”

I wanted to just accept the apology and move on, but I couldn’t. “So why didn’t you?”

“Stellar… I—”

“You don’t have to tell me if you don’t want to.” *Did you just cut her off? Shut up, stupid!*

“Did Nick ever say anything to you about me?”

*Wait, what?* “Uhh… well… I know he asked you out at Christmas. I know you said no and broke his heart. I know he’s basically had a crush on you since he even knew what that word meant.” *Why are you talking about Nick? Shut up about Nick!* “I know he would do anything for you—”

“Yes,” she interrupted. “You’re right. He would. But that’s not what I’m talking about. None of that. Nick never said anything to you about me and Josh?”

“Nothing I should probably repeat.”

Lauren laughed again. “I think you’re answering my question by not really answering my question.”

“Okay.” *I was lost.* “I’m not quite sure what I’m supposed to say.”

“Nick didn’t tell you what happened at my birthday party? What Josh did to me at my birthday party?”

“No.” I was suddenly both concerned and pissed at Nick, and I didn’t even know why yet. “What did he do?”

Lauren spilled everything then—everything about what happened that night. *Everything Nick knew and didn’t tell me.* She told me what Josh had done to her. I was ready to jump off the ferry and swim the seven or eight miles back to Montauk to go after him. She joked—at least I think she was joking—that was why she’d taken me out to Block Island to have this conversation.

I was mad at Josh. I'd never liked him—not him, Caleb, Elliott or any of the other minions who hung out with him. But now my feelings for Josh went *well* beyond dislike. Everyone who knew me considered me one of the least violent people in the world and yet those who knew me best had intentionally chosen not to say anything to me about this for fear of what I'd do in response. What did that say? Better yet… what did it say that they'd probably made the right decision?

I honestly didn't know if I should feel betrayed or grateful. Nick knew all of this. Kate knew all of this. Taryn knew all of this, Ken, Carrie, probably even Calvin and James—all the people I'd spent the most time with the past three weeks. They knew why Lauren wasn't coming by to see me, and they all let me believe what I was believing—that she just didn't care for me. Sure, they offered up some possible explanations, but none of them were credible—not to me. Lauren would have come to see me. The girl who gave me that incredible drawing... she'd have come to see me. I knew that. And when she didn't it hurt me like no fractured bone could. It broke my heart.

I was most mad at Nick. *No doubt.* And then Lauren told me about her conversation with him at RB's that morning—before she'd come over and invited me to Block Island. Then I couldn't be mad at Nick.

Then I couldn't be mad at anyone.

## ←★★★★★ LAUREN CHAMBERS ★★★★★→
**Journal Entry**

**←Friday. August 5, 2016→**

I rode my bike to Ray's Bait & Boats just after sunrise to find Nick. We needed to have a face-to-face talk. He was helping load Ken's charter boat when I pulled up, and came over as soon as he saw me. "Hey. What are you doing here?"

After a few minutes of pretending I wasn't there for any specific reason, I finally addressed the elephant on the dock. *I don't mean Nick.* "I wanted to ask you something," I said.

"Sure. Anything," he replied.

"Hypothetically speaking—"

"Lauren." He cut me off. "Just say it."

"Okay." I took a deep breath, before basically continuing in hypotheticals anyway. "If I asked you to do something I knew you wouldn't like—that might even hurt you—but you knew it was what I really wanted, would you do it for me?"

I watched his face cloud over. "Lauren, I'm not sure I'm following your code here, but are you asking me if I would respect whatever it is you want enough to let you have it?"

I nodded. "Pretty much."

"How long have you known me?" he asked.

"Fifteen years."

"And you have to ask that?"

I nodded again. "I do for this."

"Okay."

"Do you remember when you asked me out?"

"Like it was yesterday. That's kind of my point. I think I've proven how much I care for *and* respect you."

I swallowed hard. *He wasn't going to make this easy on me.* "You're right. You have. But at the time it was implied that I was saying 'no' to dating you because of Josh."

"Right." Nick looked away. "Which you didn't deny."

*True*. I hadn't. "But it wasn't because I was *dating* Josh."

"Then why—"

"Because there was someone else." I cut him off—a little harsher than I'd intended to.

Nick took a deep breath. "Stellar?"

I nodded. "Yes."

"So why not just tell me that then?"

"Nick, I don't know. I didn't know what I was supposed to do. I've liked you since I was little—always thought you and I were going to get married. When I played with dolls I'd be Barbie and you were Ken. Other than Taryn you've always been my closest friend. I never wanted to hurt you in any way—"

"And you don't think that did?"

"Nick, I know it did. I said I didn't want to hurt you but I also didn't want to lose you."

"How would you lose me if you were dating me?"

I could tell he was angry and probably with good reason. This wasn't going like I'd hoped. "Nick, I'm sorry."

"So why are you here?"

"Becau—"

"Wait." He held up his hand. "I think I know why. That riddle you asked earlier was about this—you're here to ask me for permission to date Stellar. Aren't you?"

I didn't nod or shake my head. My eyes had filled with tears, and I briefly saw Nick's bitter expression soften. I reached out for his arm and he didn't pull away. "Nick, it wouldn't be right for me, considering how I feel about you, not to," I whispered.

Nick had tears in his eyes too, but he wiped them away. He sighed deeply and kicked the ground. "I want to be mad at you, Lauren, but I can't be," he said bluntly.

"I understand."

"I feel the same way about Stellar," he continued, "but I know everything he's done for me. And I also know, if that boy knows anything at all about love, that he's deeply in love with you… no matter how many times he tells me otherwise."

I didn't know what to say to that. I hadn't yet considered what I felt for Stellar to be love. I just knew it was a different feeling than any I'd had for any other boy ever—including Nick.

"Nick—"

"He thinks you hate him, you know?"

"What?"

"You're the only person in the world he cares about who *didn't* go see him after he broke his arm… after he saved your best friend's life."

"Yeah, but—"

"Lauren, you made me promise not to tell him what Josh did to you, and then you never came over to tell him yourself. You've put me in a terrible position for a full month now. You did the same thing to Kate. You've basically made us lie to him every single day."

"Nick, I know, I'm sorry, but—"

"Lauren, I don't think you get it."

"No, Nick… I don't think *you* get it. Do you know what Stellar would have done to Josh if he'd found out? If he'd seen my face?"

"No. I don't."

"What would *you* have done?"

"Man, put me in a room with Josh and I'd have killed him."

"You wouldn't have, and you know that. But Stellar… with a broken right arm… what would he have done? What *could* he have done?"

Nick didn't answer right away, but when he did it was clear he'd thought this through—probably long before today. "Lauren, no one knows what Stellar would have done to Josh, or what he will do to him if you do actually tell him what happened. I can't say for certain that you made the wrong choice. If I really thought you were wrong, I could have told him at any point. I *would* have told him."

I knew that was true. I was actually kind of surprised he hadn't.

"Okay," Nick muttered.

"Okay?" I asked. "What do you mean?

"I care for you and respect you enough to let you have what you want."

"What does this mean for us?"

"Lauren, listen to me. Stellar is my best friend. If the situation were reversed he'd be standing here saying the same thing I am. *Go for it.* Stellar is *always* that selfless—whether it hurts him or not." Nick shook his head. "You and I will be fine. We always have been. I'll always be here for you whatever you need—even when it hurts me."

I stepped up to him and hugged him tightly. He didn't hug me back, but he didn't push me away either. When I stepped back and looked up at him he had tears in his eyes again. I had an awful ache in my chest as tears filled my eyes, too. "I'm sorry, Nick. I really am."

"Don't be," he smiled down at me. "He's wanted you forever." As I turned towards my bike I overheard him add in a whisper, "I've just wanted you longer."

Mom and Dad were planning on taking Taryn and me out to Block Island that morning. When I got back home I cornered my mom and asked if it was all right if I invited Stellar instead. I'd filled her in on my feelings for Nick and Stellar in the weeks she'd kept me home, so my request didn't catch her completely by surprise. "Are you sure?" she asked me. "What about Nick?"

"I took care of it," I answered.

*And yes… I was sure.*

When we arrived at the Parker's around 10:30 I rang the doorbell and Kate answered the door. When she said my name I heard footsteps pound overhead and the shower go on upstairs. I saw Kate smile, and it was all I could do not to laugh out loud. *Guess Stellar knew I was here.*

I could feel my heart in my throat as Kate and I waited for him to come down. Kate was asking me questions that I'm sure I barely answered adequately, and then Stellar came casually strolling down the stairs.

"Oh… hey, Lauren," he said. *Like he didn't know I was there.*

He tripped all over his tongue for a couple minutes before I asked him to go to Block Island with us. I could tell he was fighting mixed emotions. No doubt he was a little hurt and confused about why it had taken me so long to come by. But it was also clear he wanted to go. Kate made it easy for him. She all but shoved him out the door with me.

On the ferry ride from Montauk I told Stellar all about what Josh had done to me at my birthday party—well, almost all of it. I told him about being punched in the face, but didn't elaborate on all the groping.

I could sense that Stellar wanted to go after Josh—he even seemed willing to jump off the boat and swim back to Montauk to get it over with. I had to talk him off that ledge.

I could see him looking at me throughout our entire conversation, but Stellar didn't look at me like most boys did. He was fixated on my face—on my eyes, my lips, my smile—and my hair. His eyes didn't wander much that I saw. He looked at me like Nick looked at me. He made me feel safe, made me feel special, made me feel loved.

It wasn't lost on me what Nick sacrificed today. I had no doubts on how he felt about me. But if I didn't follow my heart, I'd never know what this was that I was feeling for Stellar. So I told Stellar about my conversation with Nick from this morning. I told him what Nick had said, and then I asked Stellar if he'd be willing to go out with me.

He didn't say yes on the boat, but he also didn't say no. He just laughed and shook his head. He seemed stunned, overwhelmed, and I didn't want him to commit to anything until he was ready… either way. We had a full day of exploring ahead of us, and I just wanted to have fun with him. I slid my hand over his on the rail and he wrapped his fingers in mine. He squeezed my hand and smiled at me as the horn sounded over our heads. "Welcome to Block Island," the captain's voice boomed.

"Well, shall we?" Stellar asked me.

He could have been asking about any number of things with that general question, but whatever he meant by it I was okay with. "Yes," I said. "Definitely."

========== LAUREN CHAMBERS ==========

## STELLAR 50 – "Block Island"

Lauren asked me out. *Twice actually.* I didn't say yes the first time. Initially I was planning to talk to Nick before I committed to anything. But after spending a full day with her on Block Island and hearing all she had to say about Josh, it seemed wrong to not give her a definite answer. She had put a lot on the line—with both Nick *and* her parents—to be where she was, with me, right now. Given my "sketchy" background and surfer/skateboarder appearance, I couldn't have been the former mayor's preferred suitor for his only daughter. *To have been a fly on the wall for that conversation.*

Lauren was making a significant statement in the "popularity circles" too, simply by branching out into mine. *There was plenty of room in mine!* That move took a level of commitment that wasn't lost on me.

She had a lot to say about Josh. She explained why she sat with him at lunch, laughed at his jokes and pretty much always ignored me at school. It all made perfect sense… now. *She could've told me this a LONG time ago though.* When she sat by me, talked to me, or was even seen with me at school… that was when Josh bullied me. That's when everyone tripped, pushed, kicked, mocked, cursed and otherwise picked on me—at Josh's command, of course.

On the other hand, when Lauren stayed away from me the bullying stopped. If Josh didn't feel like he was competing against me for Lauren's attention he left me alone. On the surface, there was an easy solution. She let him claim they were dating. That was okay with her until the beach party. After that, enough was enough.

The restraining order against Josh, and his being booted from school, gave Lauren an opening to pursue what she really wanted—*me apparently*—without having to worry about Josh running interference or coming after me. At least that's how she saw it. It was somewhat ironic that she now seemed to be trying to convince me not to go after Josh—though probably not for *his* safety. I wanted to, trust me, but Josh could've killed me—or broken my other arm. I couldn't get to him *physically.*

It was a beautiful and memorable day on Block Island. It wasn't safe for me to bike anywhere so we just walked… everywhere. Lauren's parents were a little leery about letting her out of their sight, though her mom made it clear it had nothing to do with me. *Something about being a wealthy political figure's daughter.* They were every bit as protective of Lauren as Nick always said they were. And the beach party had probably made them even more so.

Lauren didn't let it affect her though. She wasn't shy about holding my hand in front of her parents. It was a bold statement—one I'm not sure I'd have even been comfortable with in front of Ken or Kate yet.

It's also worth noting that my earlier assumption about not being able to see her in a swimsuit on this trip turned out to be partially false too. When it got hot Lauren took her plaid shirt off. When it got hotter she took the white cami off. And then, in that black bikini top… she got even hotter.

At the southeast corner of Block Island, not far from one of the two lighthouses out there, a staircase of 144 steps leads to the base of what's known as the Mohegan Bluffs. We stopped on a landing near the bottom—just above Bluffs Beach—and Lauren pointed towards the point. "I've always wanted to snorkel over there," she said.

"You've been down here before?"

"Many, many times. It's my favorite place on the island. I think when I die I'd want to have my ashes scattered here."

*That was a weird thing to say.* "You want to be cremated?"

"Oh, I don't know about that. I just think it sounds better than saying I want someone to throw my body off this staircase and let the ocean swallow it up."

I laughed. *She was right.* Cremation did sound better than that.

"Where would you want to be buried?" she asked.

I'd always figured I'd be buried with my parents somehow. But considering their bodies had never been recovered, that they were now a part of the 9/11 memorial, that didn't make any sense. *Where would they put me?* "I don't know." I shrugged. Her cremation idea didn't seem so absurd now. "This does seem as good a place as any."

Lauren smiled. "That's kinda what I thought, too. But you haven't answered my question."

Question? I looked at her. "What—"

"*The* question. Will you go out—"

*Ah.* "Yes." I cut her off. *Absolutely!*

And she leaned in immediately and kissed me—lips to lips—her eyes closed, mine wide open. No tongue… but all heat. I took a mental snapshot of that moment—one that would be framed on the ceiling of my room every night, for a long, *long* time. I was never going to forget the sight, the smell, or the taste of her in that moment. It was unbelievable. *To every average looking kid in America… don't give up on your dreams.*

"Thank you," she said.

Umm… "Yeah." *Nice comeback. You should be thanking her.*

She told me some pirate and shipwreck stories, including something about a burning ghost ship, but I don't recall much of them. *Just a little distracted.* As I said, I'll never forget that moment—that kiss. And that landing at the base of those steps, well, that was the closest I've been to heaven in my life so far. I'm certain I loved that spot on Block Island every bit as much as Lauren did then. *If not even more.*

## ←★★★★★ NARRATOR ★★★★★→

### ←Sunday, July 3, 2022→

Kate arrived at 8:30 a.m. She stepped in the front door, and maneuvered her way around my belly for a hug and a kiss. "Gosh, Lauren, you look beautiful," she said.

*For a whale maybe!* I shook my head. "I sure don't feel it."

"Honey, trust me, you *define* beautiful." She glanced over my shoulder. "He still here?"

"No. He left early."

"Of course," she said. She didn't intend for it to come across bitter or sarcastically, but she sensed I might have taken it that way. "I mean—"

"I know." I took her hand. "It's fine."

"I just want to see him."

"I know you do."

"Did you tell him I was coming?"

I nodded. *I begged him to stay.* "Yes. I told him you didn't want me to be alone in case the baby came early." I led her over to the couch. "Are you sure you want to go through with this?"

Kate took a deep breath and nodded. "It's part of his story. I think it should be in there." she handed me several sheets of paper. "Are you pretty close to that part?" she asked.

"Close enough. I'm at September of 2016. We just left Block Island."

"The first time?"

"Yes."

"Ooh…" She nodded. "I remember that day."

*Me too.* I nodded with her. *I remember it all too well.* "I printed out a copy of what I've written so far. Would you mind giving it a general run through for me—make sure I didn't mess anything up? I'll start working on these." I held up the handwritten pages she'd just given me.

"I'm sure it's fantastic." Kate put her hand on mine. "And of course I'd love to read it all, but on one condition."

"Okay?"

"I need a box of Kleenex."

I laughed. "I may have used them all up last night."

Kate smiled softly. "I'm sorry."

"Don't be." I pointed towards the cabinet. "There might be another box or two in there. I stocked up on Monday. I knew what I was in for."

"Has it been as hard as you thought?" Kate asked.

"Yes." *Much harder.*

## ←★★★★★ KATE PARKER ★★★★★→
### Letter (Part 1 of 4)

"Can you love someone at fifteen?"

I remember the night Miles asked me that. He'd just gotten back from Block Island with Lauren. He called it the best day of his life. I tried not to take offense to that—we'd had so many great ones together. "You can love someone at two, dear."

"You know what I mean. Do you think it's possible to actually be in love with someone at fifteen?"

"Miles, high school sweethearts get married all the time."

"So it's not outside the realm of possibility?"

"Is anything?"

He made some comment about the New York Jets but otherwise ignored my question. "But how would I know? And I mean 'know' know."

"Slow down, cowboy. Today was the first of many wonderful days you two will hopefully have together. There's no need to decide your entire future the very first night. Maybe she's the one, maybe she isn't—"

"She's the one," he replied instantly.

I smiled. There was no point in trying to talk him out of it now. I stood and shut off his light. "Sweet dreams."

"No problem there," he answered.

As I was stepping out into the hallway I heard him say my name.

"Yes?" I peeked back in.

"How long was it before you knew you loved me?" he asked.

"Didn't take long."

"So she might love me too already?"

I laughed. "It's not outside the realm of possibility."

←←←←←→→→→→

***"It takes hundreds of good golf shots to gain confidence, but only one bad one to lose it."***

- Jack Nicklaus

←←←←←→→→→→

## STELLAR 51 – "Lefty"

Teachers are likely as repulsed by the idea of their students kissing as we are imagining the same of our teachers, so I'll spare you most of those details—since that's pretty much all I remember about the rest of August. I was as obsessed with Lauren's lips as I was with, well, there was *nothing* I was more obsessed with—nor had there ever been. I always thought kissing was weird; some people made it look so gross, but consider me a convert to the practice. I should probably leave it at that.

The 2016-17 school year was about to start and I was actually excited about going into 9th Grade now—particularly since it meant being back in the same building with Lauren and Nick. I also *finally* got to remove my cast the day before school started. *And. I. Could. Not. Wait.*

Nick and Kate were also ready for school to start, if for no other reason than they'd no longer have to listen to me bemoan my temporary handicap. I'd been driving them absolutely crazy with all my whining about not being able to golf. Of course, I never said a word of it around Lauren. *People you're trying to impress get the edited version of you.*

Kate finally decided she'd had enough. She had Calvin pick me up a left-handed sand wedge and a Phil Mickelson instructional video, since he's a lefty. Cal even claimed she'd asked him to get some left-handed golf balls—a charge Kate vehemently denied. It's hard to pick the more honest person between the two of them, but I believed Cal on this one.

At first I thought all the left-handed business was a stupid idea. And then Cal said, "You can complain about not golfing or you can golf and not complain."

So I picked up the stupid club and gave it a few swings. Turns out I was worse at golfing left-handed than even I thought I'd be. Everything was so backwards. *Thank you, Captain Obvious.* In all fairness, I was having to play *both* one-handed *and* left-handed because of my dumb broken right arm, but I didn't like to make excuses and Cal didn't like hearing them. "You's just chugging pessimism now, sir," he'd say.

*Yeah. I kind of was.*

I'm a stubborn fool though, too. After a few weeks of practice and being generally useless everywhere else, I'd actually somewhat figured it out. I couldn't pull off the same spin as I could right-handed, nor could I get any reasonable distance with just one arm, but I was pretty accurate inside fifty yards.

Cal, James and Nick were sitting on a bench watching me one day. I walked over to join them and Nick was shaking his head. "What?" I asked him.

"You swing better with one good arm than I ever did with two."

"So butter," James said.

"That's bull," I countered. "Josh is the only person our age I've ever seen outdrive you, Nick."

"Okay, so maybe that's true," Nick conceded. "But look how crazy far you've come in just three weeks? Someone who doesn't know you wouldn't even be able to tell you're right-handed."

I knew that was a compliment, but it still felt like an insult. "Well none of that will matter when I get my cast off next week. What good will all this work be then?"

"You never know, sir," Cal said, chomping on a toothpick.

"Right." I shook my head and walked inside for a drink.

I got my cast off a week later, the day before school started, and promptly pitched the lefty sand wedge into a corner of the foyer closet at home. It took me a full three weeks to get my natural right-handed swing back. Similarly, it was almost October before I could physically tolerate a full round of swings with my weaker right arm.

Cal suggested we go along with Ken to Farmington, on Saturday October 1st, and pay Coach Chandler a visit. When we walked into the clubhouse Coach was there waiting for us—with OB.

"I don't want to use up all your swings on the range," Coach said. "So I thought maybe you two could go out and play together."

It seemed like OB was already aware of Coach's plan—*and was still here*—so he must not have had too much opposition to the idea. "Sure," I said. *I just wanted to golf.* "Sounds good. Let's go, Cal."

"Umm, Stellar, I need Calvin to hang with me today... if that's alright."

I'm sure the look of surprise on my face was the polar opposite of the expression on Cal's face. He seemed to also have known this was coming. *Was I the only one who didn't know what was going on here today?* "Okay..." I looked back and forth between Cal and Coach. "Can I grab a pull cart then?"

"Sure," Coach nodded. "Let me go get one."

He disappeared for a minute and then returned. "Sorry, bud. Guess we're all out."

"They're *all* on the course?" That was more than a little bit suspect.

"Guess so."

"We gonna play today?" OB snapped, glaring at me. "You gonna be a sissy or man up?"

I wasn't going to let a two-hundred-year-old lightweight call me a sissy. I struggled to lift my bag onto my shoulder. "Let's go." I gave Cal a glare of my own.

"Good luck," Cal said with an irrepressible smile.

OB beat me by fourteen strokes. I know because after every hole he told me how far ahead he was. It was the most humiliating athletic experience of my life thus far. At one point in the round the old fart told me my swing resembled a “fat goat trying to kick himself in the face with his back foot.” I couldn’t quite visualize what he was actually trying to say, but took it as an insult. My arm was throbbing by the back nine and I wanted to quit, but with OB asking me if I was going to give up *after every single hole*—and calling me every variation of the word “wuss”—I forced myself to push through it. I couldn’t give him that satisfaction, though he got plenty more satisfaction from me elsewhere. He pointed out the yardage different between us every time he outdrove me—which was far more than I care to admit. I got to the point on the back to where it felt like I was swinging all of my clubs simultaneously instead of just one—*I was so out of golf shape.* Carrying my bag and taking all these swings had flat out exhausted me. *And I never did see anyone with a pull cart out there.*

I had nothing left when we finished.

As I staggered off the 18th green I heard OB shouting. He was gesturing for me to come over to him. I approached him, head down, shoulders sagging, and asked him what he wanted. He reached his bony fingers up and grabbed my ear, pulling my head down towards him.

“Ouch,” I cried out. “What the heck?”

He didn’t let go. “Listen, sonny, and you listen good,” he snarled. “You take your hat off and shake hands with your playing partner after every round, no matter how bad you might suck. Respect the players—”

I started to object. “But—”

“Shut up.”

*That wasn’t very respectful.*

“This game is no game for namby-pamby wimps, for lazy, denim-wearing miscreants, or for people who don’t follow the unwritten rules.”

“But—” *None of those categories applied to me.*

“What’d I just say to you?”

“OB, I… ” I’d shaken his hand after he’d drained that last putt on 18, he’d just somehow forgotten it already.

“What?”

“Nothing.” I shook my head. “You’re right. I’m sorry.”

OB finally released my ear and walked off grumbling something to the effect of “darn kids.”

I followed him up to the clubhouse to find Cal and Coach. The assistant pro informed me they’d taken off for a bit but should be back within the hour.

“Let’s go eat,” OB said.

That was quite literally the last thing on earth I wanted to do at that time—go anywhere with OB—but I did anyway. We walked into the restaurant and I waved at Brittlyn.

"Hey, Stellar," she called out. "It's been a while."

I nodded. "I broke my arm."

"She doesn't care," OB muttered.

*Nice.*

"Aww, sweetie, I'm sorry to hear that." I watched her bounce over to us. She placed a Dr. Pepper in front of me and iced tea in front of OB.

"Thanks," I smiled up at her, trying to keep my eyes on her face. For some reason—*related to Lauren I'm sure*—that wasn't as difficult a task anymore.

"You want your usual burger?"

My "usual" burger was whatever she wanted to put on it that day. I ate pretty much anything. "Sure." I nodded.

"And you, Mr. Brown?"

"Same." He didn't even try to lift his eyes from her chest, which apparently didn't bother Brittlyn at all. *She had to be used to it from all the old men in here.* His order bothered her though.

*Wait... did he just order a burger?*

"I'm sorry, Mr. Brown..." Brittlyn asked the question for me. "But did you just say you wanted a burger?"

Still staring at her breasts, he nodded.

"Okay. Got it." Brittlyn nodded cheerily and bounced away, OB following her every jiggling step. It was more than a little creepy.

"Best views in the city," He said with a smile when she was beyond earshot. "Too bad you missed them."

*How could he possibly have noticed where I was looking?* "What do you—"

"What's her name?"

"What?"

"Am I stuttering?"

I shook my head. "No."

"Then what's her name?"

"Lauren."

"She look like that?"

*Better.* "Beauty is in the—"

"Beauty is beauty, young man."

"She has beautiful eyes too, you know." I nodded towards Brittlyn. "And a beautiful smile."

OB nodded. "I do know that. Yes, I do. I love that smile."

"So why—"

"Why focus on the rest? Why stare? Why gawk? Why dream?"

*Okay...* "Sure."

"Because, son..." He pulled an old photo out of his wallet of a young woman. "My wife once looked like her. Blue eyes, not green eyes like Brittlyn, but otherwise similar—especially in her dimensions, if you know what I mean."

I did, and I could easily see the stunning resemblance to Brittlyn—and even Meghan Hardin—in that photo of OB's wife from seventy years ago. *Wow!* "But... it's still—"

"Maybe it's creepy. I can see that too. I just know I miss her. I don't have many days left on this earth, and I don't much fancy looking at older women—they don't remind me of my girl. That one... " He pointed at Brittlyn. "With that smile and those curves... she reminds me every day of my girl."

"I heard you didn't like your wife."

OB chuckled. "Did you? Well, that's not true. Not at all. She may not have liked me much at times, or even most of the time—*especially* not at the end—but I never liked anyone more. Never loved anyone else in my entire life."

"In your whole life?"

"We were high school sweethearts. Fell in love at fifteen. She was my first and only girlfriend."

I went silent then and my thoughts turned immediately to Lauren and I. *So it was possible to find love at fifteen.*

OB placed his hand on my forearm. "Love what you can in life, while you can," he said. "You never know when you might lose what you care about the most, and when you do, you'll wish every day you had it back."

That was as sentimental as OB *ever* got. "Okay... one question though."

"What's that?" he asked.

"What about all these other old guys in here. All their wives used to look like Brittlyn too?"

"I can't explain those cretins." He winked at me. "But ain't no way their wives ever looked like mine. Ain't no way a girl like that..." He nodded towards Brittlyn. "... ever fell for one of these losers."

I laughed and glanced around the room. *You know what? This guy wasn't that bad.* He was an unpleasant, obnoxious, hypocritical pain in the rear end most of the time, but I kind of liked him. And I was definitely starting to understand him. I was well aware that loneliness could gut a person—I was certain it had done so to OB. He just needed more friends...

*And maybe a hot woman over 80 to lust after.*

## STELLAR 52 – "Life and/or Death"

Bart Millard of the Christian group MercyMe once sang that, "You never know why you're alive until you know what you would die for." I guess that means I should know why I'm alive.

*Heck of a way to start a journal entry, isn't it?*

I guess you could call that a teaser because I'm not quite ready to explain just yet. I need to wrap up October 2016 first.

I was nowhere near ready for competitive golf by then. I'd qualified for the National Junior Championships in Florida because of my two victories, but I had to pass on participating this year. *That sucked!*

I was trying to get strength back in my arms, especially my right arm, and it turns out one of the most effective conditioning exercises was fishing. When Ken took me out on my birthday I discovered all that reeling and casting really worked the weaker arm muscles. So on weekday evenings I'd go out in the boat for a few hours after school, and then on weekends he'd take me to Farmington to practice and work out with Chandler. *Until the snow came, that is.*

Then I put the clubs away. At least I had every other year.

Every year Ken had closed RB's down at the first significant snow, usually sometime in late November. He'd still take his boat out fishing whenever he could, but the rest of the boats were hauled up and moved to our storage sheds. I honestly had never been inside either of those buildings—didn't even know both of them were ours.

Anyway, when he'd close up shop there was nothing left for James or Calvin to do during the winter. They might come out once a week to help with a maintenance checklist, but that wasn't paying their bills. Without my knowledge they'd been working with Ken on a plan to change that. A plan that would directly impact me in several ways this year.

One afternoon in late-October I was biking down to the marina and saw a large sign being erected just off the highway by our store. What it said was unmistakable, and as a result I almost drove my bike off the bridge into the canal. "Long Island Indoor Golf Center" it said in huge bold green letters with "Simulators & Practice Greens" below that.

I raced down to the shop and flew in the door. Ken and Calvin were chatting behind the counter. "Did you see that sign?" I pretty much shouted at them.

They both stopped talking and turned towards me. "Sign?" Ken asked.

"There's a Golf Center opening around here somewhere, down here by us." I couldn't contain my excitement, and couldn't believe they didn't know anything about this either.

"That's strange." Ken looked at Cal.

Something about the way he said those words tipped me off. *He knew about it.* "You know about it!" I challenged Ken.

"I might." He had a sparkle in his eye.

"Where's it going to be?"

"Right behind us," Ken replied.

"What? *Where?*"

"Come on. We'll show you."

I glared at Cal. "You knew about this, too?"

"I may have, sir."

I followed them out towards the large red shed behind the RB's building. I'd never noticed a road leading to the other side before. As we walked around to the opposite side of the shed I found an entire parking lot there. *That had definitely never been there before. When did they do this?*

"Wasn't this your shed?" I asked Ken.

"Yes."

"When did you sell it?"

He laughed. "I didn't."

"What do you mean? Did you lease it to someone?"

Ken stuck a key in the door. "Anyone ever told you that you ask a lot of questions?"

I ignored his question and focused instead on the key turning in the lock. He held the door open for me and flipped on the lights as I stepped inside.

"Surprise!" a group of people suddenly shouted at me as my eyes adjusted to the sudden brightness.

I was floored. *I literally knelt down on the floor at one point.* I felt like I was going to faint. Kate rushed over and steadied me. "You okay?"

"You knew about this, too?" I whispered.

"Of course, dear."

"So that errand you just sent me on for Ken… you were setting me up for this?"

She looked at me and smiled. "I'm sorry."

She knew how I felt about surprises. But this one was different. I didn't hate it. In fact, I pretty much loved it. Kate helped me stand as Lauren and her parents, Taryn and her parents, Nick, Carrie, James and Will, a new kid we'd been hanging out with at school, all gathered around.

"All of you knew?" I asked. "How did I not know about any of this?"

Everyone laughed as Lauren answered my question. "Let's just say it's been in the works since the day we went to Block Island."

"*That* was part of this, too?" *This was almost too much to take in.* "Whose idea was it?" I asked Kate.

She turned and nodded towards Calvin and James. "Theirs." James was pointing at Cal, deflecting credit. "But it never would have happened without the Dahls," Kate continued. "We owned the building, but they paid for everything else."

"We wanted to do something special for you," Mrs. Dahl said.

"Your card was enough," I said to Taryn.

"Nothing is enough compared to what you gave us," Mr. Dahl stepped up and put his hand on my shoulder. "We'd have been paying for a funeral instead of this," he put his arm around his daughter and Taryn smiled up at him, "... if it weren't for you."

I finally started to look around, to take everything in. Everyone moved out of my way so I could see. The building was huge, which meant the Dahl's contribution was just as huge. There were a dozen simulator stalls along the north wall of the building. There were big screen TVs covering the east wall in a bar area. There was a massive chipping green in the middle of the building with a giant mural on the wall behind it of an eagle with the word "WINGS" painted above it and "Long Island Indoor Golf Center" painted below that. *Will had painted it—that's why he was there then.* And finally, there was a putting green at the south end of the building—biggest one I'd ever seen. "You can change the contours of that there green," James said, admiring it with me. "It has sixteen sections you can toy with on that there computer." He pointed towards a large jukebox/ATM-looking machine in the corner.

"Sections like the squares in Cal's yardage guide at The Hills?"

"Exactly." James nodded. "All his idea too."

It was genius.

"You can even lay it all perfectly flat if you'd like," James continued.

"Wow!" I noticed a couple rooms in the southwest corner of the building. "What's in there?"

"Well," Ken said. "There's the office and then there's your room—the Lounge."

"My room?"

"Go check it out," Lauren whispered in my ear.

I didn't need further encouragement. I ignored the door marked "Office" and opened the other one marked "Lounge." *Holy crap!*

There were two more simulator stalls in the Lounge. There were also two couches, a loveseat and two recliners, a pool table, a ping pong table, a pop machine, a refrigerator, two giant TVs, four large arcade games, weightlifting equipment, a treadmill and a table with eight chairs around it. "This is awesome," I mumbled. I could feel tears welling up in my eyes as Lauren took my hand.

"You like it?" she asked.

All I could do was nod.

Nick stepped up on my other side. "You can do pretty much whatever you want in this place."

"It's yours as much as it's mine," I replied.

"It's golf," Nick stated matter-of-factly.

"Doesn't have to be," Ken pointed out. "Those simulators will play any satellite TV channel you want. You guys can even play video games on those walls."

"This is straight out of that "move that bus" TV show Kate used to watch."

Kate laughed. "Extreme Makeover?"

"Yes." I nodded.

"Golf edition," Mrs. Chambers added, which drew several more laughs.

"I don't know what to say." I turned around and faced everyone. "This is way too much."

"Look at it this way," Ken said. "Now Cal and James have a place to work all winter—they'll be here every day. You and Nick will each have your own key and there's a video security system here so you just type in your code when you enter the building and we'll know where you are from home. This is your escape, your sanctuary, this is something Kate and I never could have given you but always wanted you to have."

"It's more than I could have ever imagined," I replied.

"Son," Mr. Dahl clapped me on the back, "you deserve it."

"Cake and ice cream anyone?" Kate asked, and everyone cleared the room, everyone except Lauren, Nick, Taryn, Will and me.

"This is awesome," I said for probably the hundredth time.

"You have everything you could possibly want now," Nick said what I was thinking. I knew he was referring to Lauren as well, but I didn't sense any bitterness in his voice. He'd been amazingly supportive the past two months.

"I can't believe I didn't know about any of this." I looked around at each of them. "All of you knew about this and I had no idea."

"Lauren's a good distraction." Taryn said with a laugh.

*Yes. Yes, she was.*

The local name for the place was going to be WINGS—straight from Will's incredible mural—though we weren't going to serve any. It was more of a reference to birds—to golf terms like eagles, birdies and even the albatross. I liked it. Scratch that. I *loved* it.

And now I had a place to play all winter.

WINGS opened to the public on Friday, November 4, 2016. It was packed every single day the first two weeks. It was open 9 a.m. to 9 p.m. Tuesday through Thursday and 10 a.m. to 10 p.m. Friday through Sunday. *Closed on Mondays.* I mentioned we didn't serve wings—neither chicken nor buffalo—but we had popcorn machines constantly running, and the bar served candy, ice cream, pop and beer. It was the kind of place a golf nut would design on paper knowing full well his vision would never come to fruition. Oh, but this one had. Cal's had.

Cal's vision became my dream come true.

*Until November 18th.*

I was lying on the couch in "my room" around midnight on Sunday night when I heard the scream. Chills shot through my body and I jumped to my feet, my headphones falling to the floor. I must have fallen asleep and not noticed that my music had ended. That scream had been so loud, it had seemed like it was in the room, like it was on TV. But the TVs were off. Then there was another scream. That one was right outside my window.

I had all the lights off in my room and almost turned them on but decided to look out the window first. What I saw made every hair on my body stand rigid. There were two men standing over a woman just outside. They were both wearing masks. One of them knelt on top of the woman. And then I saw him punch her, and watched her head bounce off the ground. I raised my fist to pound on the window, to hopefully scare them away, but that's when the masked man on top of the woman turned her over. Everything changed in that instant.

The woman was Kate.

## ←★★★★★ KATE PARKER ★★★★★→
**Letter (Part 2 of 4)**

**←Friday. November 18, 2016→**

None of us will ever forget that day. Each of us for our own reasons. I had to write all of this down at the police station, or it probably never would have been recorded. I don't want to think about this. I don't want to talk about this. I don't want to remember any of it. But this day changed all of our lives, and since only two of us could have told the story… that means I have to.

I can recall, in the clearest of details, all but a couple of minutes from that Sunday night.

I tried to call Miles at 11:45 p.m. No one knew where he was. James had locked up WINGS at 11:15 and taken the train home. He said the lights were out in Stellar's Lounge so I figured he must be somewhere with Nick. But then Carrie said Nick hadn't been feeling good and was already in bed. I texted Lauren to ask if Miles was at her place. She texted me back immediately. "No."

Then I began to worry.

Ken was still out on a boat. I wasn't expecting him back until around 1 a.m. if even then. I also knew Ken had taken Cal with him that night, so I didn't even try to reach Cal. I didn't want to worry Ken but I was running out of options, so I tried calling him. He didn't pick up, so I asked him to call me as soon as he could.

At that point I decided to go down to the marina myself and look around. I thought maybe Miles was out on the docks, or sitting in the shop waiting for Ken. When I got out of the car, everything was dark. It was freezing cold and I immediately wished I'd thrown on a jacket instead of just the hoodie.

There were two people sitting out on the docks by the shop so I approached them thinking it might be Stellar and someone else. As I got closer I saw the beer bottles and noticed the men were wearing black jackets and ski masks. *Again, it was freezing out so that wasn't exactly suspicious… or any kind of red flag.* I greeted the two men and asked them if either of them had seen a boy around.

"A boy?" one of them said and chuckled. "No."

The other one stood then and walked towards me. "What's a pretty lady like you doing out all by herself on a cold night like this?" *Strong Jersey accent.*

As he stood next to me and lustfully looked me up and down, that was the first moment I felt a twinge of fear. I reached for the phone in my back pocket but it wasn't there. I realized I'd left it in the car. *Crap!* Chills washed over me and I knew they weren't just from the cold. I tried to contain the panic I suddenly felt in my chest. "My husband and I are just out looking for my son, and I thought I'd check with you two," I said. "Thanks for your help."

I turned to walk away, but the man beside me grabbed my arm and turned me back towards him. He gave me a creepy gap-toothed grin, and looked over my shoulder towards the car. I'd stupidly left the door open and the dome light had remained on. He could plainly see there was no one else in the front seat… but he couldn't see Avery in the back from where we were.

"Your husband, eh?" he sneered. "Your invisible husband?" The mask didn't cover the white around his eyes or mouth, and nothing could mask that accent. *He was definitely from New Jersey.*

"I don't want any trouble," I said as calmly as I could manage.

"Good," Jersey man said. "Cause we don't neither."

The other man stood up then. He was shorter and stockier than the guy next to me. I started to back away from the tall one, and the split second he glanced back at the shorter man I sprinted towards the car. But the tall one was also super fast. He caught me by the end of the dock and once again grabbed my arm. Somehow, when I tried to pull away, he lost his balance and fell, rolling past me. In doing so he ended up between my position and the running car. That's when I saw the knife in his hand. The moment he spit on the ground and stepped towards me I became relatively certain I wasn't going to make it to the car alive.

With the shorter man closing in on us from behind, I made the split-second decision to run for WINGS. I hoped to lead the men away from the car and Avery, and hopefully call the police if I could make it inside. The station was just down the street. They'd get here quickly. *That was my thinking anyway.*

The tall one came after me, cursing me with every step, but the shorter man was more interested in the car. I heard him call out for the tall one to stop chasing me and come back—that they could just take the car. I slowed to make sure that didn't happen. The tall one continued his pursuit, yelling back, "Cut her off the other way."

I watched the short man comply and take off around the other side of the bait shop past my car, and at that point I committed fully to making it into WINGS. I made it to the door and punched in the code but somehow got it wrong. *I didn't know Ken had changed it. He hadn't mentioned that to me.* I was frantically trying to punch the number in again when the tall man caught me.

I screamed as he threw me to the ground. My face hit the gravel hard and I was momentarily stunned. At that instant the shorter man came around the building and joined us. "What are you doing?" he asked the taller one.

Just then a car passed by and I knew that might be my best—or last—chance. I screamed at the top of my lungs, just before I was punched in the face by the taller one. My head hit the ground hard again and this time I almost blacked out.

"Hold her down," the tall one barked.

*Please, God, no.*

The shorter one did as he was ordered, but voiced his objection. "I'm not okay with this. We should get out of here."

"Turn her over," the taller one commanded.

"Wade… "

"Shut up fool," the taller one snapped. "I said turn her over."

The shorter man did so but I saw him shaking his head.

"You don't have to do this," I whispered to the short one before the tall one punched me in the face again. I tried to blink away the stars in my eyes but to little or no avail. I was so close to blacking out. I closed my eyes tightly as the tall man settled on top of me. And then suddenly there was a bang behind him like a door being slammed shut, or open. The tall man lifted off of me for a split second, and I saw a brief glimmer of silver before whatever it was connected with his head in a sickening crunch. Then he was lying back on top of me again. But now he wasn't moving and now my face was getting wet. I could taste that it was blood.

I heard another sickening crunch and a painful cry. I struggled to push the tall man off of me, to turn and see what was going on, but he was heavy and I was so groggy. There was one more loud crunch, another cry, a loud metal crash and then a few solid thumping sounds like someone being kicked. I saw one shadowed form get shoved against the side of the metal building while the other stood and staggered across the parking lot. I still didn't know who specifically was helping me, though the shadowed form leaning against the building clearly was. And then I heard him crying. Then suddenly I knew exactly who it was. *Miles.*

I whispered his name. A second later he was kneeling over me, crying though seemingly less from fear than physical pain. I felt him tug on my arm, trying to pull me up, but I couldn't move. "Mom," I heard him say. "Let's go. Let's get inside before this guy gets back up."

He helped me up with his left arm and guided me inside. "Avery," I said.

"What?" Miles asked.

"Avery. She's outside. In the car," I whispered. I was so out of it. *I now know I had a serious concussion.*

"I'll get her," Miles said. "We need to call the cops."

"No… Miles—"

"Yes, Mom… we do."

I remember him calling the police and then cleaning me up with a washcloth, wiping all the blood off of me. Somewhere in there he ran out and brought Avery in the back door. I wrapped my arms around her as the parking lot filled with flashing lights. Then they came in and took Miles away from me. I remember asking what was going on—why they were taking him away—but no one would tell me. "Don't say a word," was the last thing I whispered to him. "Not a single word. Promise." I still hadn't noticed how badly he was hurt.

"I won't. I promise," he said.

And then he was gone.

An officer took Avery and me home and stayed with us until Ken got there. Ken said he'd gotten a few details from one of the officers down at WINGS, and that he'd given them all the security camera footage, but he still had tons of questions for me. I told him I'd fill him in on everything when I got back, but that I needed to go to the police station to be with Miles. Ken wanted to take me to the hospital first but I insisted I was fine—it could wait. I needed him to stay here with Avery. I hugged Ken, told him I loved him, and told him I'd be back soon.

And then I went to help my son.

When I got to the police station Miles wasn't there. Panic set in immediately, but the police officer with me quickly found out they'd taken him to the emergency room. He had several broken ribs and his right arm was fractured again. But this time it was a much more serious break and there were several smaller ones. He needed immediate surgery. The officer escorted me to the hospital where I sat in the waiting room surrounded by four police officers like I was a dangerous criminal. Finally an officer came in who I knew well, Captain Joe Mapps.

"Kate," Joe said. "Are you okay? I just heard what happened. Ken called me at home and told me you were here. I came right over." He turned and looked at the other officers. "Can you guys give us a minute?"

I was extremely grateful for Ken's foresight with that call. Three of the officers in the waiting room heeded Joe's request and left, but the one who'd been assigned to me at the marina was lingering. "Sir, I'm supposed to—"

"Just give us a minute, Ethan."

"Yes, sir." He nodded and walked down the hall about twenty paces.

"So what happened?"

"Joe," I burst into tears immediately as he wrapped his arm around my shoulders.

"Shhh… Kate… "

"Joe," I sobbed, "I can't say much to you… you know that. Just tell me you've seen the surveillance video. Tell me you know Miles didn't—"

"Kate… no… I haven't. I don't really know anything yet. But I can take your official statement if you want me to."

I shook my head. That wasn't a smart move. "Joe, I'd love that. But you and I go back twenty years… I can't have—"

"You're right," he agreed. "I'm going to have Simms do it though. He doesn't know you, but he'll treat you right."

"Just tell me one thing…"

"If I can, I will," Joe replied.

"Did that guy live? Is he still alive?"

"No."

The waterworks began again. "And the other guy? You know there was another guy?" *I needed to make sure they knew there was one.*

Joe nodded. "We know there's another guy, and there are cops out there looking for him right now." He hugged me again. "Fortunately, there was a trail. We'll find him."

"Thank you, Joe. I can't thank you enough."

"Anything else I can do for you, Kate?"

"Please make sure they're taking care of my son."

"Consider it done." Joe waved for Ethan to come back over. "Kate, if you need anything whatsoever… if anyone treats you poorly in any way, you call me immediately."

I knew he was partially saying that for Ethan's benefit. "I will, Joe."

"Ethan, I'm going to send Detective Simms over here to take her official statement. You don't let anyone else ask her any questions about what happened, you got that? You stay with her until Simms is done and then you take her home."

"Yes, sir."

"Thank you, Joe," I said again.

He gave me another hug and whispered in my ear, "I'll take care of Miles. You… watch your words. Remember what helps you, forget what doesn't." He stepped back and looked at me to make sure I understood. "Be smart, Kate."

I nodded. *Got it.*

I had a lawyer friend of mine, Paula, present when Detective Simms took my statement. I elected to write it down instead of voice record it, and chose my words carefully to make sure they couldn't be taken out of context. I even had Paula take pictures of my notes just in case.

Detective Simms seemed like a nice, honest, guy, but I knew a couple shady detectives and was personally—and professionally—aware of how they could manipulate the truth in court. I was careful not to set Miles up in any way. In case, heaven forbid, this went to court.

When Miles came out of surgery Paula sat in with him for his statement as well. Simms was kind enough to stay behind and keep an eye on the detectives conducting his "interrogation." I, of course, wasn't allowed to be anywhere near Miles for any of it. After I hugged and kissed him the detectives had insisted I go home. Paula in turn had promised to stay with him until they either took him away or let him come home—in which case she would bring him to me.

Ken rushed to greet me when I got home—around 2:30 a.m.—and he wrapped his arms around me. "Are you okay? Is Miles okay? Please—"

I just started crying, the pressure in my chest almost squeezing the tears from my eyes. "Will you just hold me?" I asked him.

"Of course," he said. And he did, without asking any more questions until there was a knock on the door around 5 a.m. I opened the door before the knocker had lowered his hand. It was Officer Ethan.

"Yes, officer?" I couldn't read his expression.

"Ma'am, I'm just letting you know they're sending me home. There are two officers in the car right there." He pointed at them. "Here are their cards. But you should know they're not here to keep you here. They're just here to watch your house for a few hours, just protocol."

"Wait, are you saying—"

"You are not a suspect."

*That was fast.* "How—"

"I really can't say, ma'am."

"And my son?"

"He'll be home soon."

*Oh, thank God. Thank you, God.* I knew I probably shouldn't have done what I did just then but I wrapped my arms around Officer Ethan. He should have pushed me away but he didn't. "Thank you," I whispered in his ear.

"Of course, ma'am. Goodnight to both of you." He nodded to Ken.

I closed the door and turned to Ken. "How did they—"

"The surveillance videos," Ken said. "Has to be. They had to have caught everything. It had to be open/shut to be so quick."

*That made sense. Man, I hoped that was the case.* My phone buzzed in my back pocket. Text message. "That was Paula," I said. "She's bringing Miles home."

And then the tears began to flow again. I could see Ken really wanted to hear my side of what had happened. He had been far more patient than I ever would have been. I hurriedly gave him the short version so that he'd at least be ready to face Miles when he got home.

We didn't know what to expect. We sat on the couch and waited for the door to open. When it finally did Ken and I both stood. Miles glanced at us then shuffled up the steps towards his room. Paula stepped in the door behind him, and watched him go upstairs. There was a lump the size of a softball in my throat. I felt like I might faint so I sat back down. "Please," I patted the couch beside me, looking at Paula, "please sit for a minute."

She did. "The district attorney won't be pressing charges," she said.

I looked at Ken and he asked her the question for me. "Was it the video?"

"That and they found the other man." Paula confirmed. "Or rather, I should say the other man turned himself in. He was actually at the station when they were out looking for him. He came clean to clear himself—didn't hold anything back. His statement confirmed everything the surveillance footage showed."

"But how would that clear him?" Ken asked.

"Because he didn't do anything," I replied. "Not to help or to hurt me. Not really."

"Kate—"

Paula held her hand up to stop Ken's objection to my quick dismissal of faults. "He's not free and clear. He still has some accessory and assault charges he's facing. He's going to do time. But, he made it clear to the police that your son did no wrong… that Miles had *no choice* but to do what he did, in order to save you. Miles is completely clear in part because of that man's honesty. He could have stayed quiet and this could have lasted months, or even years longer. The man deserves *a little* credit for that." She said that last part looking directly at Ken. He nodded, recognizing as much.

"But…" Paula continued. "All that other stuff will sort itself out. Just worry about Miles. Get him to a counselor. I've put three cards in this folder of people I recommend, though you probably know some good ones too from your practice… just be there for him. Take care of your family. That's the best advice I can give."

I nodded. I was fine. I wasn't worried about me. Nothing had happened to me that a few ice packs, some ibuprofen and a little rest wouldn't cure. All my concern was regarding Miles. I thanked Paula repeatedly, and told her to let us know if there's anything else that we needed to do. *Or anything I could ever do for her.*

When she left Ken and I talked for another ten minutes or so. I convinced him I was fine, that none of tonight's events would scar me in any way, save for what was affecting Miles. I didn't really go into the details any more than I had to. He wanted to talk more but I wanted to go check on my son.

I crept into his bedroom and tiptoed around to the other side of his bed. I knelt down by his face and could see that his eyes were closed. “Miles,” I whispered. He didn’t budge. I didn’t think he’d be asleep yet, but it seemed clear he didn’t want to talk… not now. I kissed him on the forehead. “I love you. If you can hear me just know that. You and I… we’ll get through this together.”

As I was leaving his room I heard him whisper, “Kate.”

“Yes.” I slipped back over to his side.

“Will you lay with me awhile? I just don’t want to be—”

“Sshhh… of course,” I replied. “You don’t have to explain.” I lay down beside him and slipped my right arm under him. He rested his head on my chest and within minutes was fast asleep.

I stayed with him for another twenty minutes or so and then quietly slipped out of the room, but not before kissing his forehead one last time and whispering a most heartfelt, “Thank you.”

## ←★★★★★ JAMES DUNNE ★★★★★→
**Letter**

**←Friday. December 16, 2016→**

"I killed a man once."

Stellar looked up at me, seemingly gauging my sincerity. He remained silent. We were sitting out on the end of the docks all bundled up watching a barge shove chunks of ice through the canal. It was cold out but not unbearable. Mr. Parker was due back any minute from refueling the boat.

"I did," I continued. "I was driving. Had a little much to drink. My car crossed that middle line and struck him head on. He never made it out."

Stellar looked at me again. *Still not a word.*

"It troubled me something fierce. Can't say I've ever gotten over it." I was watching him carefully, not sure how he was taking this. "Oh, I went to rehab. I got all cleaned up. Haven't had a single drink since, but—"

"But you killed someone," He finished the sentence for me.

"Yes. Yes, sir." I could see him nodding slowly with me. It was time to make my point. "There's one big difference between what you did and what I did."

"And what's that?"

"You saved a life, too. You did what you did for the person you've loved most for most of your life." He was quiet again so I continued, "Whereas what I did was all wrong."

"And what I did wasn't?"

Stellar was staring intently at me right now and I chose my words carefully. "Taking a life can't ever be right—it shouldn't never happen. But if there's a gray area, boy, you are smack in the middle of it."

"It's murder."

"No, son, no it isn't. Not what you've done. What you've done is more sacrifice… it's love."

"But how can killing be love?" I could see his eyes fill as he spoke. "When I first saw them, I saw those two guys who killed Bernie and I was afraid. I was going to pound on the window, but I was afraid. Then I saw Kate and… well… then I saw Bernie in that alley again and I remember feeling like I let him die—like I was the reason Bernie died." Stellar wiped his face with his sweatshirt sleeve and turned away from me. "I didn't want to lose Kate like that, too. I was angry. I *wanted* to kill—"

"And you didn't lose Kate," I interrupted. "Son, there are people in this world that ain't no good. I was a good man, but I did something really stupid… real wrong. I had to own up to that. You, you did no wrong, Stellar. Not a thing."

"Well—" he began to object.

I cut him off. "Would you have hurt those men if they hadn't been hurting Kate? If they hadn't been doing wrong? No. No way, sir. But know this… you sure saved Miss Kate a lifetime of pain, of terrible memories she would've never forgot. That's worth more than you know. Ask anyone who's, well, been through a… well… an assault like that." I placed my hand gently on his shoulder. "Stellar, bad as it seems, you did this right."

"People keep saying that but—"

"Stellar, they ain't lyin'." This was the one time I raised my voice at him. "Ain't a soul who cares about you who would lie to you about this. That district attorney who spoke to you—she told you this wasn't your fault, that you should have a clear conscience. Those people don't just say that. If they felt you messed up at all, trust me, you'd know. Their job is to put the bad people away. They didn't want to put you away. They had *no* cause to." I could feel that I was getting through to him by his body language. He was definitely listening now. "And that other man, the one who messed you all up, his statement said you could have killed him. That you held back. He says you let him go." Stellar nodded now. "He was right, wasn't he?"

Stellar nodded again. "I guess."

"Look. I know you're avoiding Miss Lauren. I know you're even avoiding Miss Kate. I know you don't want to hear about God forgiving you, or hear anyone calling you a hero. But you have got to get past this, whatever it takes. You can't let this ruin your life. Not this. You did this right."

There was a long silence as we watched Mr. Parker's boat approach from down the canal. "So what did you do?" Stellar asked me quietly. "How did you ever forgive yourself?"

"I couldn't at first," I told him honestly. "I had a terrible guilt. I found the man's obituary. I tracked down his wife with a cop friend's help. For years I put gift cards in her mailbox to pay for whatever she needed, but don't really know if she ever needed anything. She had a real nice house but lived all alone. She walked everywhere and I followed her around town doing little things, helping her any way I could think of. I put flowers on her husband's grave every year on the anniversary of his death and eventually, on the fifth such anniversary, I met his wife there. Or she surprised me there. She was waiting for me. She knew who I was, and all that I'd been doing, all along. She'd seen me hundreds of times over the years—even reported me to the cops on a couple occasions for stalking."

"She did?"

"Yes, sir." I nodded. "She wasn't ready to forgive me those years. She was still plenty angry. But at her husband's grave that fifth anniversary she offered me an olive branch—an invitation."

"Invitation?"

"Yeah. This'll sound weird, but she gave me a key to her house, told me she had a downstairs apartment that was all mine if I wanted. Said it would be less creepy to have me live with her than follow her around all day." I laughed and Stellar smiled. "She said she'd rather not live alone anyway. Strangest thing, that was."

"I'm sure." Stellar nodded.

"Long story short she forgave me so I could forgive myself—and I did, best I could. She gave me a kind of peace and, well, long story short *again*, I've lived with her ever since."

I saw the sudden surprise on his face. "So you actually live with her?" he asked.

"I do."

"You married her?"

"No. No, sir." I couldn't help but smile. "Rose is almost eighty now—will be next year. Was never anything romantic between us. She's more my, well…" I shrugged. *She wasn't exactly my mother either.* "We just make a different kind of family is all."

The earlier surprised look on Stellar's face had now become more one of realization. "Ah, so that was the woman who answered the phone when I called you that day?" he said. "She's the one who didn't know a Jake. She didn't know people called you Jake."

"Yes," James chuckled. *That was years ago*. "Yes, that was Rose." The boy had a great memory.

"Why didn't you tell me this story before, James? Seems like it was about the biggest thing in your life."

*It definitely was.* "You didn't need it, sir," I replied. *And I don't like to talk about myself. I could relate to the boy that way too.*

Stellar nodded again as Mr. Parker pulled the boat up beside us.

"You two okay?" he asked, looking back and forth between us.

"Yes, sir," I answered.

"Yeah," Stellar replied.

He looked at me and smiled, and for the first time in a month I caught a glimpse of the boy I'd always known before this.

When Mr. Parker and I were alone for a minute he asked me how his boy was doing. "Did he say anything to you?" he asked.

"Oh yes, sir, Mr. Parker. He said plenty."

"And?"

"And... I think he's on the way back to Stellar."

========== JAMES DUNNE ==========

## ←★★★★★ LAUREN CHAMBERS ★★★★★→
**Journal Entry**

**←Saturday. December 31, 2016→**

Stellar is dead.
At least that's what it feels like.

It's New Year's Eve and I'm angry. And happy. I'm pissed. And ecstatic. I spent ten hot minutes kissing a boy tonight, but it wasn't the boy I love. Or maybe it is. Maybe it will be. At least it's not the boy I thought I'd be kissing tonight. I don't know what happened to that boy. He hasn't spoken to me in over a month. I used to stop by his house every day. Now… it's been over a week since the last time I checked in on him. It seems pretty clear to me that Stellar doesn't love me anymore. You don't shut someone out that you love. Not like this.

I get that something happened to him. I've read the story in the paper. I understand he broke up a fight that somehow involved Kate, and managed to severely re-break his arm in the process. I know that someone died in that fight. I get that it's serious. I mean, Stellar's in rehab for his arm. He's actually seeing a shrink for what Nick referred to as PTSD. He needs help. He needs me. *Shouldn't he come to me? Doesn't he trust me?*

He can't. I must not mean as much to him as I thought I did. That has to be it. I'm no more informed on his life now than a guy in Botswana, or wherever-the-crap-in-the-world, who read the story on CNN or whatever on-line. I shouldn't feel guilty for moving on.

But it's not just Stellar. That's what's even more strange. I feel like I'm being shut out by the entire Parker family, even Kate. Nick's getting the same treatment. That's what he told me before I kissed him tonight. That kiss… I don't know that I should have kissed him. I don't even know if Nick wanted me to. He's probably as conflicted and confused as me. But anger and passion apparently are quite fierce together, and they took over on my front porch tonight. One minute we were freezing cold. The next we were rather hot. My mom broke it up when she caught us. I don't think she's all that happy with me. "You don't know what you've just done," she said. Whatever. Oh well. Nick didn't seem to mind. He likely got a lot more than he thought he'd be getting at this party. Stellar's loss.

I was just going to go to bed. I certainly didn't feel like writing. I've torn out all the mushy pages where I raved about "my first love", where I doodled Stellar's name a billion different ways and imagined our house, pets and kids, planned out our entire future together. That future is history now.

I've thrown away all the entries full of whining and crying about him not answering my calls or letting me into his house. It was pretty much the same thing every day and would be as redundant for you to read (*Mrs. Willett*) as it was for me to write. Besides, none of that is anyone's business.

But now I'm angry and I need to vent—I need to get it out. It didn't seem right to wreck Nick or anyone else's New Year's Eve with this tirade, so this is just between me, this pen, and this paper. For now.

When Nick left my house tonight I called Stellar and left him a lengthy voice message. *Of course he didn't pick up!* I told him about Nick and me—told him we're together now, that I kissed Nick tonight. I told Stellar he'd ruined his chance at the best thing he ever could have had. I let him know that he messed up, that we were permanently through. I told him I didn't ever want to see him again.

Crazy harsh, and probably a little over the top, but I made my feelings known in no uncertain terms. Maybe I shouldn't have done that. *You think?* I do regret it a little. But I've run out of ways to express my frustration. Enough is enough.

========== LAUREN CHAMBERS ==========

## ←★★★★★ NARRATOR ★★★★★→

### ←Sunday, July 3, 2022→

I slammed the journal shut and Kate jumped. She whipped her head around and saw the tears trickling down my face. I already knew this part. I'd read it and regretted it a million times over, but for some reason it was hitting me harder now. I didn't want to put it in the book… but how could I possibly leave it out? How else would the reader know that none of this was Stellar's fault?

"Hey, you okay?" Kate asked.

"No." I shook my head. "Not really."

"Where you at?"

"New Year's Eve 2016. The night I… the night I kissed Nick."

"Hey, Lauren—"

I waved her off. "I know, I know… I know it doesn't matter anymore. But I was so cold. I could have been more insistent that he see me—that he talk to me. I could have pushed you, too. I was so stuck on how I felt I didn't even think about how he felt. I was so angry—so childish."

Kate was kneeling beside me now. "Lauren—"

"Stellar would have never given up on me."

Kate didn't disagree. She knew that to be the truth as much as I did. "Lauren, it all worked out."

I nodded. "I guess. But it's so dang hard to read this in my own writing, especially after we just went through your whole story together. Knowing what he did for… "

"For me?" Kate finished my sentence.

I nodded again. "That and all he went through after. Revisiting all his pain through you and through the letter from James. I just wish he would have talked to me."

"Lauren, you're preaching to the choir. I felt the same, trust me, very much the same. I wanted to understand where he was—to help him any way I could. I couldn't imagine what it must have been like for him to think that what was happening to me was like watching Bernie die again to him. I couldn't imagine what it must have felt like to know you'd killed someone at sixteen years old. I wanted to hold him, to take all that pain away. I was just as lost as you were. Trust me."

I did trust her. But that didn't make me feel better about my own choices. "But you knew—"

"Yes. I knew the whole story. I probably should have said more to you, but I wanted it to come from Miles. In fact, forget 'probably.' Hindsight being what it is, I definitely should have said more to you… even though legally, well, I knew I wasn't supposed to say anything at all."

"Legally?"

"Not until the end of December when it all wrapped up, that is. Just in case anything had gone wrong with all the official court stuff we were supposed to keep quiet. And then when we got the okay, well, Miles wanted to…" I watched her shake her head, then she continued. "I don't know…" She sighed deeply. "I messed up, Lauren. I'd change an awful lot of things too. We all could have done things differently."

Kate was right. We all could have handled those months better. But everything I thought I never was I saw clearly in myself in those journal entries. I was harsh, cold, unforgiving. I was selfish. I was the opposite of Stellar at a time when he most needed me to be like him. I would never absolve myself of that—even if I knew he had.

If only God granted everyone a do over. *I'd have used my mulligan there.*

Ken and Avery stopped by and picked up Kate a half-hour later. Kate hugged me tightly in our doorway and kissed my cheek. "Thank you for doing this, Lauren." She placed her hand over her own heart as tears pooled in her eyes again. "You have no idea how much—"

"Of course I do," I replied. "It means just as much to me. Trust me. I'm honored to be able to do this for all of us."

I waved as they pulled out and turned to find my husband standing behind me, wiping his own eyes. "Where did you come from?" I asked him. "What's wrong?"

"The garage. And nothing." He shook his head. "Just something in my eye."

I didn't believe him. "How long were you in the garage?"

He shrugged. "A while."

"They would've liked to see you, you know? Especially Avery."

He nodded and turned away from me. "Yeah. Next time."

"You always say that."

"I know."

"Hey, you know they don't—" He turned with a glare that stopped the words in my mouth. *They don't blame you.*

"Doesn't change a thing," he said.

## STELLAR 54 – "Fisher's Island"

I went over to Lauren's house on New Year's Eve just as I'd done every night the two weeks prior, every night since I'd spoken to James. I'd never been able to knock on Lauren's door, but that night I was going to. That night I was determined to. It was New Year's Eve—the perfect time for a new beginning. Kate had called Mrs. Chambers to make sure Lauren was home. Mrs. Chambers knew I was coming. The adrenaline was coursing through me. I had a letter in my hand, a significant gift in my jacket pocket and the biggest apology in my heart. And then I saw Nick and Lauren on the porch. I didn't want to watch… but I couldn't look away.

I listened through tears to her message when I got home. When Lauren told me she never wanted to see me again I made a commitment to comply for as long as possible. The eight-page letter of apology, of explanation—it went in the trash. I didn't blame her. I didn't blame Nick. This was my fault. I could have easily talked to her at any point. I wasn't officially under any kind of legal gag order, just struggling to get all my emotional ducks in a row. I blew it. She made it pretty clear how she felt about me. And, like I said, I didn't fight it. I would have, I absolutely would have, if I hadn't seen them kissing—if I hadn't known that they were now together. I didn't want to get in the way of that. And I didn't want to lose Nick, too. Besides, I've said it before, I've always considered them the perfect couple. *A real-life Ken and Barbie.*

I'll admit that it hurt terribly. It still does. But I moved on.

*Right.* So it was a little harder than that. People like me don't just "*move on*" from a Lauren. I'm no Brad Pitt. There's not likely to be an Angelina Jolie after my Jennifer Aniston.

Avoiding Lauren turned out to be rather easy, physically. *Emotionally was another story.* I didn't have to work Ken or Kate too hard to let me finish out the academic year on a home school curriculum with some help from a few empathetic teachers. My broken arm was a wreck—a casted collection of pins. Recovery was much more slow and painful this time, a rehab that was only made less painful by Ken taking me out fishing with him every day. Ken had his rules on the boat, and I had mine—one rule—no talking about Lauren. Fishing was my escape from her, and I spent as much time out on the boat as I could throughout February, March and into April. And why not? I couldn't golf. Hadn't swung a club since, well, that night, nearly five months ago now. I hadn't even been back to WINGS since that night, couldn't get myself to enter that building or even be in the parking lot.

I got my air cast off on April 1st (2017). Incidentally that was the same day several of the local courses opened. Strangely though, I had no desire to play. I noticed James and Cal would leave clubs randomly lying around the shop. Their message wasn't all that subliminal, not subtle at all. I'm sure they were curious if I could even make a golf swing with my rebuilt arm. But I didn't even want to. If I never picked up another golf club that would be soon enough, that's how I felt at that point. My life was fishing now. All fishing.

Every weekday morning Ken and I went out and made our rounds around Fisher's Island. That was our "loop." I knew every hotspot. I'd memorized the tide patterns. I knew how to maneuver the boat out and back in, through the shallows of Plum Gut, the mile-wide stretch between Long Island and Plum Island. The waves could get up to six feet high in The Gut and there were routinely strong winds and currents in that stretch of sea. You had to have your wits about you at all times in The Gut or you could scrape bottom on those shoals. You'd be a punchline in the local newspaper and fishing shops for weeks.

Ken taught me a great deal about the boats, and fishing in general, those months. We only spoke about Lauren when I had to vent—and Ken mostly just listened on those occasions. My "counselor" had encouraged both Ken and Kate to let me voice my real feelings whenever I was willing to share them—without interruption. *As much as possible.* So they did.

But then she also encouraged me to try to stay positive around Ken and Kate, and everyone else. *Again, as much as possible*. So I did. I held most of my negativity in.

My counselor was nice, pretty and seemed smart. I trusted her even if her cheery demeanor and counseling methods were a little too "sunshine and happiness." She talked about finding rainbows in thunderstorms, making molehills out of mountains and lemonade out of lemons. She could write the book on clichés. Easily. "Think positive, be positive," she'd say, and her favorite line was *always*, "You can do it." *She liked to exorcise her inner Rob Schneider (The Waterboy).*

I tried to follow all her advice. I'm still trying.

Some days it was positively hard... others it was positively impossible.

Honestly, things were good between Kate and me again, thanks mostly to James and the counselor... and the case being completely closed, of course. Kate felt terrible about Nick and Lauren being together, but there was nothing any of us could do about it now. She was just happy I hadn't let it ruin my friendship with Nick. *As far as she knew.*

Yeah, Nick and I were still getting along, though some days were harder than others for me to handle. *Like any day I saw him or spoke to him.* He'd often join us on the weekend fishing trips, even if we weren't talking much. He likely enjoyed those trips as much as I did. (Heavy sarcasm.) Fortunately, you can fish without talking and, in theory, even catch more that way. *We tested that theory out a lot.*

Nick knew I didn't want to hear about Lauren, and I'm sure he didn't want to talk about her in front of me. Those weekend fishing trips with Nick were only uncomfortable because I was insanely jealous of him, and couldn't escape the visual of him kissing *my* girlfriend. I measured my actual level of anger with him by how many times I thought about pushing him off the boat each trip, and considered my good days the ones where it was less than a thousand. So I did have a few good days.

Ken often said he was proud of me. He was impressed I could keep my cool and be such a good friend to Nick under the circumstances. Yeah, if he knew how much I was boiling inside, well, I don't think he'd have been so complimentary. I missed Lauren with all my heart, and I don't doubt for a second that I still very much loved her. I can't imagine it possible that anyone could have loved or wanted her more.

The truth hurts is *very much* one of the world's greatest understatements, and I might just have to seriously hurt the next person I hear say it. These days I can relate more to the "life sucks and then you die" mentality.

*But that's not very positive, is it?*

## ←★★★★★ NARRATOR ★★★★★→

### ←Sunday, July 3, 2022→

I didn't even notice my waters break. At least it didn't feel like I expected it would. I was in the shower, desperately trying to wash the tears from my face and the aching from my heart. I couldn't get Stellar's words out of my head. And then suddenly it happened, suddenly I realized what had happened.

I wasn't expecting it. It was too early. The baby couldn't be coming yet.

The doctors apparently agreed. When we got to the hospital they acted like I had four years to deliver. "Waters breaking didn't necessarily mean birth was imminent."

*Interesting.* I'd never done this before, so maybe I was overreacting but there was seemingly no sense of urgency whatsoever. In fact, an hour later, when Ken, Kate and Avery rushed into the waiting room, I was still in there, and Nick was still pacing and having a staring contest with the receptionist.

Kate came straight over to me. Avery made a beeline for Nick. Ken stood at the fork in the road and watched both interactions. I saw Avery wrap her arms around Nick.

"False alarm?" Kate asked me.

"Not to my knowledge."

"But they haven't taken you in yet?"

I shook my head. "They asked me a bunch of questions about contractions and my water breaking, but maybe I gave the wrong answers. They don't seem concerned. Maybe I'm acting too calm."

"You want me to rattle some cages?"

I nodded towards Nick. "He's done plenty of that."

On cue my OBGYN, Dr. Caruthers, *finally* pushed through the double doors and strolled towards us. "Mrs. Birch?"

"Yes," I replied.

"We're ready for you."

Dr. Caruthers led Nick and me down the hall to an empty room. He and the nurses checked "under the hood" and confirmed that, "I still had plenty of time."

"So the baby's not coming tonight?" I asked Dr. Caruthers.

He looked at my chart, presumably to check the baby's sex and likely seeing that we didn't want to know. "Oh, it is." He smiled at both Nick and me. "Just probably not for few more hours. You did the right thing coming in. Now I just need you to relax and get comfortable."

Nick told me he was going to go call his mom.

"Kate already called Carrie and my parents," I told him.

"I know." Nick nodded. "I just want to update her. I'll call your parents too."

I figured they were on their way to the Charleston airport now. "Nick, will you send Kate back?"

"Sure."

A few minutes later Kate slipped into the room. "Hey, honey," she whispered. "You good?"

"I didn't know if they'd let you back in here."

"I can be persuasive when I have to be." She sat beside me and took my hand. "What'd the doc say?"

"Basically, it's going to be a long night." I sighed.

"So what can I do for you? How can I help?"

I pointed at my bag in the corner of the room. "My laptop is in there." Kate glanced back at it. "I was wondering if you'd type for me."

Kate looked surprised. "Are you sure?"

I nodded. "If you don't mind. I'd like to keep working on it as long as I can. I'm all the way up to May 2017."

Kate smiled. "So you kept working after we left tonight?"

"Of course." I returned the smile.

Kate retrieved the laptop. "Lauren?"

"Yes?"

"I wanted to tell you something earlier today, but couldn't figure out how to say it."

"Okay…"

"I lied to you about that journal."

I didn't immediately know what she was referring to. "Which journal?"

"You said you were missing a journal from Stellar."

"Yeah, one of the first ones." I wasn't yet sure how exactly she'd "lied" about it.

"I know where it is," Kate continued.

"You do?" *Why would she have lied about that?*

Kate nodded. "Stellar has it with him."

I hadn't even considered that possibility. "But…"

"It was all about you." Kate had tears in her eyes again. "Everything he ever thought about you, everything he ever felt about you, it was just… all you. Poems, letters, jokes, notes… those pages… they were full of love, full of…" She couldn't finish.

I nodded as my mind filled in the adjectives for her. *Happiness, passion, loyalty, betrayal, pain, sadness and utter disbelief. But also love. Mostly love. Dear God…* Tears flooded my own eyes then too.

"I'm sorry," Kate whispered. "I don't know why I didn't just tell you."

I reached over and took her hand. "Don't be sorry. Please. Don't be. I'm glad you told me now, and I completely understand."

I guess I was wrong before. I'd never read that journal—not one all about me. I'd have remembered that—probably even word for word. I closed my eyes. *Stellar, I'm so so sorry.*

But Kate wasn't done. "The letter was in there too, Lauren. So was that photo your mom took of you and Miles on those steps on Block Island… and his favorite shot—the one of you, Squirrel and Avery."

I knew what pictures she was talking about but... "The letter?"

"The letter he was going to give you on New Year's Eve."

"But he threw it away."

Kate nodded. "Yes and no. I found it. I kept it." Kate shook her head. "I always thought—"

"Why didn't you tell me that before… years ago?"

"Miles wouldn't have forgiven me for that."

"Why?"

"Because even he didn't know I had it… that I'd read it. I honestly believe if you'd read it, knowing you, it would have changed your mind. It would have hurt you. It would have hurt Nick. I probably wouldn't be here today with you for a number of reasons—none of us might be for that matter."

"But maybe…" I couldn't get myself to say it. *If she were right about the impact that letter would have had, then maybe…*

"Stellar would be here too?" Kate said it for me. "Yeah. Maybe," Kate murmured. "Don't think I haven't considered that a billion times."

There was a lengthy uncomfortable silence as I pondered her words, and she tried to figure out what to say next—if anything. "He loved you, Lauren," she finally added. "And he loved Nick, too. He'd have wanted you two to have this day together. He would be very happy for both of you."

Everything Kate said was true—dead on. *That was Stellar.*

"It's not right," I finally said.

"What isn't?" Kate looked afraid of what I was going to say next.

"It's not right for you to feel any guilt for this. Not anymore. And it's not right for Nick to avoid you like he does. Kate, it's—"

"Lauren, shhhh… it's okay. Honestly. This was probably terrible timing for—"

"No," I interrupted her. "It wasn't." I squeezed her hand. "I'm grateful, trust me. Everything you said… everything you've done… I'm beyond grateful."

Kate nodded, standing up. "Lauren, I should—"

"Kate." My voice took on a more serious tone. "Please don't leave. Please stay with me. I… I need you here."

She looked surprised. “Okay, but—”

“I need your help.” I tapped the laptop. “If you’re still willing—”

“Of course.” She nodded. “Whatever you need. You know I will. But can I get you anything first?”

“I’m guessing a bacon cheeseburger with supersized fries is out of the question?” I smiled up at her.

“Probably.”

“How about a small glass of water then?”

“I can do that.”

Kate brought me the water and readied the laptop. “Okay,” she said. “Where do I start? What’s next?”

“May 2017.” I replied. “I think I’m up to OB.”

## ←★★★★★ CALVIN JACKSON ★★★★★→
### Letter (Part 3 of 6)

Was late April or first of May I got the call. Mr. Oscar "OB" Brown had passed.

Mr. Chandler Green, he called me and told me about the funeral, asked if I might be able to get Stellar to attend, said he had a letter from OB for the boy.

Stellar, had been having a hard time of late. I'd kind of kept my distance, knowing me and golf were tied together in his head. I ran WINGS for Mr. Parker. James ran RB's. Stellar didn't come over to WINGS—hadn't in months—so I hardly saw him. Still, when I got the call from Coach Green, I figured the boy would want to know.

I approached him on the end of the docks that day.

"What's going on, Cal?" he asked me.

"Just got a call for you, sir."

"A call?" Stellar looked at me in curiosity.

"From Mr. Green—Coach Chandler."

Stellar waved at a passing boat whose occupants called out to him. He didn't look back at me. "Cal, I don't want to see him. I don't want to talk to him either."

"Ain't about that, sir. Ain't about golf."

"Well, what is it then?" He still wasn't looking at me, and there was a sharp edge to his voice.

"Mr. OB. He passed."

"Passed?" Finally he looked at me.

"He died, sir."

Stellar nodded, and I watched his shoulders slump. "Coach called just to tell you that?" The edge in his voice was gone.

"Yes, sir. Well, kind of."

Stellar sat on a wooden crate. "Okay. What else did he say?"

"He has a note for you, from OB, and was wondering if you might attend the funeral on Wednesday."

I was expecting him to say no but watched him nod instead. "Of course," he said. "But I don't want to talk about golf."

"No problem, sir. I'll be sure Coach knows as much."

Wednesday morning, May 3rd, the Parkers, Nick and I climbed into Mr. Parker's truck and drove to Farmington. It was a dark and gloomy morning, perfect for a funeral. I was surprised Stellar had invited Nick along. No matter what he claimed to his parents about the healthy status of their friendship, I was unconvinced.

When we pulled into the cemetery I initially thought we'd been given bad information. There were only two cars parked near the burial site, and I could only see three people standing under the canopy by his casket.

"Where is everyone?" Stellar asked.

"'Fraid this might be it?" I mumbled. "Weather may have scared people off."

"The weather?" Stellar replied bitterly. "That's bull."

Mr. Parker and Mrs. Parker tried to calm him. "It is what it is," they said.

But Stellar wouldn't let it go.

We approached the Pastor, Coach Chandler and a beautiful blonde in a low-cut, body hugging black dress who I almost didn't recognize—Miss Brittlyn.

When she saw Stellar she immediately hurried over to him and wrapped him in her arms. "I'm so sorry, Stellar."

I watched Nick check Brittlyn out in awe. She tended to have that effect on people, in any circumstances.

"This is Brittlyn, Nick." Stellar introduced them.

"Pleasure," Nick replied.

*No doubt.*

As Brittlyn hurried back under the canopy I heard Nick whisper to Stellar. "That's the girl you told me about in Hawaii? She's real?"

"Of course she's real." Stellar smiled.

"Wow," Nick added.

"Yep." Stellar nodded.

A fourth person did join us just before the service started. She appeared to be in her fifties or sixties, and only Coach Chandler seemed to recognize her. I figured her for a sympathetic club member or bartender—something along those lines.

The service was short, but would have been much shorter if Stellar hadn't spoken. Considering he'd specifically told me he didn't want to say anything, his interruption of the pastor took me very much by surprise. It irked him to no end that more people hadn't shown up to pay their respects. I don't remember everything he said that morning, but here's what I do recall.

"I wish I'd known him better. I wish I'd known his wife. I wish so many of the things that have happened to me recently hadn't happened so I could have spent more time with him. It wouldn't have bothered OB that no one but us showed up today—he truly wouldn't have cared at all. When he lost the love of his life..." Stellar paused and shook his head.

"All he had left was golf. All he had left was you, and you, and you. All he had left was us. Which is too bad. He was a great guy—blunt, but great. He was funny, inappropriate, rude, but honest. We all let him get away with a certain number of things," Stellar looked directly at Brittlyn, "because we understood why he did what he did. We at least got to know him enough to get it. We knew enough to care."

Stellar stepped towards the casket and placed his right hand on it. "OB told me in our last round together that if anyone sang Amazing Grace at his funeral he'd kill himself. He told me that on the fourth hole at the club, which appropriately, I understand, is where he died putting out a three-inch gimme." Stellar laughed. "The old man wouldn't have even given God that as a gimme." Stellar bowed his head. "I hope you can see us OB, wherever you are, and I hope you know that we're here for you. You did so much you'll never get credit for—people just didn't get you—but we got you."

That was pretty much it. They weren't brilliant words. I doubt he'd even planned to say them until seconds before he did. But they said enough. They made their point. Stellar was saying "thank you" for him and for everyone else who couldn't, hadn't or didn't even know they should be.

He returned to Miss Kate's side, and she put her arm around him and kissed his head. I heard her whisper, "That was perfect." And I heard Stellar say, "Thanks."

Then the mystery woman spoke. "I don't have much to say," she began. "I heard you call him OB." She pointed at Stellar. "I can imagine what those initials stood for. My kids knew him as Oscar the Grouch, but then… they didn't really know him. I didn't really know him either—not anymore—not like the rest of you anyway. But I will say I distinctly remember him hating Amazing Grace." She smiled at Stellar then looked around at the rest of us. "Other than that, I wanted to thank all of you for coming on this appropriately miserable day."

Had to be a club member by that comment. Or a relative.

She turned towards Brittlyn and continued. "And I don't know you either, but you have to know you look an awful lot like Mom did when she was your age. It's really quite startling. But trust me when I say that's the greatest of compliments. I can only hope the old man didn't make you too uncomfortable with that fact."

*Mystery solved.*

Stellar and I exchanged a quick glance as she stepped back. His surprise was evident. I just nodded. Made sense. OB's only child.

We didn't sing Amazing Grace. *Or "I Love Trash."* Nor did we sing "Take Me Out to the Ballgame" which Stellar claimed had been OB's actual request. We settled for "It Is Well With My Soul." I think OB would have accepted that.

After the funeral Coach Chandler approached Stellar with a manila envelope. Coach handed it to him and said, "I've got something for you in my car."

We followed Coach to his car and he popped the trunk. He lifted out a bag of golf clubs, OB's set of hickories—or rather his wife's. "Supposedly it's in his note," Coach said. "He wanted you to have these."

I could tell Stellar considered refusing. Instead, he bit his lip and took the bag of clubs. He shook Coach Chandler's hand and thanked him.

"Come see me sometime will you?" Coach asked. "We miss you over there."

Stellar shrugged but said, "Okay."

Miss Brittlyn leaned in and kissed his cheek. "I've missed you," she said.

"I've missed you, too," Stellar replied.

Stellar watched Brittlyn walk away and slide into the car. I felt I could almost read his mind. She's amazing. But she's no Lauren.

I didn't think the boy would ever get over that girl.

On the car ride home Stellar opened the envelope. It contained two keys, a check and a note. Stellar glanced at the check but didn't react. He handed it up to Miss Kate and she reacted. In fact, she was barely able to muffle her scream. I could see the numbers over her shoulder. TWENTY. MILLION. DOLLARS. I did a double take but there was no doubt that's what the check said. I looked at Stellar again, but the money didn't interest him. He was reading through the letter.

When he finished reading I waited for him to say something. We all were waiting. Instead he leaned his head against the window and rode the rest of the way home—eyes closed—in silence.

The next day I was polishing the counter at WINGS when Stellar walked in the door carrying the bag of hickory clubs OB had given him. I did my best to hide my surprise as he approached the counter and placed the envelope in front of me. He hadn't been in there in six months! "I'll be in the Lounge," he said and walked towards the room once designated as "his."

I quickly skimmed through the letter. This was the gist of it:

The check for $20 Million was—in Miss Kate's care—to be divided up equally six ways between Stellar, Coach Chandler, Brittlyn, OB's daughter, the new Junior Clinic at the golf club, and to completely pay off the townhome OB had recently purchased between Farmington and Bristol. That townhome was left in Ken and Kate's name.

OB had given Stellar over $3 million dollars, and the boy didn't bat an eye. He never had cared about money. *Bernie had definitely done the boy right!*

OB thanked Stellar for giving him a chance, for seeing past the surly exterior and being the closest thing to a new friend he'd made in years. He asked Stellar to occasionally pinch Brittlyn's rear end for him (though he used a different word)—something I was certain Stellar would never do—and to tell Coach Chandler to spend some of his $3 million on a new putter and shoes cause "the one is broken and the others are too broken in."

OB praised Stellar's composure, his all-around game, and stated plainly that he'd never seen a golfer with more talent, at any age. He believed Stellar would be a multiple-major winner on the PGA tour. He insisted that Stellar understand that, "Sometimes sucky things happen in life that just plain suck and the remedy is to blow—to exhale—and seek the positives. Find the silver linings. They're there," he said. "And if a grumpy old fart like me can find them, a brilliant kid like you surely can."

And finally, there was a paragraph about a Hickory Golf Tournament in Galloway, New Jersey that OB's wife had wanted to play in but had died before she could. OB had signed up for it this year, but also died before he could participate. His last request of Stellar was that Stellar enter and use the hickory clubs in that tournament—to play one round for OB and his wife, if OB couldn't.

That's why Stellar was here now, why he was in his "studio." This wasn't a reconciliation with golf. He didn't want to be here. But he was in there testing out his arm and those wooden clubs to fulfill the final request of an old man with very few friends, but one true friend in Stellar.

I tell you, just when you think you're too old and dried up to shed a tear, that boy just gets to you. Just when you think you're too old to learn anything new, he teaches you.

I walked across the room and tested the handle on the door to his studio. It was locked. I leaned my head against the door and could hear the familiar sound of clubs hitting balls. But I could also hear something else. I could hear crying, and cursing. There was sobbing, and sounds of someone in physical pain. And it tore me all apart.

========= CALVIN JACKSON =========

←←←←←→→→→→

***"Golf is the closest game to life.***
***You get bad breaks from good shots;***
***You good breaks from bad shots;***
***but you always have to play the ball where it lies."***

- Bobby Jones

## STELLAR 54 – "May 2017"

First of May I found out I lost another friend. OB died. He had it coming. He wanted it to come. I'm sure he was rather relieved to die—his last words were probably even "thank you" to God, and that man seldom had anything nice to say to God. He missed his wife—the love of his life. I understood. If she'd have still been on earth I'm sure he'd have fought to keep living. But with her gone, he was ready to go, too. As long as he ended up the same place she was.

I'd only spent a handful of days with that old man in my life, but I knew I was going to miss him. I even said a few words at his funeral. And then he goes and gives me three million dollars. Well, I didn't want his money. There were only two things I wanted in life. I had one (family) and couldn't have the other (Lauren).

I hope Nick knows what he has. It kind of burned me that he was so impressed with Brittlyn. Sure, she's hot, but she flaunts it. She puts it all out there for public consumption. That's not Lauren. Lauren has the super hot going for her too, of course… but it's far more private and reserved. She pulls it off in a t-shirt, jeans and ball cap. She pulls it off in a snowsuit where you can't see an inch of skin. She overwhelms in subtle waves of heat. *I'm probably not making any sense.* Let's just say she has that certain "I don't know what" quality—or "je ne sais quoi" as the French put it. I clearly can't describe it… but I'd trade ten Brittlyns for a Lauren, and that's no knock on Brittlyn. What she put up with for OB—her selflessness and compassion, some guy is going to be lucky to get her, too.

What got me about OB's letter was that last paragraph—the paragraph about golf and the golf tournament. I was done with golf, never wanted to play it again. And then I go and read the words of a man who seemed to hate everything, telling me how I should find the "silver linings" in the darkness, make the best of the worst.

That man didn't want me to end up as disgruntled as he was. If that were even possible. He didn't want me to miss the opportunities he claimed I had. He believed in me, actually said as much, and wanted me to pursue this stupid game of sticks and balls.

I didn't see the point. But then he went on about this Hickory tournament in Galloway, New Jersey that his wife had wanted to play, but she'd died before she could. OB had pledged to play it for her and then he also died. He somehow had the foresight to write this letter and ask me to play it for him—for both of them—if he couldn't make it. *Which was obviously the case.* I didn't feel like I had a choice. I had to do this for him. Even if it killed me.

There were several major problems. First, the calendar said I only had five weeks to get ready. I hadn't swung a single golf club in six months, hadn't tested my arm with anything other than a fishing pole. It ached every night as it was, just from basic day-to-day movements. Swinging a golf club was going to be excruciating.

The other major problem… this was a "hickory clubs only" event. I couldn't recall ever having swung a single wooden club in my entire life. And hickories are nothing like modern golf clubs. They don't have all these power pockets in the faces, no array of enhancing shafts, and forgiveness is a foreign word to their manufacturers. Hickory golf is a game of finesse, of bump-and-run play. It takes far more intelligence, creativity and accuracy than modern golf. Tour players with their 200 mph swings would snap a sack of them in half in just a few holes. They would really struggle with this game. *I was going to struggle with this game.*

When I got home from the funeral Nick and I were hanging out. He had the money on his mind—imagining what all he could do with $3 million dollars. I honestly considered offering it to him for Lauren, but that would have been a messed up transaction either way.

When Nick read the letter and got to the part about the Hickory Invitational in New Jersey he laughed. "That's dumb," he said.

And those two words are what made me 100% certain I was playing. That comment sparked the five-alarm fire that ensued. "You don't think I can do it?"

"Stellar, I'm not saying that… but you haven't swung a club in six months. *You* don't even know if you physically can. Is it worth risking your arm for a stupid golf tournament?"

"I'd do anything for a friend," I replied. "And what would you do? What would you do for a friend? Or should I say… what would you do to your best friend?

"Stellar, that's not fair."

"Not fair?" *Lighter fluid.* "*That's* not fair?""

That's when the fire in me raged out of control.

I yelled at Nick. I screamed at Nick. Kate came running in and I screamed at her, too. Nick knew how much I loved Lauren—he'd always known. How could he do that to me, to his best friend? I said things I didn't even know I was feeling, unleashed pain I didn't even realize I had.

I don't know how Nick took it, how he just stood there and accepted my anger, but he did. And when I was done screaming at him and cursing him *he* apologized. *Nick apologized to me.* And it was so genuine—so obviously heartfelt—that I couldn't help but accept it.

"Stellar," he said calmly. "You're absolutely right. If you want me to end it with her right now, I'll go over there and do it."

I shook my head, though I did consider challenging him to turn those words into actions.

"Nick," Kate said softly. "Can I have a moment with my son?"

"Sure." Nick nodded. And he left the room.

"Kate—"

"Miles. I just want you to take a deep breath."

"Kate—"

"Miles, I know you've been holding onto that for a long time. I understand that. But that was harsh. Forget what you said to me. You just tore Nick to pieces. He honestly would go end it with her right now… I believe that.

"Kate, I don't want Nick to end it with Lauren."

"That's not what it sounded like to me. That's not what your face is still saying."

"Well of course I want him to end it with her then. Is that what you want me to say? I love her. I want her. I don't want anyone else to touch her, to kiss her, to have her in any imaginable way. I want her."

"So where does that leave Nick?"

"I don't care."

"You don't mean that."

"But I want to." That was it right there. I wanted to not care what Nick felt for Lauren. I wanted to be selfish with this. I wanted Nick to give in for me without me asking him to. I didn't want to be the one to sacrifice this time.

Kate shook her head and turned to leave the room. I reached out for her hand. "Mom…" She stopped and looked back at me, a twinge of surprise on her face. "I love her."

"I know," Kate said. "But how much?"

"What do you mean?" *After all that wasn't it obvious?* I couldn't think of anything I loved more.

"Do you love her enough to give her what she wants?"

"Of course."

"Then…"

I got the message. *Get out of the way. Let her go.*

I wish I could say Nick and I hugged it out, but we didn't. When Kate opened the door he was gone. I was certain he'd heard every word, and I didn't even regret it. He stole my girl. He knew how much I loved her and he stole her. I didn't care if his feelings were hurt now. He had Lauren to kiss his pain away.

Kate fielded a call from Carrie later that evening. From what I could hear through the vents Nick was crushed. He'd skipped dinner and just gone to bed—completely unlike him. Carrie wanted to know what had happened, what it was all about. "Girls." I heard Kate say. "Stupid girls."

I went to bed content.

I woke up a malcontent. I was such an idiot. I went looking for Nick to apologize, but he wasn't home, wasn't at the marina, and I didn't see his bike at Lauren's when I rode by. Carrie didn't pick up when I tried calling her either. I stopped back by the house to pick up the hickory clubs and angrily rode over to WINGS.

Cal was surprised to see me, of course. It had been six months since I'd set foot in the place. I dropped the envelope on the counter in front of him, told him to read it and locked myself in the "studio" with the hickories. I then proceeded to hit golf balls in the simulator until I could barely move my arms.

I eventually collapsed on the couch and fell asleep. I'm not sure how many hours went by before I woke up to Cal wrapping my arm in a sleeve of ice. "Owww…"

"Don't move your arm, sir," Cal said.

"Don't think I could if I wanted to," I mumbled.

"You hit too much." He shook his head. "It might be broken again."

"That might not be the worst thing."

"Can you explain why you did this? Why you took it so far?"

"I was angry. And hurt. I needed something to take it out on, to make the pain go away." *The irony was not lost on me.*

"This about Miss Lauren?"

"It's always about Miss Lauren, Cal." It was about Nick too though. I knew I'd hurt him.

"You could say how you feel, tell her how much you love her."

"It's too late, Cal."

"Ain't never so, sir." Cal shook his head.

"Until you're dead," I replied sarcastically.

"And you ain't dead," was his immediate and impressive comeback.

*True.* Quite true. *But irrelevant nonetheless.* I looked at him. "Cal, sometimes maybe you shouldn't say what you're thinking."

Appropriately he didn't respond to that remark. Which actually made me wonder what he was thinking.

## ←★★★★★ CALVIN JACKSON ★★★★★→
### Letter (Part 4 of 6)

May was a rough month for Stellar. The girl he loved was with his best friend. His best friend wouldn't speak to him. Nick's mother was upset with Stellar. Stellar's parents were upset with him. It seemed he could do no right when, unfortunately, that's all the boy tried to do. Everyone had such high expectations for him, wanting him to handle everything like an adult—at sixteen. It's no wonder he felt so overwhelmed. It's no wonder he felt so alone.

Stellar's approach to "running away" was to lock himself in a room at WINGS. He took his considerable pain and frustrations out on golf, and golf only hurt and frustrated him more. He wasn't the player he'd been before breaking his right arm—twice. I'm relatively certain that if he were to see a sports psychologist right now the doctor would tell him to give up the sport, or, at the very least, give up hickory golf. This wasn't the game he'd excelled at before. This particular golf was bad for his health—mental, physical and emotional. He was only getting more and more frustrated with each passing day, each day he got closer to the Hickory Invitational in New Jersey.

So there we were, June 3rd, less than a week away from the event, and he was nowhere near ready to play. His right arm was bruised fifty shades of purple. We iced it every day, and I could tell he was still in considerable pain. He'd refused to have it checked out by a doctor, because he was certain they'd shut him down—probably even put on a new cast. He'd kept his arm hidden from Ken and Kate and begged me not to tell either of them about it. That put me in a terrible position. At a time when the boy trusted almost no one, I risked alienating him even more by breaking his confidence… but there are some secrets you shouldn't keep, and I knew this was one of them. I knew Miss Kate was worried about him. I needed to make her more than that. I needed her to intervene.

Miss Kate wasn't fond of coming down to WINGS either. *Understandably.* It took Stellar half a year to come back here, and when Miss Kate would come down to pick him up she'd stay in the car. She hadn't once been inside since mid-November—since the attack.

I watched her pull into the parking lot this time and walked out to meet her at the car. "I'll walk you in, Miss Kate," I said.

"Thank you, Cal. You didn't have to come out."

"Of course, I did." I could tell that she was grateful I had.

She couldn't wait to ask what this was about. "You wanted to talk to me?"

"Let's go inside." We walked towards the building.

"Cal, you're scaring me."

I turned towards her. "I don't mean to, Miss Kate. I just… I think Stellar needs a friend."

"What do you mean?"

"He has no one. He needs you. With all he's been through… of anyone in the world who should be there for him now, Miss Kate, it's you."

I didn't intend to say it so bluntly, 'twas way out of character for me, but it just came out that way. What had to be said was said.

"Hold on a minute." A very rare anger flooded Kate's face. "Are you implying I'm not doing enough for my own son? How... Cal, you don't have the right to—"

I swallowed hard. I knew this could cost me my job and my relationship with Stellar. This conversation could easily destroy my present and future.

"Miss Kate, I don't mean to overstep." It was hard to maintain eye contact with her glare. "But you don't really know what he's going through."

"You've got to be kidding me right now. I know far more than you do about—"

I shook my head. "No. No, Miss Kate, you don't." It was too late to turn back now.

"How dare you?" She looked stunned. "Where is this coming from? What are you doing?"

"Miss Kate." I swallowed hard again. *Drive it home.* "You have a boy in there with an arm possibly broken thirty ways, crying out with every swing, trying his heart out to win the girl he loves and please the woman he loves—you—and you are not with him. You don't know what he's doing to himself. You don't know how lonely he is." I watched her mouth drop open as she looked towards the building. I knew I had to make every word count. "Now Stellar, he says not to say anything to you—that you're already angry with him and that you don't care, but I know you do care and I felt this needed to be said."

"Cal—"

"I can collect my things, Miss Kate, and be gone in minutes if you'd like. But that boy, he needs you. He feels he has lost everything he loves because he risked his life to save you and *trust me*, he doesn't understand why you are not there with him."

Her rigid demeanor had evaporated. I've always maintained Miss Kate is the most understanding person I know, but I had pushed it here. For a man who most often said too little, this time I feared I'd said too much. I was expecting the worst.

Instead Miss Kate took my hand. "Calvin… *you* are *not* going anywhere. I've known you several years now and never heard you say more than twenty words for any reason, so I don't know how you managed this, but I certainly believe that every word you've said was calculated and true. I can only imagine how difficult that must have been for you. I'm sorry if I—"

"Miss Kate, please…"

"Calvin… I'm sorry."

"Stellar will not be pleased with me."

"He'll get over it." She continued towards the front door of the building. "He's in there now?"

I nodded and led her inside, then over to the Lounge door. I grabbed her arm. "Listen," I whispered.

She put her ear to the door but she didn't need to. We could plainly hear the clubs hitting balls, the grunts, groans and moans coming through the door. "How long has he been doing this, Cal?"

"Four weeks."

*"Four weeks?"*

She probably wanted to ask me why I'd waited so long to tell her, but she didn't. I could see she felt terrible. She had no idea. "Yes, ma'am." I nodded. As she reached for the door handle I took her hand. "Miss Kate, this will sound stupid to you… but he needs to play in that event next weekend."

"Cal, no—"

"Miss Kate." I reiterated. "He must. Or he will never forgive either of us."

"But Cal, it's golf."

"Not this time it isn't. This isn't about golf at all."

"Okay…" She looked puzzled but nodded. "Okay, if you insist it's that—"

"Yes, Miss Kate. I do." I turned to walk towards the counter and this time she grabbed me.

"Cal," she said. I glanced back into her soft brown eyes. "Thank you."

"Anything for that boy," I replied.

========== CALVIN JACKSON ==========

## ←★★★★★ KATE PARKER ★★★★★→
**Letter (Part 3 of 4)**

**←June 3, 2017→**

For someone with 20/20 vision I'm pretty dang blind. Cal opened my eyes to something I shouldn't have missed—not once, and certainly not for twenty-nine consecutive days. My boy was hurting. And it was pretty much my fault.

It's easy with Avery to know when she needs something. She'll tell me bluntly. She can be rather direct, rather bossy. She pretty much screams, *"MOMMY!"* But that's never been Miles's style. His connections are more emotional and less verbal. He's more subtle—more of a whisperer. Sometimes his needs are harder to see.

That's *no* excuse for my ignorance.

I've always asked Miles to level with me—to never lie—to always tell me exactly how he feels. Most parents ask that of their kids then get angry when their child is actually honest about their mistakes. The child sees that and determines there's less risk to lying. It's easier to lie.

I was *NOT* going to be *that* parent. That was *NOT* going to be my kid. I've always appreciated my son's honesty—that he's been a straight shooter. I feel that's made our relationship what it is. He's proven to be worthy of my trust day in and day out. What's more he was willing to pay the ultimate sacrifice for love, he was willing to give his own life to save mine. That should have earned him even more credibility than anything.

Instead, when he leveled with me about Lauren I didn't want to hear what he was saying, I wanted his words to be different—to be more sensitive of Nick. I was critical of him for it. That wasn't fair. It wasn't fair of me. Guess I was *that* parent after all. *Thank God Cal had the guts, and love for my son, to point that out.*

It's hard to talk to people about your emotions. There's always the risk they won't understand, that they may even mock you. Those reactions damage you and make it far less likely that you'll trust that person—or maybe even anyone else—with such feelings again. I hoped it wasn't too late with Miles.

When I entered his studio at WINGS I found him with his head in his hands on a chair facing the golf simulator. He didn't hear me come in, but as soon as I announced my presence I saw him jump and pull the right sleeve down on his shirt.

He spun towards me. "Kate. What are you doing here? Did you try calling? I didn't—"

"Can I talk to you?"

"Uhh… sure."

He walked over to a couch and sat down and I sat beside him—to his left. "How's the golf?"

I knew he wasn't sure how long I'd been in there. "Okay, I guess," he replied.

"Cal told me—"

"Uggh…"

"Miles. I'm sorry."

"What? Why—"

I am *not* a crier—contrary to all the evidence otherwise these past several months—but the tears poured out of my eyes then. "I'm so sorry."

"Kate, what—"

"Listen." I took his face in my hands. "I love you. You deserved better than this from me."

"Kate." He pushed my hands away with his left arm. "It's—"

"Miles. I'm sorry about Lauren. I'm sorry about Nick, about Carrie, about Mr. and Mrs. Chambers, about everyone. I'm sorry that none of us have been there for you." I'd interrupted him so many times now he wasn't even trying to get a word in anymore. "You have every right to be upset with Nick and with Lauren. You have every right to be upset with me. You break your arm saving Taryn. You break your arm saving me. You lose Lauren. You lose OB. You've done all these things for other people, and what has anyone done for you?"

"Kate I'm not looking for anyone to do anything for me." There were a few tears in his eyes now, too. "I just want someone to be there for me. I want to be able to tell someone my feelings without being judged, to be able to tell you I love Lauren without you telling me that I can't."

There it was. Plain and simple. Fair and square.

He continued. "I'm not asking people to give her to me. I don't want Nick to give her up—to have to sacrifice his love and happiness for my benefit. But when you ask me a question I need to know whether or not I can tell you the truth *as I feel it* because the truth hurts me, a lot, and if you can't take it, then please don't ask me for it."

*Again. Dead on.* "Fair enough." I nodded. "I'm sorry."

"Please stop apologizing."

"Miles…"

"It sucks to lose Nick's friendship."

"I'm sure you haven't."

"Of course I have. He *can't* be friends with me. He knows I want her. He knows I'd do anything to get her."

"That's not true."

"What wouldn't I do?"

"You wouldn't stab him in the back. You wouldn't betray either one of them or throw either of them under the bus to the other. You could have given Lauren that letter and made her feel like a fool—"

"Wait—" Miles tried to cut me off but I didn't let him.

"You could have let Nick read that letter and made him feel like a fool."

"Kate—"

"There's a lot you wouldn't do, but they're not going to give you any credit for it because they don't know. Lauren doesn't know you legally couldn't talk to her about the attack. Nick doesn't know that either. You could have found your way out of this mess if you'd been willing to sacrifice either friendship but you weren't." I'd said what I needed to. I could let him talk now.

"How'd you know about the letter?"

"I found it in the trash."

"And you read it?"

I nodded.

"And you were still upset with me for what I said to Nick?"

*Now I felt like an even bigger idiot.* "Miles… I can't explain that. I was thinking about losing Carrie if you lost Nick." *Which had actually happened.* "I was thinking about what it would mean for us and the Chambers family if you, I don't know. I was stupid. I was really selfish."

I deserved the nodding head I got in response. "You shouldn't have read that letter," he said quietly.

"But I'm glad I did," I replied. "Especially now. All those words have kind of sunk in now. If Lauren would ever read them—"

"She *can't*. She can't know what I was going to say that night… what I was going to do—"

"I know."

"Not *ever*."

I nodded. "I understand."

"You have to promise me that. No matter what, she *never* reads that letter. You never tell her what it said. You never tell anyone. You take it to work and you shred it tomorrow."

"Miles—"

"Promise me that."

"Okay." I lied. "I'll take care of it tomorrow."

For a second it looked like he didn't believe me, but then he nodded. "Thank you."

"No, Miles, thank you." He leaned his head against my shoulder and I wrapped my arm around him. It was impossible to miss the giant flinch when my hand came to rest on his right arm. He pulled away from me instantly.

"Miles?"

"Kate."

"Let me see that arm."

He shook his head but didn't move away from me. I slowly rolled up the sleeve and almost threw up on the spot. I've never seen so many bruises, so many variations of yellow, red and purple color tones on skin. "Holy—"

"Kate. It's fine."

I looked him in the eyes. "How—" I shook my head.

"I have to play in that tournament next week."

Every part of the mother in me wanted to say "no way" and yet I found myself going back to Cal's words on the matter. Cal had been right about me, he'd been right about pretty much everything I'd *ever* heard him say. He was the only one who knew how badly Miles was hurt and yet he'd insisted I not mess with this. I took a deep breath and shook my head again. "I know."

That's what I said. Not "over my dead body" which would have been entirely inappropriate for other reasons, but "I know."

"You do?" Miles looked rather surprised.

"Like it or not… yes. I do. But I have two conditions." I held up two fingers.

"Okay."

"One—you come home with me right now and let me treat the swelling for you. And two—after your round I take you straight to the doctor."

"It's a three-round event, Kate."

I laughed. *Of course it was! No way he even made it through 18 holes.* "Whatever you say."

## ←★★★★★ NARRATOR ★★★★★→

### ←Monday, July 4, 2022→

The fireworks started at midnight—12:07 a.m. to be exact. That first significant contraction doubled me over and had the monitor beside me beeping like crazy. A nurse scurried in and pushed a couple buttons.

"That was a good one," she said.

"No kidding," I snapped. *Be nice. She didn't do this to you.* "Sorry."

"Ma'am, it'll get a lot more personal than that in the next few hours," she replied with a smile.

"Especially if you keep calling me ma'am," I replied.

"Sorry." She nodded. "Habit."

"No worries."

Kate was still typing away in the chair beside my bed. She'd just finished entering and editing one of her own letters to her satisfaction. "It's too bad you don't have more from this time period," she said.

"What do you mean?"

"Well, Stellar's not saying much about you at this point. Nick isn't saying anything about either of you at this point—"

"You feel like there needs to be something from me?"

"I do. I feel like you're the centerpiece of this entire part of the book and your voice is missing. In fact, five pages from your journal on this time period are torn out—entirely gone."

I had intended to have all of this done before I got to the hospital. It was not part of my plan to have Kate doing any of this conversion for me. It was unfortunate that she'd noticed those missing pages.

"Listen, Kate, you and I both know why I can't put how I was feeling at that time in this book."

"Because you were regretting leaving Miles?"

"Because I still loved him."

"But Nick knows that."

The look on my face said otherwise. "Actually—"

Kate put her hand on my arm. "He didn't know?"

I shook my head. "Only my mom. And then my mom told you." Kate's stunned expression prompted me to say more. "I couldn't tell him what I was feeling. He was so angry at Stellar. He was so insecure—so worried I'd leave him. I… I never told him."

"But… he knows you loved Stellar."

"Yes, of course, he knows I loved Stellar before he and I were... together." I glanced at the door to make sure Nick wasn't standing outside. "But he doesn't know that I love Stellar more."

"Loved," Kate corrected.

"Nick doesn't know that every day I regretted kissing him on New Year's Eve and every day I wished Stellar would come over. Every day I wanted to see him... Nick doesn't know that if Stellar had simply asked me to leave Nick I would have in a heartbeat, every single day until..."

"Wow."

*What else could she say?* "Exactly. So I didn't tell him." I watched Kate's face as she absorbed what I'd just said. I felt terrible.

"I always assumed he knew."

"Just my mom," I replied, "and you."

Kate was silent for a full minute, staring out the window. Finally she spoke. "Looks like you made the right decision."

"Did I?" I wasn't so sure. *If I had just been honest with Nick then. If I'd just apologized to Stellar—just told him how I felt. Maybe then...*

"Definitely doesn't do us any good to dwell on "what ifs" now."

*Preaching to the choir.* I'd done it for years anyway.

"How does Nick feel about you writing this book?"

"He's fine with it." *I honestly believe that.* "We all owe something significant to Stellar. Nick has his own things to say, as well as his own regrets and his own secrets, I'm sure." I paused. "We all need this book."

"Each in our own way," Kate agreed softly.

"Are you mad at me?"

"Far from it." Kate shook her head.

"So you understand?"

"There are things Ken doesn't know about me too. Even some significant things." Kate stood up. "We all make..."

*Mistakes.* She didn't say it—she caught herself in time.

"We all make some choices we feel we have to make," she reworded, with an almost sad smile, then stood suddenly. "I need a bathroom break. Can I get you anything?"

Another tremor ripped through my mid-section. I winced until it subsided. "A little more water maybe."

"Sure thing."

Kate stepped out into the hall and I laid my head back on the pillow. I'd tried hard to move on from those days. I loved Nick now—I had for years—I knew that to be true. But there was always going to be a part of me that wondered what life would have been like with Stellar. There was always going to be a part of me that regretted not having the chance to find out. And deep in my heart, in the locked away most honest part of me, I knew it was impossible for me to ever love anyone more than Stellar. And that wasn't Nick's fault. But Nick could never know that.

Those missing pages would never be a part of this book.

←←←←←→→→→→

***"I don't fear death,***
***but I sure don't like three-footers for par."***

- Chi Chi Rodriguez

←←←←←→→→→→

## ←★★★★★ CALVIN JACKSON ★★★★★→
**Letter (Part 5 of 6)**

The morning of June 8th I thought we were going to have to drop out of the event. I'd say Miss Kate was closer to allowing an amputation than she was to letting Stellar play, but somehow we got out the door. I told him this was stupid, that even OB would say so, but he didn't want to hear it. He's a strong-willed young man to say the very least.

We drove to Galloway, New Jersey and completed the registration. Kate freely applied a variety of gel-like anesthetics to his arm while all the other tourney participants loosened up on the range. When our tee time was up we headed to the first tee and I handed Stellar his wooden BelleAir driver. He took a single practice swing and then stepped up to his customized, orange, McIntyre "Park" ball with OB printed on its face. I told him those initials were bad luck to put on a golf ball.

"I can't have much bad luck left," he said, paraphrasing a quote of mine from an earlier golf event.

*That should've been true.*

Stellar's first hit with the driver shattered its face. One swing and he was already down a club. The ball itself barely got off the ground, but at least it went straight—about eighty yards. This was going to be a long day.

He deserves credit for at least trying to stay positive. Approaching that first tee shot he joked that he probably still would've outdriven OB with that ball. I smiled, but the golf gods must not have been amused.

Stellar bogeyed the first six holes and parred each of the next six. He even broke his E.E. Beverly Brassie—his three-wood equivalent—on the twelfth hole.

His day was done. He'd need to birdie the last six holes to make the cut, and he didn't have a single birdie yet.

And then somehow he had six. Somehow, he made the cut… on the cut line. I'm certain you don't need more details of that round, it was miserable in every way. His playing partners cringed every time he hit the ball—the pain so obvious and magnified on Stellar's face with each swing. I heard both of them at multiple points call him stupid. It only motivated the boy more.

Miss Kate, for her part, could barely watch. On the other hand, Stellar's group had gained quite a gallery following. There were so many murmurs, so many expressions of shock and awe. For someone who despised attention he was certainly garnering plenty of it.

When Stellar stepped to the tee for his second round the starter actually crossed the tee box to wish him luck and shake his hand. He even mentioned he was pulling for him. The starter didn't shake hands with the other two men—something they both couldn't help but notice.

People were carrying newspapers around with them and pointing at Stellar throughout the round. *I guess there'd been a small story on his last round.* There were photographers everywhere—a day after we hadn't seen a single one. Somehow this small event had become a major local news story. I was overwhelmed by all the commotion. Stellar ignored it. He kept swinging, kept salvaging pars from double-bogey tee shots. The former Mrs. Brown's GB-V putter was a lightning rod in Stellar's hands. But there wasn't a smile on his face, not a wave in his arm. He was fighting, persevering, through more and more pain. This wasn't fun for him, not a single swing of it. It was sad to watch. It was painful to watch.

There were throngs of people crowding him on every shot. They'd never needed player security at this event before. People were on the tee boxes, climbing trees, all over the greens—it was like this was some big historic event, and they all wanted to be a part of it. "Surreal" doesn't cut it. It was all I could do to keep people from grabbing Stellar or touching his arm. I felt like I was guarding the President of the United States.

Stellar was 2-under on Saturday with ten pars, seven birdies and a snowman (an 8) on a par 3. That 2-under had him in a tie for tenth… and on the front page of Sunday's paper.

I didn't know what to say to the boy. If I had to guess, in the first two rounds there were probably less than ten words said between us. Total. That changed on Sunday. Sunday morning, on the first tee box a lunatic fan charged up to Stellar and hit him in the arm. There was no malicious intent. This wasn't Happy Gilmore. It was a rowdy yet celebratory move, I knew that, but when Stellar crumbled to the ground in agony a police officer and about sixty other angry men tackled that fan. I could hear the man screaming while they collectively whaled on him, but I was more concerned with my boy.

That was it. Stellar could no longer swing his right arm and these sticks weren't reversible. He couldn't play them left-handed.

"I can't do it," he moaned, weeping on my shoulder.

"It's okay, sir." I wrapped my arms around him. "Ain't no need to go on. You did your part."

Kate joined us, and Stellar dissolved into tears in her arms. I stood to fight off photographers who all wanted that windfall shot. "He's just a boy," I pleaded. "Please leave him alone."

"He's the Magician," one of the reporters said. "The Montauk Magician."

"He's not…" I started to say, but no one was listening. *He's not from Montauk.*

No one cared. And no one heeded my pleas. Kate and I protectively escorted Stellar through halls of cheering fans, through the pandemonium that this old-school event had become.

Stellar officially withdrew. He was marked as a "DNF"—Did Not Finish—but the papers barely noted that the next day. It was all about this sixteen-year-old kid with wooden clubs who "would have won the whole event if he hadn't been assaulted by a rowdy fan."

I felt bad for all the participants ahead of Stellar who no doubt still would have beat him—they deserved better than that—but I certainly couldn't deny one absolute truth.

I had just witnessed the third of Stellar's five *golf* magic acts.

========== CALVIN JACKSON ==========

## STELLAR 55 – "June 2017"

stupid stupid stupid stupid stupid stupid stupid stupid stupid
stupid stupid stupid stupid stupid stupid stupid stupid stupid
stupid stupid stupid stupid stupid stupid stupid stupid stupid
stupid stupid stupid stupid stupid stupid stupid stupid stupid
stupid stupid stupid stupid STUPID stupid stupid stupid stupid
stupid stupid stupid stupid stupid stupid stupid stupid stupid
IS stupid stupid stupid stupid IS stupid stupid stupid stupid IS
stupid stupid stupid stupid stupid stupid stupid stupid stupid
A stupid stupid stupid stupid A stupid stupid stupid stupid A
stupid stupid stupid stupid stupid stupid stupid stupid stupid
stupid stupid stupid stupid STUPID stupid stupid stupid stupid
stupid stupid stupid stupid stupid stupid stupid stupid stupid
stupid stupid stupid stupid WORD stupid stupid stupid stupid
stupid stupid stupid stupid stupid stupid stupid stupid stupid
stupid stupid stupid stupid stupid stupid stupid stupid stupid
stupid stupid stupid stupid stupid stupid stupid stupid stupid
stupid stupid stupid stupid stupid stupid stupid stupid stupid

I heard it from my caddie, two nurses, three doctors, a lawyer, a pharmacist, a man watching the Red Sox on TV, six golfers, and my little sister all within a matter of hours, all referring to me. Well, except the Red Sox guy. I don't think he knew anything about my arm. Or what I'd done with that arm.

There are certain words you just grow up hating—underpants, liver, Jets, stupid and, well, hate. Those are my big ones. I'm not much for curse words in general—*not that any of the ones I've mentioned would be considered as such* (*except maybe Jets*)—and I'm not just saying that. There are merely far more intelligent and creative words to insult someone with or to use in general descriptions than the various forms of reproduction, dark recesses of your anatomy, dog and donkey references, and/or nouns of bodily emissions.

Stupid, if you think about it, is just another way of saying all of those things. It's seldom actually used as a reference to someone's intelligence, which is actually all it should be used for. And calling someone with a high IQ stupid is actually. Well… pretty stupid. So let's just say that I didn't appreciate everyone referring to me as that word all day. It got old quickly.

I knew what I was doing, and I knew the hickory tournament could very well be the last time I ever golfed—maybe ever even used that arm.

But, if I'm being absolutely honest, I didn't care. I started golfing because I loved it—because I was good at it. I started playing competitively to beat Josh, for Lauren. I only played in this tournament for OB. *Okay, and his wife.* What else was there to play for?

It wasn't fun anymore, not when every swing brought tears to my eyes, and when the results were far from what they used to be. So why would I ever want to golf again? I wasn't good. It wasn't fun. There was no incentive.

*And then suddenly there was.* The doctor told me I'd probably never play again. After essentially calling me stupid he said I'd used up my last swings, that I'd be lucky to write with my right hand again after I got this THIRD cast off.

That pissed me off. I'm sorry, but it did. You don't tell me what I can and can't do—what I will and won't do. You don't know me.

Kate asked me in the car on the way home what I was thinking.

"He's wrong," I said. That's what I was thinking.

"You have to be smart about this, Miles."

"And not stupid," Avery chimed in.

"Avery," Kate scolded. She didn't like that word either.

I glared at my little sister. "I will be."

We rode in silence back to Southampton. As we passed the sign for our Long Island Indoor Golf Center I saw a familiar figure on his bike heading towards our golf shop. "Kate, can you drop me off here?"

She pulled over. "Sure. You okay?"

"Yeah, I'm fine. Just want to go talk to Cal."

"Want me to come pick you up later?"

"Okay if I call you?"

"As long as it's before nine."

I knew she meant 'before dark'. I nodded. "No problem."

I crossed the road and ran down to WINGS. I opened the door and stepped inside. Cal waved from behind the counter. As my eyes adjusted to the lack of natural light in the room I looked around at all the simulator stalls and practice areas. *Where was he?*

"You l-l-looking for someone?" Cal asked as I approached him.

"Did I see Josh come in here?"

Cal pointed towards the putting green. Sure enough, there he was.

"You let him come in here?"

Cal nodded. "Can't keep him out."

"But—"

"He's done no harm. Been downright cordial in fact."

"How long has he been coming here?"

"Since May 5th."

I looked Cal in the eyes. He didn't have my memory so that was oddly specific recollection. "And you've never felt like sharing that?"

"What's it to you?"

"This is our place."

"And he knows that." Cal seemed to be fighting back a smile. *He was enjoying this.*

"What about Caleb and Elliott?"

"No, sir." Cal shook his head. "I didn't invite them."

What was he saying? "Wait, you invited Josh?"

"Yes, sir."

"But—"

"Correct me if I'm wrong, sir, but didn't you say yesterday you ain't never golfing again?"

"Yes, but—"

"So if you're never golfing again, what's it matter if Josh comes here? His money becomes our money—it's as good as anyone else's."

"I don't think you understand. Do you know what he did to Lauren?"

"Do you believe in second chances?"

"Forget it." I shook my head and walked towards the putting green. *Not for Josh.*

"Sir," Cal called, but I waved him off.

I pulled a barstool up by the putting green and watched Josh putt. I watched him roll the ball with near perfect speed on every putt, but the ball refused to drop. He had no idea where the breaks were, and it appeared as if he'd set them all. I literally watched him miss twenty putts in a row from all distances before I'd had enough. "Good grief," I muttered loud enough for Josh to hear me.

"I suck," he said.

I shook my head. "Yes and no. Your pace is perfect, but it's like you're blind."

"Don't hold back on me now."

*That was fair.* "Did you set the slopes yourself?"

Josh nodded. "Yeah."

"Okay, so you've actually got the hard part down." I walked towards him. "There are pros who don't have your pace." I held my left hand out for his putter. He handed it to me without hesitation. I looked it over and tapped it on the green a few times. "The problem is not your putter—though a Scotty Cameron center-shaft mallet would be a great upgrade for you."

"That's what you have?"

I nodded. “Cal can hook you up.” I scanned the undulation of the putting surface near the hole he was putting towards. “So, what… you have this set at around 3 or 4 degrees in C4?” I pointed out the slope in that particular section.

“Yes. Four degrees in C4. Exactly.”

“Well, when you put the ball out here from back there you have to think mathematically. Over these last five feet that four degrees is only going to break about two and a half inches—at the most—towards the hole.”

I illustrated my point by putting a ball, single-handed—and left-handed—along that very line. It broke just the right amount, right where I’d indicated, but it was going too fast and just missed the hole.”

“Wow. How do you know that?”

“I memorized this chart Cal gave me on slope variance years ago. I could tell you based on the degree of slope how much a ball should move either way over any distance. If I had your pace I’d never miss.”

“Thanks,” Josh mumbled quietly.

I hadn’t intended to compliment him, but realized I had done just that. “Sure. So here, take your putter and take eight paces in any direction.”

As Josh paced away from me I glanced across the room at Cal who was beaming. I shook my head and concealed the smile that almost escaped. I wasn’t willing to concede any sort of victory to him, and I certainly wasn’t in the mood for any of his subtle gloating.

I worked with Josh on his putting for over an hour. It was amazing how much he improved just in that short time. *Man, to have his touch with that club!* Cal brought some snacks over to a table by the putting green and Josh and I sat down to devour them.

There was an extensive uncomfortable silence while we ate which neither of us knew how to break. Eventually Josh went for it. “Why’d you do that?”

“Why’d I do what?”

“You could have just gone in your Lounge like you usually do—”

“You’ve seen me in here before?”

“Many times. Many, many times. What—you’ve never seen me in here?”

I shook my head. “Nope. Never.”

“Wow,” Josh laughed. “Guess I didn’t know I was so invisible.”

“I wouldn’t have thought that either.”

“Yeah. I suppose not.” Josh jammed another handful of popcorn in his mouth. “Guess you probably would have tried to kick me out long before now, eh?”

I nodded. “Something like that.”

“So, you didn’t answer my question. Why’d you help me?”

“You were hurting me.” A smile cracked my lips.

Josh let out a loud laugh. "I was hurting you?"

"It was super painful watching you miss *TWENTY PUTTS IN A ROW*!" I reached out towards him and gave him a friendly shove.

A much easier silence settled over our table for the next few minutes while we finished off the popcorn. "So that's it?" he asked.

"That's it." Though I wasn't entirely positive that was actually the only reason. Calvin *might* have been in my head.

"I don't feel like a 'thank you' is enough."

"It is," I replied. "I don't do hugs."

Josh laughed again. "Got it." He started to walk away from me and then stopped. "Hey, Stellar."

"Yes?"

"That Arizona ace was wicked awesome."

"Unicorn."

"What's that?"

"I call it a unicorn. Par four like four legs, one hole like one horn… legendary… surreal."

"I like that," Josh laughed. "Unicorn. Cool."

"Thanks."

"You shouldn't quit," he added.

"Quit?"

"Cal says you're thinking of quitting the game completely."

*Ah.* I nodded.

"You shouldn't." He looked away for a second. "I hope you don't. Never seen anyone who can play like you."

And then he was gone. I watched him shake Cal's hand as he walked out the door and looked away as Cal turned his focus towards me.

*What the heck had just happened?*

I called Kate a few minutes later and before long she and Avery entered the building. I saw her stop and talk to Cal briefly before she waved at me and I hurried to meet her. "Heard you had some fun," she said with a smile.

I turned towards Cal, but he wouldn't meet my glare. "I don't know about fun… but it wasn't the worst night of my life."

We walked towards the door and I heard Cal call out. "Goodnight, sir."

I ignored him. *It was my turn for the mind games.*

## STELLAR 56 – "Lesser of Two Evils"

"Heard you made a new friend last night." James welcomed me to WINGS with a huge smile.

"Gosh, someone in this room has a really big mouth." I glared at Cal, and crossed the room to grab my backpack out of the kitchen.

James laughed heartily and Cal just shook his head.

"And friend is jumping the gun." I added coming back into the main room.

Cal turned and handed me a wet towel. "That kid deserves a friend like you, you ask me."

"If only someone had asked you."

Cal smiled. "You gonna wipe some tables or just stand there and be ungrateful?"

"So I'm supposed to thank you for inviting Josh to come practice at WINGS now?" I gave him a second to respond, but he didn't. He just stood there with that smile.

"Forget that," I continued. "And no… no work for me today. I'm supposed to be at school at 10. Mrs. Willett has some big plan for my summer."

"You don't sound all that excited," James chimed in.

"Is there a good combination of summer and school that I don't know about?" I walked towards the front door.

As I swung it open I heard Cal say, "Man, that boy is grumpy."

"Shut up," I yelled over my shoulder. "Shut up already."

Kate was waiting for me in the parking lot. "Who exactly are you telling to shut up?"

"It doesn't matter," I replied. "He won't."

When we got to school, Mrs. Willett was there waiting for us. The meeting was thankfully short yet anything but sweet. She was worried about my writing. *Like every other teacher I'd ever had.* Supposedly it was still terrible—horrible—though she claimed to have seen and fixed worse. As part of my "negotiated" homeschooling plan with Ken and Kate I'd agreed that I'd work on it this summer. So here I was.

Ultimately, I had two choices—summer school three days a week for four hours each of those days, or a daily journal where I write about my entire life. It was like going to a Jets-Ravens game as a Patriots fan and having to cheer for one of those other teams. First of all, it's the last place in the world you want to be. Secondly, there doesn't seem to be a lesser evil. It's a coin toss that lands and sticks on the edge.

It came down to convenience. I didn't want to be sitting here alone in a hot classroom twelve hours a week with a teacher who thought I wrote like a first-grader. The idea of writing about my life, as depressing as that seemed to be, was actually far more interesting. And Kate told me it would be good "rehab" for my broken arm—an opinion my doctor seconded.

Mrs. Willett made it clear that I was to start at the beginning, as far back as I could remember, and to write about any event, every year, that was of any significance. "If you do a good enough job," she said. "You won't have to do it again next summer."

I made the pledge right then and there to become the best writer in America. Carve my name on the Pulitzer. *No way* was I doing this again next summer.

And so—in June—that's how this project began. This is what I've been doing for most of the past three months. This is how I've been rehabbing my right arm—writing journal entry after journal entry, retelling my entire life. I've got two days of writing left before I'm done—August 31st and September 1st. Two more journal entries before school starts. This hasn't been as bad as I thought it would be. But I'm definitely glad it's almost over.

## ←★★★★★ JOSH CARTER ★★★★★→
### Letter (Part 1 of 3)

### ←Wednesday. August 18, 2021→

Can't say I've ever met anyone like Stellar. I hated him before I knew him, hated him for years, for things I later found out weren't even true. Not sure what that says about me. *Actually, I know exactly what it says about me.*

When Lauren asked me to write a letter for him—to write about what I remembered most about him—I didn't so much as hesitate before I said, "Of course." I was thrilled she was writing a book about him, thrilled to potentially contribute to it. *Thrilled to have evolved enough to be given this chance.* A story needed to be told about this guy's life. He was more special than the rest of us put together—he just never acted like it. For most of my life you could say he was the polar opposite of me.

I'm not quite sure where to start, though I guess you could say I already did. I'm sure my contribution to this story began infinite chapters before this letter fits in. I'm also relatively certain I was the villain. *Deservedly so.*

There isn't a device capable of measuring my regret for the donkey I was for however many years to Stellar. When I found out he liked Lauren, I made it my mission in life to make him look like a fool in front of her. The things I did to him publicly, the things I said to him privately, the lies I told about him, and the person I made him out to be… those all are things a bully would get expelled for nowadays. Those are the things that today would tragically put many victims under tombstones. I'm deeply ashamed of those years and wish more than anything I could have a mulligan on them. Thank God, Stellar was a stronger kid than most—a far better man than me. He never did anything back… except humiliate me in golf, of course. That was what mattered the most to me, the thing no one my age was better at. I was untouchable. Until Stellar decided I wasn't. Until he realized that was my kryptonite.

The funny thing is, he came after me for what I did to his best friend, Nick. It wasn't what I did to him, or even to the girl he loved. He came after me because of Nick. The way to get to Stellar was never to attack him directly, trust me, I'd done it many times. The way to get a reaction out of Stellar was to go after the ones he loved— think Avery, think Kate, think Lauren, James, Cal, Ken and yes, Nick.

Nick was a great golfer, he was good at anything he wanted to be good at. I think it's a safe bet he could have been just as good as me in golf. But he didn't want it. After his dad died, he wanted nothing at all to do with the game. Nick didn't have the heart to come after me in golf. But Stellar did. Stellar came after me for him.

Stellar couldn't out-bully me at school. He couldn't get to me through my "posse," couldn't humiliate me with jokes or pranks, or do anything at all to lower my social stature, which was all that mattered in school then. But Stellar had this talent with a golf club and this keen sense of determination that few people this side of Napoleon and Genghis Khan possessed. And apparently all it took to get his fire started was putting him in a tournament with me. I never beat him in a golf event and the stories from those events are ridiculous.

I'm convinced he'd have beaten me infinite more times if he hadn't broken his arm saving Taryn—an accident I was almost exclusively responsible for. I'd lost control at that point in my life. I was given an avenue to alcohol through my dad and my brother and I used it every chance I could. That resulted in me being expelled from school, humiliated in the community, kicked off the junior golf tour and very nearly losing the girl I've since married. I wouldn't have my wife and a beautiful little boy if it weren't for Stellar saving her that night.

But I'm getting ahead of myself. Stellar didn't just break his arm saving Taryn. He broke it again saving his mom—saving Kate. You can argue "right place right time" all you want, call him a "lucky hero"—like I did way back when he and his dog saved his sister, Avery—but I'd like to know what other human HONESTLY would have intervened as Stellar did in ANY of those situations. I wouldn't have. Even as someone who hated him, I admired him. Sure, I was jealous as heck. The girls were going crazy for him. He could have skipped every class except for Mrs. Willett's and probably still gotten straight A's. Every reporter and paper on Long Island ran features on him. He was this mega-hero. It made me sick.

And then I talked to Taryn—or Taryn talked to me—and she told me how Stellar didn't want any of it. He didn't want the attention, didn't want the praise. He didn't care about the girls, the glory, didn't even care about golf anymore. And I didn't get it. *How was that possible?* The kid was gifted—supernatural even—and all that mattered to him was the people he loved, and doing the right thing. It was ridiculous. But it made me admire him more. And then I heard what he agreed to do for that old man—OB. Then Calvin invited me to their new indoor golf center and I heard and learned firsthand what Stellar put himself through every day to play in that hickory event. And I started to realize the problem wasn't Stellar. It was me. My life was in my way. I was in my way.

I disassociated myself from my other groups of friends. It was a sudden but necessary severance—an amputation that probably saved my life. They were trying to pull me deeper into all the alcohol, smoking and vandalism cliques. I wanted a shot to be like Stellar instead. I didn't want to be the outcast—the bad guy. I still wanted to be on the PGA Tour someday. I only had one shot at that. I needed to become a better person.

My dad had similar demons he was fighting at the time. We kind of helped each other get through it all. Taryn helped me quite a bit, too. But no one helped me get there more than Stellar.

I remember working on the putting green one day at WINGS, and he came over and helped me. He didn't have to. There was absolutely no reason for him to even consider it. I was his rival, pretty dang close to perhaps his one and only lifelong enemy. And, with what I'd physically done to Lauren, I was certain he'd have poured gasoline on me if I'd been on fire. If the roles had been reversed… I absolutely would have never helped him.

But he did. He came over. Stellar saw a perceived need and he tried to meet it. He rose above—like always. It was that day that I believed I could make it, that day that I decided to try to catch onto Stellar's coattails.

I guess you could say that's when our friendship began.

========== JOSH CARTER ==========

## STELLAR 57 – "The Last Entry"

This is my last journal entry. Today is September 1, 2017 and I finally get to put this assignment behind me. Appropriately, I'm going to cover the last thing I thought I'd be covering in this journal… or in any context. I'm going to talk about my "friendship" with Josh.

Even though I lived it, I still can't believe things worked out like they did with Josh. I hated him for so many years. When I read stories about people drowning, getting hit by a bus, or about golfers getting attacked by alligators—things like that—I always hoped it was Josh they were about. I always wanted that for Josh.

I hated him for Lauren, even if they were never actually together. I hated him for Nick, for Taryn, for the royal all-around jerk he always was. I could write a page or more listing all the reasons I would never waste a minute of my life helping Josh—ever. And then I spent two hours with him working on his putting. And then I kept helping him with other things. I can't explain it. *Though Cal probably can.*

What changed? I would have to say that Josh did. *A miraculous transformation if there ever was one.* There was a time, literally only three months ago, when the only positive adjectives I'd have used to describe him would have been in sentences like, "What's the antonym for (*insert positive adjective*)?"

There was certainly one adjective I never would've associated with Josh before June: humble. He had never been that. So, just imagine when he seemed to be asking me for help, and actually did ask me for help later, how much that must have floored me.

I wanted to say no. I really did. He didn't deserve my help. I wanted to walk over there and tell him to leave. Instead, when it finally was time for him to go, I didn't want him to. He was kind of a substitute for Nick. Kind of. He was definitely a substitute for loneliness.

I feel like I need to say this again. Golf was dead to me. I hated it. I didn't care if I was good. I didn't care if I ever picked up a club again. And then I became a teacher for a few hours one night, and suddenly a surge of longing burned through me. Suddenly I wanted to play again. I even went home that night and got my putter out of the garage. I took it up to my room and putted left-handed for another hour until Kate came up and told me the ball rolling back and forth across my wood floor was driving her and Ken crazy.

I went back to WINGS day after day, after that, and worked with Josh on various aspects of his game. A few weeks later he was every bit as good of a putter as I was—if not better. His short game was astonishing. He could kill the ball off the tee. He had everything working and would've demolished any junior golfer in America at that point, of that I'm nearly certain.

The only problem was, he still hadn't been reinstated by the ruling junior golf bodies and wouldn't be until next May. He was, however, able to play in club events at The National. And with the Club Championship coming up the first week of August he asked me to caddie for him.

"Seriously?"

"You don't have to if you don't want to."

"No." I shook my head. "I mean, yes, of course I do. But you could have anyone caddie for you."

"Far as I'm concerned, it's you or I carry my own bag."

*Who was this guy?* "I'll do it," I said.

And so I did. It wasn't a fair fight. Josh was like Rory at the Kiawah PGA Championship, or Spieth in the 2015 Masters—nearly lapping the field. Josh won the two-day event by 14 strokes, at 18 under, with back-to-back 63s. Then he stood up there for his acceptance speech and deflected all the credit to other people… to Taryn, his dad, and me.

*Whatever happened to the guy I hated?* I liked this guy.

This summer has been the weirdest three months of my life. It's been hard to deal with the reality that Lauren will probably never be mine. *And that I've never wanted her more*. It's been hard to lose Nick, my best friend, a guy I'd still do anything in the world for if he asked. It's been bittersweet giving up golf and then finding my love for it again. I'm fortunate that my shared tragedy with Kate has resulted in us bonding so tightly together. I've loved spending so much time on the boats with Ken this year, and watching Avery become more and more beautiful/annoying every day. I can't tell you how much I owe James for straightening my head out, nor can I understand how Cal always seems to know exactly what to say to me and even more what to do *for* me. I'm even grateful—I'm serious—that you (*Mrs. Willett*) gave me this absurd summer assignment. For all I know, you may hate it. I could even fail it, but I actually wouldn't mind doing it all again next year if you feel I need to.

I guess you could say, through all of this I've taught myself a heck of a lot. But I won't pull a cliché on you here—you won't get me to say I wouldn't change a thing. I haven't lied in this assignment yet and I'm not going to start at the end.

There is most definitely one thing I would change, one "thing" missing from my otherwise perfect life. Pretty sure it goes without saying.

I'll wrap with Kate's favorite Bible verse—1 Corinthians 13:13—the one stenciled above our family picture at home. It's rather appropriate at this juncture.

***"And Now These Three Remain: Faith, Hope and Love. But the Greatest of These is LOVE."***

# ←★★★★★ CALVIN JACKSON ★★★★★→
## Letter (Part 6 of 6)

### ←Monday. June 4, 2018→

This was a day I'll never forget long as I live. It was the day of the Monday Qualifier, the sectional qualifier round for the 2018 US Open, that this year was being held at The Hills on Long Island.

If it weren't for Josh, Stellar wouldn't even be participating in the event. If it weren't for Stellar, I don't believe Josh would be good enough to participate in the event. Them two boys, they helped each other get here. And the other reason, perhaps the real reason Stellar was here for this qualifier, was because of where the "here" was: the country club in Farmington, Connecticut.

Coach Chandler coerced Stellar into giving the local qualifying round a run with the knowledge that the sectional round was being held at his course. He invited the boys to come out and play as much as they'd like, and Josh and Stellar had looped perhaps a dozen rounds in the past two months. They breezed through local qualifying despite the fact Stellar was quite rusty from a ten-month "doctor mandated" absence from swinging sticks. But make no mistake, rusty or not, Stellar had his groove back. That smooth whoosh, the effortless turn and dead-center click of ball on iron face. He was all over his game.

Without Stellar caddying for him Josh struggled a bit. A few careless errors cost him a stroke here and there. He ended up one behind Stellar when they wrapped up eighteen. But, like I said, they both cleared the field. They both moved on to Farmington.

So there we were on Monday, June 4th. Stellar in all black—a tribute to OB he said—and Josh in all white. *I reckon there wasn't no tribute to that.* On any other course the odds of a seventeen- and eighteen-year-old having a legitimate shot at an Open spot were slim to none. The best amateur and former PGA players in the world were in Farmington today—and scattered around the ten or so other national qualifying spots—and each of them had the game to match or beat these boys. Make matters worse, only two moved on automatically from here to Southampton—to the Open at The Hills.

I can write this so well because I remember most every shot of Stellar's round, and with James carrying the bag for Josh, I can account for Josh's general game as well.

The Sectional Qualifier for the US Open is a one-day 36-hole event—a true test of endurance and skill. You can't get lucky and make it. You have to be all good, all day.

Being relatively local to Southampton, our boys had a friendly audience. Some of the gallery was expected and some was not… like Miss Carrie and Nick. Miss Kate and Mr. Parker was here, of course. Coach Chandler was there step for step with Miss Brittlyn, and even Miss Lauren had come with her parents and Miss Taryn. I didn't dare tell Stellar that Miss Lauren was here though. That boy didn't need no such distractions today.

Turns out it wouldn't have mattered if Tom Brady, Derek Jeter, King Kong, and Captain America himself had been standing there outside those ropes, Stellar was that focused that first round. He wouldn't have noticed.

The pins were in tough spots those first three holes. They were all par spots and we played them accordingly. Wasn't no sense in digging us a hole to start. Three down, three pars. Even keel. Then we stepped to the fourth tee and Stellar saw the location of the flag. For a brief second I caught a flicker in his eye, the slightest of smiles on his face. I knew then Coach Chandler had coordinated that pin placement—it was Stellar's "home field advantage" and he took full advantage.

The split second the ball was in the air Stellar called it. "All over it," he said. "Might be in."

*Now why would you jinx yourself like that? There's no way you could possibly... This isn't like calling a three-pointer in basketball.*

That little white ball landed soft, hopped high once and low twice, then pulled back on a rope to the pin. There was a light clang and a roar from the crowd lining the ropes. It went in. *Holy...* Hole-in-one.

Stellar called it, but he didn't react much. The gallery lost their collective minds for him. Walking behind him towards the green I saw him look to the sky for a moment and if I'm not mistaken he said something, though I couldn't quite make it out. *My guess would be a few words to OB.* That was OB's favorite pin spot too—the last pin he'd ever played to.

Stellar may have been ignoring the gallery, but I took them in. I saw Miss Kate and Mr. Parker hugging Avery and screaming. I saw Nick looking down the rope at Lauren—first time they'd seen each other in a couple months. *So I was later told.* I saw Coach Chandler smiling and hugging Miss Brittlyn, and Miss Brittlyn in her short shorts and tightest tight t-shirt hollering at Stellar, who somehow managed to pay her no attention. Yes, as jubilant moments go, this was near the most epic I'd ever seen. Another magic act for Stellar—I count it as his fourth.

He wrapped up the first round strong—bogey free with three more birdies. He was at five-under at the halfway point—18 holes to go—a shot behind Josh and four others. I figured he'd played his best.

Turns out I was right. He lost that impenetrable focus between rounds somewhere around the moment he saw Miss Lauren and Miss Brittlyn talking.

Every other boy, and man, that walked by those two was drooling over Miss Brittlyn's, well... assets. Stellar's distraction went the other way, with Miss Lauren.

"Was Lauren here this morning?" he asked me.

"She was." I nodded.

"Why didn't you tell me?"

"Must you ask?"

"Was she with Nick?"

"They did not appear to be together, no."

"So she came with Taryn?"

"It's possible." I waved my hand in front of his face. He was trying to catch Lauren's attention. But she wasn't looking his way. "Sir, you must stay focused."

"I'm focused," he replied, as Lauren finally smiled his way.

*Right. He wasn't. Not at all.*

With Stellar knowing Lauren was following him he brought out a different game. I suggested he play the first three holes as he had earlier in the day. He went after the pins instead. This morning's three pars were replaced with three bogeys this afternoon. And yet he strode to the fourth tee unshaken. This was *his* hole and he was acting like he owned it.

Before the ball had even left the club's face though I swear his head was shaking. He knew he'd messed up. He was long, over the green, and buried in the deep rough. He managed a bogey out of a lucky putt.

Finally the course had his attention. Finally he realized that not only could he not coast in, but he might get his rear end handed to him on what was essentially his home course. He was giving away The Open opportunity.

As we waited our turn to hit on the fifth tee he finally spoke up. "What am I doing?"

"Do you want to know?"

"Of course."

"You're playing to impress, sir. And as impressions go, you're not."

"You really believe that?"

"I do."

"So how do I fix that?"

"You have to want to. It has to be more important to you than—"

"That's not possible. Nothing is."

I glanced over at Miss Lauren who was watching me talk to Stellar. "Sir, you have fourteen holes left. My advice would be to make these last fourteen holes all you think about for the next fourteen holes. Miss Lauren will be there waiting to congratulate you at the end, and you'll either accept the results knowing you didn't play your best, or you'll accept them knowing that you did."

Stellar looked up at me and nodded. "Good point." He took the 3-wood from my hand. "How 'bout I play my best then?"

"I'm all for that," I said with a smile.

I can't say he played his best. From time to time I'd still see him glancing over at Nick and then at Lauren. But he managed to get his round to two-under by the end, finishing at seven-under overall through 36 holes and in a five-way tie for first. That meant a sudden-death playoff for those five—which included both Josh and Stellar—starting with the first hole. Only *two* could move on.

A bogey cost one of the five on the first hole, knocking it down to the final four. All four players saved par on the second. They lost one more competitor to a par on the third hole when the other three birdied. And so they moved to the fourth hole, just three of them: Stellar, Josh and a former PGA star, and I dare say there may never have been a larger gallery around a single hole in amateur golf history.

The former tour player put his ball in the middle of the green, a mere six to eight feet remaining for birdie. Josh went next and was a little long, but pulled his ball back to ten or so feet to set up his own birdie attempt. The pressure was all on Stellar.

"What club did I hit last time?" he asked me.

"Nine-iron. Same as this morning."

He looked at me with a frown. "There was wind this morning though, right?"

"Wouldn't have mattered either way," I replied.

"So you still think nine is the club."

I was still holding it out to him. "I do."

He reached out for it but I pulled it slightly back. "What?" he asked.

"You don't have to go for the pin, you know. Nine-iron to the middle is a safe easy shot. You can make that putt."

Stellar nodded and looked up at the trees. They were absolutely still. He glanced back at me. "Nine's the club."

"Agreed."

I've played this moment over and over in my head a billion times in the past few years. Stellar hit the ball and didn't watch it for a second. He turned almost immediately to look at me. I thought he'd messed up.

Initially I followed the flight of the ball, until, out of the corner of my eye, I caught him still staring at me… he was smiling at me. I lowered my gaze to meet his.

He gave me a thumbs up and nodded.

*He can't possibly... There's no way... not again.* I was back to watching the ball. Stellar paid no attention to it. He walked towards me, nine-iron extended. You could hear the crowd suck in their collective breath as I reached for the club. The murmur escalated to absolute chaos as this ball landed eight to ten feet short of the pin and took a series of small soft hops before settling in the bottom of the cup. Twice in one day. *Magic act number five. Holy...*

Josh went crazy. He picked Stellar up and would have carried him all the way to the green if it hadn't been hurting Stellar's arm so much to be carried that way. The arena was engulfed in total pandemonium. This was the stuff of legends. In that moment I was certain he was going to win the Open at The Hills the next week. He and Lauren were going to be together again—they'd probably even get married. Karma—long overdue—was paying up. It was in the cards, in the stars, in whatever. Stellar, if he wasn't already, was going to be the greatest golfer ever.

The former PGA tour player made his birdie putt. Josh missed his. Josh was on the outside looking in for the US Open, later confirmed as the third alternate to the field. There was little chance he'd get in. He was disappointed, but boy was he also thrilled for Stellar. I don't much use the word "cool" as an adjective, nor "awesome" for that matter, but seeing those boys together as friends with Nick right there with them, that was awesome. That was cool.

I watched Miss Lauren give Stellar a hug. I watched her give Nick a hug. I watched them sit at a table and eat hot dogs and drink soda with Josh and Miss Taryn, and I flashed back to when they all were so much younger—before love went and got in the way of all that freedom and innocence. Never thought I'd see the day. *Especially not with Josh there.*

Miss Kate walked up and stood beside me, sliding her arm through mine. "So great to see isn't it, Cal?"

"Miss Kate." I nodded. "There aren't words."

"Pretty sure this is all thanks to you," she said.

I laughed. "Hold on. Afraid I can't take credit—no more than you for sure."

She didn't answer. Just smiled. There was no point in arguing over an outcome we both appreciated. "What a beautiful day." She sighed.

"Indeed."

"My boy is going to play in the US Open."

I glanced down at her with a grin. *Stellar knew that Hills course like the back of his hand.* "Miss Kate, your boy is going to win the US Open."

========== CALVIN JACKSON ==========

## ←★★★★★ JOSH CARTER ★★★★★→
### Letter (Part 2 of 3)

### ←Wednesday. June 13, 2018→

Largely thanks to Stellar and his mother, I was readmitted to our local high school, midway through my senior year. Mrs. Willett also campaigned to the board on my behalf and graciously they granted me a "final chance." I was on my best behavior, wasn't so much as summoned to the office once all year. I kept my nose clean and got my high school diploma. I had a shot at college.

For our "EoY Party" on June 13th, our class decided to go out to Block Island. Lauren's parents wanted this trip to be special, so they leased three boats from RB's for the occasion—and brought their own. We all met down at the marina and Stellar was there to see us off.

From what I understood Nick and Lauren were no longer a couple. Or they were still together but were taking some kind of a break. Taryn was Lauren's best friend and she didn't understand it, so I didn't try to either. All that really mattered was that everyone was getting along.

Stellar was more an unofficial member of our class than he was an official member of his junior class, if that makes any sense. He only hung out with us. We all wanted him to come along, and to be fair no one said he couldn't. But the next day was a HUGE day for him and if I were in his shoes—on the eve of the US Open—I probably wouldn't have gone out and exhausted myself on Block Island either. I would have traded places with Stellar in a heartbeat for his opportunity. I would have given anything to be in the US Open here in Southampton. Conversely, I'd gathered it was a similar guarantee that if Stellar could have had Lauren, he'd have traded places with me and gone with her to Block Island instead of playing golf.

Taryn's dad, Mr. Dahl, was operating the boat with Taryn and me, Lauren and Nick, and Mrs. Gehrke and Mrs. Willett—our class chaperones. Mr. Parker was operating the lead boat with six kids. Another parent had the third boat with five of our classmates, and Mr. Chambers was at the helm of the last boat with his wife and the last four participating students.

I remember Stellar and Cal untying each of the boats and waving as we pulled away from the docks. I recall Lauren hanging at the back of our boat giving Stellar a final wave, and I can't forget the expression on Nick's face as he watched her do so. He was smiling. He wasn't bitter—didn't appear jealous, he seemed at peace with whatever connection his "girlfriend" had to his best friend at that moment. (*I later learned the "significance" of Block Island to Stellar and Lauren. Then her reluctance to leave him and Nick's understanding of that all made far more sense.*)

Lauren hung out at the back of the boat, with Nick not far from her, until Stellar had disappeared from her view. Then she and Nick joined the rest of us.

We had an awesome clear-sky day out on the island, but it was cut short by an impending storm. Mr. Parker was concerned about the speed and ferocity with which it was descending on our area, and urged the other parents and chaperones to quickly round everyone up. We left Block Island a quarter after four. The occupant lists of the boats had shifted a little. Taryn, Lauren and Nick were all with Mr. and Mrs. Chambers now in the last boat off the island. I was with Mr. Parker in the lead boat with a few other students. Mr. Parker's instructions to me were simple—make sure everyone followed our boat, and alert him if anyone couldn't stay with us.

That was no problem until the rain hit not far from Plum Gut. Then the wind picked up, the visibility dropped to a matter of ten yards or so, and the waves were breaking hard against the boat. Plum Gut was dangerous enough to navigate in perfect weather for veteran sailors—like Ken. It was a nightmare in a squall for anyone, especially the less experienced—like the other three boat captains.

I could tell Mr. Parker was nervous. We could barely see Mr. Dahl's boat behind us, and neither of the two boats behind that. The wind and rain weren't letting up. If anything the conditions were worsening. I heard Mr. Parker calling in a mayday, and that's when I started to really worry. I listened to him give the last known position of the boats over the radio and heard the Coast Guard operative confirm on the other end. That's when I felt the fear in my chest, the panic pounding in my heart.

The rest of the students on our boat were huddled together—puking, crying… terror on all their faces. I returned to the back of the boat and held tight to the railing, straining to see the other boats. Admittedly I was most worried about Taryn on that last boat. I just wanted to see their boat.

We made it through The Gut with a little luck, and all of Mr. Parker's experience, and I was relieved to see the second boat—Mr. Dahl's—had made it as well. But as we neared the marina I became aware of two things. In the brief moments when the rain shifted and I could get more distance on my vision there were still no other boats in sight beyond our first two. The other thing I noticed was another boat coming towards us from the marina. I assumed it was the Coast Guard and for the briefest of moments I felt a sense of relief… of security.

I was wrong. As it passed us, I recognized the lone occupant just seconds before I heard Mr. Parker scream Stellar's name above the wind. *What the heck was he doing out there? And where was he going?*

I figured out then that he'd been listening to the mayday over the radio in the boat shop. He heard Mr. Parker identify the boats by name and knew the last boat—the "SS Mayor"—was the Chambers' boat.

I heard Mr. Parker pull back on the engine. He slowed us down as Mr. Dahl pulled the second boat up beside us. The water was so rough we couldn't get too close to each other, so Mr. Parker was screaming over the water at Mr. Dahl. "I have to go back," he yelled.

"No, Ken," Mr. Dahl replied. "We can't. We've got twelve students here we have to get back to the marina."

Mr. Parker looked like he wanted to argue but finally nodded and gunned the motor. He raced us back to the marina, dropped us all off and then turned back—streaking towards Plum Gut with Cal. I'd offered to go with him but he'd refused. He told me to go home and promised he'd call when he got back. So I did just that. I went home.

========== JOSH CARTER ==========

## ←★★★★★ LAUREN CHAMBERS ★★★★★→
**Journal Entry**

**←June 14, 2018→**

Yesterday was supposed to be a celebration. The senior class trip to Block Island commemorated the conclusion of 13 years of pre-college education, the end of high school. It should have been one of the best days of our lives. And it was for a while.

But it was also a little bittersweet for me. Block Island always held a special place in my heart because of the day I'd spent there with Stellar. Nick knew all about that day from Stellar, and he was most gracious in accepting how much it still affected me. There wasn't a hint of resentment in him, no sign of jealousy or disgust. That said an awful lot about Nick. It was one of the many things I loved about him.

It was hard standing there on the back of the boat watching Stellar fade away in the distance while I returned to the place we'd first kissed… while he watched me sail away with Nick—with everybody but him. It had to break his heart. I didn't want to do that. I wanted Stellar to come along though I never explicitly asked him to. Nick, Josh and Taryn had, and I felt my desire was implied, but he declined for various reasons. He claimed he needed to rest for the US Open the next day but while that gave sufficient reason to everyone else, in my heart I didn't buy that. He didn't need rest. He wanted to be on Block Island with me as much as I secretly wanted him to be. He wanted to kiss me again. He wanted to return to the landing at the base of the Mohegan Bluffs with me. *My heart was pounding like mad just thinking about it.* Yes, I'm certain he *wanted* to come along. He was just too afraid of the emotional toll it would take on him to be there with me—to be there with me and Nick—to feel like a third wheel on a bicycle. Okay, so his decision made perfect sense. No doubt it was for the best. It would have been just as hard on me to stay away from him—to not constantly be staring at him—just as hard for me to not be thinking about him every doggone minute.

I pretty much did anyway though. I wished all day that he'd been there. It wasn't much of a party for me. That spoke volumes to what my heart wanted and yet I wasn't unhappy with Nick either. We didn't have any physical contact out there—hadn't in months, in fact. But he respected our mutual decision to cool things off a little and gave me plenty of space. We were good. He was an absolute gentleman in every way imaginable. He knew where my mind was, and he accepted it. Maybe it wasn't fair to him, no matter our standing, but he took it like a man. A very, *very* good man.

I'd made the trip between Long Island and Block Island one way or the other over eighty times in the first eighteen years of my life. Most of those loops were by ferry from Montauk, but a handful of times my dad had taken us on his boat, the "SS Mayor." I preferred it that way, of course. It was much more peaceful, much faster, much more fun. It was almost always smooth sailing, even in high winds, even in the Plum Gut. There were many stories about The Gut—many warnings, myths and tall tales. But never once when we'd been out there had we reason to worry about the shallow shoals, the waves or currents, or even the passing ferries. Dad would try to play it safe—to time it right and pass through in slack tides when fishermen deemed it the safest. But it never seemed to matter when we passed. We never felt like we were doing something dangerous.

The storm descending on Long Island from Canada caught us all by surprise, including virtually every meteorologist. It was expected to stay well north. It was menacing, but not deemed a menace to our area. Mr. Parker had his doubts though, and corralled everyone to the boats about an hour before we'd planned to leave. He wanted us to play it safe and be certain to beat the storm back to Long Island in case it did hit. No one had a problem with that at the Block Island marina. If anything they were still mocking the notion we were in the storm's path.

We were almost to The Gut when the rain hit, and it came down in black blankets. We couldn't see through it. The winds were suddenly whipping us around, and we couldn't even see the boat in front of us. My mom was visibly nervous, constantly pleading with my dad to slow down so we wouldn't run into anyone else. If we didn't have radar on the boat we'd have been completely lost. But even the radar wasn't functioning properly. It wasn't showing us any of the other boats. We trolled along slowly for a good ten minutes, pretty much holding our collective breath the entire time. We were deep in The Gut now, and my dad was just hoping the boats in front of us wouldn't turn around and head back towards Block Island. Unfortunately that's exactly what Mr. Mays did in the boat in front of us.

Mr. Mays had never taken a boat through The Gut, and all the flashing lights on his screen indicating dangerously shallow water, rocks and various other hazards had really spooked him. He couldn't see any better than us but figured he had plenty of space to turn around and head back to Block Island, since his radar screen didn't show us right behind him. He was hoping we'd see him and follow suit. But neither of us saw each other until we broadsided him and our boat rolled over his like a monster truck. Our boat didn't smash his. It tore it in half. The impact was so direct and so severe it hurled Taryn and me at least twenty feet through the air into the freezing water of The Gut. I knew we were in trouble then.

I had no idea where Nick was—if he was still on the boat or in the water with us. I didn't know what had happened to anyone else in the other boat or even if my parents were okay. I couldn't see either boat, and the only thing I heard other than the roaring ocean was a soft pinging to my right.

Taryn had a nasty gash on her head, but she was still conscious. "Are you okay?" I yelled at her. She was fighting to stay above the surface and didn't respond in any way, not even a nod. I could see the terror in her eyes. And that's when the first big wave crashed on us.

I felt something tear into my side as the wave dragged me under and scraped me against some rocks. I fought towards the surface and looked frantically around for Taryn. She broke through a second after me. I reached my hand out for her just as the second wave pounded us down again. I hit the rocks again, but this time with my head. The blow stunned me and though I kicked back up to the surface I didn't look for Taryn this time. I was just trying to find my own bearings. I was just trying to save myself.

I figured I had to be really messed up, because I couldn't see anything but a brilliant white light shining right in my eyes. My ears were ringing. I was swallowing water, and didn't feel like I was moving even though I was trying to. It was a weird sensation, a freaky sensation.

And then I thought I saw someone flying through the air. I heard a giant splash beside me and heard someone say, "I'll be right there, Lauren." It sounded an awful lot like Stellar. If I was dead this was the strangest purgatory. I shook my head again, and suddenly my ears stopped ringing and my senses cleared. There was a boat about twenty feet from me and I saw someone pulling another person up the ladder on its side. And then that person launched himself through the air again towards me. Then that person was wrapping his arm around my chest and pulling me towards the boat. "I've got you," he said. It *was* Stellar.

He got me to the ladder and asked if I could climb. I nodded but didn't move. He got behind me and pushed me up the ladder. As I lay on the floor of the boat he knelt beside me. "Are you okay?"

I forced myself to sit up. "How are you here?"

"Lauren, who else is out there?"

I shook my head and looked around. Taryn was sitting a few feet from me shivering and crying. *Where was Nick?* "Nick," I said. "Nick's out there."

"You're sure?"

I wasn't. I shook my head. "No."

Stellar looked over the side of the boat into the torrential rain. "Lauren—"

"Where are my parents?"

"They're fine. Their boat is still up. I saw both of them."

"We drove over Mr. Mays."

"His boat. Yes, I know. I saw it. I think everyone got out of their boat fine. But you said Nick was here, too? And Josh?"

I nodded then shook my head. "No. Not Josh. Just Nick."

Stellar stood then, and I reached up to grab his hand. "Stellar, stay here."

"Lauren, I can't." He pulled his hand free. "There," he said suddenly, pointing through the dark rain. "There's the other boat."

I only saw it for a split second, but Stellar was right. It was about twenty yards to our left. Stellar stepped towards the edge and I suddenly found a burst of energy sufficient enough to lunge towards him. I grabbed him with both of my arms and held onto his leg. "Stellar, don't. Please… you don't have to— Don't leave me."

"Lauren," he bent down to pry my hands free from his leg. "It's okay." He smiled at me. "I love you," he said. He kissed me on the lips and then he was gone.

I screamed as he jumped overboard. I screamed his name as I pulled myself up the railing to look into the water. I didn't see any sign of him for several minutes… and no sign of the other boat. "Stellar!" I screamed again and again.

Taryn wrapped her arms around me from behind. She pulled me back towards the center of the boat. I fought to break away from her grip, to return to the edge of the boat and watch for Stellar, but suddenly there was another set of arms wrapped around me. "Lauren," a man's voice said.

I turned and looked up into Mr. Parker's face. "Ken—" *I had no idea where he'd come from.*

"Where's Stellar?" he asked.

I couldn't muster a word from my lips, so I just pointed over the edge where I'd last seen him.

"Why?" Mr. Parker yelled. "Why'd he jump in?"

I still couldn't answer. I was in shock. I was trembling. Taryn had to say it for me. "He went after Nick."

I suddenly realized that there was another boat beside ours—must have been where Mr. Parker had come from—and now there was yelling coming from that boat. Mr. Parker ran to that side of the boat and yelled back. Then I saw him jump into the water. A couple minutes later he hauled a body up the ladder into the other boat. *Stellar?*

I hurried over to the side of our boat and yelled at the other boat. I finally recognized Cal as the person on the other boat—the person Mr. Parker had been yelling back and forth with. "Who is it, Cal? Is it Stellar? Do you have Stellar?"

Cal shook his head. "It's Nick," he yelled back.

"Thank God," I whispered. I turned to Taryn. "They've got Nick."

"What about Stellar?" she croaked back.

I turned back towards the other boat. “Where’s Stellar?” I yelled at Cal. He just stared back at me with an empty expression. “Hey,” I yelled again. “Where’s Stellar?”

The last thing I remember was Cal shaking his head. His look said it all. I hit the floor.

When I came to, the boat was moving. The rain was still pounding the roof above me, but the sky was a little lighter outside the windows. I looked around the cabin and saw Taryn and Nick wrapped in towels. I noticed Cal was driving our boat now. I looked back at Nick and Taryn, and they were both crying. *Something was very wrong.*

“Nick,” I whispered. He didn’t look at me. “Nick,” I said it again. He still didn’t look at me.

Just then Cal pulled back on the throttle. We were pulling up to a dock. I forced myself to stand and looked outside. It only took a matter of seconds for me to take everything in. I saw Ken step from another boat parked in front of us carrying a lifeless body—the body of a boy. I saw Kate running down the dock towards Ken and fall at his feet. I watched Ken lower the boy’s body to the dock and saw a hysterical Kate throw her own body over the boy’s. I knew who the boy was.

Stellar was dead.

Calvin caught me before I hit the floor this time.

*I wish he wouldn’t have.*

## ←★★★★★ NARRATOR ★★★★★→

"I can't do this," Kate said. "I can't do this anymore."

I didn't have to ask where she was. The torrents of tears streaking down her face told me she was typing the part I'd been dreading—the part I didn't know if I could do myself. She was typing my journal entry from the day Stellar died. She leaned forward and buried her face in the bed beside me.

"Kate, it's okay." I reached out and placed my hand on her head.

There was a knock on the door then and I looked up to see Nick. "Sorry, I don't mean to—"

"It's okay, Nick." I waved towards him. "You can come in."

Kate stood up then and excused herself, briskly walking past Nick without looking at him.

"Reliving a few things I guess," Nick said, watching her disappear down the hallway.

"She was helping me type and… well… it's just at that part."

"That part as in—"

"You're alive, and her son isn't."

"Ah." Nick nodded. "Awesome. Don't suppose this whole thing is gonna have a happy ending somehow?"

I took his hand and placed it on my belly. "This is the happy ending, babe."

"And Kate?"

"She just needed a break."

"Sure she's coming back?"

"Kate doesn't hate you, Nick. Doesn't even dislike you. And she doesn't blame you… no one blames you, Nick."

"Pretty sure you're wrong there. Ken—"

"Stellar made his own decisions." I squeezed his hand as a contraction attacked me. "Today… today is the perfect day to accept that once and for all. Hopefully, today, we can all start over *together.*"

He'd heard it from me a hundred times—"It's not your fault." Mostly because his greatest fear was that I also blamed him… that I secretly wished it had been Stellar who had survived that day instead of him. I knew I'd never fully be able to convince him otherwise, especially when I wasn't certain he was wrong.

But Stellar was dead. He was gone. What good did it do any of us to blame anyone else, or regret something we couldn't change?

We all needed this book to end. We all needed to move on. I loved Nick and always had in some capacity. I was happy with him and having this baby with him. My life was with him. My future was with him. At some point that had to be enough for Nick and I. At *some* point that had to be enough for *all* of us.

Nick wasn't ready to let the subject drop yet. As Kate came back into the room he dropped my hand and turned to her. "You know I'd trade places with him if I could, don't you?"

"Nick, come on—"

Kate waved me off. "It's okay, Lauren. Nick, we've had this conversation. But…"

"But what?" He was *super* sensitive now.

"But," Kate continued. "From the second that child is born, I don't ever want you to say that, or even *think* that again." Nick opened his mouth to reply, but Kate held up her hand. "Let me finish. Let me be clear because I don't really like talking about this either… but Miles knew the risks when he went out there to save you. He—"

"Stellar didn't come out there to save *me*, Kate," Nick replied. "We *all* know that."

I had to look away. I felt terrible that Nick was doing this right now.

But Kate was up for the fight. "Okay, so he didn't. But after he saved Lauren he intentionally went back in for you. He didn't have to, but he did, and I need you to respect the fact that my boy made it possible for you to be here today. And anything you say about wishing you could trade places with him—that you'd rather be dead than here with your wife and baby—well that hurts me, personally. Miles wouldn't want that. I don't want that. And most of all, I don't want you to ever claim you want that again."

Nick dropped his head in silence and stared at the floor. Her message was received loud and clear.

Kate took Nick's face in her hands again and lifted his eyes towards hers. "My boy loved you, both of you." She glanced at me. "He wanted both of you to be happy *forever*. So do it together. Nick… do it for him." Kate referred to Stellar. "Or do it for her." She pointed at me. "No matter what, you both need to make sure that child is loved as much as our Stellar was—that he or she always feels that loved. That's what we *all* want from you. Do you think you can do that?"

Nick covered Kate's hands with his own, and she finally let go of his face. He nodded, still looking in her eyes. "Of course."

## ←★★★★★ NICK BIRCH ★★★★★→
**Letter (Part 3 of 3)**

**←Friday, June 15, 2018→**

I'm going to write this down now so I never forget it, not that I ever think I could. The last thing in the world I want to do right now is write. I don't want anyone else to know how I'm feeling, or what I'm thinking, but… it's what Stellar would do if he could.

I watched Lauren wave goodbye to Stellar on Wednesday. She on the boat to Block Island with me. Him on the docks at the marina. It was tearing me up inside, but I did my best to contain that. Lauren had stressed numerous times over the past few months how there was nothing more important to her than me working things out with Stellar. She wanted him to be a part of both of our lives. She told me that, until she believed he and I were good, she wouldn't kiss me, wouldn't hug me… she wouldn't touch me. I told her that was stupid. She told me to take a hike.

So I walked. I walked all the way home from her house, and by the time I got to our place I had determined that she was too valuable to me to let go of. What she was asking of me was something that shouldn't have been a tough request at all to fulfill. Stellar had been my best friend for years. *For years!* He had done everything for me… so much I could write a book on it. The least I could do—the very least I could do—was try to make things right between us. So, I called her back and agreed to try. I told her I didn't want to lose her. I promised her I'd try.

Naturally I was afraid this move would cost me Lauren—if I hadn't already lost her—that she'd start spending more time around him and realize I was the "D" to his "A+." And so I was paranoid of everything. Every compliment she gave him made me cringe. Every time she mentioned his name it was all I could do to not shake my head. And then Stellar did something… unimaginable.

Somehow, someway, he made friends with Josh. Josh, my bitter enemy. Josh, *OUR* bitter enemy. The guy who had done so many things to Stellar, who had tormented him since the first day I met him… *and even before that.* The guy who physically assaulted the girl we loved. That guy! *Stellar and that guy were now friends!*

I couldn't imagine what brought that on, or what it must have taken for Stellar to look past all the bullying, slights and abundant negatives in their past. At first I thought he was doing it to throw it in my face. And then I just felt stupid. Absolutely plain stupid.

*Of course he wasn't.*

Josh was alone. Stellar was alone. *The latter because of me, I might add.*

Here Lauren wanted me to make up with my best friend—to give him a chance so we could all be friends, together. *And I was fighting it!* That was the message I was sending to the girl I loved.

And then there was Stellar, laughing, high-fiving, and hanging out with the guy he should have hated the most. He had accepted Josh. *JOSH!* Stellar had given Josh the benefit of the doubt… given him a second chance. That was the message *HE* was sending to Lauren. Or at least that's what she saw.

Once again, Stellar was in a class of his own. Me, on the other hand, every time I looked in the mirror I expected to see a horse's rear end staring back at me. That's what I felt like. I realized I wasn't living up to my end of the bargain. And so I called Lauren again and told her I thought we should take a break. It wasn't that I didn't love her. It's that I needed to respect her more. I needed to honestly be able to do what she'd asked me to do regarding Stellar and I hoped when I figured it out she'd still be there, that she'd still want me. She wasn't asking for my endorsement for her to be with Stellar. She may or may not have loved him still… I'll never know that. But I do know that she wanted to be able to talk to him, to hang out with him, she wanted that friendship back with Stellar. And I was getting in the way of it. I owed it to Lauren to figure that out. I owed it to Lauren to try to get my best friend back.

Stellar made it easy on me. *Big surprise.* He acted as if I'd never hurt him—as if I'd never kissed his girlfriend on New Year's Eve and basically stolen her from him. He acted as if he was just as happy to have me back to hang out with as he was to have Lauren looking at him, waving at him, and saying a simple "hello" to him now and again. There are people in life who are just too good to be true. And then there's Stellar. He's too good… and true.

But back to the boat ride. It was tearing me up inside watching Lauren watch Stellar fade into a speck and then disappear. *Just not the way you'd think. I wasn't jealous.* What tore me up was remembering how excited Stellar was when he got back from Block Island with Lauren on their "first date." I remembered his second-by-second, full-sensory, description of their first kiss, and his thrill at all the simple little things, like how they'd held hands while counting all 144 steps near the Mohegan Bluffs. I remembered the energy in his voice, the joy on his face, the impact that day had on his heart, and I knew he was standing there on that dock thinking of all those things right now. The same had to be true for Lauren. *It wasn't right.*

That moment took me back to when Stellar and I had never been closer—to when he'd have done anything in the world for me. And I felt terrible. Stellar should have been there with Lauren instead of me. Lauren should have been with Stellar… instead of being with me.

I made up my mind then and there that I was going to break up with her. I didn't want to do it on our senior trip—didn't want to scar Block Island for her in any way—so I'd wait until we got back to Long Island. And then I'd go find Stellar and tell him how much Lauren still loved him and how much he meant to me. I had it all worked out in my head, even if it wasn't completely settled in my heart. I knew it was the right thing to do. This time I—Nick—was going to do the Stellar thing.

I never got that chance. When Mr. Mays turned his boat back into the path of ours, and we went over the top of them, I was launched into the rails of our boat. My body hit the rails so hard it knocked the wind completely out of me. I flipped over the top rail and landed on the cabin roof of the other boat, which had been split in two. I could barely move, couldn't breathe at all, and was just holding on to the mooring line as tightly as I could, until I could regain my bearings. The waves were slamming against the two halves of the boat. I hadn't yet seen anyone else—didn't know if anyone else was even alive. And then the boat started to sink. Now Plum Gut isn't super deep, not in parts of the shoals, and the half of the boat I was on hit bottom pretty fast. The waves began to flip my half of the boat over, but I suddenly had a much bigger problem. I was stuck in the mooring rope.

A giant wave crashed across the deck of the boat and shattered the window. Shards of glass went everywhere and I grabbed one of them. It sliced my hand instantly, but I held tight to it—I needed something to try to cut the rope.

Another giant wave completed the flip of my side of the boat, and I was now completely underwater. My years of swimming, diving and practice holding my breath underwater were being put to the defining test as the boat rolled and I struggled to free my left arm.

I couldn't move my left arm, and not just because it was tightly wrapped in rope. It felt like it was either broken or dislocated. And then the waves rolled the boat again and I emerged long enough to take two big gulps of air. I could've sworn I saw another boat not far to my right, but before I could get a better look my half of the boat was rolled again, and I was back underwater.

With one hand and very little leverage I was having almost no success at all cutting the rope. The grim reality was starting to set in. The most decorated high school swimmer on Long Island was going to drown.

And then there was someone beside me, someone taking the glass from my hand and hacking at the rope. And then the boat rolled again. As we came to the surface I recognized Stellar. "How did you—?" I gasped.

"Hang on," he barked. He planted his feet into the wood and pulled on the rope, but it wouldn't give. Another wave was rolling in and he leveraged all his weight into one last effort, lifting as much of the rope as he could. He loosened it just enough for me to slip free but now Stellar was trapped beneath it.

"Stellar—" I called out, grabbing his hand with my one good arm, trying to pull him free. But it was no use. He was at least as stuck as I'd been. "Why—"

"Nick," he yelled. "Love her for me." And then he kicked me as hard as he could in the chest just before the giant wave slammed into the boat. I fell back, free from the wreckage as the boat flipped away from me into the shallowest part of the shoals. I literally heard it smash into the rocks this time. I backpedaled a few feet and screamed Stellar's name. I slapped the water with my right hand and screamed it again. And then someone was grabbing me from behind.

"Help him," I pleaded.

"Where is he?" a man's voice asked. *Ken.* "Where's Stellar?"

I pointed but couldn't speak, and Ken dove below the thrashing ocean surface. He came back up a minute later empty handed. He swam over to me and pulled me, screaming the whole way, towards the boat I had indeed seen earlier. *There were actually two there.* Cal helped me up into one, and I remember hearing Lauren's voice yelling from the other boat, asking if they'd found Stellar. *Nope.* I remember thinking. *It's just me.*

Ken eventually got Stellar free from the wreckage. He led us back to the marina—he and Stellar in one boat, the rest of us in the other—and carried his lifeless body onto the dock. I watched Kate sprint down the dock, screaming the whole way. It was obvious to everyone that Stellar hadn't made it. The only person who didn't go on the Block Island trip that day was the only one who didn't come back alive.

Stellar's last words echoed in my head. He could have been talking about Kate. He could have been talking about Avery. He could have been talking about Lauren. *I knew he was talking about Lauren.* But I was determined then and there that I would do everything I could to carry out his last wish with *all of them.*

I haven't gone to church since my dad died years ago, but I've gone to Catholic school all my life. I know Jesus pretty well—his story at least—and he is considered by millions as the greatest man to have ever lived. That's hard to argue with if you believe in the Bible.

Jesus was a magic man himself, a loving man, a selfless man. He didn't deserve to die, especially not like he did—not for any reason—but certainly not after all that he did for the world. He was so good and deserved so much better than what he got in the end. As a child I remembered that story feeling so many different kinds of wrong. Why should someone like that have to die for anyone else? Where were all the angels? Where was God? Why wouldn't God intervene? How did taking the life of someone so great make anyone else's life better in any way?

I think you can see where I'm going with this. I don't get it. I don't get that. I don't get this. I'm not comparing Stellar to Jesus in any religious or philosophical way whatsoever. But none of us got to physically meet Jesus. We have to rely on faith that he existed and that hopefully we'll meet him someday. Well, I got to meet Stellar. I got to know and love him. I've never known anyone like him—no one so magical, so loving, so selfless. He deserved so much better than what he got in the end. He deserved to be the one here writing this now about losing his best friend. He deserved to be the one knocking on Lauren's door tomorrow and sharing this sorrow with her… to then share the rest of his life with her. Where is the justice in this? Why wouldn't the God of the universe see fit to save someone who made such a big difference for so many people? Why didn't you intervene for him? Why did you save me instead?

How am I supposed to make sense of this?

I don't get it.

======= NICK BIRCH =======

## ←★★★★★ JOSH CARTER ★★★★★→
### Letter (Part 3 of 3)

### ←June 14, 2018→

The storm knocked the power out last night. I plugged my cell phone in when I got home, took a shower and climbed into bed in my pitch-black room to wait for Ken's call. I had asked Dad to wake me up in an hour, so, worst-case scenario, if I slept through Ken's call I'd call him right back. I only intended to rest a little while.

Next thing I knew Dad was tapping me on the shoulder. "Phone call, bud," he said. "It's someone from the PGA." I shielded my eyes from the sunlight streaming in the window. *Where did the sun come from?*

"Hello," I said, as I looked at the clock which read 6:03 a.m. *Son of a gun... Dad let me sleep all night.*

"This is Corey Manning from the PGA."

"Yes, sir."

"I'm calling to inform you that you have been moved from the alternative list to the active list for the US Open."

I was stunned. "What? Seriously?" I jumped up out of bed. I was no longer mad at my dad. "What time do I need to be there?"

*This was the greatest call of my life.*

"Actually, sir," the voice said. "The event has been postponed a day due to the tragic death of an Open participant."

"Who?" I asked. *Had to be somebody big.*

"Sir, I'm afraid I can't say."

"Got it. No problem."

"Sir, your first round tee-time is tomorrow morning at 6:40 a.m. I'd advise you be there at least an hour beforehand."

"Wow. Okay." That was pretty close to Stellar's tee time. Maybe we'd even be playing together. I needed to turn on the news. "I'll be there at 5:30," I said. "Thank you for the call."

"Of course. Have a good day."

"Thank you. You, too." I tapped the button to end the call and shoved my dad. "I'm in," I hollered, laughing. "I'm in the Open."

My dad was just as excited as I was. He hugged me tightly. "So happy for you Josh," he said.

"Hey," I pushed back from him, "did Ken call last night?"

"No."

"You're sure?"

"Positive." He nodded. "I checked your phone and my phone every hour or so until 1 a.m. then just went to bed. You seemed like you could use the rest yourself. Didn't see the point in waking you with nothing to tell."

"He should have called."

"Call him now. With Stellar in the event the PGA would have notified them, too about the delay."

"True." I picked up my phone. "Dad, turn on the TV and see if you can find out who died."

"I'll check downstairs," he said.

I nodded and punched in Stellar's number. It went straight to voicemail. I called their home phone next. Kate answered. "Hey, this is Josh," I said. "Could I talk to Stellar?"

I heard what sounded like a muffled sob come from Kate's mouth. *What the heck?*

I heard her say, "Ken" and then Ken was on the phone. "Hey, Josh," he said.

"Did you guys hear?" I asked. "They pushed back the Open a day… something about someone dying."

"Josh—"

"But, because of that, I got a call from the PGA saying I'm in."

"Josh—"

"Mr. Parker, I'm playing in the US Open with Stellar."

"Josh… you won't be playing with Stellar." I heard a strange guttural sound come from Mr. Parker's voice over the phone.

"I'm sorry, what?" I asked. "What'd you say?" Somehow, before he even replied, I knew exactly what was coming and it nearly stopped my heart.

"Stellar is dead." Ken whispered hoarsely. "Stellar is the one who died."

Mr. Parker hung up the phone on his end, and I dropped mine. I covered my mouth with my hand and turned in shock to look at my dad who had come back into the room. By the look on his face I knew I didn't have to say anything—he knew who had died.

"I am such a dumb—"

"There's no way you could have known," Dad said.

I shook my head in disbelief at my own stupidity. They'd given me Stellar's tee time with Rory and Phil. I *absolutely* should have known.

I half expected the phone to ring again at that moment, with the Guinness Book of World Records on the other end, ready to award me the record for biggest "foot in mouth" occurrence in history.

*That was the worst phone call of my life.*

I played the first two rounds of the Open—though I've never felt more conflicted. On the one hand I believed Stellar would have wanted me to play. The Parkers and Lauren even assured me as much. On the other hand, it felt wrong in every way. I was taking *his* spot. Add in all those people celebrating on the course, all the drinking and boisterous laughter… yeah, it felt all wrong.

I know none of those people knew Stellar. They didn't know this was essentially his course—that he had known every inch of every green better than any other human alive. They didn't know he quite possibly would have won this entire event with that knowledge and the way he'd been playing. They couldn't see the headline I saw: A 17-year-old nicknamed nobody from Long Island—Major champion. They didn't know what they were missing. How could they? They weren't trying to be disrespectful. But it was like no one out here cared about Stellar at all. I couldn't accept that. I wanted to make some noise.

I made the cut and surged up the leaderboard on Day 3—Sunday. I was in the second to last group going into Monday, two shots back. Then I withdrew. Stellar's funeral was Monday morning. I wouldn't have missed that for a million dollars, not even for a legitimate shot at a Major championship.

A reporter asked me why I withdrew, if I was injured or what? I nodded and thought about my answer. My heart was hurt, no question, but I kept my answer a little more coded. "Some things are just more important than golf." Yes, *those* words came out of *my* mouth.

"Even though you could have won?" she asked in disbelief.

"I already lost." I bowed my head for a moment then looked up at her again. "And by playing tomorrow, I'd only have lost more."

A former friend of mine asked me later why the Parkers couldn't have respected my opportunity at the Open, and bumped the funeral back a day.

I proceeded to punch him in the face.

The irony wasn't lost on me. A year ago I'd have been the selfish jerk asking that question. To date though, in truth, the thought hadn't even crossed my mind.

========== JOSH CARTER ==========

## ←★★★★★ KATE PARKER ★★★★★→
**Letter (Part 3 of 3)**

Miles told me where he wanted to be buried. He told me on August 5, 2016 to be exact—the night he got back from Block Island with Lauren. I had always figured it would be near his parents in Manhattan, or near Ken and me on Long Island. Instead he said he and Lauren were on the same page—in fact he'd stolen the idea from her. "So, where?" I asked him.

"As close to heaven as I've ever been," he said.

"And where's that?"

"The Stairway to Heaven," he replied. "That's what we call it." *He and Lauren.* "On Block Island."

I knew the spot well. "You do know those steps go *down*?" I asked.

He smiled. "Steps go both ways."

As you can imagine I was initially against the idea. In fact, I didn't even acknowledge the possibility until Lauren asked me if he'd ever talked to me about it.

"I'm not cremating my boy," I snapped. "And I'm not taking him out there. I'm never going out there again."

Lauren left me to steam and respectfully didn't bring it up again. After three times my usual glasses of wine that night—three glasses if you're wondering—I threw the glass against the wall across the room, and Ken came sprinting down the stairs. "What the heck was that?" he asked me. Then he saw the glass all over the floor. "Never mind," he said.

"Miles wanted to be buried on Block Island."

Ken didn't say anything. I wanted him to pick up another glass and throw it against the wall but he didn't. "Okay." That's all he said.

"Okay?" That was *not* on my list of acceptable things for him to respond with. "He wanted to be cremated." I still didn't get an objection from Ken. "And he wanted his ashes to be scattered at the base of the Mohegan Bluffs." *Still no objection.* "I mean, that's stupid… I can't—"

"Kate." He sat down beside me on the couch.

His calmness pissed me off. "Why aren't you as angry as I am?"

"Oh, I'm angry," he replied. "But not about this."

"But why?" I raised my hands in the air. "Why aren't you?"

He was silent for a minute before choking up and looking away from me. "Because if it's what Miles wanted…"

I knew he was right then. "But," I shook my head, "but the ocean took him from me, from us, and we're just supposed to give him back?"

"Kate, that place—those steps—they're not just any place."

He was right. Ken had proposed to me at the base of those steps. Miles had originally intended to do the same to Lauren there someday—or so he'd said. It was among the most special places in the world to him, if for no other reason than his life's greatest highlight was from there. In a matter of minutes I realized I couldn't hate the idea as much as I wanted to—not anymore. *If that's what Miles wanted.*

"But we have the funeral scheduled at—"

"I'll cancel it," Ken said.

"But we don't have a cremation—"

"I know a guy," Ken cut me off again. "I'll take care of it."

"But we'll have nothing left of him." That reality hit me like a ton of bricks. No one I knew had ever been cremated. *How would we...* "How will we visit him?"

"We'll have *everything* left of him," Ken corrected. "And we'll visit him at those steps as often as you want to. He will always be there."

I stopped by the Chambers house Thursday night and asked to speak with Lauren. She came downstairs with bloodshot eyes, a sniffling nose and the saddest imaginable face. We easily could have passed for identical twins, albeit from different generations. I told her what we had decided to do, and she didn't say anything in reply at first. She just hugged me and wept into my shoulder. Finally she said, "Thank you."

"No." I shook my head and lifted her chin. "Thank you. You were right. This was what he wanted."

I always thought he'd made his cremation wishes on a whim, that he'd merely copied Lauren's idea because he had nothing better. *Or to impress her.* Lauren told me that night that wasn't the case. She explained how Miles had told her that he loved Ken and me like we were his real parents, but he knew where his real parents were. They were ashes among the ashes scattered beneath the streets somewhere in the vicinity of Ground Zero. There were no actual tombstones saving their place in this world. Likewise, he didn't want one for himself either. Then it all made sense. Finally, I found my peace with the idea.

Ken booked a private ferry for the funeral on Block Island, on Monday, June 18, 2018. There were nineteen of us and the pastor. I didn't like being out there on that water—not five short days after Wednesday's storm. It didn't matter to me that Monday was a perfectly calm, crystal clear, blue-sky day. It was still a haunting expedition. My heart was in my throat, my hand tightly gripping Lauren's the entire way. I was an internal wreck.

Lauren, on the other hand, handled herself with admirable calmness, grace and maturity. Externally, anyway.

I couldn't imagine what that ferry ride was like for her, or Nick, or Taryn, Ken, or anyone else who was out on the water on Wednesday. Lauren did most of the talking at the service. She even brought a journal along and asked that everyone in attendance write a few words—a farewell note to Miles.

Ken carried the urn until it was time to scatter the ashes. I was too afraid I'd drop it—that I'd drop Miles. I followed Ken up the hill to the steps, a path we'd jubilantly walked together a hundred times. There was no joy in this journey.

I watched Lauren escort Avery just ahead of us. They held hands and Lauren talked to her the entire way. The big sister who'd never had a little one, the little sister who'd never had a big one.

Nick and Josh hung back behind us with Taryn and her parents, Lauren's parents, Ray and his wife—Michelle, James and Rose, Carrie, Brittlyn, Chandler, Calvin and the pastor.

Lauren stopped at the top of the steps and knelt down. Avery knelt beside her and the rest of us followed suit as we reached them. I could hear Lauren crying. I could hear Lauren praying. I watched her hug Avery and they stood together. They walked down the steps, and we followed them to the bottom.

The pastor spoke, but admittedly I tuned him out. He couldn't tell me anything I didn't already know about my boy. I didn't need to hear him say where Miles was or was going, what he was thinking or doing. It was as simple as this...

*If my boy wasn't in heaven there wasn't one.*

When Lauren took over I listened. I hung on her every word, we all did. A few other people spoke, Cal, Nick, Josh, and then I said a few final words.

Finally, we walked down to the beach below the steps and scattered my son's ashes into the Atlantic. I wept as they poured from the urn while Avery gripped my arm and Ken and Lauren hugged me. We watched the cloud of gray merge and submerge into the clearest of blue. Miles was gone. But he would always be here.

We sat on the steps for a while, as everyone took their turns writing farewell notes in Lauren's journal. We stared out towards the vast expanse of ocean and thought of Miles, thought of Stellar. We told stories, did a lot of crying, a lot of hugging, and even a little laughing. It was sad but therapeutic. It was hell, but it was heavenly.

I should probably write down what I said though it wasn't what I had prepared to say. I'd typed out a full page at home, but spoke just a few sentences from the heart instead.

*"Miles. I love you. This isn't fair. No parent should outlive their child. I'm blessed that I couldn't have kids, that Ken and I couldn't have kids, because then we got you... we got you and Avery. You saved my life, Miles. You did for me what I couldn't do for you. I'm so sorry. I'm so, so sorry. But, I want you to know that everything you did for me—and for every one of us here—was worth it. It will never be forgotten. You, my love, are in my heart. I will carry you with me everywhere I go... forever."*

They say there's no pain like childbirth. I guess I'll never know if that's true. But I do know I can't imagine it compares to losing a child—can't imagine it's even close. At least there's reward in the one, most of the time. There's never reward in the other.

Physical pain can't possibly compare to losing Miles.

## ←★★★★★ NARRATOR ★★★★★→

"Kate." I tapped her arm.

She jumped, startled, and looked up at me. "Yes?"

"Go get Nick."

"What?"

"Go get Nick."

I was sweating profusely, and the contractions were almost on top of each other now. I'd noticed the doctors and nurses gathering. They were coming in. It was time.

Kate snapped my laptop closed and stood up. "Got it."

"Hey," I whispered between sharp breaths. "Come back with him."

"Are you sure?"

I nodded. "Please."

Kate hurried out of the room as the maternity staff swarmed me. I was stretched, poked and prodded for the next few minutes. I guarantee you the vitals of every one of my organs was checked in triplicate, at least. Eventually Nick and Kate were back in the room with me, and the doctor was directing Nick to the chair by my head and Kate to my other side.

Thanks to the epidural I didn't feel everything, but I felt enough to know that next time—if there is a next time—Nick was doing this. *How do people ever willingly do this twice?*

To his credit, Nick was great. He held my wrist the entire time, wiped my forehead, kissed my hand. He encouraged me through every push, kept his eyes on mine—he did the best that he could do. I wanted Kate to be a part of this from beginning to end, as humiliating and embarrassing as it may have been to me if I'd actually thought that through… if I'd known what it would actually entail. That she'd never get to do this was both a blessing and a curse. I don't know… it just seemed right to have her there.

Nick didn't pass out when the baby came out, but when they wrapped her up and handed her to him he looked like he was about to. She was beautiful, a head full of hair. She was perfect.

Kate got to cut the cord. She fought back tears as she did so. *Amazed she had any left.* She even got to hold my daughter before I did, though, honestly, I didn't mind. The doctors asked Nick and me if we had a name picked out yet. We shared a smile and nodded. As Kate turned towards us I said, "Stella."

"Kate, you're holding Stella."

***← NOT THE END →***

## "FUNERAL TRIBUTES (2018) & FINAL NOTES (2022)"

### ←JOSH CARTER→

**(2018)** - I feel like I should be congratulating you for winning the US Open instead of this—you'd have been the youngest Major champion since Old Tom Morris won (also at age 17) in 1868. I wish I could take back the decade of my life I knew you before I got to actually know you. I owe you so many apologies and so many thanks. I don't know where to begin or end but you'll be missed by all of us. Thank you, Stellar!
**(2022)** – Sometimes I wonder where I'd be, or who I'd be, if I hadn't met you. Can't believe it's been nearly four years since we lost you. Lord, my life has changed a ton since then. I should have said more four years ago—at least thanked you more. To make up for it I'll say more now. I'm on the PGA Tour now full-time. Cal caddies for me most every event. *The man certainly knows how to bring out the best in you.* He sure misses you, Stellar. Even makes me go one club short every round just to carry that wedge of yours. *And he's never once let me hit it.* I don't mind though. It's an honor. Taryn and I were married on Block Island a year ago (so you could be there)—we wouldn't have each other were it not for you. We now live in Port Orford, Oregon and have a beautiful little girl named Abbey—middle name Miles. She's perfect. Life is perfect. Well… almost. Wish you were here!

Thanks for everything, man. I can't possibly express it enough. – Josh

### ←TARYN DAHL-CARTER→

**(2018)** – I have peace knowing I got to know and appreciate you before we lost you. You saved my life—not once but twice—and every day I get to live after this one is solely because of you. I won't waste them—I promise you that. You were a great neighbor and a great friend. I'll miss you and all the times your little sister whipped us both in UNO. Thank you, Stellar!
**(2022)** - Stellar, I hope you can see how much you changed people's lives. Your forgiveness and selflessness changed me years ago, but more than anyone—in the years since—you've changed Josh. Good Lord. From time to time we talk about how hard we were on you when you moved to Southampton—trust me it's not something we're proud of—but as much as we've both changed we can't help but marvel at how you never did. You were always the same awesome person. We wanted to name our daughter after you, but when I asked Lauren for permission—who was also pregnant—she told me why we couldn't. *Great minds think alike I guess.* But with the "Miles" middle name, we still kind of did anyway!
BTW – I blew up and framed that black and white group "selfie" we took at the Hills, that night you, Nick, Lauren and I were out golfing. I'll never forget that night. And Lauren *still* hasn't golfed since then. Not once! She says she can't. I guess I get it. I haven't either, but that's just because I'm terrible. (ha ha) Oh, well. We all miss you.

All my love and gratitude. - Taryn

## ←MR. & MRS. DAHL→

**(2018)** – There's something to be said for the impact you had on people, Stellar. Before you we never talked to our neighbors—your parents. We despised them, probably as much as they despised us (not that I can actually see Kate disliking anyone). You brought us together even before Taryn's accident and afterwards, well, we've been inseparable since. It's hard to believe you saved Taryn's life twice. We couldn't thank you enough the first time, and this time we didn't even get to thank you in person. Doesn't seem right to only be able to do it like this… but thank you!

**(2022)** – Your dad wanted to get out of the boat business after he lost you, so we bought him out. Your parents and Avery moved out to Block Island the next spring, and they've lived there ever since. We go out to see them a couple times each year, and every time Kate and I will walk down those steps to say hello… and thank you. For all you did for Taryn, and for my son-in-law Josh… and for allowing us to have our first grandchild through them. Thank you, Stellar!

## ←RAY & MICHELLE PARKER→

**(2018)** – If it weren't for you and your selflessness, Michelle and I wouldn't be back together. You might not have seen it by the way I acted, but you were impacting me every day. You made me want to be a better person, and eventually I figured out a way. I don't know why I couldn't say that to you while you were alive—maybe I thought it wouldn't mean anything to you, or you couldn't comprehend the depth with which I felt I owed you. But I have to write it here now. I'll never forget Bernie for all the meaningful ways he inspired my son—my Jordan—before he died. And I'll never forget you for helping me find a reason to live, and to love living again, when you moved out to Southampton to live with me. Took me a while. Took me too long. Sorry I was who I was. But thank you for being who you were. Thank you for leading me back into the light… Thank you for leading me back to my wife.

## ←BRITTLYN SAYLOR→

**(2018)** – This is the saddest day of my life. You were the sweetest kid I've ever known. I loved your smile, your encouragement and maturity. What you did for OB was remarkable. I wish I'd known you better—wish you'd been a little older—but I loved you just the same. I'll miss you.

## ←CARRIE BIRCH→

**(2018)** – Oh, Stellar. What a life you lived. What an impact you had. Not quite sure where my boy would have been without you—especially when his dad died. Not sure who he would have become if you hadn't guided him with such good example. Most of what I have to say is "thank you" for all you did for him, and all you meant to him. I know things weren't the best in the end—and trust me that tears Nick apart now—but he loved you. You always were his best friend. Maybe Lauren and Kate deserve consideration for this truth, but I don't think anyone in the world will miss you more than Nick.

**(2022)** – It's been a rough four years for me. Your mother and I haven't spoken as much as either of us would like to. I had so much guilt—as did Nick—that first year, that we ended up moving away from Southampton. The move pulled Kate and I even further apart. Nick and Lauren barely even spoke that first year after… well… Losing you drove them apart, but loving you is what eventually brought them back together. They found a unique comfort in your memory, and you remain the glue that binds them. Nick is the greatest husband. Lauren is a perfect wife. They'll make you proud as parents—of that I have no doubt. I'm sorry for however Nick and I let you down or hurt you. You were so good to us… so instrumental to helping the Nick then become the Nick of today. I think I said it before—in Lauren's journal at your funeral—but I'm even more convinced of it today… no one misses you more than Nick.

## ←MR. & MRS. CHAMBERS→

**(2018)** – Oh, this hurts. It hurts to know how much Lauren loved you. It hurt to know what you were going through when she did what she did to you. It hurts so much. She has missed you so much. She was coming back around. You two were going to be together again… I just knew it. Lauren always had a special place in her heart for you—pretty much from the first day she met you. She'd hung around Josh for years and seen him bully many a poor kid but there was something about you that made her stand up to him. There was something about you that made her talk her dad and me into letting her see you. On the surface you weren't the type of kid we wanted her with. The little we knew of you was nowhere near who you were though, and I thank God every day for that trip to Block Island when we got to know the real you. You were everything she said you were, *and more*, and now we understand why she loved you like she did. You're the kind of person every parent hopes their child finds and loves—I mean that. Lauren was lucky to know you, love you and to be loved by you.

**(2022)** – Kate and I have been best friends for years now. We've helped each other adjust the hopes and expectations we had in 2018 into the opportunities we both have today. I can't say I've ever met a better person. Of course, she always redirects that praise to you. Man she misses you so! We just found out a few months ago that Lauren and Nick are pregnant. We're going to have a grandchild. Their wedding a year ago was certainly interesting. I always thought Nick would be the best man at your wedding—with Lauren. Instead, you were the best man—in absentee—for Nick. He didn't physically have one there—just a framed picture of you and him. The fact that Josh was one of his groomsmen was almost as impressive. They actually still spend time together every now and then when Josh comes to town. If that isn't a testament to your continued incredible influence, I don't know what is. My daughter misses you every day. I can say the same for Ken, Kate, and your stunning little sister, Avery. You are always loved, always appreciated… always missed.

## ←COACH CHANDLER GREEN→

**(2018)** – I don't know what to say. I could say you changed my life, but I see pretty much everyone has taken that already. I'll always remember the times you spent at the club with OB. That man hated everyone and yet he so loved you. It all happened so quickly, that transformation. One day the man never wanted to golf again. The next day he was begging me to call and invite you out, all the while insisting I never tell you that. Ha. I know when I spoke to you about your impact on OB you gave Cal all the credit, and no doubt he deserved a good sum of it, but it was you (and who you are) that got through to that old hack. I wish there were more people like you. And Brittlyn wishes you'd been a couple years older. *I know that made you smile!* She insists she'd have stolen your heart from Lauren, had that been the case, and kept you alive somehow. *If only.* We miss you bud. Say hey to OB for me, will you? *If God's a man of unlimited forgiveness, he should be up there.* (*ha ha*) *And let him know I bought a new putter!*

**(2022)** – I'm coaching Josh now. Have been since he withdrew from the Open. That was such a classy move—one I didn't even think about at your funeral. Says a lot that he'd skip out on a chance to win a Major to be there on Block Island for you. Made it easy to say yes when he asked me to help him. Cal's caddying for him, too, by the way. They're a force. He's won four times on Tour so far and is the spokesman for the PGA's Anti-Bullying campaign. Taryn says that would say more to you than it does to me—but it's impressive in any regard. They make such a great couple. He's a real good man. I'm guessing that says a lot too. Hey - I do also work with Avery every now and then still—whenever your dad brings her over. She's such a sweetheart—has your heart in fact. That girl is going places in golf, which leads me back to me. I'm still at the club, and mostly coaching Josh "long distance," but I just accepted a job in Bandon, Oregon that begins this summer. That's basically where Josh and Taryn live now, which will make a few things easier. It's a bittersweet move, but it's time. I haven't played a round of golf at the club since your last round here. Just can't get myself to… not even with Nick. He comes out once a week, every week, to "talk to you" for 18 holes. *Well, 17 actually.* He never plays the fourth hole. Just walks up there and drops the ball in the hole and leaves it there… writes a "1" on his scorecard. Cool tribute. He really misses you. But then we all do. You were one in a zillion, kid. I'll never forget you and can't wait to get a copy of this book Lauren's writing.

## ←JAMES HILL & ROSE→

**(2018)** – It's terrible to be writing you under such circumstances. I wasn't in when you left the docks, or I'd have been on that boat with you. No way I'd have let you go out there alone—not in that tempest, not ever like that. Perhaps then I wouldn't be writing this. *Or maybe people would be writing these eulogies for two.* I brought Rose out here with me today as she's heard so much about you. She knew you like a grandson she hadn't ever met, asked about you all the time, and wanted to be kept up to date on all I knew about you. We've had your picture on our refrigerator for many years—or different pictures anyway. You were a part of our life then—every day—and you always will be from here on. Stellar, it was chance that we met and my good fortune that we became such fast friends. You'll never know how much it meant to have you always stand up for me as you did—to endure all you did in my honor. There aren't sufficient words for my sorrow today, no description for the depth of our loss. Rose asks that you save a spot for her in heaven—she expects she'll join you soon. I beg to differ on that—think I'll keep her with me long as I can.

**(2022)** – Mr. Stellar, how you been? Been a few years already… some long and tiring ones. How's my Rose? I so miss her and her coffee. Figure you know your folks live out on Block Island. Suppose you also know I've sold Rose's house and joined them. Your dad, he left the boating business—has his contractor license now. I help him out much as I can, tend that southeast lighthouse too, by those steps of yours and Bluffs Beach. I watch from time to time at dusk, as the beacon first flickers across the water, I watch the shadows grow long by them steps—where you rest—and I listen to the swish of the waves passing beneath them. It's a familiar swish in good weather, sounds a lot like your golf swing cutting through grass. Brings a smile to my face sometimes when I need it, and some tears at other times. Yes, sir. You're still on my mind. I ain't good with words, not like all these other folks, but I miss you. I miss you and Rose both plenty. Save a place for me, will ya?

Until we meet again… been an absolute honor, sir. - James

## ←CALVIN "CAL" JACKSON→

**(2018)** - Apology in advance for my words. I fear they won't be sufficient. No way they can say what I wants to say. No way they can amount to what they should mean. I've known you the shortest of most, but feel I've known you much differently. I watched firsthand in you a boy become a man, a lamb devour a lion, and an apprentice teach a master. You had no ceiling, no cap—no limit. Who's to say what you could have been as a golfer, not that it matters. It's more important what you were as a young man, as a son, a brother and a friend. But on the course you impressed me like no one has, or probably ever could. Your ability to modify your game hole-by-hole and shot-by-shot, to take advice in any mood and make it work as it was intended was (simply put) unbelievable.

You gave the most insecure of men a confidence I'd never imagined. You accepted me as a trusted friend, treated me as more than an equal, bought in to my mentoring like no one could be expected to, and for all the credit you gave me you deserved far more. I used to tell you before each round to "Be the best version of you." We're all here for you today, because you lived that mantra beyond the course. You were the best version of anyone.

I wish you wouldn't have pushed me off the boat that day. I was only trying to keep you home—to keep you safe. I failed Miss Kate that day—failed in my vow to always protect you—but I suspect this all went down as you'd have wanted it to... if someone had to die that is. You wouldn't have accepted letting anyone else lose anything for you. So I hope you understand how hard it is for me... to accept our losing you.

**(2022)** - I ain't a fan of the ocean. Every year I like it less. It took you from me and I still can't accept it. Don't imagine I'll ever. I live in Montauk now, your parents bought me a small house on the shore. I can look out to sea and walk on the beach, but I won't touch the water. I confess this, *though I'm sure you already know it*, because I know what you said to me when you pushed me off the boat. You told me to take care of your family. "If anything happens to me," you yelled, "take care of my family."

Yeah, I heard you. But I can't move out to that island with them. I can't be out there, I just can't. I'm sorry if that means I've failed you... but I pray you understand. James agreed to move out there instead—I told him what I'd promised. He's with your family every day. They're safe... safe as they can be. James doesn't bear my guilt. He doesn't bear my fears. He doesn't bear my specific pain.

I've been caddying for Josh much as I can. Can't escape that irony. *Considering he cost me my job at The Hills a decade ago*. He's doing quite well. He listens—even better than you at times—but he's not you. That's no offense to him—I like him plenty, but I don't see golf the same no more. Now it's just a game again. For me, you made it life.

Miss Kate comes to see me couple times a month. Most times she'll bring Miss Avery. Boy, that sister of yours is a star. She doesn't have your natural talent—not sure anyone else on earth does—but she has your focus and maybe even more determination. She wears a locket round her neck with a picture of you two in it—from that first night in the hospital when her dad died. She says it's to remember where she came from, but I reckon otherwise. I think it's to remember what real love does for someone and how real the love you had for her *always* was.

I've got a picture of us, too… walking the fourth hole in Farmington after that last hole-in-one. It's taken from behind, you're looking at me and laughing—our fists about to meet in the air. I clipped it from the newspaper and cut away the words—left only the headline above it. I don't need anyone else to tell me, or remind me, about a minute of that day. But that picture and that headline, "The Magician", are framed on my wall. *Still can't believe you essentially called that shot… twice. Crazy.*

You were always Stellar… you were magic to so many of us in so many ways. We all were blessed to know you. I'd maintain no one more so than me. Wish I'd said this while you were alive, but it ain't a normal thing for a grown man to say to a boy who ain't their own "I love you." But I did, son. Ain't no doubt 'bout that.

I'll always remember you as the best version of anyone.

Your humble partner and friend. - Cal

## ←AVERY PARKER→

**(2018)** - I've known you *half* my life though sometimes it seemed more like *twice*. (ha ha) You were the best brother a girl could have, better than a girl could ask for. You always took care of me. I don't feel like I ever did much for you except raise your dog. Squirrel is going to miss you. I'm going to miss you. I don't feel like saying "I love you" is saying enough but I don't know any stronger words.

**(2022)** - At fifteen I have a little better grasp of what I could have said. I could have thanked you for giving me a family after my dad had died and my mom as well. We never really talked about either of them. We didn't talk about Dad and how you stood up to him when he was drunk, how he pushed you in the water when you couldn't swim and how you wouldn't back down no matter what, all to protect me. We didn't talk about how the police and paramedics had given up on me when you and Squirrel didn't, and how you slept on the floor in the hallway of the hospital for hours, to be there when I woke up. We didn't talk about my mom, or the fact that she decided to work out an adoption with the Parkers, because even my mom loved you. *You had that much effect on her in just a few hours of ONE DAY.* Imagine how much effect you had on me—after I had the chance to reflect on the wonderful YEARS we had together.

I had no idea how to even miss you when you died, but trust me I learned how to in the next year—in the past four years. I keep hearing all these stories of you, from Mom, from all her friends, from classmates, from James. Everyone has so many magical wonderful memories of you and I love them all. I just wish I had more of my own. It's not fair that you're gone, not before I got to comprehend how great you were, not before I was able to understand absolute love and to see you the way all these other people do/did. I miss you in a way none of them can—I was your sister. That means I also love you in a way none of them could. I was your only sister.

I love you Miles… as only I can. - Avery

## ←KEN PARKER→

**(2018)** - I love you son.

**(2022)** - I couldn't say it then. Couldn't say what I felt. Couldn't say what I meant. I'd always wanted a son but couldn't have one. Finally got one, then I lost you. I couldn't put that in words. I respect that everyone tried, but I'd never hurt so much. Reading what others wrote, it felt like a competition—who missed you most, who loved you most. I did. But I couldn't write that. I barely could write what I did, but I did love you, son. I do love you still.

I miss you every day. I go for a run to your steps, I run down them and up them. I'll sit on them and talk to you, then I go home and your mom goes out and does the same. We both know it. We both do it. But we don't talk about it. What's there to say? It's not a contest—we can't compare what we miss. We each loved you in similar ways but knew you completely different.

I missed you most on the boat. I had to give that up, too. We moved to Block Island because Avery wanted to, because Kate wanted to, they felt it brought you closer to them. I understood—but didn't need that. You are with me everywhere. I don't need the island. I don't need the ocean. You're with me in the car when a stupid song comes on. You're with me in the restaurant—any diner that serves pancakes. I see you as every kid on any bicycle, imagine you with every puppy, and every Sunday I go to all three services just to hold the church pew arm like I once held your hand.

I pulled you from the water just a couple miles from here. I used to go down to that end of the island and look out there—try to figure out why you did it. Nick stole your love, he stabbed you in the back. How could you give your life for him? Who cares what he says he was going to do—he didn't do it when he could have. I can't look at this like Kate, I can't give him the benefit of the doubt. He took my son from me. I can't forgive him. You and Lauren should be together. You and Lauren should be having that kid. You always sacrificed, never took. Why did you have to be like that? Why did you have to be that good?

These are the kind of things I feel, the kind of things I wanted to say back then. I doubt this will make it in the book, but it's the only truth I know. I miss my boy, and I resent the heck out of anyone who doesn't get that—who wishes I were more PC and would say otherwise. Nick took Lauren from my son and my son from me. I'm not Kate. I'm not Miles. I can't get past that. *Sorry, Lauren.*

I love you, Miles. – Dad

## ←NICK BIRCH→

**(2018)** - I'm sorry. This service should be for me instead of you. One more time you were the better man—the best man. I shouldn't even be out here today. No one else out here betrayed you like I did. And knowing that—as I know you did—no one but you would have come to rescue me like you did. I didn't deserve your friendship in the end. I didn't deserve Lauren, not more than you. She should have never gotten between us, because I knew how much you always loved her. I should have never been in the way. I owe you both and the whole Parker family an apology. I messed up. I'm sorry.

**(2022)** - Seems everyone read the journal entry I wrote at the funeral. Everyone but Ken tracked me down and told me not to blame myself. Or, if I couldn't do that, to at least forgive myself. Even Kate did, and Kate knew more than anyone how much I'd hurt you. I certainly didn't blame Ken for his feelings. I agreed with him. Wholeheartedly. If I put myself in his shoes and someone did to my kid what I did to you… if my kid died to save another kid who didn't deserve it… yeah, I'd be pissed at that other kid, too.

I hid out for two months after you died. Finally I convinced my mom we needed to move. She wasn't able to face Kate any more than I was able to face *any* of your family. We could have done it a better way, I admit, but we left in the middle of the night one night. It was just easier than having to try to explain what we both figured your family didn't want to hear. I wrote Kate and Ken a lengthy letter of apology. I told them both all the reasons I hated myself and blamed myself. I told them my intentions with Lauren—to end it all. Somehow Kate tracked me down. She tracked us down. Took her less than a week in fact. She pulled into our driveway and barreled into our living room. She made mom and me both sit down and she ripped us each a new one.

You're probably smiling now, but we weren't. And Kate really wasn't. She wasn't okay with us leaving like we did, didn't want us to leave at all for that matter, and she wasn't okay with me taking any blame or committing to leave Lauren—*especially not on your account.* She said that would have *really* pissed you off. She asked me again if you said anything to me before you died—she'd asked me that question a dozen times before—because she figured you did. It couldn't have gone down like it did without you saying *something.*

I think she was hoping you said something about *her*, but I couldn't lie to her, or even take the chance I was lying. I finally admitted you had said ONE thing to me. "Love her for me." That's all you said. That's what I told her.

"Are you happy now?" I asked her. "Now do you believe me?"

"No, I'm not happy," she replied. "But yes… I believe you."

"What made you so sure he said something?"

"Because I don't believe my boy would have given his life for you without making absolutely sure that you knew what to do with your opportunity."

There it was. *What do you say to that?* I mean, she was right. *But...* I lowered my head. "You think Lauren actually wants to be with me?"

"Nick, I *know* Lauren wants to be with someone who will love her like Miles would have. Everyone wants that, but especially Lauren… because she knows what that feels like. So, what I'm asking you is, did Miles gave his life for you for *nothing…* did he *totally* waste his last words—his last wish—on you?" I was shaking my head as she continued. "Or are you going to rise to the occasion and be the man he thought you were… the man he challenged you to be?"

At that point I was nodding. It was a good point. "But Lauren knows I was going to leave her—to get out of the way for her and Stellar." That's what I replied with.

"Well then, it's up to you to make sure she knows you'll never think of leaving her again."

I wish I could say I ran out the door then and there and proved myself to Lauren. But that's not at all what happened. To her credit Kate never came back and pushed me. Perhaps she understood I needed to get there on my own.

It took me a while—ten months to be exact—but I finally got to the point where I forgave myself enough to go talk to Lauren. When I told her your last words she hit me. I figured she'd have heard them from Kate by now. She hadn't. She hit me over and over and over. And then she hit me. Then she hit me again. Finally she collapsed at my feet, and I sank down beside her. I tried to put my arms around her, but she pushed them off. I figured that was my signal to leave, but as I was standing she spoke. "Can you?"

"Can I what?" I whispered, kneeling back down beside her.

"Can you love me like he did? Can you stay with me like he would have?"

"Lauren, I will love you forever the best that I know how. But I'm not Stellar. I can't do anything that he could do. So maybe the better question is… could *you* actually love me?"

She shook her head and looked at me. "I don't need you to be Stellar. I need you to be you—the guy who loved me before either of us even knew Stellar. In the simplest form… in all the smallest of ways. Nick… I loved you back then when you were that guy. If that's still you, if *that* you is in there somewhere, then I… then yes, I can love that you."

We got married last year. That was the first time my mom had seen Kate since Kate busted down our door.

Ken didn't come to the wedding. I still didn't blame him. Not one bit. But it bothered Lauren—that much was evident—and she talked to Kate about it.

Things have gotten better (and they haven't) in the 18 months since then. Kate and Mom are on speaking terms again. They get together with Mrs. Dahl and Mrs. Chambers and have tried to at least work everything out among the four of them. Ken and Kate (or Kate at least) gave us OB's condo near Farmington for a wedding present—a 1.1 million dollar wedding present with all taxes paid for 10 years. Kate said it, though she didn't have to, "It's what Stellar would have wanted."

I hope that's true. I hope that's what you'd have wanted.

Kate came to Farmington occasionally to visit us, but I hadn't been able to face her since the wedding—not even since she and mom had made peace, so she'd only seen and spoken to Lauren. I hadn't seen Kate, or Ken, or Avery since late 2018. And then the baby arrived and there they all were in the waiting room. I didn't know what to expect. I half-expected Ken to punch me.

But he didn't. Avery hugged me. She told me she'd missed me. Kate hugged me. She told me she was proud of me and that she loved me. Ken didn't approach me, didn't shake my hand, didn't look at me. And I still didn't blame him.

I had intended to wait in the delivery room with Lauren. I certainly didn't want to stay in the waiting room with Ken. But then Lauren started talking to Kate, and Kate started helping her write, and Avery was pleading with me to play checkers with her, and then Avery wouldn't let me go. Long story short, I sat in the waiting room with Ken and Avery while Kate helped Lauren finish this book up.

And then my nightmare scenario ensued. Avery got up to use the restroom and left me alone with Ken. We watched each other peripherally for a couple minutes until I couldn't take it anymore. "I'm sorry," I finally said, still not looking directly at him.

He looked at me though and sighed. "I know."

"Is there any way I can… Is there anything I can…"

He shook his head. "Nick, you don't owe me anything. I decided to try to beat the storm back that day. I can blame myself plenty too. Truthfully, I'm as much mad at me as I ever have been at you. You're good. You are… you've done everything Miles asked you to do." He paused as Avery came back towards us. "I can't ask you for more."

Avery caught that we were talking, so she quickly spun towards the vending machines. Neither Ken nor I missed her intentional deviation.

"I don't want you to hate me," I said, tears stinging my eyes.

And then I saw the tears on his face. "I don't and I won't. Promise." He wiped his face. "I wanted to blame someone else… thought it would help… but I can't and it didn't. We can't… we have to move on."

I stood but didn't approach him. He stood and came towards me. I held out my hand, but he ignored it and wrapped me in a hug. He didn't let go for awhile. He sobbed and hugged me tightly like he was hugging you… he gave me the hug I'm sure he wished he could give you. *Talk about gut wrenching.*

He didn't have time to say anything else. *Nor did he have to*. Mid-hug Kate came running into the room and skidded to a halt, staring at us. We both looked at her as it took a second for the shock to leave her face. "Nick," she said, "it's time. You need to come with me."

And then Kate and I were in the delivery room with Lauren, and Lauren had the baby. Kate picked her up, and we told her the name Lauren and I had decided on months ago: Stella.

No one will let me say this, Stellar, but my heart knows it's my truth. This should be your life. This beautiful baby… she should be *your* daughter, and I should be the one with God. Instead… your goddaughter's name is Stella… and I'm the one who gets to raise her.

That's not me being ungrateful for what I have. It's exactly the opposite. I'm eternally grateful… and I'll prove it to you. You'll see. I'll always love Lauren for you. And I'll love Stella for you forever, too.

Til I see you again. Your best friend. - Nick

## ←KATE PARKER→

**(2018)** - I refuse to say goodbye. I refuse to believe you're not coming back. I keep waking up thinking I hear you talking or calling me. And then I can't sleep. Then I don't want to go back to sleep. I don't want to write in this book. I refuse to acknowledge any form of goodbye. I'll talk to you tonight. I'll talk to you tomorrow. I won't give up. You have to come back.

**(2022)** - It's been four years since you left. You didn't come back. And even still, not a day goes by that I don't think of you. I've had the chance now to read this entire book of Lauren's, I've even helped her finish it. I've had the chance to read all these notes from all these people who loved you like they've never loved anyone before and—as sad as it makes me—I can't help but smile. I can't help but say, with each incredible note, "That's my boy." That's you they're talking about. I'm so proud of you—so proud to have been your mother.

I had that journal burnt with you, same with that letter and your scrapbook of pictures from your earlier life. Of course I wanted to keep them for myself. (I did keep one of you as a little boy swinging a golf club left-handed.) But the rest were yours. The promises I made to you to never share them with anyone else—that was how I kept them. They're out there in the ocean with you… those memories, those words, those images—all that love—it's out there with you.

That ring you gave me to sell years ago… I couldn't do it. I held onto it, and couldn't get myself to throw it in the ocean with everything else. Instead, I had it melted down into a pendant with Stella's birthstone, and gave it to Lauren on Sunday. I told her it was a present from all of us—including you. I hope that's okay. She may not wear it every day… but I'm relatively certain she'll keep it for life.

That baby girl of theirs is an angel. They called her Stella Nicole. Lauren and Nick agreed on the Stella. Lauren made the call on Nicole—the name you two were going to use for a girl if you'd ever had one together. (Ironically to honor Nick) She's beautiful… but how could she not be? I mean look at her parents!

I know I've been talking to you a lot, on my walks, about Ken—about your father. I've been worried about him for years. I think he finally had a breakthrough last week. He and Nick hugged it out in the hospital waiting room—not once but twice—and they spoke on the phone last night.

Nick wants to come out to Block Island with Lauren and Stella. You have no idea—*actually…* forget that. *You do.* You know it's a huge step for those two—Nick and your dad. Nick wanted to make sure that was okay with Ken first. Ken said it was. So we're really getting somewhere. I think Stella may have broken the ice so to speak, so thank God in even more ways for her. I hear they've even designated you as the godfather. Pretty appropriate, I think. Who better to watch over her than you?

You know I'm going to keep up my end of all this. I'm going to take care of your love. I'm going to be there for your best friend. I'm in this for the long haul, and I'll do everything I can to make sure those two love each other as much as you wanted them to, that Lauren gets every bit of everything you'd have given her. I get it. The best way for me to love you for the rest of my life is to love them.

I'm not going to say as much as others will, I know that, but words are no measure of my love. I'll keep most of that in my heart. I'm also not going to say goodbye. I still refuse. But Lauren needs me to get her this letter so she can wrap up this book. It's an incredible book—an incredible story—about the greatest kid I've ever known. I'm so honored to have been more than "Kate" to you—at least a few times anyway (ha ha). I'm so honored to have been your mom. I love you, Miles, with every breath I breathe. It's not possible for "I love you" to mean more than it means when I say it to you.

Forever – Mom

## ←★★★★★ NARRATOR ★★★★★→

### LAUREN CHAMBERS-BIRCH

**(2018)** - I'm with Kate on this. I refuse to acknowledge this is it. I refuse to say goodbye. We shouldn't have had any "lasts" yet. Not that last wave, those last words. That last kiss. There should be *so* much more. When Nick and I spoke last night he told me it should have been him we were burying today. I didn't disagree, not vocally, but I know you'd have wanted me to. If someone had to die then this went according to your plan.

You knew what you were getting into, just like with Taryn, just like with Kate. You knew that water and those rocks better than anyone. You knew what you were doing and what would happen if you didn't quite pull it off. I don't want to insult you in any way by saying this should have happened any other way. I know how you would feel if anyone else had died out there instead of you. No. I know you, Stellar, so I know this is true… this is how, given the circumstances, you'd have wanted it to be.

But I don't have to like it. I can hate it all I want. *And you know I do.* I wish with all my heart you hadn't died last week. I wish I'd had the chance to say all the things to you that I wanted to say. I wish I'd have broken things off with Nick before that trip instead of waiting until we got back—and then I never did. Nick ended it. *The irony.* Seems we were all on the same page after all. You wanted me. I wanted you. He wanted me to have you. We let love mess the three of us up or, I should say *I did that to us.* That kiss was my idea, my fault. You think Nick was going to turn that down? No. I'm the one who owed you the apology of a lifetime. I just never got to give it to you. *I missed a million chances.*

It's too late to say I'm sorry. I guess that's kind of cliché. But a lot of those clichés fit me right now. I didn't know what I had until you were gone. I took you for granted. You deserved better than me. Yeah, they're all true. But that begs the question why you even wanted me so much. There are so many beautiful girls out there. Take that stunning blonde girl at the funeral today who even wrote she "wished you were older." Who was that? And why didn't you pursue her? Why me? Why was I so special? Why did you love me so much?

I wish I could have asked you all these things in person. I'd have loved to hear the answers. But now I guess I'll never know. I'll never know what I did to deserve your love—to make you so loyal, so forgiving, so everything I've ever wanted and was too dumb and blind to know I had. I'm sorry, Stellar. Turn and ask God… He'll confirm this: I've *never* loved anyone more than you.

**(2022)** - Okay. So now I know the whole story. I've gone through every journal, every letter, every tribute, every note. I've read every take from every angle, and I know every regret, every mistake, every secret and every truth. I know it all and it's harder for me to handle than I'd ever imagined.

What's it change though, knowing everything? *Nothing.* That reality hit me even harder. This changes nothing at all. You are still gone. I still love you. I still love Nick. And now I have a beautiful baby girl—Stella Nicole Birch—who I will love for the rest of my life.

Kate asked me never to read her final note to you. She made me promise. *Right.* I broke that promise the first chance I had. I knew I was missing a journal. I found out about the letter. I found out about the ring. *A ring?* I figured out you were going to give it to me that New Year's Eve—the night that I kissed Nick. *With that mysterious letter.* And now that ring is a pendant around my neck. Kate's right. I'll absolutely keep it for life.

I could tell you that I'm kicking myself, that I regret this or that decision, but I'm not. I don't. *I can't.* If I've learned anything through writing this book, and reading every word of it over again it's that you, Stellar, would simply want me to love and live the life I have. That is the greatest tribute I can give you. You had no ulterior motives. You never tried to manipulate anything to your advantage. You loved your family. You loved your friends. You loved Nick. And you loved me.

I wanted to tell this story as completely as I could and I couldn't have done that alone. I needed everyone else to give me "Stellar" as they knew you, as they remembered you, as they loved you. And everyone did just that.

I don't want this to be complicated. That's what I told Nick last night. I wanted him to know that I loved him with most of my heart but that a part of my heart would always be yours. *That's the truth.* He responded as I hoped and thought he would. He didn't expect it to be any other way.

Nick called your dad last night for the second time in a week. Nick wanted to know if we could come out there sometime, to bring Stella out to the steps to "meet you", to see where they lived now. Ken said "Of course." *Pretty sure we'll be there next week.* That's huge for those two! *But I'm sure you know that.*

I guess I should mention the golf part too. Cal was over here today. He, Nick and I went to the club in Farmington and played the course. Cal caddied for both of us. He's a much better caddie than I was for you—that one time you let me tag along, and tried to teach me how to play.

Nick, Cal and I walked the entire eighteen holes together—just the three of us. Cal insisted I play the full eighteen, just this once. *No matter how many hundred I shot.* It was pretty exhausting, but I can see why you loved to walk and golf so much. It was so peaceful, so therapeutic. Hey, Nick even played the fourth hole for the first time since you last aced it… for the first time since we lost you. He got a three, and said that was pretty good. *I took his word for it.* Cal gave me a one… he said only my last putt counted. *My first—and probably last—ace!*

We cancelled our membership at the club tonight. It was bittersweet, no doubt about that. Chandler and Brittlyn are both gone now and Nick finally got all he wanted out of the place—he got me to play one round there with him. Nick said that was enough for him, that he'll never play the course again. I hope that isn't true. I hope, if we're still living here several years from now, that he'll take Stella golfing there, maybe even with Cal, and that he'll tell her the legendary stories about "The Magician".

*The best golfer most have never heard of…*
*The best friend he'll never forget.*

I love you, Miles "Stellar" Parker. ----- Lauren

***"As you walk down the fairway of life you must stop to smell the roses, for you only get to play one round."***

\- Ben Hogan

# THE AUTHOR'S INSPIRATION FOR "THE MAGICIAN"

"STELLAR"

## GOLF HUMOR

# HAPPY ENDING

***(Figured You Might Enjoy a Few of My Favorite Golf Jokes)***

**JESUS and MOSES** are playing golf and come to a par-3 hole with a long carry over water to an island green. Moses safely reaches with a 3-wood but Jesus pulls out a 5-iron and says "Arnold Palmer would hit five-iron from here."

Jesus tees off and his ball ends up 25 yards short of the green in the middle of the pond. He turns to Moses and asks him to part the water away so he can hit the ball where it lies, but Moses refuses, so Jesus steps out on the pond surface and walks towards where his ball sank.

At that moment a foursome of golfers approach the tee box, and see Jesus walking out on the water. One of them turns to Moses and says, "Who does that guy think he is? Jesus Christ?"

"No," Moses shakes his head. "He thinks he's Arnold Palmer."

**A GOLFER** is standing on a tee box overlooking a river and sees a couple of fisherman. He turns to his playing partner and says, "Look at those two idiots fishing in the rain."

**A MAN and his WIFE** are playing the fifth hole at their club when he slices his ball so far to the right it rolls into an equipment barn. He finds the ball and is about to take a drop when his wife says, "Let me go down to the other end of the barn and hold the door open. Then you can hit your ball through the door and back onto the fairway with no penalty stroke."

He agrees, but as she's holding the door open for him he takes a big swing and strikes her in the head with his ball, instantly killing her.

As luck would have it, two years later the man and his new bride are playing the same hole when he again slices his tee shot into the barn. And again, as he's about to pick up his ball, and accept the penalty stroke for an unplayable lie his new wife says, "Let me go down to the other end of the barn and hold the door open."

But this time he cuts her off. "No. No way. The last time I tried that shot I got a triple bogey on this hole."

**TRUTHS of GOLF**

- 99.99% of all matter is empty space, but that last 0.01% will stop a golf ball dead.
- You will always make that 40-foot putt for a 10.
- Nothing straightens out a nasty slice quicker than a sharp dogleg right.
- If you're ever golfing in a lightning storm carry a 2-iron. Even God can't hit a 2-iron.

*(For the comprehensive purpose of this next joke please accept the term "women's tee" vs. "forward tee.")*

**IT was a SUNDAY MORNING** and Larry was beginning his pre-shot routine, visualizing the upcoming shot, when a voice came over the clubhouse loudspeaker. "Would the gentleman on the ladies' tee please back up to the men's tee?"

Larry remained in his routine, seemingly unfazed by the interruption.

The loudspeaker came back on. "Excuse me, would the man on the women's tee please back up to the men's tee?"

Larry came out of his stance, turned towards the clubhouse, and shouted. "Would the announcer in the clubhouse kindly shut up and let me play my second shot?"

**A PRETTY PATHETIC GOLFER** was getting frustrated with his terrible round and began blaming his mistakes on his caddie.

As the round came to a close the golfer refused to tip the caddie and said, "You have to be the worst caddie in the whole world."

"I don't think so," the caddie replied. "That would be too much of a coincidence."

**FOUR RETIRED MEN** played golf together once a week for many years. One day, on a hole that runs along the highway, a funeral procession passed by and the oldest man hissed at the others. "Show some respect."

The other three took their hats off and stood solemnly until the cars had all passed. Then one of them turned and asked the oldest man what had gotten into him. "In thirty years I've never known you to show anyone respect on the golf course."

The man nodded. "That's fair. But I was married to that woman for 65 years."

**A BAPTIST PASTOR** decides to play hooky on a Sunday to play golf. He's playing the best round of his life when an angel asks God. "Are you going to let this slide? Do something."

So God says, "Watch this."

The pastor hits a 425-yard tee shot that goes in the hole for a double eagle. The angel turns to God and asks, "Why in the world did you reward him?"

God smiles and says, "Who's he gonna tell?"

**Thank You For Reading "THE MAGICIAN." Please Leave a Review.**

50354132R00171

Made in the USA
Lexington, KY
12 March 2016